Of Bonds and Daggers

The Curse of Gods, Book One

Dakota Monroe

Contents

Content Warning

If you're looking for an enriching fantasy world with an epic plot, this is not the book for you. This book is a dark romantasy—heavy on the romance. It is an easy-to-follow story, with very light world building, and contains insta-love vibes (for those who prefer slower burns). Within are topics that some may find disturbing or triggering.

The triggering content includes adult language, alcohol consumption, anxiety, child abuse, child rape, death, consensual non-consent, depression, exhibitionism, explicit sexual scenes (F, MF, MFM), graphic descriptions of torture, grooming, mental illness, physical abuse, praise, psychological abuse, rape, sexual abuse, trauma, verbal abuse, violence, voyeurism

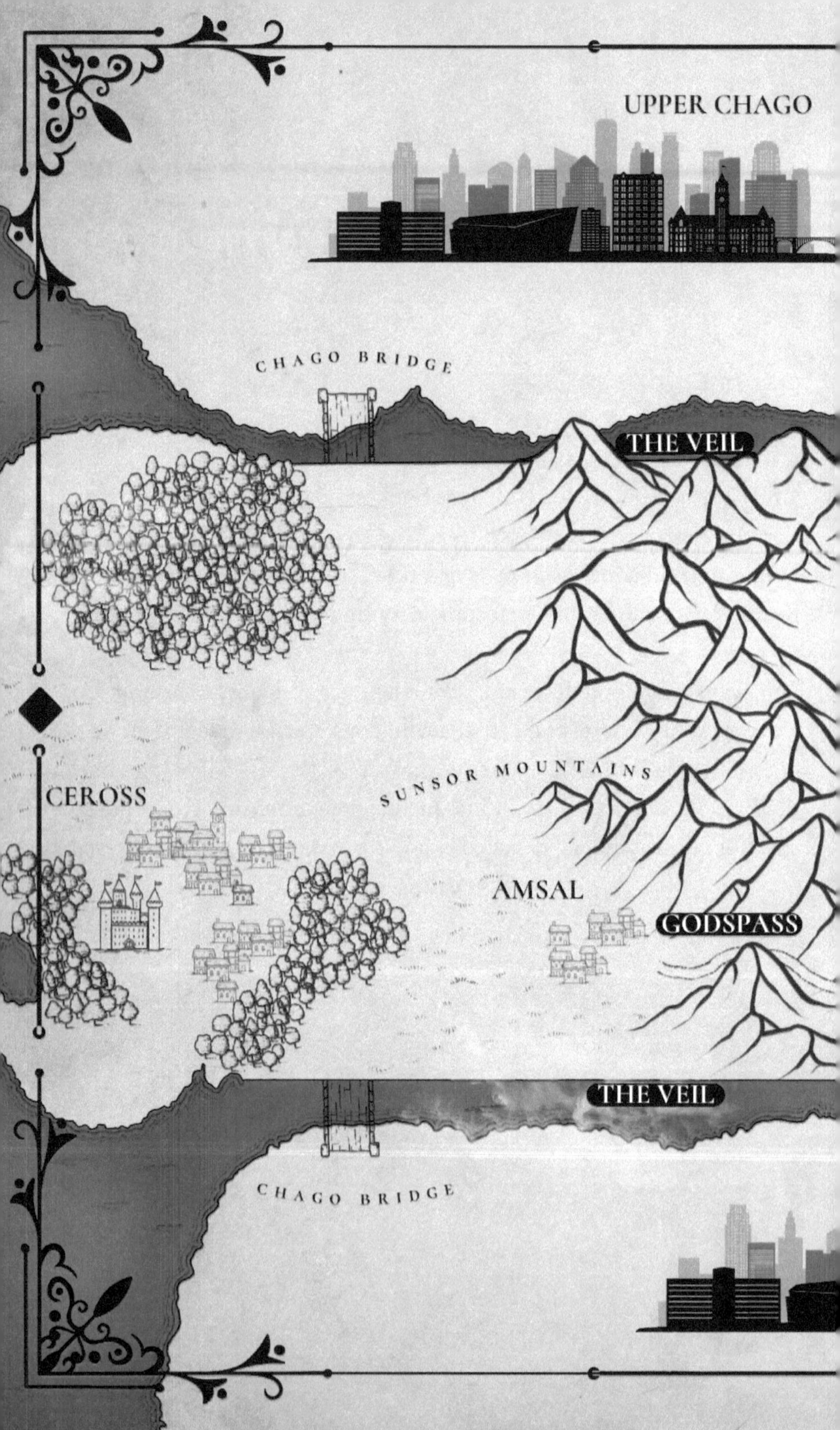

UPPER CHAGO
CHAGO BRIDGE
THE VEIL
SUNSOR MOUNTAINS
CEROSS
AMSAL
GODSPASS
THE VEIL
CHAGO BRIDGE

The Curse of Gods

Playlist

Bad Omens - The Death of Peace of Mind

Kim Dracula - Superhero

Joel Sunny - Luminary

Arankai - Paint it Black

Joel Sunny - Streets (Violin)

Elvis Drew - Make Me Feel

Isabel LaRosa - Heartbeat

Glasswaves - Dead Dreams

Joel Sunny - Under The Influence (Violin)

Witchz - Drowning

Movement - 5:57

Ex Habit - Love Me

Trevor Something - The Ghost

Meg Myers - Desire

Joel Sunny - Middle of the Night (Violin)

Gangs of Youths - Achilles Come Down

Omido, Ex Habit - Please

Mansionair - Easier

Scratch Massive - Dancer in the Dark

Dicktionary

If you're here for the smut, you can find it in these chapters:

- Chapter Eight
- Chapter Ten
- Chapter Twenty-One
- Chapter Twenty-Three
- Chapter Twenty-Seven
- Chapter Thirty

To those who want to be fucked by two sassy fae males at the same time.

This is for you.

Prologue

Dark. Always dark.

I don't remember the last time he allowed me to see the sun. The only light that pierces my eyes is the one he uses when he wants me to watch him fuck me or hurt me.

I am nothing.

I am a vessel to serve him and please him at his will. I'm not even permitted scratching an itch. I haven't moved my own limbs for three years—unless he allows it. The smell of urine is heavy in the air; my nose wants to scrunch, but I do not even have control of my face. Just my eyes and thoughts. He hasn't allowed me to relieve myself in two days. I wonder if he'll be disgusted and cease fucking me.

I watch the ceiling. The dark plays tricks on my mind, scratching at the torn threads of my sanity. It makes me see things that aren't there…or maybe I'm only seeing the things I wish were there. It's funny what your mind makes up when all you have is your imagination.

I imagine killing him—a different way each time. My favorite is seeing myself pin him to the ground with daggers holding him in place. Then I would slice his dick off with a dull knife, making sure it hurt in the worst way. He would scream my name and beg me to kill him.

I wouldn't…yet.

I'd use a small, double-sided blade to hold his mouth open and place it on the inside, so that if he tried to close it, the blade would pierce him deeper. I would take his severed cock and shove it to the back of his throat, forcing him to choke on his own depravity.

I try to smile, though my body doesn't move. The thought of watching the light leave his eyes—knowing that I'm the one who brought him to his end—is what keeps me going. Keeps me sane. I will find a way out of here. Somehow. I just need to time it right. Stay patient until his ego eases his routine; then I will wring his miserable life from his body.

Escaping has to be my number one priority. He can do what he wants to me, but it's not just me he's hurting.

I need to warn them. I must tell them they were wrong, and I'm paying the price for their ignorance. A twinge of heaviness creeps through me; they have no idea I'm here. They won't expect to hear from me for years. They won't come looking for me, or worry about me.

No one will save me. I must save myself and the others. I'm the only hope they have.

Footsteps approach and I sink further into the numbness that has become my friend. The door creaks open, and I keep my eyes staring at the ceiling; I don't bother pretending to be asleep when he arrives anymore. That just makes him angry.

He talks to me about his day…about how hard it is for him to live this life. I sense he's frustrated and displeased, and I sink into myself as I know what that means for me.

The numbness greets me with open arms.

He's generous today, he says. He won't hurt me with his dazzling sharp tools, but instead will let me enjoy my punishment.

He doesn't call it a punishment.

My body sits up on its own, turning over and waiting there just how he likes. I try to move, but he has control. My attempts never work, though I still try. I hear the clinking of his clothes hitting the ground. I hear him slither toward my unwilling flesh, positioning himself where I cannot see him.

The numbness wraps its fearless arms around me. It covers me like a blanket, and I hide from reality.

I feel nothing.

Chapter 1

I take a deep breath, immense satisfaction running through me at being undefeated. I've won against each of my opponents thus far and only have one left to go. His name slips my mind, but I know he's the strongest of the males I'll be facing.

I look to my left, my parents watching me with smug looks on their faces. It feels nice to have their approval. I wish I didn't have to nearly kill fifty males in order to get it, though.

That's the competition: me against them. I'm the best warrior they've seen in centuries. Stronger, faster, and more powerful than each of them.—as I'm proving today. But my next opponent is the one who trained me: my best friend. His name is on the tip of my tongue.

I look down at my clothes, grimacing at the blood soaking into the black leather. I frown at how difficult it will be to clean. These are my favorite leathers. My knuckles burn where the skin is scraped off, and there's a large gash running up my forearm. The blood seeping out slows as everything heals before the next match.

I stretch my body, putting extra focus into my legs. I need to be fast to beat him…I could overpower him in a strength test any day, but in hand-to-hand combat? He already knows all of my tricks and go-to maneuvers. I'll have to do something different; give him something he won't expect.

My skin tightens, fully sealing as I take another deep breath, forcing myself into a state of calm. He will attempt to mess with my head, and I need to stay focused. I have to win this, because if I don't…my parents will be disappointed. I cannot let them down anymore—I'm already too much of a failure in their eyes.

I turn to face my opponent, planting a smirk on my face that I know will piss him off. He doesn't give me a chance to see him before he's on me, tackling my body to the ground. Dirt flies up my nose at the impact, and I wince at the crack in my shoulder. That bastard.

I throw my elbow back, though he sees it coming and slides from me. Exactly what I wanted…a moment of his distraction. I summon water to blur his vision, only for a moment before I rear back to kick him in the throat with my leather boot. His hands fly up as he sputters for air and instinctively backs up. I use that movement to jolt forward and slide through his wide stance, grabbing his knees and pulling him with me. His face smacks into the dirt, nose cracking as I smile at his inability to take a full breath.

Just to piss him off more, I do not attack while he's down. I stand back and wait for him to right himself. Letting everyone in the arena know that this is an easy game for me. That I'm toying with him and could take him down at any time; that I'm only dragging this out to humiliate him further.

He growls, muttering how much of a bitch I am under his breath. He's right, I am. Best friend or not, he will never get special treatment from me in the arena. As far as I'm concerned, he's just like every other male. Right now, they all either want to kill me or fuck me. My opponent is definitely in the former group.

We go back and forth for several minutes; he tires quickly, not pacing himself as he should. He knows better than that, but he's angry with me. He'll lecture me about it later…but whatever, this is fun.

I give him a sweet smile and in a mocking voice say, "Do you yield yet, or must I embarrass you more?" That does it. He charges, throwing his arm up to send a large wave of water at me. I smile genuinely at his effort, knowing he's aware that I'm much more powerful than he is.

I do not move a muscle as the water inches closer, my opponent just behind the swirling blue liquid. I wait until it's directly in front of me before raising one hand to stop it and turn it into an impenetrable wall, forcing my adversary to smack right into his own creation. I lift the palm of my hand, encasing him in the water and pushing the wall down to slam him into the ground hard enough to end this match.

The arena silences. For a moment, a pang of worry glides through my chest as I wonder if I hurt him badly. The water dissipates, some coming back red. My eyes shoot up to my friend and widen when the crack in his head glares right at me—a reminder of what a disappointment I am. I cannot even win a competition without fucking something up.

I'm too stunned to move, staring at the steady stream of blood flowing from his wound. Why can't I think of his name? I'm vaguely aware of others rushing from the stands to his side, doing what they can to help him heal before it gets to the point of no return. My breathing falters as my heart beats out of my chest. I feel cold sweat coating my body, and everything becomes blurry as I...

"Nell?"

I jump in my seat and look over to where Sarah waits, giving me a worried look. She must have said my name a few times. I take a deep breath and settle back into the ridiculously comfortable armchair in her office. The afternoon light shines in through the floor to ceiling windows that overlook part of Chago and the river dividing the city in two.

"Sorry, what did you say?"

She creases her brows and makes a brief note on her tablet. "I was asking if you would perhaps be interested in discussing medications yet?"

Sarah is pretty; almost too pretty to be a therapist in this part of Chago. She has stunning long blonde hair, skin that would make a baby jealous, and teeth whiter than the walls of my apartment. Well...that's not difficult to achieve. The place is old, and the walls cling on to years of other tenants who treated it worse than me. Gods know management would never repaint the walls. They'd have to double our rent.

Sarah looks expensive, and no one on this side would be able to pay for an hour of her time. I'm her charity case, as I cannot even afford to feed myself properly; so she sees me once a week—for free. I wonder if she just comes over the bridge to meet with some patients pro bono, and her central office is over *there.*

Chago is separated into two classes: the poor and the not poor. Years ago, the mayor decided that anyone who couldn't afford to live somewhere that costs a minimum of two thousand dollars a month was poor, and got shipped to this side of the river. That's not all, of course…you don't look pretty enough? Gone. You lost your job? Gone, because chances are you won't get another one before you become homeless. And if you do become homeless? Gone faster than I could jump off the bridge connecting both sides of the city. It's disgusting.

We're forgotten about over here; the roads were paved before the city was separated and haven't been touched since. Buildings are not taken care of and lawn work is not a thing because who has the time or money? And best of all…our grocery stores only receive the second-hand food from the other side. Anything that did not sell—or is expired—graciously becomes ours at an overpriced rate.

Even knowing each of those truths, I still daydream about living there and being able to feed myself and Xamira. To have an apartment that isn't falling apart and a job that doesn't suck the life out of me. To walk down the paved roads and see people smile, while going outside to do something other than work. That's the dream. I'm unsure if that would fill the emptiness in my chest, but I would rather be empty and fed instead of empty, hungry, and living in a colorless world.

"Oh...um, no thanks. I would rather not take any medication." That's a lie. I would love to help myself feel *something*, but Xamira is more important than some pills.

"All right. If you change your mind, you have my number. That is our time for this week—I hope your evening at work goes well."

"Thanks, I'll see you next week." I stand and turn to make my way out of her office. Even this room seems out-of-place over here; with pretty, deep green walls, dark hardwood floors, and a rug that feels like the gods themselves made it. She has a bookshelf lining the entire wall opposite her over-sized windows, and paintings filling up the rest of the space. I bet just one of those paintings is worth more than I have made in my entire life.

"Oh, and Nell." I pause in front of the door and look over my shoulder. "Please reach out to me any time between our meetings if you feel you need extra help, or cannot seem to keep from wandering into daydreams."

I nod slowly and walk through the door, closing it behind me. Strange. Why would she care if I'm daydreaming? At least it gets me out of this shitty place for a little while.

Chapter 2

"Y ou like that, baby? You want me to come all over your tits and make a mess of you?"

No, I don't like that—and no, I don't want to clean up your nasty cum. But instead I say, "Mhm," hoping that will get him to finish faster.

I'm not sure why I keep doing this to myself. I just want to feel something, and hope that the next guy I find will be able to fill that empty void in my chest. But not only do none of them help the hollowness, they don't even make me come. So, I'm left feeling empty and disappointed. Not that they could make me come even if they tried—they think their dicks are the gods' gift to me, when in reality two of my fingers could do better work than that. Plus, I doubt any of them have ever even heard of a clit, especially what's his name poking me from the back right now.

I want this to be over, so I arch my back and do a nice little practiced moan into my pillow and—of course—that sends him over the edge. He makes a weird grunting noise and practically seizes on top of me. *Gross.* How is he sweating this badly? It's literally been three minutes? At least he's still wearing the condom and didn't follow through on his threat to get his cum all over my chest.

He lays there for a minute, and I swear to the gods I'm about to break his nose if he doesn't get up and get the fuck out. I would like a little peace, and a shower, before I need to go to work.

"Wow…that was great, thanks. I kind of need to get to work, if you wouldn't mind…"

"Oh, yeah, sure."

He pulls out, and I'm sad to report that I'm not even a little sore. He slides on his clothes while I slip a robe over my nauseated body and wait. I look at my mattress on the floor, wishing I could afford more than just a blanket. I saved up several months just for that mattress, and buying sheets just never seems high on the priority list. Although, it would be nice to wash them and be able to sleep in a clean bed—but I've been through worse, I guess.

I usher him to the door, ready for this whole experience to be behind me. "Hey, you were wonderful. I would love to see you again. Could I get your number?"

First—ew—no, I wouldn't give him my number even if I had one. But I don't. I found the phone that I have on the street a couple of years ago and can only use some apps when it's connected to the Wi-Fi. No way could I afford a phone plan; and no plan, no number.

"No, I do not give out my number. Thanks though. I'll see you around." I not so gently push him out of the door, and shut it before he can turn around to say something else. I lean against the creaky wood and wonder what the hell I'm doing with my life. How do some people simply have everything handed to them while the rest of us must suffer perpetually? Gods, can I just get a break?

My parents didn't want me, so I grew up going home to home with men who would look at me too long, or touch me in places they shouldn't…and women who would beat me for their husbands doing that. I had no friends in high school to talk to; and when I got a job, ready to save anything to help myself out of the situation, my last foster care mom—Mary—stole it all and claimed that I owed it to her for staying in her house. It didn't matter that she got paid by the state for having me, and several other children, under her care. We still owed her.

So, I left as soon as I could and found a job as a server—I've been there ever since. After a few months, I was able to find this apartment, and it was one of the happiest days of my life. I didn't care that there was mold in the ceiling, that the locks didn't work, or even that there was no actual kitchen-just a fridge and a microwave. It was mine, and I was finally able to do something for myself.

Now, I'm still in the same apartment, with the same job, and I don't think I can keep this up much longer. The only thing that keeps me going is Xamira. I found her outside not long after I moved into this apartment, and she seemed just like me: lonely and sad. I brought her back here, and we have been best friends ever since. She always seems to know what I need; whether it's a hug or to laugh, in which she struts around the apartment like it's her stage doing weird noises and stunts. She is the funniest cat, and I'm so thankful to have her in my life.

That's why everything I do is for her at this point. She deserves the best of everything. I know I'm not able to give her the best, but I give her what I can. I always buy her food before mine, because I refuse to not take care of her like she does me. Sometimes I will even splurge on a little toy for her—instead of getting myself dinner—because her happiness is the only thing I look forward to these days. If I lost her, I would lose myself...and probably not live to see my next birthday. There would be no point for me to struggle through anymore.

Speaking of the little cutie, she must sense my need for some love after that incident we will never speak of again. She runs over to hop up into my arms and give me a hug. She wraps her little arms around my neck and purrs into my chest—this is the best feeling in the world. I wish I could just sit here forever, holding her and giving her nose kisses.

But that's not possible. I need to leave this shitty apartment to go to my shitty job to make shitty money, while being treated poorly by a shitty boss and shitty customers. And then do it all over again tomorrow. Xamira was right…I really needed a hug from her right now.

I pull her back a little to look into her beautiful, golden eyes. "Thank you, my girl. You are the best thing in my life—I wish I could repay you for everything you do for me." She watches me like she's listening and understanding what I'm saying to her. I lean in to kiss her on the nose, a smile forming when she closes her eyes and rests her forehead on mine. Gods, you would think this cat is more intelligent than most humans I know.

"I have to go to work. But as soon as I'm done, I will come right back here and we can cuddle all night." I set her down, and watch as she saunters over to my makeshift closet—just two cardboard boxes shoved up against the wall—her shiny, black fur being done no justice by the lighting in this place. I smile to myself; *to be a cat living freely, with no job or responsibilities.*

I take one more look in the mirror before leaving the apartment. My auburn hair is tied back, with a few pieces hanging in my face; my grey eyes look dull and sad. A heaviness runs through me at the girl I see in my reflection. She's not happy. She's too skinny—showcasing her wide jaw and puffy, chapped lips. Her pale skin looks like it hasn't seen the sun in years, seeming nearly as dull as her eyes. She needs help…something better than this life she's forced to struggle through. Unfortunately for her, another night at her soul-sucking job calls.

I turn away from the mirror, pushing back the tears I feel at knowing how great I could be, how much good I'd do, if I could just get myself and Xamira out of this hell.

I am six hours into my eight-hour shift at the diner, and I'm so overstimulated I might explode. Today is just not my day. Chago's Best is a diner just down the road from my apartment—the damn place has been open since before I was born. The owner, Jim, started this place up when he was twenty-nine and from what I hear, he used to be a good boss. Now the man is pushing seventy and treats his employees like shit; I can't say I would be upset if he were to find himself in front of a car and gone from this world. Gods know he deserves it with the way he treats all the women who work for him—including me.

One time I asked him for a raise so I might buy myself some actual food instead of instant noodles for a change. He smirked and said, "Sure, I'll give you a nickel more if you get on those pretty knees and open your mouth for me." Yeah…I haven't asked for anything since that day. I wanted to kick him right in his saggy balls, tell him to fuck off, and leave this place for good.

Unfortunately, finding another job would be very hard. Especially as most places are shutting down due to low business. And I doubt I would find another job that gives you a free meal during working hours. So, I am basically option-less.

"Nell, hurry your ass up. You got table 6 that just walked in."

I ignore him, shovel the rest of the hash browns and eggs into my mouth, and make my way to the front. One look at table six and I just know my day couldn't get any worse at this point. Four men around my age are sitting in the booth making a show of who can be the biggest douche bag. They most certainly came over from the other side of the river—they are wearing clothes I wouldn't dream of owning. They all have decently styled hair, each sporting muscles that only those who are well fed—and have enough energy to go to the gym—can have. They likely came over the bridge to laugh at those of us who *live* here…because this breed of man likes to feel powerful, even if it means feeding on the weak.

Jim slaps my ass, shoving me a little toward the table. I bite down on my tongue to keep from saying anything, as I may go off like a bomb if I talk to him right now. What has gotten into me today?

I take a deep breath and count to ten as I survey my surroundings. This place has seen better days, though it looks well for its age. Red and white stripes line the back walls, connecting to the front windows that overlook the sidewalk. There is bar-style seating next to the kitchen—with stools spread out in front—and a kitchen hidden mostly behind the wall full of pictures that display Jim and his customers over the years. It could be cute if you took away the dirt, grime, smell, and location. Oh, and the owner.

Feeling calmer, I stride over to the table. The guys notice me heading their direction and slap each other on the arm. They whisper something I cannot hear, though I have a good guess about what they're saying. "Hello, welcome to Chago's Best. Can I get you guys started with anything to drink?"

"Yeah honey, what's the cost to get a drink of you?" Wow, haven't heard that one before. My eyes drag to the one who spoke; he's attractive, with a baby face and slicked-back blonde hair. His dark eyes look more soulless than mine, and he's smiling at me like he just said the funniest thing ever—it's clear this man has never been told no.

"If you're not going to choose any drinks, I will be right back with waters and to take your order." I walk away, my jaw clenching whent they burst out laughing.

A while later, the diner finally begins to slow. I only have two tables at the moment, one of them still being the four men with sticks up their asses. I've been avoiding them as much as possible, and thankfully they haven't given me any more trouble.

I am so tired. So angry. Tired of the unfairness of this world…angry at whoever decided this was the way everything should work and that I don't have the power to change any of it.

"Hey, sweetheart!" a man yells from behind me. I bite my tongue as I walk to their table, where hungry eyes watch me with intent.

I don't even bother smiling anymore; it's not like they were planning on tipping, anyway. "What can I help with?" They already finished their food and paid, so I know whatever they plan to say will cut the last string I have holding me back from knocking their teeth out. I need to get a grip, but fuck has this day been horrible—I'm truly struggling to hold down my emotions.

"Why don't you come sit in my lap? You look like you're having a bad day, and I just want to make it better. Give you something *big* to smile about."

My eyes flit to each of theirs before I spin to leave without responding, but blondie has other ideas. He snatches my waist and pulls me into his lap, his friends laughing at my squeal of surprise. A large hands hold me tightly while the other trails up my leg, shoving it open until it's held in place by his knee.

Hot breath brushes my neck—I might throw up. He rubs his sticky face against my ear, and my nose scrunches from the overuse of cologne. "Come on, baby…I think you could use a good fuck, and the four of us are more than happy to show you how it's done. I've seen you watching us—wishing you could ride our cocks. I bet you've been fantasizing about it since we walked in here. You're probably so wet right now…" The others laugh and spew a mixture of comments I attempt not to hear.

"Let's take her to the alley out back. She won't mind a little mess; probably used to it."

"Come on, Duke. We could walk out of here and fuck her until she's bloody on the street, and nobody would do a damn thing."

"I'm not normally into slum rats, but she's pretty enough to get my dick hard."

Duke smiles into my hair, a prickling running through my skin at the movement. "You hear that, baby? You're pretty enough for us. That should make you feel special…I think you owe us a little something for showing you the attention I know you crave." He presses his fingers into the waistband of my leggings, and instinct claims my body. I lean forward to throw my elbow back into his face—his nose cracks loudly, saving me from his grip as he releases his hold. I stand up, angling my leg to kick his throat, the hit hard enough to throw his chair backward. He slams against the chair behind him and falls to the side, landing on his cheek with a slap. His friends stand in unison with murder in their gazes, but Jim steps in before they touch me.

"Hey fellas, we don't want any trouble here. Either we have a problem, and Ricky in back gives the cops a call; or we don't have a problem, and I forget what I saw you doing to my best server. Your choice."

The guys give each other questioning looks, not realizing the cops do not give a shit about us on this side—they wouldn't show up here even if we paid them to. The standing men grab Duke from the floor and practically drag him from the diner, pinning me with dirty looks and names they think will hurt me. Guess it pays to have been called a bitch, slut, and street rat every day as a child, because I don't even blink at their comments. Instead, I smile sweetly and wave my fingers at their departure.

Now that I have a moment to process…how did I know where to hit him? And where did I get that strength from? I shrug and stare at the small puddle of blood—I guess I can be a bad-ass when I need to be. Where were those instincts every time my foster parents decided to shove their hands down my pants?

"Nell, goddammit! What the fuck was that?"

Is he serious right now? "Did you not just see what they were doing to me? I was defending myself, Jim. I wasn't about to be raped in the middle of the diner—sorry that caused some blood to get on the floor."

Jim laughs, throwing his hands up dramatically. "*Raped*?" He laughs harder. "Honey, they were just copping a feel. As boys do. Learn to live with it because men touch women's cunts all the time. That's not rape, it's just the way of life. And besides, I don't blame those boys. You're a pretty thing."

He continues chuckling as he walks away. "Clean up that blood and head out for the night."

My wide eyes stare at his back, my mouth struggling to close from its agape position. I can't help but wonder if I have *"please harass" me* tattooed across my forehead. That is clearly the only explanation, because what the actual fuck? I have no idea how some humans can be so cruel to others…but you know what? Xamira seems to think I'm worth more than this, so I am done letting people walk all over me and use me for their pleasure. Fuck that.

I stalk to where Jim stands at the counter, my fists clenching while heat fills my chest—I'm certain I could kill a man with one look. He turns at my approach, eyes widening; I do not give him the chance to open his mouth before my fist connects with it. He rears back, and I swing my foot up into his balls as hard as I can.

"Fuck you, Jim."

I untie my apron and drop it on his bloody face. I run from the diner and down the sidewalk, a big grin on my face. That felt *so* good! I've wanted to hit that man since the day I started working for him, which was also the first day he "accidentally" grabbed my ass.

I feel free. Like I could take on the world. Fuck him, and fuck that place. I don't know what I plan to do about another job, but I will figure that out tomorrow. I could ask Sarah…she must have some connections or need an assistant? The moment I enter my apartment, I send her an email using the upstairs neighbor's Wi-Fi. Why haven't I thought of asking before? Surely I'm not too prideful to ask for help…especially when it could be good for Xamira, too.

Chapter 3

After emailing Sarah last night, I curled up on my mattress with Xamira and slept better than I have in a long time. The therapist responded to my email within two minutes, though I had already shut my phone off to save the battery and didn't see it until this morning. It was after midnight...is she always up that late responding to patient emails? My brows furrow as I wonder if the woman sleeps at all, because she insisted on meeting at 8:00 AM *sharp*.

I'm thankful Xamira woke me in time to see the email—I am never awake this early, so I certainly would have missed the meeting. I'm not complaining, though. I feel a lightness in my chest that tells me today will be good. Just a small seed of hope…because growing up like me, you learn not to expect anything.

I wring my hands as I walk to her office building, noticing how quiet it is for a change. I suppose I'm never out at this time of day—only when I need to work or get things for myself and Xamira—so I do not hurry as I study my surroundings. The buildings here are tall, two-dozen stories for most of them, though they mostly look abandoned. The windows are broken in random places, and spray paint covers much of the lower parts. The streets and sidewalks are cracked so badly that I'm not sure how anyone would drive a car through here and not pop every tire. Grass and weeds cover every surface, and if it weren't for the one or two businesses I see every block, I'd be convinced this place was completely deserted.

I reach Sarah's building, which also looks rundown—but at least it has a working door. I step inside and nod to the woman at the front desk; she wears the same black cardigan and cream top every day, it seems. She scowls at me with beady eyes, and it's a struggle to not roll my own. I do not want to get on her bad side…she'd likely put an "out of order" sign on the only working elevator here, and I'd be forced to walk up hundreds of stairs just for an appointment. No thanks—I will just continue to pretend her angry stares are fine and not creepy.

I step into the musty elevator and press the worn button that will take me to Sarah's office. The lights flicker, and I convince myself the metal doesn't groan as it moves. Honestly, there *should* be an "out of order" sign on the front of it…I hum, wondering how long until it quits working—with any luck, it will be with me in it, so I can fall to my end with a smile on my face.

No, I shouldn't have those thoughts. What would Xamira do without me? I tell myself I'm only allowed to think that again if I ever lose her. I won't, because she's my cat…which means she has to at least live as long as I do. I do not make the rules, that's just the way it has to be.

The elevator stops, and the doors take so long to open that I wonder if it'll grant my wish after all. But—lucky for me—they do open, and I come face-to-face with the words *Sarah Gardner, Psy.D*…I am feeling uncharacteristically nervous to talk with her today.

Not only have I never asked for an impromptu meeting before, I also have never asked for help from anyone. Except the gods, but they don't listen to shit. I'm not a naïve little girl anymore—I know better than to think they're real. And even if they were, that they would ever think to help someone like me.

I rehearse one more time what I plan to throw into our conversation, shaking out my hands.

Sarah, I know you see me for free, and you have been so kind and helpful all these years…I do not want to take advantage of anything you do for me, though I was wondering if you could help me with finding a job?

Yeah, that sounds totally professional and not weird at all.

Before I can finish hyping myself up, Sarah opens the door. "Nell! I thought I heard the elevator. Please, come in!"

"Thank you." I smile and step into her office.

I stroll to the armchair she has for patients—a mirror to the one she uses—avoiding the sharp corner of the table just ahead. A log as a table is an interesting decor choice.

A flash of light catches my eye through the window, and my eyes widen at how different the water looks; I'm usually here during the afternoon, but maybe I should adjust my appointment times because the water sparkles so beautifully…I could watch this for hours. I definitely understand why Sarah wanted to meet this early.

Dragging myself out of my poor attempt at stalling, I lower myself into the seat. My body tenses when I notice Sarah already sitting in hers…staring at me with a look I cannot decipher. I make quick work of finding my seat, not wanting to upset her or waste her time.

"Sorry, I didn't realize how pretty everything looks this time of day and couldn't help admiring."

She smiles at me, though it doesn't quite reach her eyes. She doesn't respond to my babbling, instead tilting her head slightly as she continues to stare at me.

Okay, this is awkward. Is she mad at me for emailing her? She said I could reach out whenever I needed…she can't be mad at me for that. She doesn't look upset, though—it seems like she's trying to figure something out that I must have the answer to.

Matching her stare, I wait for her to break the tension. Most people would be uncomfortable and blurt out the first thing that comes to their head, but not me. While I try to be a nice person in general, I have no problem standing my ground; and if that means staring at my therapist for an hour while she stares back and doesn't say anything—so be it.

While I endure the silence, I study her. She looks very put together and not at all tired like I would expect, considering her late reply to my email. Her hair falls nicely over her shoulders in soft waves. She has done a brown smokey eye that would take me three business days to complete; and she's wearing a matching light blue set with wide leg pants and a slightly fitted top. That material looks so comfortable…maybe I'll ask her where she bought it, though I could never afford a set. Probably couldn't even afford a piece of the fabric. But a girl can dream…and window shop.

She narrows her eyes slightly, nostrils flaring. "What prompted you to email me last night, Nell?"

I can't even take pride in my silent win that she spoke first because I'm so thrown by the question. She usually isn't so direct, preferring to dance around topics until I itch to pull my hair out.

"U, well, I wanted to see you. And you had mentioned I could reach out if I needed."

"Yes, but you saw me yesterday. What happened between then and now that you felt you needed to see me again today? Are you all right?" Her tone says she's not concerned at all.

I suppose I should ease into the conversation I really want to have. "I quit my job last night."

Her eyebrows raise and she makes notes on her tablet, leaving my big announcement sitting between us for a couple of minutes. When she looks back up, her lips purse before she speaks. "And what led you to quit your job so impulsively? I assume it was not something you were planning, considering you did not mention it during our session."

I agree and then go through the events of the night. I mention how I was already feeling overwhelmed when I went into work, leaving out the fact that I had a very disappointing hook-up—I get the feeling she'd judge me for it—and finish with what happened during my shift.

"I see…and do you think that was a good decision on your part?"

I can't tell if *she* thinks it was a good decision or not, but of course I'm going to defend myself. I know I made the right choice. "I think it was a good decision. I was being treated poorly—repeatedly—harassed by my boss and customers, and not taken seriously even when my well-being was threatened. I'm not sure I can think of a better reason to quit a job."

She gives me a smile that hints at malicious, almost like she's trying not to laugh at what I'm going through. Why would that be amusing to her? Is it not her job to help people? This must be some kind of game to her…a way for her to gather information on the poor and then go home with plenty of stories to tell her friends while they laugh and sip on their expensive wine.

Stop it, Nell. Not everyone is out to get you. She could just be tired and not in the mood for giving actual smiles. Either way, I think I should feel her out a bit more before asking her about a job.

"It sure is an interesting reason to quit your job, though you know that is just a woman's calling in the world, and no reason to go rashly making big life decisions." She gives me a pointed look that says I've disappointed her and continues before I have the chance to speak, "After you left yesterday, did you have any more daydreams?"

What is with her and my daydreams? How does she even know I have them? It's not something I have brought up to her before, because then she'll really think I'm crazy.

But they're only dreams…distractions from the lifeless, colorless world that I live in now. I'm not sure why I feel like I shouldn't tell Sarah, but the way she's acting today urges me to keep those thoughts to myself.

I crease my brows, shaking my head. "What do you mean daydreams? Like wishing for a better life?"

"Is that where your thoughts take you when you get distracted from our conversations?"

This is…uncomfortable. I'm concerned with why she is so interested in this. "Sure—sometimes, I guess. Other times I think of my cat, or what I need to do before work. But I wouldn't consider that daydreaming; just regular thinking."

I attempt to keep my face neutral when she stares at me like she knows I'm lying. I swear I see a hint of red cloud her eyes before it disappears, and she snaps out of her death glare to give me a sweet smile. That smile has always calmed me before, but now I'm wondering how many times she has used it to control herself around me.

"Right, of course. Just mundane, human thoughts are the things capturing your attention lately." She is visibly trying not to tremble. "I would really like to talk to you about medication. I think it could be very helpful. The one that I recommend would help reduce your impulse nature and running thoughts. It would also make you feel more okay with the world around you, so that you don't find yourself questioning things, or quitting your job after a minor incident.

"And before you answer, I understand that money is a concern—especially now. Just know that this medication is something I can give to you for free. My services in providing it to other patients allow me to help those who cannot afford it, because it can be pricey for some."

Fuck, I really need a minute to process everything she just told me. First, she thinks I need medication that basically forces me to be more compliant? Second, she didn't even mention the medication helping the one issue that I actually see her for…the emptiness in my chest that's been plaguing me for years. Third, she's once again minimizing what happened to me yesterday. As if I should just accept being touched by strangers and have them tell me they're going to rape me in the middle of the street and get away with it. I would think another woman would understand when I say that scared me, and that I feel it was a good reason to quit my job. Lastly, she's trying to give me an expensive medication for free. That doesn't seem strange *at all*.

I can understand doing some sessions for no charge if she is passionate about helping people; but after today, I am getting the sense that is not her motivation.

This wasn't such a good idea…I need to just thank her, leave this suffocating office, and not come back. She is acting strange, and I don't feel like being a part of her game anymore. I have enough to worry about as it is.

"No, thank you. I understand where you're coming from, but I would much rather not be on medication. Actually, I think I'm feeling much better about everything. I'm very sorry to have interrupted your day—thank you for meeting with me."

I stand up and spin to hurry from the office, but I nearly run into her very full—but nice—breasts. Has she always been this tall? And how did she get over here that fast?

"Nell," she breathes, grabbing my shoulders. "I'm worried about you, that's all. I want to see you thrive and be happy, and I think these pills could be so useful to you." She's now holding a bottle of said pills. Strange.

"How about this…take one now, and then you can take the bottle home, try them out, and let me know how you're feeling at our next meeting. If you still hate them, I will stop bringing it up. What do you say?"

I have to tilt my head to look into her eyes. I feel like a child being scolded by their mother. Is she going to let me leave if I don't take the pills? I suppose I could just take the bottle and pretend I'm taking them if I see her again—I don't plan to, so it shouldn't matter.

Hesitantly, I grab the pills and give her a shy smile. "Thank you, Sarah. You know how embarrassed I get by admitting I need help or can't afford things. I wouldn't ever want to take advantage of you like that. But I will take these and try them. I trust your opinion, and I do hope they can help me."

She beams. "Oh, I'm so happy to hear that! You are going to love them. Take one right now, won't you?"

"I'll take one today, though I thought I would wait until I get back to my apartment just in case any side effects hit me right away. I don't want to be walking the streets and suddenly feel exhausted or anything." Please, just accept that and let me out of here. What even are these pills, anyway? She didn't tell me anything except what they'll do to me.

She examines my for a moment before relenting. "Of course—they can make you more tired. Take one right when you get home, though, so you can start feeling the full effects within a couple of days.

"And please reach out to me again if you need to meet sooner. I am always willing to see you, and I'm glad you trust me enough to help when you are having troubles. That is what I'm here for." She squeezes my shoulder before dropping her hand and stepping to the side.

I smile and thank her again before walking to the door. It's more difficult than it should be not to rip it from the hinges, though something in my gut tells me she wouldn't let me leave if she suspected anything was awry. I look up to wave goodbye when I enter the elevator, the hairs along my arms rising when she's standing in the same spot with the same smile on her face. Gods, she is definitely strange in the mornings—and definitely not the kind person I thought she was.

Once the elevator doors close, I let go of the heavy breath I've been holding for what seems like an hour. She's just a creepy woman who wants me to take some weird, unnamed pills. Nothing to be worried about. I've dealt with much worse.

Chapter 4

It's early afternoon when I wake from a much needed nap. I cuddle Xamira into my chest, chuckling at her purr. I lie with her for a few minutes, brushing my fingers through her long, soft fur. She looks up at me with those golden eyes, staring as if she wants to tell me something. This is an expression she gets frequently; she is such an intelligent cat, but unfortunately I don't speak feline and she doesn't speak human. The language barrier really sucks.

"I love you, too." I give her nose a little rub with mine. She huffs and stands up to pad her way over to the window. "Hey, what was that for? Was that not what you were saying to me?" She looks back, and I swear she rolls her eyes.

Laughing, I grab the bottle of pills Sarah gave me. I didn't inspect them before, so I only now notice that there isn't even a label on these. There's just one hand-written word in marker: Nell.

Why would she have had these already set aside for me? Also, why would she take the label off? Isn't that illegal or something? Well, giving them to me like she did was illegal as well, so I don't believe she cares.

I open the bottle to inspect them and find nothing interesting—just capsules filled with white beads. No writing or imprint on them, either. It's like she just makes these at home, throws them into an old pill bottle, and hands them out to random patients. I am for sure not taking any, no matter how much Sarah thinks they will help me.

For all I know, she's waiting for me to take one so she can come to my apartment, kidnap me, and sell me to sex traffickers. She has the perfect cover to do something like that…

I shake my head; I need to stop getting off track and figure out what I'm going to do about a job. I look over to Xamira who is—very intensely—watching birds sitting on the tree outside. What are my options here? I could go back to the diner and beg Jim for my job back. I snort; absolutely fucking not. I refuse to walk back there with my tail between my legs and apologize for something that was done to me. He should be begging *me* to come back, if anything. But I know he won't. There are so many people who would kill for that job and he probably already has someone else hired, anyway.

I could check the job board, though I do not feel hopeful about that option. I turn on my phone and connect to the neighbors Wi-Fi. They need to get a password on that, because I'm definitely not the only one who uses it. Pulling up the Chago job board, I filter the results to include only listings within my area, and I see one posting. Just one.

Secretary—Sunrise Tower
Hours: 7:00 AM to 5:00 PM, Monday thru Saturday
Rate: $7.25 per hour
Qualifications: High School Diploma

You've got to be kidding me. Scowl lady is quitting her job? Guess I can't blame her…I would, too. Those hours are horrendous, especially for so little money. Even if I was a little daggered in that job, I refuse to work where Sarah's office is.

I turn over to bury my face in a pillow and scream. The pillow isn't very thick—so it doesn't do a great job of blocking sound—but it's good enough to not have any wandering ears knocking on my door. While

I'm taking deep breaths to calm my racing thoughts, Xamira jumps on my back and lies down.

Laughing, I say, "Xamira, you can't just jump on me like that! How am I supposed to get up to do anything?"

She makes a little grunting noise that I take as her telling me I wouldn't get up to do anything, anyway.

"You're right, as always," I sigh. "What should I do? I'm out of options here, and I don't know how I'm supposed to fix that." She starts making biscuits against my shoulder blades. She could definitely make a living as a massage therapist if she weren't a cat.

"I can't go back to the diner, and there are no job openings on this side of the river." Xamira uses that moment to pounce on my back while meowing. My nose scrunches as I turn around and pull her onto my abdomen. "Are you trying to play, silly girl?" I move my fingers, knowing she likes to chase them around, but instead she stills and stares at me like I've offended her.

"You don't want to play, then? Just had a little energy to get out, and that was it?" She stands and pounces again, making me grunt a little at the force to my abdomen. Before I can ask her what's going on, she meows loudly at my face, and my body jolts from the strange behavior.

"What is it? Was it something I said?" She makes biscuits on my shirt, and I take that as a yes.

"Okay, I'll bite. Was it just now when I was talking about jobs?"

Pounce.

"When I was looking at the pills Sarah gave me?"

Pounce. Does she actually understand what I'm saying?

"What else did I say?" I hum and tap a finger on my chin. "Did you want to take another nap?"

Double Pounce.

Okay, clearly I'm upsetting her by not understanding. "Let's try this: I was talking about not being able to go back to the diner," *pounce*, "and having no job openings on this side of the river." She begins making furious biscuits.

"Okay, I think we're getting somewhere. It wasn't about the job openings." A*nother pounce.* "So that must mean it's about this side of the river?" More biscuits and meowing.

Why would she know what it means to be on this side of the river? I suppose I found her on the street…it's possible she came from the other side. That would make sense—she is beautiful and definitely belongs over there.

"What about this side of the river, Xamira? Are you saying you want to leave to the other side?" She continues to make biscuits and gives meows again, her eyes shining a brightly as they stare deeply into mine. My forehead creases…I'm conversing with my cat.

"We can't just leave…how would that even work? I have one hundred forty-seven dollars in my savings. I doubt that would be enough to get a motel room for the night, let alone find us a permanent place to stay."

She pounces again. I can't decide if she actually understands or not, but she keeps responding accordingly to what I'm saying. This is strange. I've never seen her act like this before. "Do you understand that you're telling me we should go to the other side of the river, where we would definitely be homeless, and probably could only afford food for maybe a day or two?" She makes more biscuits.

I watch her for a minute. I've always thought she was more intelligent than other cats, though I've never had another cat to compare. Even so, she just seems like she knows things that even I don't know. Which is crazy—she's a *cat*! How is she comprehending my words and responding to them?

Throwing that thought to the side, she has a point. I suppose it wouldn't hurt to just walk over to the other side to see if we had any options? We can easily walk back if not. I already paid this month's rent, so we have a place to sleep for at least twenty-six more days.

Well, what the hell…why not just listen to what my cat is saying and go look? Even if we don't end up coming back, it's not like it matters. I have a mattress, a blanket, two boxes of worn down clothes, a few hygiene items, and some cat food. This place is empty otherwise.

"Okay, here's the deal." She stops making biscuits, listening intently. "It's not a far walk over to the other side, so we can just see what we find. We'll come back here if we don't see anything that works for us and think more about this tomorrow?"

She seems content with that, because she meows as she hops off me and struts to the door. Gods this is so strange, but I guess we're doing it.

I grab my hidden savings—behind the toilet, of course. Then I put some cat food, my toothbrush and toothpaste, and an extra pair of clothes into a reusable shopping bag. I walk over to Xamira, who is sitting patiently by the front door, and chew on my lip.

"Are you sure about this?" Her answer is to stand on her back legs and reach for the handle. "I'm hearing you loud and clear," I laugh to myself. "I might be crazy for listening to my cat and thinking she can talk to me; but you've treated me better than all the people in my life, so that must mean something."

Xamira and I have been walking for about fifteen minutes, and we're already approaching the entrance of the bridge. Xamira walks slightly ahead of me, making it feel like she's the one leading me to our destination. She's always been great with walks; she loves to be outside with me, and I bring her everywhere that I can. Which isn't many places around here, so I try to walk with her every day. She's never needed a leash, and always seems to know exactly where we are and where we're going.

After a few more minutes, we stop at the entrance of the bridge. It's mid-afternoon, so the sun is still pretty high and it's decently hot out. But thankfully it's not the middle of summer, otherwise I would be in a puddle right about now.

The bridge itself is simple. It has two lanes for cars passing through to either side—not that they do often. Few want to come over here, and those who are here can't afford a car to leave. We have to walk. There is a small area to the side of each lane that's not exactly a sidewalk, but can be used as one if a car does pass. I keep that in mind, should I need to grab Xamira.

The water is stunning this close. I've never taken the time to come over by the river before, but it's beautiful. It sparkles in a way that makes me think there are better things out there for us. It's uncanny to see such beauty right next to the rest of this side of the city. But if I look the other way, the river fits in perfectly. The pleasant side of Chago has extra tall buildings—all of their windows intac—and the walls are so clean they look freshly painted. Just from here I can see a park with a small beach and garden next to the river. There are children laughing and running around in the water, their parents taking pictures of their happiness. My heart aches at the sight. I wish that was something I'd experienced growing up; even if it was with a nice foster family instead of my actual parents. Just something nice, where I wasn't constantly afraid for my body or sanity.

Holding back the liquid blurring my vision, I peek down at Xamira, who's watching me with a knowing look in her eyes. The sun makes them look like melted, swirling gold. She is so beautiful…and waiting for me.

"All right. Let's go see what we find, shall we?"

She walks alongside me now, staying on one of the lanes because there's no cars around. And I doubt we'll see any before we make it across. The bridge isn't very long, so it should take us ten minutes at the most. As we walk, I study just how different everything on that side looks. It makes me nauseous to think that the people over there are living so well, while we just get their scraps. And now I'm heading over there to try to become one of them. *It's for Xamira*, I have to remind myself. She deserves better. We both do.

When we're almost halfway across the bridge, Xamira takes off into a run…and I don't know if I should run after her or if she's just chasing a bug. But then she speeds up—faster than I ever thought a cat could go—and I don't hesitate this time. I run after her. "Xamira, wait! Where are you going?"

Gods, she must remember that side of the river. I wonder if she knows how to get back to her old family, and she just doesn't want to stick around with me any longer. I can't lose her though, so I keep running and suddenly she disappears. I stop, eyes widening as I breathe hard and frantically look around. Did I take my eyes from her? No…I just saw her. She was right there running one second and the next she wasn't.

Did I take one of those pills? Am I losing my mind here? No. There's no way she could've fallen into the water. I was watching her, wasn't I? Oh my gods, what if she's drowning? I drop my bag and sprint to where I last saw her, ready to jump over the bridge. There is nothing I wouldn't do for her, and there's no way in hell I'm about to let her drown.

I'm almost to the spot I saw her last and beg my legs to run faster. I must get to the edge—there's nowhere else she could be. This bridge is flat and empty, and I'm the only living thing on it. As I come up to the railing to look over, I try to slow down my panicked breathing and reach for the stone to check the water, but my hands do not latch onto anything. No…I'm falling.

Fuck, this must be how she fell. There was a hole in the railing, and I didn't see it, either. I scream, though it only lasts a second before my face slams into *something*. This is definitely not water, and that was too quick of a fall for me to have made it to the river. I'm on the ground? I'm scared to open my eyes, so I take a second to catch my breath and feel my surroundings. This is grass. Where the hell did grass come from?

Chapter 5

X̲amira. My eyes snap open, and I ungracefully stumble up to my feet only to be met with a…meadow? Where the fuck did the city go? Instead of buildings in front of me, there are luscious green trees, a lavender field, and other pink and yellow flowers filling out an open space under the blue sky. There's a forest on the other side of the meadow and snow-capped mountains in the far distance. I drink in the crisp air and immediately calm down a little. It smells floral and peaceful, if that's even possible?

The temperature feels different, too; it's warm, but not as hot as it was a minute ago on the bridge. How did I get here? Did I actually fall in the water, and this is where the gods greet me?

A confident meow sounds next to me, and I jump as my soul leaves my body—I force myself to dampen my emotions because I recognize that meow. My head turns to the left, where Xamira sits as if she's been waiting for me.

I crouch to pick her up. "*Oh my gods,* I thought something horrific happened to you…how did you find this place, Xamira? Do you know what happened?" I'm feeling all over her body to make sure she's okay. She seems just fine and appears real, so maybe I'm not going crazy and didn't just fall off a bridge into a different part of the world.

While my heart settles now that the immediate danger is over, I spin to ingest the rest of my surroundings, a scream catching in my throat.

The gods must be fucking with me and laughing so hard at my expense. In front of me now is the bridge, but looking toward my part of the city. And there's this strange, pink-ish, translucent wall between me and the road. I turn back around expecting a city, but see the meadow again. I'm definitely going crazy. There's half the Chago bridge on one side and this…*place* on the other. The wall separating them runs so high I can't see where it stops. It cuts right through the clouds. It also spans as far as I can see in either direction on the ground. I briefly wonder who built it, but that's the least of my worries right now.

I hear the noise of an engine, and look over my shoulder to a car coming straight at me…not slowing down. Hello! How rude is it to hit a woman and her cat? I hold Xamira tighter and run out of the path of the car. Once I'm sure we're safe, I wave so the person driving doesn't freak like I did and get into an accident.

"Hey! Buddy, slow down. You're going to crash into the tree—stop!" He's not even looking my way…gods people are so rude. Well screw him, I will not be a part of this crime scene. Tensing, I back up to a tree behind me and circle around its large trunk to cover myself and Xamira. I peek at the car, hoping the driver will swerve before he crashes. He's so close to the wall now. But instead of hitting the tree, he goes *through* the wall and disappears.

What is my life?

I thought yesterday was bad but, fuck, take me back because this is insane. At least I know how to handle a few guys who can't keep their hands to themselves. But this? A wall that looks like floating gelatin, separating a bridge that takes you to a whole different place? Yeah, okay.

"Well, girl…you have some explaining to do. You must have known this was here. Don't lie to me." I hold her in front of my face and give her my best mom look. She meows in agreement.

"And how is it you knew this place was here? Have you been here before?" She meows again and tries making biscuits on my chest. Cute as it is, I need some answers from her. She has been hiding things. "Are you saying we have both been here before?" Another meow.

I need a drink.

"Okay…well, since you brought us here, you must have a reason for it. So I suppose I will continue to follow you. But please, for the love of all the gods, do not find another bridge and jump off it. I don't think my heart could take that kind of terror again." She meows and reaches to kiss me on the nose. I set her down and wait for her to decide where she wants to go.

She begins walking through the field of flowers, and I reluctantly go with her. Everything here is beautiful; the colors seem more vibrant, the air is alive, and I almost feel like the emptiness in my chest has filled up slightly. I'm grazing my hand along the flowers as we move across the meadow. I pause in front of the forest, sucking my teeth when Xamira doesn't stop, and prances right into the trees. I laugh to myself and follow, because what else would I do at this point?

"Hello, I'm Nell Harper, and I just followed my cat through some magical wall. And I will continue to follow her because she seems to know what she's doing and where she's going—and I, apparently, don't have a fucking clue about anything." I'm so focused on berating myself that I don't notice another presence until it speaks.

"Hello, Nell."

I squeal and—in my haste to jump back from the forest talking to me—trip over a log and land on my back. Groaning, I cover my face with my hands. "Can I get a fucking break? Not only is this the second time I've fallen since I got here, but now the trees are talking to me, too?" I point up at the sky. "Oh yeah, I bet you're having a blast thinking about every single thing you could do to fuck with my life. Well, fuck you, too!"

I flip the treetops off with both my hands and someone—a man—laughs. I freeze. *Oh shit*, the trees weren't talking to me. Of course they weren't. They're *trees*. And I'm just a crazy woman making a complete fool of herself, while some random man in this forest—that nobody knows about—laughs at me. I push up onto my elbows where the man stands in front of me with his arms crossed, smiling like I'm some comedy act at a festival.

But wow, what is it with this place? Is everything here beautiful? He has sandy blonde hair, short and styled to look a little messy, but it's clear he has a product in it. Darker eyebrows but they suit the harsh lines of his face; you would think someone carved out that jaw with a razor with how sharp it is. His eyes are so blue they're hard to look at—as if you were staring at water when the sun hits it just right and blinds you for a moment. He's wearing black trousers and a loose-fitted maroon top that dips to some of his light chest hair.

He's quite attractive, and I'm at a loss for words because attractive does not mean kind. Will he hurt Xamira or me just because he thinks he can take whatever he wants?

I shuffle my legs around to stand, never looking away from his stare. He's not much taller than I am—just a couple of inches. I think I could take him in a fight if I needed. He has large, hard muscles lining his arms, and I'm certain he trains to look like this. He also has a little point at the top of his ears…interesting.

"Are you all right?" He's smirking at me and has a curious glint to his bright eyes, but he makes no move to come toward me. I should ask him about this place…he seems like he could have some answers, and I don't get predator vibes from him. Though there's something familiar I can't put my finger on.

"Yes, I'm fine." I look over to where Xamira waits, glaring at him. "Do you know where we are?"

He raises an eyebrow, still not moving. "We're in the Veil."

That stops me short. "The what?"

"The Veil. It's a place in between the mortal city Chago, and can only be accessed by those with magic in their blood. Like fae." He's studying me now, though I'm unsure if it's because he's waiting to see my reaction to what he said or if he's playing a joke on me and finds my confusion amusing.

Wait…

"You mean like faeries and magical powers like mind control?"

"I would not have described it that way, but yes…that is the general idea."

I burst out laughing, unable to control my emotions at the moment. Does this guy think I'm that gullible? *Magic* and cute little faeries with wings? I don't think so. I'm not falling for that one; though I wonder why he would lie about something like that while keeping such a straight face?

"Yeah man, I appreciate a good laugh, but I'm just wondering where we are and how I got here. One second I was on the Chago bridge, and the next I'm in a field of flowers." No need to tell him about the other fall I had earlier. I'm embarrassed enough.

"Male," he says sternly.

"I'm sorry, what?"

"Male. You called me a man—however, that is a term for mortals. For fae, we are males and females."

He's still sticking with this story? "Okay." I clear my throat. "I didn't mean to offend you at all…*male*. Could you just point us in the direction of—" I pause because I actually have no idea what I'm looking for at this point. I ended up in this weird place, and have no plan for what Xamira and I should do from here.

A pleasant breeze passes us, brushing pieces of hair across my face. It smells sweet? Almost like there's a bakery just down the path…I wonder if there is? I realize I'm looking in the scent's direction when the male speaks.

"I am not lying to you, Nell. We are in the Veil. Though I am interested that you do not know of this place, considering you could cross through. Also," he gives me a knowing smile, "what you're smelling are scents from the city—Ceross—that you will find on the other side of this forest."

"Wait, a *city*? How is there another city on top of the Chago bridge? That makes no sense…"

"The Veil encompasses the lands of the fae in the mortal realm, which includes two main cities: Ceross and Anloria. You entered from the wall of the Veil back there." He gestures to where I ran through the wall chasing after Xamira. "If you were to go to the other side of the veil, that way," he points to the opposite direction, "you would come across the second wall that makes up the Veil. Crossing through that wall would take you right back to the same spot on the Chago bridge."

He smiles at me like he didn't just tell me the most impossible thing to exist—ever. I look around at the trees and the vast landscape I can see from here, though this place must be quite large if I can see all of this from where I'm standing. Xamira still sits to my left—watching me—and I think about how she knew this place was here. The male said only those with magic in their blood can cross through to this Veil, so that must mean both Xamira and I have magic in our blood…and she's aware of this. Have I truly been here before, like she said? I'm pretty sure I would remember a place as beautiful as this, but I don't.

There is a sense of familiarity, though; not just with the male in front of me, but with the land we're standing on. It almost feels right, and I'm beginning to think both Xamira and this male are telling me the truth. But if that's the case, why do they know about this place and I don't? I'm getting a headache.

I scrunch my eyes closed, rubbing my temples, and the male shifts. I peek to see him pause his reach for me. "My apologies, I don't mean to startle you. Are you hurt?"

I narrow my eyes at him. I've learned better than to just trust people who do not show their true colors right away.

"I'm okay, just a headache."

"We can get you a tea for that, if you'd like. I was heading back to Ceross before I heard you," he purses his lips to keep in his laugh, "speaking. You and your companion are more than welcome to join."

I watch him for any signs that he's trying to trick me into something—I find none. I don't know why he would offer to help us, especially as we only just met. But as I look at Xamira, I realize she was taking me in the direction of the city anyway, and it could be helpful to have someone who knows the area lead us through. I can't trust his intentions just yet, but he seems okay enough to accept this one thing.

"Thank you."

He smiles, the action making him look much younger and even more beautiful than he already is. He walks toward Xamira, who hisses at him and jumps off the rock she was on to walk closely on my other side. His mouth tightens and the lines around his eyes crinkle a bit, but the expression is gone the next second as he gives her one of his boyish smiles. "She is lovely—cats sometimes have trouble with fae and their magic. She doesn't seem to take issue with you, though."

"I found her when she was just a baby. That's probably why." Though it is strange…Xamira is usually friendly with strangers. She's most likely on edge, considering how crazy today has been.

We walk for a few minutes as I try to process everything that has happened in the last couple of days—I pause when what he said catches up to me.

"What do you mean she doesn't take issue with me? Are you saying I'm like you?"

"Well, I would assume so. Mortals do not have pointed ears." He glances at my ears like that proves his point.

"I don't have pointed ears like yours, though? I've been living in the *human* city, with my *human* ears, my whole life."

"I may be old compared to your," he flattens his lips, "*human* years, but my eyesight works perfectly fine. Your ears look pointed to me."

I roll my eyes and lift a hand to my ear—*oh my god*s, they're pointed. The blood rushes from my face and if my eyes get any wider, they'll pop out of my head.

How is this possible? Did they change when I came through that jelly wall? The Veil. I felt nothing happen, but I was running for Xamira's life and then face planted, so I probably wouldn't have felt it.

I look at him, my brows furrowed deeply. "Why are they like this? I know for a fact they were not pointed like this before today." Right?

His forehead creases like he's worried for me and he speaks softly, "There is no magic outside of the Veil, and this includes any features that would identify you or me as a fae. So when a fae steps through the Veil, anything that separate them from a mortal are changed;. You wouldn't have had those ears before today."

We continue to the city he mentioned while I ponder this information, and I silently slap myself for forgetting my manners.

"I didn't ask what your name was?"

"My name is Andras. It's a pleasure to meet you, Nell."

Chapter 6

After walking for an hour, we pause at the top of a hill and my breath catches in my throat. The scene before me looks like something out of a fairy tale; the sun is setting behind the mountains, gently highlighting the buildings of Ceross. The first thing I notice is a beautiful, white castle resting on a hill above the city. I can just make out some of the intricate carvings along the walls, statues that look like people—or fae?—holding different elements. One is standing with their arm outstretched above them and a flame in their hand, while another is sweeping their hand across what looks to be water. Two of the others are in similar poses, holding what I am assuming are air and earth, if they are sticking to the elements theme.

But I look a little harder at the last statue, narrowing my eyes as if that will help me see better. Maybe I'm just missing something, but they do not appear to be holding anything? I make a mental note to ask Andras what those mean, if we have any time before departing from one another.

The statues are a bit creepy, as none of them have faces—in place of those features is just a smooth, flat piece of the white stone all the statues are made of. Interesting design choice.

My eyes skim the rest of the city and can't help but notice just how different it is from Chago. Walking down the streets of Chago, I wouldn't be able to see anything past the tall buildings that make up every block. Here, all the buildings look to be one or two stories and they feel almost…homey. They're not run down and painted all over—nor do they have floor to ceiling windows and large signs running across them. They're just the perfect mixture of structurally sound and pretty.

There are people moving around the streets—their laughter carrying all the way up here—and the light breeze offers the same scent I first noticed in the forest. It smells like fresh baked dough and cinnamon; but now that I'm closer to the city, I'm gathering a mixture of different herbs and leather.

I don't realize I'm sniffing the air like a dog until Andras laughs. "Yes, I would expect you are not used to your senses being so strong. Mortals have weaker ones than we do, so everything you are experiencing right now must be overwhelming." He looks at me with a hint of affection gleaming from those bright eyes.

I nod, unable to respond with the fluttering in my chest. And at that quiet moment, my stomach chooses to grace us with her song; rumbling so loudly I'm sure the fae on the far side of the city can hear it with their superior ears. I wince, though I shouldn't be embarrassed because everyone needs to eat. But, I'm not about to ask Andras for any more help.

"Well, thank you for showing us the way. I'm sure you have a family to get home to, so we can be on our way now." Xamira jumps into my arms and purs as she kneads my shoulder.

Andras gestures to the castle, a faint smile forming on his face. "I was hoping you would stay with me as a guest until you find what you are looking for. You and your cat will be provided for…I would not feel right leaving you here to learn the ways of the fae—and this city—on your own. I would be honored to help."

"That's okay—I wouldn't want to impose." And I really hate feeling like I owe someone.

His eyes darken a little before his smile returns. "I insist. It is no trouble, and you are a welcome guest."

I look between Xamira and the city—this would be my best option to feed and care for her…I have no fucking clue what this place is, and I doubt I could navigate my way back to Chago. Do they even have currency here? How would I buy her food or a place for us to stay? Andras must be someone important since he pointed to the castle when inviting us to go with him; but would the king…queen…royal…*whoever* owns that place allow two random strangers from the human world into their home?

My eyes find Xamira's, and for once she seems to have nothing to say about the choice she wants me to make. I suppose that's a good enough answer. I can swallow my pride for her, knowing she'll be able to eat and sleep comfortably tonight.

"Okay, thanks Andras." I give him a small smile as that is all I can conjure up; I am so tired I almost contemplate sleeping right on this hill. Seems fine enough. The soft grass and warm breeze are way nicer than Chago, and if I'm honest with myself…probably more comfortable than my apartment.

As we step up to the castle, my jaw drops. It is so much more beautiful up close. It appears to be made of the same white stone as the statues—marble, possibly? I'm not certain that's what they call it here. A prickling slides over my neck, and I look at Andras to find him intensely watching me take in my new surroundings.

"Are you sure this is okay? I don't know if you guys have royals, or whatever, but wouldn't they be upset with you bringing strangers into their castle?"

He quirks one side of his mouth up. "I can assure you that you being here will not cause an issue, Nell. You are safe and welcome." That almost makes me feel like I'm *not* safe and welcome.

We enter through the large, dark wooden door at the entrance and are greeted with an even larger room. Gods…you could fit twenty of my apartments just in this room alone, and there's still an entire castle left after that. Everything is made of marble—the floors, the walls, even the staircases on either side of the room; though the railing is the same material as the door. I can't see very far on the second floor but I'm not surprised to see it is all marble, as well.

It doesn't feel very warm and welcoming. I shiver, squeezing Xamira tighter. I suppose this is to be expected when you have a home like this—still, it wouldn't hurt to see some color in here instead of having mostly everything white.

A man scurries out of an archway to our right, stopping in front of Andras and bowing. "Your Highness, my apologies. We were not expecting you back so soon."

"Please have accommodations readied for Ms. Harper and her companion, Piers—and ensure their dinner is brought to their rooms." Andras doesn't say anything else, choosing to stand with his hands locked behind his back as he stares at Piers.

"Right away, Your Highness. Will you be dining in your rooms as well? I can have Serena make your favorite." Piers seems to be a bit jittery, though I'm not sure if it's because of Andras himself or because he wasn't prepared for him.

Did he say *your highness*? Have I been running my stupid mouth all day to the fae who runs this castle? My eyes slide to Andras, and I decide it's just best to ask since I've been doing that for hours.

"Your Highness? That's why you were so sure about bringing us here. Are you the king or something?"

Andras chuckles, his eyes darting around the space as if there is something to look at. "No, I am the prince of Ceross. We do not have kings or queens in the Veil. That title is loosely reserved for the gods." He almost seems to spit that last part out, like he can't stand the tang of the words on his tongue.

I study him, noticing details I didn't before. His clothes look like they cost more than a years worth of my wages, and they're perfectly clean with no holes or stains to ruin them. His boots are made of leather and not worn, indicating he either has other shoes or doesn't walk very often…and I don't get the sense that the prince is someone who likes to relax on the couch and watch reruns. He also carries himself in a way that screams royalty; tall, chin high, and a sense of confidence that only his status can grant. I am frustrated with myself that I didn't notice these things sooner, considering a lot of my time at home is spent picking apart the people who are from the other side. I was very overwhelmed earlier, so I will not scold myself for it.

"Well, you could have mentioned something sooner and saved me from so much anxiety about pissing off the ones who lived here." Andras smiles at my attempt to cover up how awkward I'm feeling. I do not belong in a place like this. He probably just feels sorry for me and offered a place to stay—not unlike Sarah, who gave me free therapy for the same reason.

"Piers will show you to your rooms." I don't miss how he keeps saying rooms, like it will be more than just a bed in there. "And there will be food sent up for you and your cat. Please rest, and call for Piers should you require anything else. I look forward to seeing you in the morning."

He reaches over to grab the hand that is not holding Xamira—I let him. He bends down to place a light kiss at the top, his warm skin barely brushing over mine as he holds my gaze. I suck in a small breath, my lips parting at the magnitude of his icy gaze. I don't think I've ever had anyone look at me so intensely before…it's disconcerting, but kind of nice at the same time.

The vibrations of Xamira's growl flit through my chest. Andras's eyes flick to her for a moment before he straightens and gives me one of those smiles I'm starting to really like.

I wake to the room lighting from the rising sun, illuminating Xamira on the bed next to me. She's sleeping on her back, with her paws mantis-style in the air. I smile to myself; she must have gotten just as good of sleep as I did. This bed feels like lying on a cloud; and to have something this nice in a guest room? I cannot even imagine the luxury Andras has in his.

After I said goodnight to Andras, Piers showed me to my *rooms*. And they meant rooms…not just a space with a bed. I opened the doors to what I can only describe as a luxury apartment. It has a large couch and two armchairs surrounding a fireplace in the main room. On one side is a door that leads to the bedroom, with this enormous bed. There's another sitting area with a fireplace that—upon further inspection—looks to serve both this room and the sitting room, as I can see the couch through the back of it. To my left is a door that opens to a walk-in closet—which I was shocked to find was already filled with all kinds of clothing options. Another door leads to a bathroom that is certainly larger than my apartment. It has a vanity with sinks covering an entire wall; a beautiful, white soaking tub that I intend to make use of, and an all-glass shower that is conveniently placed in front of the mirror.

On the other side of the sitting room is an open archway to a dining room—which holds a perfect view of the back gardens—and a round, wooden table. That seems to be the only color besides my clothing choices. Everything else in these rooms, including the furniture and bedding, is the same white as the marble. It feels cold and uninviting, but who am I to complain? These may not be my decorating choices, but this isn't my house—or castle, I guess.

Scratch that…the food they brought Xamira and me also had some color to it, and it was some of the best food I have ever tasted. Everything in this Veil must be better than outside of it, which had me thinking for a brief moment if that also means the males. Just from what I've seen so far, I have no doubt that's also the truth.

One of the castle staff—Fen—brought an array of options and my jaw fell from my face. I do not think I've ever seen so much food, or such good looking food, in my life. There was roasted chicken covered in an herb butter, candied sweet potatoes, steamed vegetables, rolls that looked like miniature versions of this bed, and creamy gravy. They also brought a stunning chocolate cake, along with some unseasoned chicken and wet cat food for Xamira. She devoured the chicken, though wasn't too happy with the cat food. Now that I think of it…she's always seemed to prefer sharing my food with me rather than eating the kind made for her species.

I tried to eat as much as I could without making myself sick, as I didn't want to waste anything or upset the staff who most likely spent hours cooking it all. Everything I tried was extraordinary. I must have seriously fallen off that bridge and died yesterday—because there's no way I am currently in a castle, after being escorted in by its prince, lying in a bed made of clouds, eating the greatest food to ever exist. It's just not possible.

I reach out to give Xamira belly rubs, causing her arms to stretch over her head and fall back asleep. What do I do now? This one night of luxury was magical and undeserved, but that doesn't mean I get to stay here forever. I need to figure out the next step for Xamira and me, though that will be difficult without having any information about this city, or the fae who live here. I should find Andras and ask him about this place, so that I can decide if this is where Xamira and I should stay.

But first, I need a shower. I felt bad enough sleeping in this fluffy, white bedding without washing up first; but I was so exhausted I could barely keep my eyes open. Anxiety does that to you. I roll from the bed—as that's clearly the only graceful way to move around on this thing—and walk to the bathroom. It takes me a minute to figure out the shower, with all the buttons and handles, but I eventually get hot water spraying out.

I wash with the soaps provided and feel cleaner than I ever have…everything here must be touched by the gods or something, because what could the soap here possibly be made from that makes it a million times better than the soap I'm used to? I turn the shower off—though I debated sitting in there all day—and grab one of the towels. These are also extremely soft. And white.

I'm standing in front of the mirror after drying my body, and look at myself for the first time since coming through the Veil. Someone screams, the high pitch tickling my throat. Is that me? I know Andras said I have a point to my ears now, but that's not what causes me to startle. I have markings all over my body that look like tattoos, but I don't remember ever getting a single tattoo…

All the markings are a deep reddish brown color and swirl nicely around my pale skin. My left arm has three lines circling it above my elbow, while my right has a swirling pattern that rises up to my shoulder, curves down under my right breast, and then climbs to wrap around my neck, ending behind my jaw just under my ear. It's beautiful. There is also a line circled around my right thigh. I turn to see if there's anything on my back and there is. It's another twisting pattern going up my spine and looks to be in the shape of a dagger, though it's difficult to make out.

I think Xamira was right…I have been here before, because these tattoos did not just randomly appear on my skin. They had to come from somewhere—but where would I have gotten them that I don't remember it? And what do they mean?

The door to the bedroom slams open and Andras bolts into the bathroom, looking positively frantic. "What is it, Nell? I heard you scream. Are you all right?"

He halts when he sees I'm wearing only towel, and suddenly I'm feeling a little self-conscious. I pull the fabric tighter around me before answering.

"I'm sorry, I didn't mean to scare you. I came out of the shower and when I looked in the mirror, I saw these tattoos all over my body and freaked out a bit."

He relaxes at my confession, shoulders slumping as he huffs a laugh, "You mean your markings? Those are something you will find on most of the fae here, depending on their upbringing." He inspects the ones he can see on my shoulders, and his eyebrows scrunch. "Though I have to admit, I do not recognize the markings on you. The fae in the Veil are given the same ones for each piece of education or training they complete. But the ones on your skin are not ones I've seen before."

I look into the mirror again and study the markings that I can see. "So the only way to get these is by completing certain things? Would it have been possible for me to get these outside the Veil?"

"No. The markings are specific to physical and mental training that fae complete in their younger years; a new marking appears with each training that is completed. It would not be possible to obtain these in the mortal cities, considering magic cannot be present outside the Veil."

"Do I have magic, then? And why wouldn't I remember getting these? You make it sound like it takes years to earn them, but I've been living in Chago my whole life." I rub my face, feeling fuzzy with everything that's being thrown at me. "I don't understand any of this," I groan into my hand.

Could I have an entire life I remember nothing of? There's no way…the last twenty-seven years have been full of trauma and struggle, not whatever it is fae do to get these markings. I would surely remember if I lived through something other than daily beatings.

"I was coming to your rooms to ask if you would care to join me for breakfast? We could discuss more about this when we are both clothed and have clearer heads." I turn to him with wide eyes. I don't think I've ever heard a man say that before…they usually try to get me out of my clothes. But he did say he was a *male,* not a *man.*

Instead of commenting on the interesting behavior, I give him a smile and tell him I will find some clothes and meet him in the dining area. He informs me that it is just under the foyer stairs, and to call Piers if I get lost.

I find a pair of loose-fitted, white trousers and a pale blue, long sleeve top. Comfy and cute—just my style. Though there is a lot more white in this closet than I originally thought. Must just be the favored color in the castle. Or Andras just really likes the clean look. I step out of the closet to find Xamira waiting for me at the end of the bed. Her long black fur and golden eyes are a stark contrast to the rest of the castle; I don't think she will ever be lost here.

"Are you ready, big girl?" She gives me a small meow and jumps lightly from the bed. I've always appreciated her desire to be by my side and do everything with me. I have a feeling she'll be allowed just about anywhere in this city, so I think we are both going to like it here. She will get to be with me whenever she wants, and I won't have to feel bad about leaving her at home all day because she's not welcome in many places.

We eventually find our way to the foyer—I may have gotten lost if it wasn't for the smell of food I was following. Andras was right, this whole heightened senses thing is quite amazing. Just something else to add to my crazy long list of things I need to process.

Chapter 7

I walk into the dining area to find Andras sitting at the head of the table; his back is straight and his hands rest on the arms of his large, colorless chair. Today he wears a hard expression and a deep forest green shirt. His sandy hair is combed through and his blinding eyes are fixed on me as I step to the seat next to him.

Staff members stand to the side of the room, each with their hands folded in front of them—not speaking. It's strange when none of them turn my way as I enter—as if they don't wish to step out of line without permission. I understand not wanting to piss off your boss because your job is more important than the shit you want to say to them.

Andras doesn't appear to treat them poorly, though; he's just not overly affectionate with them from what I've seen. But I wouldn't expect him to be…he is the prince and likely has a lot on his plate, with not much time to socialize with the castle staff.

As soon as I'm seated, the staff spring into action—they bring various food options and place them in the middle of the long, wooden table; its deep, rich color is a heavy contrast to the rest of the room. There're many smells to take in, so I try to focus my eyes on what's being set before me. The spread includes eggs, bacon, various types of fruit, what looks to be oatmeal, and biscuits. I cannot remember the last time I could afford something as nice as fruit. There's also some type of flat pancake and different syrups.

Andras fills his plate, and I follow his lead—in the process, I notice another place setting across the table from my seat. Andras catches my curious stare at the empty chair and comments, "I normally have my personal advisor here. However, she is out completing a task for me at the moment. She should return within a few weeks, and you will be able to meet her."

"Weeks?" I nearly choke from my shock. "As in, you expect me to be here that long?"

"Yes. I assume you have nowhere to go—considering before we met yesterday, you had no knowledge that the cities in the Veil even existed."

I open and close my mouth twice, not knowing what to say in response. Sure, he's right...have nowhere to go. But I didn't expect him to be so blunt about my situation and so casual about extending my stay in his castle. I'm still weary of him, and I have good reason to be; I cannot remember the last time someone was nice to me just because they wanted to be. Taking Sarah out of the picture, because clearly she had other motives for giving me free therapy sessions.

"I guess I was hoping to talk to you about that. I don't know anything about this city or its people and was wondering if you'd be willing to teach me some things? So that Xamira and I could find our own way?" I give him a small smile, his face hardening a little at my words. I shift in my seat—I'd rather not offend him or his hospitality.

"You are welcome to stay here as long as you would like, Nell. I will, of course, teach you of the city and the fae. However, not under the assumption that you will leave to live on your own so soon." He slides his piercing gaze to me, and I get the sense that I don't want to know what would happen if I were to refuse the prince.

I don't want to refuse him, anyway. I have no knowledge of my surroundings and likely wouldn't do well on my own right now. Plus,

I will not complain about the luxuries staying in the castle offers…because this is very nice. And maybe having not to worry about housing and food would allow me to figure things out instead of rushing into it and ending up in the same situation I just left.

"Okay. Thank you, Andras."

"It's settled then. You will stay here until I believe you are ready to live on your own. Now, I would like to discuss the matter of your memory."

"My memory?"

"Yes, you are fae. I may have been convinced that there was no third-party involvement in your life that would have you living outside of the Veil, had you also not had markings across your body—and quite a few of them from what I could see." My face heats at the memory of our encounter this morning. "That indicates that you have been in the Veil before and completed training."

I blink and nod slowly. He continues before I can think further, "I will admit, I am intrigued in discovering what your markings mean and where you would have gotten them."

I chew on a piece of melon and consider his words when something he said earlier comes to mind.

"You mentioned there were two cities in the Veil…would the other city give markings like these for their trainings? Could it be that I am from there?"

He takes a few seconds too long studying me, and I wring my hands together at his assessing stare. "No, I have seen the markings given in Anloria and they do not look like the ones on your skin, either."

He seems to consider his next words. "I also would be selfishly interested in knowing who would have manipulated your memories enough that you do not remember this part of your past. Not only is the manipulation of another's mind immoral and illegal, I am not aware of any fae in this realm who possess the essence magic required to do such a thing."

"Essence magic?"

He raises his brows and nods, leaning forward to place his head on top of his fists. "Ah, yes. You are not aware of the types of magic that fae can have. Simply, there is elemental magic and essence magic. The elemental magic includes fire, air, earth, and water. Essence magic is a type that has not been seen on this realm in centuries—it is said only gods are able to possess it, since it could be quite dangerous in the wrong hands."

Intrigued, I sit forward and press for more information. "What does essence magic do?"

He smirks, the movement softening his face, and moves to grab a piece of bacon. "Essence magic is very powerful. It allows its wielder to control the essence of anything, including other fae. Essentially, someone who has that magic also has all elemental magic—but it also allows them to manipulate another's mind and body, in addition. That is why it's dangerous. And also why only gods can wield it."

We sit in silence for several minutes while I process everything Andras just told me. He believes my memories have been messed with, but it would've been a god that did it…why would a god want to fuck with my head? Why would I be important enough for that? Did they change any of the memories I do have? I didn't think the gods were even real…but I had no idea about the Veil or fae, either.

Another question sparks in mind. "Would I have magic?" I ask, sitting back in my chair and turning toward Andras. He gives me a slow nod, observing my reaction, but I'm too excited by the idea of having my own magic that I ignore it.

"How would I find out what kind?"

He considers my question for a moment, running a hand over his clean-shaven jaw. "There are some things we could try to pull it out of you, but my assumption would be that you cannot access it without your memories."

"So I'm stuck until I figure out who took my memories and ask them to give them back?" He raises his eyebrows at me, and I feel the need to explain my thought process, "Well, you had mentioned that essence magic is the only thing that could do this to me, and only a god would posses it; so I presume they would be the only one who could undo it?"

"That is correct," he nods. "I would propose that finding anything we can about your memories would be the best use of your time here. There is a library in the castle that you can utilize at your leisure. Fen will be your personal aid and will show you where the library is, as well as anywhere else in the castle you might like to see."

"What about the city?" I blurt out before I'm even done thinking the words in my head, too excited to explore this new world. "Would Fen be able to show me around there as well?"

"It may be best," his jaw flexes, "to have you remain on the castle grounds for the time being. I would not want to see you overwhelmed by the new environment."

I'm not sure how that would be any more overwhelming than every-thing that happened yesterday; but I give him a smile, not wanting to push my luck with all the help he is already offering. He must notice the disappointment in my eyes because he sits forward and grabs my hand. "Why don't we give you a few days to rest before introducing the city, and I will take you there myself to show you around." He smiles and softly kisses my fingers, grazing his lips over my skin. My stomach flutters at the intimacy; it's strange having the touch of someone who doesn't want to take anything from me.

I spend the next two days doing what Andras suggested: resting. As much as I want to devour every book in that library, and question any fae who have been here for a while, to see if maybe they recognize me…I also want to have a clear head when I start this new journey. Once I dive into this whole mess, I know I won't be able to stop myself until I have some answers; so, I figured taking a couple days to rest and process my new life was an important thing to do. Fen showed me around the castle, only introducing me to a few of the staff. Everyone I meet seems nice, though it's as if they're afraid to talk to me. Even Fen—whom I've spent the most time with—is very professional and not one for small talk. I understand, though. This is their job, and I'm a guest of the prince; so it makes sense they wouldn't want to say anything around me if they think I'm going to repeat their words or actions to Andras. I would never want to get anyone fired, as I'm sure working in the castle is their livelihood. But it would be nice to have a friend other than the prince and Xamira.

"That is about all there is to see in the castle," Fen explains. "The rest of it is just empty space, mostly." We're walking down the hallway toward my rooms after Fen gave me a small tour of the place; and I mean small. *She showed me the kitchens, the dining area, and how to access the back garden. This castle is large. There's no way the rest is just empty rooms.*

I ponder that for a moment, wondering if she would think I'm rude for asking follow-up questions. "Why is it there's barely any staff here?"

Her eyes shoot to me before looking ahead again. Her voice is quieter, "Prince Andras is quite private, and wishes to only employ the staff he needs, instead of having many fae here."

"And why doesn't the staff like to talk? I've tried speaking to a few that I've seen, and they say nothing back…" She tenses, her clasped hands tightening in front of her.

"There is much to be done around the castle each day; we do not have time to speak with anyone unless it is necessary for our duties." That was vague.

We reach my room and she turns to leave before I have a chance to ask another question. I frown, wondering if I've offended her at all. That wasn't my intention. Though she seemed to get uncomfortable with what I asked. She's probably just a private fae, as well. Not everyone is social; plus, she's working, and I'm trying to gossip.

I sigh and walk into my rooms to spend the rest of the night with Xamira, making a note in my head to try and leave the questions be from now on.

Andras has been pretty busy, and I've only seen him during dinners. I know I shouldn't be upset about it. He doesn't owe me anything; but I would like to get to know him more, considering he's allowing me to stay in his home. He has asked me many questions about myself, and all I know of him is he is a prince, and he likes cleanliness and routines.

In my time exploring the castle, I've found that the fae don't have electronics like we do outside of the Veil. No phones, internet, or television; not that I had any of that in Chago, but it's strange to not see them at all here. I wonder if it's just that they don't know they exist, or they don't want those things here?

I'm walking down a hall—which, not surprisingly, looks the same as all the other halls, and I'm always afraid I'm going to get lost because of it. Xamira is walking next to me; she hasn't left my side since we arrived in Ceross. It's really nice to have her with me; at least I know I can always count on her when I need a friend. Another reason I shouldn't be upset that Andras is so unavailable…I never relied on anyone except Xamira and myself in Chago, and that shouldn't change here. I need to keep reminding myself that I can only trust us, regardless of anyone else's kindness.

I hear footsteps behind me and turn around to see Andras approaching. Xamira still must not like him for some reason, as she growls or hisses each time he comes around. They say cats can tell when someone is not a cat person, and Andras does not seem like the type, so maybe she just knows he's not fond of her species.

He stops in front of me, giving me that gorgeous smile that makes him look like he's happy and stress free. Something I've noticed he does not give out often. I take him in, and am not surprised to see him wearing the same thing he does every day. I'm undoubtedly right that the male really prefers his routines, and that translates to how he runs this castle as well. He is way more put together than I have ever been. Which is why I'm not a prince, or princess, I guess; because this place would be run to the ground faster than you can say *fuck*.

"Good morning, Nell. I trust your stay here has been well?" He looks at me with an intense stare, and I find myself feeling nervous in his presence. Strange. I've never felt nervous in front of the opposite sex before. But I've never been around my own kind before, either.

I give him a genuine smile. "It has been...nice. I still can't believe others live like this. I keep pinching myself because I swear I'm dreaming."

He chuckles and takes a step closer, leaving only a small space between our bodies. "I apologize I have not been available much since you've arrived. I have been drowning in work I need to catch up on. However, I thought you might like to get started on research today," he gestures toward the direction of the library. "I have something I would like to try with you if you are open to it. It would test if repressed memories are what we're dealing with here."

"Would it hurt?" That earns me a laugh, and I'm mesmerized by the glimpse of the male behind the mask he holds over himself as prince. He truthfully is quite beautiful. He sees me grinning at his reaction and closes the distance between our bodies, reaching his hand up to lightly run his fingers along my jaw. He reaches my hair, pushing some behind my ear, and his brow furrows as he takes in the details of the auburn strands. I'm afraid to breathe and can feel my heart racing. I hope he can't hear it and give away my reaction to such a small touch. Sure, I've been touched plenty of times before, but not like this. This is different. He smells of linen and roses, though not fresh roses. No, the scent reminds of the soap bar I found in my bathroom, which holds the faint aroma of the flower.

He seems to realize what he is doing, as he drops his hand and takes a step back. "My apologies. I just find myself fascinated by you. To answer your question: no, it will not hurt. I merely wish to ask you some questions of my own." I catch my breath and do my best to smile, trying not to expose how much he affected me just now.

"Okay" I move to walk in the direction he pointed to. "That sounds great, I'm excited to get started."

We enter the library, and I'm surprised to find it's darker than the rest of the castle. I would have expected everything in here to be white marble, but Andras informs me that it's best for the books. Instead, everything in here is black marble, including the shelving that holds the books. It's colder than the other areas of the castle I've visited, and I wrap my arms around myself instinctively. There are a couple of areas for seating and lamps spread throughout the space. It is larger than I expected, though I'm not sure why I thought it wouldn't be; especially considering how big the castle, and every room in it, is.

I wait next to Andras as he talks to the librarian; a fae who appears to be older, though it's hard to tell. He has hair that seems to have a silver hue to it, along with a few wrinkles around his eyes. But even with his features, he could be thirty or three hundred and I don't think I'd be able to tell the difference. Fen told me that fae age differently than humans do. While humans age quickly and pass away after a few decades, fae stop aging annually at twenty-five years old, and our life spans range into the hundreds. Knowing that I'm going to live longer than a couple more decades will take some getting used to, I think.

We thank the librarian—Cyrus—and Andras leads me to the second floor; we come to a dark, back corner that is full of large, dusty books, looking like they haven't been touched in centuries.

"Cyrus believes these," he picks up one book, "would be a good place to start. These volumes contain information on essence magic. And also the gods. If we can narrow down who possesses the proper magic for something like this, we may be able to figure out why they did it and how to reverse it."

I take a deep breath, holding back the cough that tickles my throat. I'm already tired and overwhelmed, and we haven't even gotten started yet. "You talk about the gods as if they're real and still alive today. If that were true, where are they? Why don't they make themselves known or help people?"

Andras's blue eyes find mine, growing several shades darker, almost like swimming in the ocean at sunset. "The gods are very real, and they do live. The gods do not have a life expectancy, so to speak, which makes them nearly immortal."

"Nearly immortal?"

"They will not die of natural causes, like aging or sickness; but they can be killed, though that would be quite difficult to achieve." He turns away to scan across other books on the shelf in front of him. "The gods are the balance of the realms. They hold everything together and make sure that the balance does not deviate, as that would cause much devastation. While they control the balance of Earth, they do not live in this realm. They live in a realm called Europa, a place that can only be accessed by gods; so I imagine it is going to be complicated trying to speak with one of them."

I run my hand along the spines in front of me, my fingers coming back coated in dust. Andras grabs several of the books, bringing them to a large table surrounded by lamps that will allow us to read. We take a seat, Andras seeming lost in some thought that I don't want to interrupt. So I sit and patiently wait.

After a few moments he comes back to himself, turning toward me and lifting his gaze to mine. "Before we look for information in these pages, I would like to ask you the questions I had mentioned earlier. If you are comfortable with it, of course?" He tilts his head, looking concerned, and I feel a little pang of awareness in my chest. His attention on me is strange. I'm not used to anyone looking at me in such a way. But it's also comforting; it makes me feel like I'm not in this alone.

"Sure," I try to give him a reassuring smile. He looks between my eyes for a moment, probably to see if I'm lying about being ready for his questioning. He must decide I'm not because he faces me fully, grabs my chair and pulls it toward him until our knees are touching. Sitting in this dark and quiet space with this beautiful male is inebriating. This is a bad time to feel the heat gathering in my lower abdomen…he is here to help me, not sate the curiosities and feelings of his ignorant house guest. I try to keep my breathing even.

His mouth quirks a little; as if he notices my reaction but won't acknowledge it. "Close your eyes." I shut them and feel him wrap his hands around mine. His skin is warm and rough. "Now, I am going to ask you some questions, and I would like you to do your best to picture the answers in your mind while you tell me aloud what you see." I nod.

"What was your childhood like?"

I stiffen, not comfortable divulging all the horrid details of the things I lived through. Instead, I give him a summary. I was given up by my parents, put into the foster care system, got an apartment once I aged out, and have been living on my own since.

"Think of your foster family."

"I had a few. You'll need to be more specific."

"Then think of your first foster family."

That's easy. I will never forget the family I lived with for the first twelve years of my life. Gemma and Pete. They had two children of their own; so I was always the outcast of the house, and they were not afraid to remind me of that each day. When I was seven, Pete found his way into the attic one night, where my 'bedroom' was. It was really just a few dirty blankets and a lamp. They never allowed me to have a pillow, or a mattress, because that would be too much of a privilege for The Orphan, as they liked to call me.

"Nell…are you awake, sweetie?" I hear the door creak open, seeing my foster father walk in.

The first night Pete visited, he told me he didn't like the way Gemma and the other kids treated me. He said I deserved better and he wanted to make me feel good, but that I couldn't say anything to the others because we would both get into trouble. He said they treat him poorly, too; especially Gemma, who doesn't treat him like a woman should, and he thinks that I could help him feel better as well.

I was a child, so of course I believed him; and of course I was excited, and willing, to do anything he asked. He started by tracing his fingers over my arms and stomach, which tickled and caused me to laugh each time he made a pass. Then he lowered his hand to my underwear and moved his fingers lightly, watching my face for my reaction.

"Does that feel good, Nell?"

It did. It felt nice to be touched gently, instead of being hit with a metal spoon or belt. I nodded, and he gave a serpentine smile. He then showed me how to make him feel good. That night, I learned what a dick looked like; and while it grossed me out, I wanted to make him happy. So I wrapped my hands around and squeezed like he told me to.

For years after that, he came to my room almost nightly. He gave me my first orgasm when I was eleven, which made me feel disgusting. He showed me how to use my mouth to please a man, and would ride my face so hard I had bruises at the back of my throat. Then he would force me to choke on his cum, which caused me to gag. Each night I would make myself throw up, trying to rid my body of what he put into it, and then cry myself to sleep.

One night when I was twelve, he insisted he had a new way for us to make each other feel good. I begged him not to. He covered my mouth with his hand and held my head down so hard I thought it would crack. Then he shoved his dick into me, insisting it would hurt the first time, but I would eventually like it. As soon as he was done, he left me to cry, lying in a puddle of blood and semen. That was the night I decided I wouldn't stay there anymore. I could take their words and their beatings, but that was a violation I wouldn't be able to get past.

The next day, Pete somehow found himself at the bottom of the stairs with a broken neck and cracked skull. His blood pooling all over the soft, cream rug Gemma loved so much. She and the kids found me standing at the top of the stairs staring at Pete's dead body; I think she knew I did it to him, though they could never prove it. She shoved my face into a wall so hard I passed out, later waking up in a new foster home. But I was glad for it. She had to have known what he was doing to me. I was going to throw her down the stairs, as well, if she didn't get to me first. Lucky her.

I can't say all of this out loud to Andras and admit just how fucked up I am, so I just nod for him to continue.

"Now imagine what each person in the family looked like. Describe them to me."

I imagine Gemma first. "My foster mother was a large woman—tall and bulky. She had long, brown hair that was always kept in a bun."

"What did her face look like?"

"Well, she had—" I stop because I realize I can't see her face. I can see the rest of her body clearly, but her face is blurry; it's most likely because it's been over ten years since I've seen her. "I'm sure she had a nose and eyes, normal facial features," I continue, "though I can't seem to remember what they looked like." I feel Andras squeeze my hands.

"What about your foster father? What did his face look like?"

I feel my forehead scrunch together because I'm thinking so hard, trying to remember what his face looked like, but I can't. "I'm not sure. I don't remember his, either. I was a child though, so it's been a long time and my memories could be skewed."

"Okay, then tell me what your last foster family looked like," he prompts. I think of them, but again I cannot make out their faces. What the fuck? Am I just repressing memories? I scan through people I've known my whole life. Kids at school I used to sit next to, teachers I had, my caseworker, the people at my very first job. I cannot put faces to any of them. I try to think of locations, like the homes I used to live in, and the schools I went to…I can make out general shapes and colors of the places, but no distinct features. Words are blurred out and fine details aren't there. It feels like my memories have some kind of filter over them, causing them to mesh together in one big glob of blurriness.

My breath quickens as I attempt to find something—anything—that I can grasp onto. I hate not being in control; and seeing my memories like this makes me feel very much out of control. How have I never noticed this before? Do I never think of details? I suppose not. Usually, it's just a passing thought; and I don't recall ever sitting like this, trying to think of specific people or places. I do my best to tell Andras as much.

His large hands grasp my shoulders, and he pulls me in for a hug. I realize I'm crying and trembling. I take safety in his hold, allowing myself to calm down as we sit there for several minutes while he holds me tightly. When my breathing evens out, he releases me; only backing up enough to look me in the eye, but a little closer and our noses would touch. I almost lean forward to kiss him, wanting so badly to distract myself right now. I feel heavy and dark because of the memories, but I'm also freaked out because the memories no longer seem real. I feel like I'm going crazy. Before I can claim his full lips, he speaks to me in a gentle tone.

"Nell, I am sorry. I did not intend to cause you this much distress." He cups my face in his rough palms. "If it helps you in any way, I can confirm that your memories have been tampered with. The fact you cannot see the faces or details of your memories tells me that they are not your memories, but instead images placed inside of your head to cover up your actual life."

Tears make their way down my cheeks again, and he gives me a pained look. Like he wants to help but isn't sure how. Next thing I know, I'm laughing; I find it so unbelievably funny how ridiculous this is. For years, I have lived with the trauma and experiences of memories that aren't real. Of things that I didn't even go through, that I believed I did. And unless these fake memories are taken from me, I will live with the reminders, and trauma, of my fake past life while also dealing with whatever my life was like before. This is all so fucked up, and I can't stop laughing. Andras looks highly concerned for my wellbeing, and amidst my breakdown, the warmth of his body seeps into me as he lifts me up, holding me tightly against him. The last thing I remember before darkness is Andras walking through the library doors, looking down at me with wide, bright blue eyes.

Chapter 8

W aking up and remembering my very public, very embarrassing breakdown was not the highlight of my life. Although Andras reassured me it was only him and Cyrus who witnessed my mess, it didn't make me feel any better. But I guess having little staff who are always busy in this enormous castle means you can get around most places without running into anyone. So I'm quite thankful for that.

I spent the next few days mostly alone, going through the old books Andras chose for me to read. I'd hoped he would help me get through these, though he mentioned the other day that he was catching up on a lot of things he needed to complete, so I understand why he's been absent. I have…mixed feelings about him. I've never really had feelings for a man that I can remember, and whoever gave me my false memories clearly wanted me to steer clear of them. After years of being abused, and having disappointing hookups, men were just not something I was interested in. *Andras is a* male, *though,* I remind myself as I roll my eyes.

He has been kind in bringing me here; giving Xamira and me a place to stay and helping me figure out what is going on in my head. His unfiltered reactions before he reigns himself in show me that he might not be as unaffected by me as I thought—that makes me smile because, even though I do not want to admit it, my body is also affected by him. He just feels *familiar*, which makes my body want to trust him; but my brain keeps slamming on the brakes, reminding me that I cannot trust anyone else. All everyone does is take from me. Well, everyone except Andras, it would seem. I guess that is the perk of being a prince: he doesn't need or want for anything.

What it would have been like to grow up with such a luxury.

This place—this castle—also seems familiar. Like it's somewhere I belong. That gives me hope that we're on the right track to unraveling the mystery of my past and what exactly happened to me, but it still hasn't filled the guttural emptiness I feel in my chest. There are moments when it grows lighter before slamming me back down again. Hopefully finding some answers will also help me discover what I need to not feel so hollow.

I sigh deeply, closing the book I'm reading through in my sitting room—it would be too convenient to find any information I could actually use, instead of just the history of the gods. It is quite interesting to read about, though it would be wonderful to find genuine answers. *Anything* at this point.

From what I've gathered, there were nine original gods, who were tasked with keeping the balance of the two realms: Earth and Europa. The gods mated with humans, creating demigods—the latter lived on Earth while the gods resided on Europa. Eventually, a few self-righteous demigods felt that they were entitled to live on Europa, considering they *were above the humans*. They started an uprising with one of the gods as their leader. The god craved all the power for themselves and, granted they helped kill the other eight gods, promised the demigods they could live on Europa with the god as their leader.

They needed more bodies, however, so the demigods gave their blood to a group of humans, which is what created the fae. Those who caused the uprising lost the war that they started, and the remaining eight gods executed every being involved, including the ninth god.

The remaining gods allowed the demigods to live on Europa, under the expectation they would become warriors and protect the realm should anything like the uprising happen again.

After some time had passed, the gods were struggling to keep the balance in the realms and noticed the humans causing mass chaos and destruction. They no longer wanted to live around the fae after what *'their kind'* did to the Earth. And so the gods created the Veil, which separated the fae and humans, allowing each to live in harmony on Earth. They ensured that no magic could be used outside of the Veil, forcing the humans to believe the fae were removed altogether—even when some walked amongst them. In time, new generations of humans emerged, and the legends of the fae and gods became campfire stories.

The books also mentioned that each god possesses two types of magic, while demigods and fae have just one type each. They sadly do not mention the names of the gods, or who holds what type of magic; I'm guessing that is to protect their identities should anyone try an uprising again, but it is still frustrating as I would love to know which god is to blame for my current circumstances.

I lie on the soft plush rug in front of the fireplace, placing my palms over my eyes before groaning into the thick fabric. Reading through that many words has given me a headache, and I didn't even find anything useful. Even so, I wish I had more to read—I no longer wish to think about anything relating to my memories. It's too much right now, and I really do not feel like experiencing another breakdown in front of anyone.

"Everything all right?" A deep voice interrupts my thoughts, and I squeal as my arms lash out instinctively, hitting Xamira's tail. She startles from sleep, narrowing her bright eyes in my direction. I turn my head to where Andras stands in front of me, arms folded over his chest and pursing his lips as if he's struggling to not laugh at my terror.

"Hey, that is not funny!" I laugh with him. "I didn't hear you come in, and you really scared me for a second."

"Apologies, my sweet. I did knock and came to check on you when there was no answer. Is the dust from these books getting so into your head that it's blocking your hearing, or are you just naturally so unaware of your environment?" He gives me a big smile that melts my heart, which—slightly—dampens the teasing remark. I enjoy this playful side of him. It makes me feel like I'm seeing something only a few others ever have the privilege of witnessing.

I let out a breathy laugh. "Oh, we're feeling funny today, huh? Well, I'll have you know I did read through every single one of those books and—" I stop, not wishing to ruin the mood but having nothing else to say.

Andras saves me from voicing what I don't want to admit and says, "I was not very hopeful that we were going to find anything useful in those old books. The history stopped being recorded centuries back. I would still like to look through some other books, just in case there is something useful, though I thought that maybe experiences might trigger some memories for you."

I sit up at this, tilting my head back to look into his eyes; today they remind me of a blue sky when it is partially covered by clouds. I take no time to realize what an interesting position I've put myself in. Sitting up caused me to be nearly level with his cock, and if I leaned forward a little, I could easily just stick my tongue out and lick my way up…

Oh my gods, Nell. You horny idiot. Get your damn thoughts together; the male—prince—is trying to help you and you're down here fantasizing about his dick.

Though I don't think I'm the only one who had a moment of straying thoughts as I see Andras tense, swallowing loudly, and eyes darkening just a little. Saving us both from the awkwardness, I make my way to my feet. "What—what do you mean experiences? Like going to different places here and seeing if I recognize anything?"

"Yes, that's what I mean. We could start by taking a trip through the city tomorrow, if that is something you are still interested in?"

My eyes bulge and I jump up to hug him around the neck, the excitement bursting from me. "Oh gods, yes, that would be so amazing. Thank you, thank you!" He hesitates a moment, but wraps his arms around my waist, hugging me back. I feel both of our hearts beating quickly and am suddenly aware of what I've done, and the very close proximity I've put us in. I lean back, resting my hands on his hard chest since he has not let me go just yet. Looking up to his eyes, I see the same heat in them that I feel running toward my core. I tighten my thighs together from the emotion I'm being slammed with from his gaze; he must notice because his fingers tighten, digging into my back.

After a moment, he lets me go, but I swear we could have been locked there for hours and I would've been none the wiser. I take a couple steps back, biting my lip because I don't know what to say. I've never had such a reaction to anyone before, and I'm feeling flustered from it.

Andras again saves the day, appearing nonchalant, and says, "I thought you might enjoy that. Fen mentioned you talk about visiting the city quite a bit, and I have time tomorrow to take you." So Fen reports back what I say to the prince…good to know. I definitely won't be telling her my dirty little thoughts. Nope, keeping those all to myself.

"I will see you in the morning, my sweet. Good night." His use of this new nickname doesn't go unnoticed. He reaches for my hand and bends to give it a gentle kiss, something I'm becoming fond of each time we part ways.

Once he leaves, I ready myself for bed and lie under the blankets, feeling like it's a hundred degrees in here. I'm still heated from my conversation with Andras; my core throbs painfully, and if I don't do something about it, I have a feeling it will make tomorrow difficult.

Is it weird to touch oneself in someone else's home…to thoughts of them…from an arguably innocent conversation…when they are still a stranger? It might be, but I can't bring myself to feel bad or embarrassed about it.

Instead, I reach one hand under my oversized shirt to grab my breast, squeezing roughly. I pinch my nipple in between two fingers and moan into the dark, quiet room, hoping no one with extra good hearing is standing outside my doors, but also not caring if they are. I'm too worked up at this point. My other hand traces the soft skin of my abdomen down to my underwear, feeling over the fabric to find it already soaked. It has been so long since I've made myself come, but I can't remember the last time I wanted to? I don't think I've ever been so turned on before, and now I'm so sensitive that just running my finger over the cotton of my underwear is making me shudder.

Using my left hand to switch between breasts, I move my right hand under the fabric, dipping two fingers into my slit to gather some wetness and start slowly circling my clit. My moans are loud, but I am no longer thinking about anyone overhearing me, even Andras. In fact, I hope he does. That male looks like he knows how to please a female. Not just from the hard muscles I've felt along his chest and arms, or his soft, very grab-able hair, but from his demeanor. He carries himself with a confidence I've only ever seen in one other person. He stares at me with an intensity that makes me want to fold in on myself but also makes me feel alive, and noticed, for the first time in my life.

Gods, I'm already so close to coming and I've barely touched myself yet. I need something inside of me. The ache is too great for clit stimulation alone. Though I un-shamefully wish it was Andras's cock, my fingers will have to do for now. I slide two in and start pumping them, curling them at just the right time to hit that place inside me that has me nearly screaming. There's no doubt someone hears me.

I roll over, shoving my face in the pillow, so that I can ride my hand and pretend it's the male under me that has me feeling so unhinged. Inserting another finger, I start to feel the fullness I crave, though I know it won't be enough. I quicken the pace of my fingers, my hips rocking on their own, and use the base of my hand to rub my clit. It doesn't take long before I feel the intense pleasure that has been building in my abdomen move to my core. Two more thrusts and I fall over the edge of the most intense orgasm I've ever had. My inner walls squeezing my fingers so tightly I'm surprised I don't lose blood flow in them.

I slow my hand down, riding out the waves that seem to go on forever, and when they melt away, I'm breathing hard and too weak to move. I lay there for a few minutes, reality coming back to me in pieces. The pillow under my cheek is wet. I think I was biting down on it at one point. The hand cupping my sex is soaked and I know the sheets will be, too.

I make it off the bed to clean myself up in the bathroom. I catch my reflection in the mirror and take a moment to look at my flushed cheeks and my bottom lip, which has an indent in it from me biting too hard. It's not bleeding, though it looks like it may bruise. I can't help but to laugh to myself at that thought; walking around the city with Andras tomorrow, with a bruised lip, knowing it was caused by my reaction to him.

Before I can walk back over to the bed, I notice my thighs looking a little different. Are they thicker? I lift my shirt and the outline of my ribs is no longer visible. I know it's the fact that I've been able to eat properly for the first time in years, but I didn't think I would see the effects on my body so quickly. It must have been so starved for nutrients that it's taking in every bit of what I'm eating. I look almost…healthy. Not even when I was a child did I look healthy; well I guess my fake child life, but still. I feel a lump in the back of my throat and I shake my head because, no, I will not be crying over something as simple as rib outlines.

I want to be happy for myself, and I am, but the hollow feeling in my chest is still there. I just know something is still missing. Maybe I'll find it in the city tomorrow. Or maybe I just need some time to process my new life and accept that I am safe.

Chapter 9

Andras and I are walking out of the castle gates the next morning, Xamira on my other side, to make our way down to the city. It is beautiful outside; the sun is shining, making the cool morning air warm up. The breeze is light, and everything sounds peaceful.

Back in Chago, you could hear large vehicles on the other side, or people yelling at each other going down the sidewalks. People were always screaming at each other there; I haven't heard a single bit of that here, and it has been so nice. Though I do feel a heaviness in my chest knowing that my life so drastically changed for the better when everyone else is still there suffering. I don't owe them anything—and they apparently wouldn't be able to cross the Veil anyway—but I don't think anyone deserves to live like that. I'm determined to help where I can once I get my memories back and figure out who I am.

Xamira seems happy to be coming to the city with me. She's been more tolerant of Andras today, though it's clear she still does not like him. I spend little time with any of the other staff; Fen mostly when she's needed to show me something, but Xamira doesn't appear to have a problem with anyone else. She even let Piers give her a little head scratch before trotting away to do gods know what. I still wish I could speak with her directly—I need to know her secrets. How she knew this place existed, and why she brought me here. Was she a part of my life before it was taken from me? Does she know what happened?

Thinking deeply and not paying attention to the paved path, I trip over my own feet, but Andras catches my arm before I can go anywhere. I look up at him, his harsh eyes already watching me, and smile my thanks. We continue walking in silence, and I was so lost in thought that I didn't realize how close we were. Heat slithers through my body from our arms brushing at our sides.

It's a little awkward, walking next to Andras after what I did last night. I'm not embarrassed about my body, or taking care of its wants and needs, but I wonder if he heard me at all. Or someone else did and told him of my activities…which wouldn't surprise me since the staff seem to report everything I say and do. I get it's their job, but come on, can't a girl give herself an orgasm without the whole world gossiping about it? It might be weird to explain to him if he asks, but I doubt he would even if he knew.

I glance over at him and take in his more casual clothing. It's not that different from what he wears every day in the castle, but I'll admit he looks pretty good. He's wearing loose tan pants, they look like the kind you would wear to a beach, and a fitted short sleeve white shirt. The shirt not only showcases his well-toned muscles but also the markings along his shoulder and arms that I have not yet seen. His skin looks golden under the morning sun, and there's an ease about him that makes me feel comfortable.

Since meeting Andras, he hasn't been the most open about his past. Even though I've gathered some of who he is just by watching him, I wonder if today would be a good day to ask him some questions. I don't want to ruin his good mood, but I also want to get to know him better. I realize I've been staring at him for a while when he looks over and smirks knowingly.

"Something on your mind this morning?" What do I say to that? *Yes, just admiring the view.*

I decide to just go for it and quickly say, "Kind of, actually. I was curious if you would tell me some more about yourself?" He quirks an eyebrow at me and I keep going, "I just thought that you know a bit about me, even if some of it was planted in my head, and I don't really know much about you other than your preferred clothing style and how you take your tea in the morning."

He looks forward toward the city; we are halfway down the hill from the castle. I wait, silently walking next to him, while he thinks about my request. He doesn't speak for so long. I think he may not reply at all; I feel like I already ruined this nice thing he was doing for me. I'm about to apologize for my rude question when he finally responds.

"I am finding it difficult to answer your question because there is not much to know about me. I've had a simple life," he smiles at me almost boyishly. "I was born in what would become Ceross, six centuries ago, during the War of Gods. My parents were originally humans, two of the ones who were turned fae to help in the war, though they wanted no part of it. They were killed after my birth and I was found by another turned fae, Imogen, who raised me.

"After the war, you know the general history from your readings, but it does not mention that once the two fae cities were created, there were royal houses established to govern the cities. I am the first and only prince of Ceross. The rest has been what you've seen during your time here—working to keep peace and take care of my people." He gives me a sad smile.

I have so many questions.

"Why were you chosen as the royal name for Ceross?" He laughs, tilting his head back to the sky, and I can't help biting my lip at the beautiful sight.

"Aside from my devilishly good looks, you mean?" He winks at me and my face heats. My body agreed to that sentiment last night. "I was chosen amongst the city members during a vote because I was the first *born* fae. It was thought that had to mean something important, and the citizens also believed my personality to be one that would be good for the throne and city. I accepted, and the rest is history."

"Who is the royal in Anloria?"

"It began with Niair and Teryn Vaintera as the prince and princess. They ruled for a few centuries, though their son has since taken the throne as prince."

"Have you ever had a princess alongside you?" I look away from his intense gaze, grasping how my question sounded like it had a hidden meaning. It didn't. I'm merely curious, and I could not be a princess, anyway. I wouldn't be able to handle such responsibility. How could I ever take care of an entire city when I don't even know who I am?

Andras brings me out of my thoughts by grabbing my hand and continuing to walk toward the city like he didn't just make my heart skip a beat. Who knew I was such a hopeless romantic, with intriguingly low standards, swooning over my hand being held? I feel the heat of his palm, and the tight grasp of his fingers interlaced with mine, and it's nice.

"I have not had a princess. I've not found a female I wish to mate with, though I hope that may change soon." I shift my eyes over to him, and he's already watching me with a small smile softening his face. My lips part, breath quickening as I realize what he's saying. I look between his eyes, trying to find the lie I'm so used to seeing in other men, but I see only desire. Males here are certainly different, after all.

Our moment is interrupted when I feel something rapidly flying toward us; I reach my hand out to catch it directly in front of Andras's face and it hits my palm hard, but I don't let that sway me into smacking him. Andras's eyes widen as he realizes what I just did; when the moment catches up to me, mine widen as well, along with my jaw.

"How did you do that?" he mutters so quietly I don't think he meant to say it out loud. I look at the green ball in my hand, not understanding how to answer him because I'm not even sure what that was. I didn't hear the ball coming. I *felt* it; and just somehow knew exactly where it would be and when to catch it. These fae senses are wild. Though I'm getting the impression that is not normal for other fae, given the shock on Andras's face.

Instead of saying anything, I turn to see two children—are they called children in the Veil?—waiting with similar expressions as Andras, though I'm sure that's because they almost hit the prince.

One of them runs forward, bowing deeply, and stammers, "Y—Your High—Highness, I am so sorry. I—I—I didn't see you there." He stays bent forward, and I feel concerned for him, wondering why he's so scared that his hands are trembling.

Andras steps forward and touches under the boys shoulder—he looks no older than ten—silently asking him to stand up. The boy stands but has trouble looking into Andras's eyes; I can see tears clouding his vision, but he stays where he is. The other boy, maybe this one's younger brother, is standing with his arms folded around himself, looking worried.

"I accept your apology…" Andras indicates he would like the boy to give his name.

"Dalton, Your Highness."

"I accept your apology, Dalton." He bends both knees, so he's level with the boy, smiling brightly at him. "It is very brave to own up to mistakes you make, and I admire that about you. There is no harm done. All I ask is that you be a bit more wary of where you throw your ball in the future. We wouldn't want to hurt someone, would we?"

"No, sir, Your Highness." Andras takes the ball from my outstretched hand and hands it back to Dalton. "Thank you!" He bows again and runs back to his brother, both of them taking off down a side street.

Andras stands, smiling, though it doesn't seem to reach his eyes. He looks over at me, heat gathering in his gaze again, most likely thinking about our small moment just before. He takes my hand and leads Xamira and me into the city; it doesn't occur to me until later that I was visiting a new place and meeting new fae while holding the arm of their prince.

The day goes by quickly and before I know it, I'm walking back up the hill toward the castle while the sun dips toward the horizon. I'm having seriously mixed feelings about everything that happened.

Seeing the city was amazing. The buildings remind me of what you would see in a cute little town depicted in a Christmas movie, except on a larger scale. The outer parts of the city are where the fae reside, though some of the shop owners, I learned, have their houses in the same building. We stopped at a bakery. The smells of the dough and spices were strong and reminded me of the day I arrived here. Xamira and I shared a pumpkin cake and, *gods,* was it good.

The bakery owner, Elise, introduced herself when she saw her prince visiting. She was a little shorter than me, with a round face and copper hair wrapped up in a bun. When she shifted just right, the sun would glisten across the reddish brown strands, making them look like muted fire. I had wondered if that was the magic she possessed, considering she looked the part and owned a bakery, but I wasn't sure if it was polite to ask, so I kept the thought to myself. I realized at that moment that I did not know what magic Andras holds, either.

Elise told us of her story, opening the bakery decades ago with her mate, being blessed with a child—which apparently, is harder to achieve as a fae than it is as a human—and how her and her family have lived a nice life since. Talking about her mate had me curious, as that's the second time I'd heard that term in a day, so I asked Andras about what it means when we left. He explained that it is sort of the same as getting married in the human world, though a bit more intense as the fae bind themselves together for life when they complete the mating ceremony.

"You will not find many fae who are mated, since it is a lifelong commitment. Some just find the one they know they will never leave and want to be bound to them. Others stay together in the same manner, just without completing the ceremony. And then you have fae who do not commit at all and find companionship with many," he said when I pried for more information.

After our time at the bakery, which left us carrying a bag full of pumpkin cakes, to Xamira's elation, we explored many other parts of the city. Visiting shops that make different types of clothing, such as leathers, shoes, casual wear, and even gorgeous dresses that had me drooling on myself. I wish I could pull something that pretty off. Actually, I wish I could afford it first.

Andras made sure I saw as many parts of the city as he could show me before the sun started setting; each place we visited had fae stopping to greet their prince. He smiled and acknowledged each one, though I got the sense that he was uncomfortable and wanted to leave. There were a few times I stepped in saying that we should go, as I didn't think he was going to do it himself. It's clear he loves his city, and its residents, but he just doesn't seem to be such a 'people person', or however you say that in fae terms. He prefers to be in his castle, or alone in nature, instead of large crowds.

After watching him today, I started feeling closer to him. He was always holding my hand, when his weren't occupied, and staring at me when he thought I wasn't paying attention. I used the time when others were speaking with Andras to take in this new side of him. He gave off a vulnerability that I rarely see from him in the castle, where I'm sure he feels he needs to be all business all the time. I wonder if he ever takes time to just relax and be himself.

I am feeling defeated after today, though. Andras tried bringing me to so many places in the city, to see if my memory was triggered at all, but I felt nothing. No recognition, no familiarity. I know that I shouldn't be so discouraged, but I can't help it. I was so hopeful that something would have helped; and I know Andras won't say it, but he's disappointed as well. This is clearly going to be more difficult than either of us thought.

We make it back to the castle, and I open the door to my rooms, Xamira running in to grab the dinner Fen brings up for her every night. I'm feeling so crushed from my hopes being let down that I just want to go to sleep and forget.

Andras must sense my internal war because his hands wrap around my waist, pulling me against his chest. The heat of his body feels so nice, and I just want to sink into him and lose myself. I feel his breath on my neck and instinctively tilt my head to give him better access.

His whispers send tingles down my collarbone, straight to my core, when he says, "I'm sorry, my sweet. I know you were hoping for some answers, and I really wanted that for you." I feel his day old stubble on my skin as he runs his nose up to my hair and takes a deep breath. If he's trying to distract me from my sad thoughts, it's definitely working. I'm nearly trembling.

A breathy 'mhm' is all I can manage at the moment, and I feel him smile at seeing just how much he affects me. He pulls me tighter against him, slowly tracing his fingers up toward my sternum. I feel his very hardened bulge against my tailbone and almost arch into it.

"Nell," he breathes, placing a light kiss just under my ear that has my nerves rapid firing. I want so badly for him to touch me that I would get on my knees and beg at this point. I mean, I could also do other things from down there…

I listen to my heartbeat, *not that one*, and turn around in his arms, my knees nearly giving out from the raw hunger I see in his eyes. I grab his face and pull him to me, smashing our lips together with the desperation that we both clearly feel. He hesitates for just a moment before pulling me so tight against him I might sink in. He takes one hand from my waist to grab the back of my hair and pulls me back, looking into my eyes; but for what, I'm not sure. He must find it, though, because he's suddenly kissing me again. This time I can feel the hunger I just saw in the blue depths of his gaze, as he's kissing me like he's about to devour me whole; and *gods* am I here for it. This is exactly what I need.

My arms wrap around his neck, grabbing his hair and pulling him harder into me, as if that's even possible. His tongue runs along my lips, and I open without hesitation. Our kiss is harsh and unrelenting, teeth clashing, tongues fighting. He tastes of cinnamon.

He bends down, not releasing our mouths, to grab my thighs and lift me. My legs wrap around his hips, and a wall smashes into my back so hard I may have felt pain under normal circumstances; but right now I'm too turned on and distracted to notice. He grinds his hips into me and his cock rubs against my core, leaving nothing to the imagination, since the only thing separating us are couple thin pieces of linen. I moan into his mouth, and he hesitates.

He breaks from our kiss. "As much as I would love to fuck you until you can't walk straight, I shouldn't tonight. I've already taken advantage of you." He plants another kiss on my lips and helps me untangle my legs and slide back down the wall. I want to protest and tell him that, if anything, I'm the one taking advantage of him, but I will never be someone who tries to guilt people into having sex after they indicate they don't want to.

So instead I nod my head, letting him know that it's okay and I'm not upset about it.

He moves toward the door, looking back at me to smirk, "Good night, my sweet," and leaves me alone in this big, white room.

Chapter 10

The last month has been a lot of nothing and also so much at the same time. I have scoured the castle library looking for anything that could tell me about the god who did this and how to reverse it. Each day I become a little more disheartened, and desperate, because I want to figure this out; to find out who I am…really, I'll take *anything* at this point. I have even resorted to reading children's fables, hoping that maybe a mention of the gods would be in some, but had no luck there, either.

I am convinced this is just going to be my life now, and I will never get my memories back. I suppose it's not the worst thing; this place is beautiful. The castle, while I still find the decor strange and uninviting, is nice. Watching Xamira thrive, having food and a warm place to sleep will make this all worth it, even if I don't figure out what happened to me.

Two weeks ago, I accidentally walked in on a meeting Andras was holding with his army council—something I didn't even know existed. But the army captain, Dominik, and his lieutenant, Bren, will apparently be staying in the castle for the extended future. I didn't feel it was my place to ask why, and I wasn't sure I wanted to after meeting the captain. His voice sounded familiar, but there is no way I would forget meeting him, so I know I was hearing things. He's a large, bulky male who looks like he eats children for breakfast. He always seems to have a scowl on his face, while being ready to decimate everything he touches. I have been trying hard to steer clear of that one—not wanting to get in his war path—though that hasn't been difficult since he keeps to his own schedule. Which is thankfully away from me, most days.

Bren, on the other hand, has been a breath of fresh air. He is a tall male, taller than Andras, with muscles to match, making it clear he trains quite hard every day. He has straight, black hair that reaches his shoulders, but he usually ties it back. He looks intimidating from the outside, like a true soldier, but really is such a teddy bear on the inside. He has been one of the kindest fae I've met so far during my time here.

One day, he was walking by the library and noticed me about to rip my hair out from frustration. He walked over to tease me about it until he saw how truly upset I was.

"Okay, sweet cakes." He has annoyingly been calling me that since he found out my obsession with the pumpkin cakes from Elise's bakery. "What's got your pant—oh, are you all right?" He changes his tune when he sees me glaring up at him.

"No, I'm not. I have been doing everything I can think of, all day, every day since I got here, to find out what's going on with me. I just want to know why this happened," I slam the old book in front of me closed and stand up, bracing my hands on the table. "I'm trying so hard to find just one piece of information. Anything. Anything at all. And I can't. None of the books know anything. None of the fae know anything. And my brain knows absolutely nothing, either, even though it's all. Locked. In. There." I'm shouting at this point. "I just wish I could get a break. I feel like I'm going crazy. Like maybe nothing happened to my memories at all. But that's not possible; something did happen, so why can't I find anything?" I slam my hands on the table, making Bren jump in surprise.

He rubs a hand along the back of his neck, looking wildly uncomfortable, like he's never dealt with anyone being angry before.

"Nell," he takes a hesitant step forward, like I'm some scared animal who's about to attack at the first sign of danger. "Listen, I don't know why you can't find anything about your memories. I wish I did. I wish I could take this burden from you because I don't want to see you get premature wrinkles." I look up at his smirking face. It's almost enough to make me crack a smile. Almost.

"So, while I can't help you with this, I can help you with something else. A way to release all of your stress and anger; because this," he waves his hands at me and the books, "is not good for you."

"I am not fucking you, Bren."

He bursts out laughing, grabbing his stomach and doubling over. That is enough to make me crack a smile. His laugh is infectious. He finally recovers from what apparently was the funniest joke ever, and looks up at me, wiping his eyes from the tears running out.

I would be offended, but then he speaks again, "You never know, sweet cakes." He winks. "But that is not what I meant. I was talking about training with me."

"Training?"

"Yes, you know, like exercising. Sometimes with weapons," he holds back a laugh.

"I know what training is, you big oaf," I fling some dust in his direction. "I'm saying, why would you want me training with you?"

"Why not? You could use an outlet for your frustrations," he looks pointedly at the books, "and I could use a partner. It's quite difficult to weapon train by myself."

"Why don't you have a partner? Wouldn't Andras or Dominik train with you?"

"Once in a while, sure, but they are always so busy running things. Please," he gives me puppy dog eyes, and I can't help but laugh at how ridiculous he is.

"Okay fine, I will train with you."

And since then I have been training with him each day. Dominik and Andras have yet to show up, though I get the impression they would rather train on their own, but felt bad for him, so they joined him occasionally. I've found that it actually is helping me with my stress and 'frustrations,' as Bren put it. We spend an hour training with our bodies, doing a mix of running, stretching, and hand-to-hand combat. Then we spend another hour weapons training, and that is what really shocked me on the first day.

He showed me the weapons room, filled with many deadly contraptions. There were daggers, axes, bow and arrows, and even spears. But what really got me was the swords. *Swords.* As in the things you read about in children's books. Sure, they didn't have technology centuries ago, and swords were perfect for wars, but we have guns now. Well, at least the humans do. I asked Bren about them, and apparently that's another thing they do not keep in the Veil, though someone could certainly bring one in if they wanted. I guess there just hasn't been any need since the War of Gods.

While the swords shocked me on the first day of our training, my skills shocked Bren. When we started our combat, he spent some time showing me basic stances and moves, and I caught on easily, my body somehow already knowing what to do. So we went right into fighting, and before we knew it, I had Bren yielding, pinned to the ground, hands stuck at an odd angle on his back. I let him go, eyes wide, having not a clue where those moves came from. I looked up after the fight to see Andras watching through the window. He looked angry at first glance, but he walked away before I could tell for sure.

Andras has been difficult to read the last month. We haven't had any more heated moments, much to my disappointment. And we also haven't talked much, either. He says that he's just busy, which I understand, but I feel like some of his 'business' is him avoiding me. Does he regret what we did, or does he think I do? I'm nervous to ask him about it, because I don't want to push him away any further…I'm starting to like him.

There have been moments where we made flirty comments or exchanged heated glances, but that's as far as it has gotten. I've never been afraid to stand up and say something before, so why now? I should just walk up to him and tell him what's on my mind. I feel fire in my veins at the thought and know that's the right decision. I will get him alone later and demand some answers. He doesn't owe me a relationship, but I feel like after what we did, he at least can have a conversation about it with me.

I spin in time to catch Bren's arm swinging at my back, twisting it and lifting my leg to kick in his throat. Not hard enough to damage anything, but enough to make him feel winded and yield the match when his back hits the mat. I smile at yet another victory, still wondering how I seem to know what Bren is going to do before he does, and exactly how to counter it.

Bren stands up, hand rubbing his throat. "Fuck, Nell. I would love to know how you beat me every time. I am a lieutenant in the army. There is no way you should be able to do that. Especially not with such perfect form."

I've been thinking a lot about that recently and decide to confide in Bren. "I wonder if it has anything to do with my old life. Like, if the god who hid my memories could only do just that: memories. The body has its own memories, doesn't it?"

Bren's eyes widen, realizing what I'm saying. "Whoa, Nell, I think you're on to something. The memories in your brain are not the same as muscle memory; that has to be why you can do these impossible things but not remember how you learned it. You have instincts like

I've never seen before…you react to things before they happen; you're so fast even I have a hard time keeping up with you. And your strength? It's insane for—" he pauses, not knowing exactly what to say.

"For what, Bren? For a *female*?" I roll my eyes.

He gives me a sheepish smile. "Well, yes, exactly that."

As much as I hate being underestimated just because of my sex, he's right. The things I've been able to do during our trainings are unexplainable. I am fast and strong, and I know how to use many weapons. I tried using a bow and arrow yesterday and hit my exact target each time. I didn't even know where to look from the bow. I just thought of my target and the arrow met its mark. It doesn't make sense to me how all of this seems to come naturally, but that's why I'm convinced it's a part of my memory issues. My contemplation is interrupted by footsteps, and I turn to see Andras approach.

"I have to agree. I believe whomever messed with your head could not do the same to your body's memories. That is why you have been discovering, and demonstrating, these amazing abilities." He takes the final steps toward the training mat, thankfully located in one of the buildings behind the castle. Otherwise we would all be soaked from the rain today.

I then see Andras's attire; he is wearing shorts and a fitted tank. He must be here to train, since I have yet to see him in something other than his usual clothes. He looks good enough to eat, and I find myself clenching my thighs together at the thought. He notices my reaction and smirks, taking his turn to look me over. My attire is a bit more fitted, with leggings and a sports bra. It doesn't take long to see the heat enter his eyes. Does it feel warmer in here, or is it just me?

"Okay, since you two are going to eye fuck each other the whole time, I'm going to call it a day. See you both at dinner." He backs away, giving me a wink before he makes it out of the room.

"Would you care for a match?" Andras says as he gestures to the mat.

"With you? Are you sure you could keep up with me?" I tease. "I have put Bren on his ass each time he's tried to fight me." I give him a sweet smile, walking slowly toward him, making sure my hips sway just right. He licks his lips, watching me.

"That is where you have it wrong, my sweet." He closes the distance between us, pressing up against me and allowing me to feel his erection. "I am not Bren."

No you are not.

He leans in, and I feel the whisper of his lips on mine; I want to close the distance but refuse to be the first to give in here. I will have him on his knees before he's allowed to taste me again.

"I do not lose." He backs away, a smile on his cocky face.

I don't respond, instead I saunter over to the middle of the mat, using everything in my arsenal to my advantage, and turn to see him watching me, not trying to hide his desire in the slightest. I ready my stance and give him a feline smile, looking up at him through my lashes, letting him know he is to make the first move.

He circles me, taking in every curve of my body; and I let him, not moving even when he is fully out of my sight. He walks in front of me again, an arms length away.

"You are making it very hard to think of anything other than your tight cunt sliding down on my cock." My jaw drops. And that was the distraction he was looking for. He swipes a leg out, catching me completely off guard, knocking me to my back. The air leaves my lungs, and it takes me a moment to catch my breath.

Angry, I jump up and face his smug face. "That was not fair."

"Sure it was. You want to use your body to distract me? Then I can certainly use my thoughts to distract you," he smiles, and I feel his eyes take in every inch of me. "And what filthy thoughts they are, my sweet.

The things I want to do to you would have you blushing until you were the color of a rose."

He's trying to distract me again. It may have worked, had I not already learned my lesson. He charges, swinging a leg toward my knees to get me down again, but I'm prepared for him this time. I flip back over his leg, grabbing his ankle and twisting as I right myself, forcing him to roll across the floor. He looks up at me, the anger I felt moments ago radiating through his eyes.

And then we dance.

We're a mess of limbs clashing and bodies slamming, one of us getting the upper hand for a moment before the other takes over. It's a hard battle, much harder than I was expecting, given how easy it has been to take down Bren. It's clear Andras is much more experienced, and I find myself pretty equal to him. Which makes me frustrated…because of course I want to win.

After several minutes of the back and forth, I'm on my back and Andras forces his body in between my legs before I can get back up. My thighs are lifted at having to accommodate his wide stance. Heat quickly builds inside my abdomen, and I'm breathing hard for a whole other reason now.

I'm too focused on the position to care about the fight any longer, even though this technically means the match is his. He doesn't seem to think about it either, as he stares down at me with his blue eyes, a deeper blue in the dimmed light of the room.

He leans down to run his nose up my sternum, forcing my jaw to the side, and breathes in my ear, "You smell delicious." He moves to kiss me, but I put a hand in between our lips before he makes contact; his eyes open, brows furrow in confusion.

"I don't think so. I want to know what's going on here before I let you kiss me again." He sits back, still confused.

"What do you mean?"

"I mean with this," gesturing between our bodies, "*us*. What is this, Andras? You nearly fuck me in my room weeks ago, and have been practically ignoring me ever since. Now, you come in here telling me you want me to sit on your cock and that I smell delicious? I'm confused about it is all," I shrug. Before he can reply, I continue, needing to clarify.

"I don't expect us to be boyfriend and girlfriend, or whatever, but I'd just like some clarity on where your head is at before mine starts making assumptions. Is this just something physical to you? If so, that's fine, but sometimes it feels like that's not the case." I close my mouth before I continue rambling. I've never had a conversation like this before. It's always been just physical to me, but this is different.

He tilts his head, studying me for a moment, a blank look on his face. He moves back to settle on the mat, allowing me to sit up and look at him. He takes another moment of thinking before he speaks.

"You're right. I have been avoiding you and did not realize how much it bothered you." I was not expecting that. My eyebrows raise and he continues, "I am conflicted on my feelings. While I am physically attracted to you, I am also attracted to you as a fae. You are beautiful, talented, and quite improper, which I find charming and refreshing.

"I seem to have some feelings for you, though I'm uncertain what those are just yet, or what they mean. I have never dealt with feelings like this before."

He looks uncomfortable admitting this, almost like he's upset with himself for feeling this way, and I find I want to share my truth as well.

"I feel the same." He looks up from his lap in surprise. "I also seem to have feelings that I can't describe and am not sure what to do with."

He nods, processing my confession, and says, "So what do we do from here? This appears to be unfamiliar territory for the both of us."

He looks so vulnerable right now, like asking me for help with his feelings has him freaked out.

I decide to take the lead. "I guess we could just do what feels right and not put a label on it?" He barks out a laugh. I wonder if he's laughing because, of course, there would be no way he would ever put a label on *this*. Whatever this is. He's a prince and I'm, well, just some random person turned fae, who lost her memories, has nothing and no one, and would just bring down his image. But he saves me from my drowning, insecure thoughts before they get any worse.

"I only laugh because that is the most mortal thing you could have said, and I find your candor amusing." He smiles brightly at me. "I do like your proposal, however. We can certainly do what feels right and not *label* anything."

I'm walking through the castle garden and scolding myself for not taking the time to visit here before. It's stunning, and so large I could get lost in here for hours. I walk by some different colored roses, smiling as it reminds me of Andras's scent.

I'm glad I stopped him yesterday to discuss what was going on between us. It feels like a weight lifted off my chest, which is nice considering how many things I have pressing it down. After our talk, I went back to my rooms to shower and eat dinner with Xamira. I decided to skip out on dining with everyone else, needing some time to process things.

The most significant of those things being my memory. I do not know what else to try, or where else to look. There are a few more books I can go through, but I no longer have hope of finding anything in them. I think I just need to fully accept that I will not be getting answers unless the god who did this decides to come back and tell me why. It's not like I can send a letter to them, or call them, so I just need to wait. Unfortunately for me, waiting is not something I'm good at. I know I will start going crazy as soon as I'm done looking through all the resources that are here.

I snap out of my thoughts when I walk up to a gazebo in the middle of the garden. I would have missed it if not for the sun on the little pond behind the structure catching my eye. There is a small path through thick foliage; I walk through it and make my way into the shaded area. It feels like a whole different world in here; it's quiet and peaceful. I look over the railing at the pond and see several goldfish swimming around. They have these here, but not cell phones or guns? I need to have a talk with whoever was in charge of the decisions when the Veil was made.

I'm leaning over the railing, watching the fish go back and forth, when I feel a presence behind me. I go to spin around to see who the hell snuck up on me when arms surround me, grabbing the railing, and their front pushing me forward so I can't move anywhere. I relax when I smell a familiar scent of roses.

"What do we have here? A female, all alone in the gardens, with no one to protect her," I feel Andras smile into my hair.

"I think I can protect myself just fine."

"I think you're right." He steps back a little, allowing me to spin and face him. He looks handsome standing over me surrounded by flowers, the sun indirectly hitting his hair, making it look like a darker blonde instead of the light sand I'm used to.

"I've been thinking," he says, his voice rough, eyes heated. I bite my lip, knowing where this is going.

"About what?" I press.

"About how I have yet to taste you." He licks up the column of my neck, causing my breath to hitch. "A*ll of you*. I call you my sweet, but do not know just how sweet you are; and I am aching to find out."

He runs his hands down the sides of my body, wasting no time in going after what he wants. He lifts the lightweight sundress I'm wearing. I didn't want to get too hot walking through the garden midday, but now I'm thanking my past self for a very different reason.

Andras drops to his knees in front of me and takes in the sight of my lace underwear. He licks his lips, and leans forward to run his nose along my center, taking in the scent of my arousal. I hear a low growl come from his chest, and in the next second he has one of my legs over his shoulder, my underwear pulled to the side, and is running his tongue up the same path his nose just took.

"Oh *fuck*," I whimper, not having been prepared for the assault of sensations. I lean one of my elbows on the railing, my other hand going straight to his hair to keep him right where I want him.

"You taste divine, Nell." The vibrations of the words send tremors through my legs. He eats me alive, leaving no part of my pussy un-licked. It's all I can do to stay upright; I'm pretty sure the railing, and his hand holding my hip, are the only things not letting me fall. I know my standing leg is not working any longer.

He sucks my clit into his mouth, and my head drops back with a groan loud enough for anyone else in the garden to hear. His free hand travels up my leg and there is no grace period from the time his fingers reach my heat until he roughly shoves three of them inside of me. The sudden intrusion burns a little, but I don't care. It all feels way too good. I shiver when he curls his fingers just where I need them, and I feel him moan against my flesh.

His tongue is dancing wickedly around my clit before he sucks it deeply into his lips, and then back to his tongue again. He's pumping his fingers at a speed I don't even understand, but he keeps them curled, never fully pulling them out, and my vision wavers. How he knows exactly where to touch me is beyond my comprehension, but I will not complain about it.

"Andras, *oh gods*, I'm so close," my voice is shaking with undiluted pleasure.

My words seem to excite him, and he sucks me in one last time, lightly biting down on my clit. I lose myself as the orgasm rocks itself through my body. I'm certain I ripped some of Andras's hair out, and scared any living thing within a five-mile radius with my scream.

As I come down from the bliss, Andras kisses his way up my body, ending on my mouth. I taste myself on his tongue, and a fresh wave of arousal coat my legs.

I pull his head back just enough to look into his eyes and practically growl, "Fuck me right now."

He smiles, biting my lip in one more kiss before spinning me around and bending me over the railing. The hand on my back holds me down; it's painful, but not enough to make me stop this. He lifts my dress again, and I feel his hard length glide through my wetness, coating himself before he enters me in one merciless thrust. I gasp at the intrusion.

He gives me no time to adjust to his size before he's fucking me hard. The pain slowly gives way to intense pleasure, and I meet each of thrusts with one of my own. This isn't sweet lovemaking. It's not something to take our time with. This is intensely violent and primal. It almost feels like a claiming. Andras is taking what's his, and will let nothing get in the way of that.

He grabs my hair and yanks me up, pulling me flush against his chest. He lifts me so my feet are standing on the bottom rail, giving him better access, and continues driving into me.

"You feel so fucking good," his rough voice says in my ear, causing my neck to tilt, giving him access to bite the spot just below that has my back arching. "I have been dreaming of this for a long time, Nell. You have no idea."

I can't comprehend what he's saying as my second orgasm hits me hard; he reaches around to circle my clit with his fingers, prolonging the torrent of pleasure. I feel him thrust hard, stilling behind me for a moment before pulling out to release himself onto my back. He grabs my chin, pulling my face to the side so he can claim my mouth.

He releases me too soon, and I just lean my head back against his shoulder, trying to catch my breath. He holds his arms around my waist and we stand in silence. My hand wraps around to grab his hair and keep him here for a while longer.

The bliss is short-lived as someone clears their throat; both Andras and I look toward the path back to the garden.

"Your Highness," Piers says. "My apologies for interrupting, however you are late for your meeting with the council regarding the Solstice Ball."

Andras sighs into my hair, "Thank you Piers, I will be there in a moment."

He kisses my neck once more before backing up, the heat from his body leaving me, and I feel my cum run down my leg. Not caring about the dress since I can just wash it, I use the bottom part to wipe myself up a little. That should allow me to make it back to my rooms to clean up properly.

Andras tucks himself back into his pants as I turn around, and we smile at each other, both relieved after letting out the feelings we've been harboring for a while. While we walk back out of the garden, I remember what Piers's interruption was about.

"What's the Solstice Ball?"

"It's a ball that is held each year on the fall solstice." He grabs my hand. His rough skin feels nice alongside my own. "The ball is held in either Ceross or Anloria—we switch years—and it is meant for our cities to see their royals come together. It shows the citizens that we are at peace with one another, and that we can work together to solve any issues that would arise and harm either of the cities.

"This year Ceross will host the ball. The prince of Anloria, and his court, will be attending; they most likely will leave their city in the coming days, as it takes several to cross the Sunsor Mountains and make it here."

I think about this for a moment; a ball sounds interesting. I wonder if it's anything like high school dances?

"Is this ball something I am to attend?"

Andras smiles down at me. "I would not force you to, however I would love for you to attend. My advisor will be returning for the event, and you will meet her."

"That sounds lovely," I look down at the grass. "Though I'm not sure what I would wear to a ball? It seems like something you wear large beautiful gowns to, and you know I have none of those. I will skip this one and attend next year's."

"Nonsense. I already have a gown being made for you. I chose the colors myself, and it will be ready in a week's time, when the ball will be held."

My eyes shoot over to Andras at this. "You have a gown being made for me?" He nods, "Not only would I never ask you to do something like that for me, but you have one being made without knowing if I would say yes to attending or not?"

"That is correct," he smirks down at me.

I huff a breath. This male is ridiculous. Thoughtful, and good with his dick, but ridiculous, nonetheless.

Chapter 11

I look in the mirror at this stunning gown Andras had made for me. It's mostly black, with a corset bodice made of lace, showcasing my skin between the openings of the fabric. The lace leads down into the skirt, which is an all black tulle that reaches the floor. There's a slit up the left side—nearly touching my waist—which boldly reveals that I am not wearing panties. The sleeves are thin pieces of tulle that hang off my shoulders, showing off some of my markings along my shoulder and collarbone. The bodice has small silver jewels adorned across the fabric, matching my grey eyes and making them stand out in the light.

I'm surprised at the design and color of the dress…when Andras told me a week ago that he was having one made, I was expecting a white dress paired with white heels. This is the complete opposite, and I wonder if that was the point. He wants me to stand out to the others, though I'm not sure why when we are not together.

Since our little gathering in the gazebo, Andras and I have had no more alone time. I am more fine with it now that we have established what is going on between us, though I imagine him seeing how good this dress actually looks on me will have him seeking me out when I'm by myself tonight.

And I do look great in this dress—I feel powerful and sensual. My body has filled out immensely in the last couple of months. Between properly feeding it and training nearly every day with Bren, I have muscles and curves that would have made me jealous if they weren't mine. I feel healthy. I can't believe this is who I am when just two months ago I was sitting in a moldy apartment, starving and working seven days a week so I could make sure Xamira had a place to live and food to eat.

I tear up thinking about it, but refuse to let any fall because I'll be damned if I ruin my makeup. Xamira must notice my shift in mood because she runs over meowing. I sit in one of the chairs in front of the fireplace and she jumps up into my lap, purring and making biscuits without her claws, as if she knows they would tear the fabric of my dress. She peers up at me with her golden eyes, and I'm almost certain she's reading my thoughts with the way she's looking at me. I lean down and kiss her nose, giving her the chin scratches she loves.

"Thank you for being here for me. I love you so much." She purrs, telling me she loves me, too.

I stand and take one last look in the mirror, grabbing the black lace mask Andras had made with the gown—I pull it over my face and adjust my wavy hair to hide the band. He didn't tell me it was a masquerade ball when I asked him about it, but I'm still excited to go; though I was hoping maybe some visitors from Anloria could tell me if they recognize me at all. Oh well, I think I owe myself a night of fun.

I'm standing to the side of the ballroom, watching Andras greet everyone he runs into. I shouldn't be disappointed…he is the prince of Ceross, and all the fae here are eager for a moment of his time. So—yes—I *shouldn't* be disappointed. But I am. The room is remarkable, though. While the floors and walls are made of the white marble, there are black curtains hanging along the walls that do not have windows. The lighting is dimmed and hidden inside black orbs, giving the illusion of mystery, even though we are all wearing masks.

There's seating in a few areas along the wall, with musicians set up in one corner, playing classical sounding music, and a bar set up in the other corner, where staff refill wine glasses, and walk around handing them out to attendees. It really is quite a beautiful ball, and I wonder how much planning goes into something like this.

I wish Andras would ask me to dance, or even Bren. I haven't been able to talk to either of them, and they are the only ones I really know here. I think I recognize a couple of the fae from meeting them in the city when Andras and I visited; but I wouldn't remember their names, and would just embarrass myself if I tried to talk to them. I'm surrounded by so many but I'm feeling quite lonely, the hollowness in my chest making itself very well-known tonight.

Out of the corner of my eye, I see Andras approaching me. I turn to smile at him, only to see he's with a female who is watching me as they approach. I take a deep breath and make sure my smile stays in place, even though I'm not feeling particularly happy at the moment. As they reach me, I wait for Andras to introduce us, hoping whatever he brought her over here for can be talked through quickly. My feet hurt from standing here for an hour, and maybe I'm feeling a little sorry for myself. We all have those days. I just want to go to sleep, and forget about all of my problems for a solid twelve hours.

"Nell, I wanted to introduce you to Imogen," my eyes widen at the name, "my advisor." And your adopted mother, apparently. How does that work, exactly?

My eyes find Imogen as I say hello. She is beautiful, almost too beautiful, like she was plucked from a painting that took years to perfect. She doesn't appear decades older than Andras, but fae aging and all. Her straight black hair is slicked back, showing off her sharp jaw down through her exposed shoulders and dip of her breasts. She's wearing a skin-tight, sleeveless, red dress that barely reaches mid-thigh, and I have to wonder what dress code was written on the invites because she looks like she's headed for one of the clubs in Chago. No judgment from me—she looks hot. I am just not sure she fully got the memo that this was a ball. She is, however, wearing a black lace mask, surrounding her intense black eyes. Are her pupils dilated or are her eyes really that dark?

Her smile, though, is where I stop to stare. There's something oddly familiar about it, though I haven't met her before. She doesn't seem to recognize me, so I'm probably just too tired for my own good at the moment, and making things up in my head.

"It is very nice to meet you, Imogen. I have heard great things about you from Andras during my time here." She bows her head and gives me another one of those smiles, something tugging in me at the sight. I need to lay off the wine.

After a minute of uncomfortable silence, I decide to break away. "Um, well, it was nice meeting you," I stupidly say again. "I suppose I will see you around." I look toward Andras, "I am going to get some air. I will find you later."

I turn from them and walk toward the closest door I can find. I need to clear my head before I scream—this night has not at all been going how I'd hoped. Before I can make it to the door, a sharp pain runs through my chest, and I stop to press my hand against the wall. It dulls for a moment before a second wave of pain hits, and I lean my free arm against the hard surface for support. Thankfully, I am at the side of the ballroom, so no seems one notices my struggle; the last thing I need is a crowd obsessing over me.

The pain dulls again, feeling more like a tug; I wait for a few moments, but no more sharp zaps come. The tugging intensifies, and though it doesn't hurt, I have the urge to look behind me. I turn around and my gaze immediately finds two males walking through the main entrance to the ballroom. The air in my lungs dissipates and the entire room melts away, leaving just me staring at these insanely attractive beings.

One of them has nearly black hair, styled to look messy on top of his head. He's wearing a black suit with a grey tie, somehow matching my attire, and I can see the bulge of his arms through the jacket. It doesn't appear to be too small on him, but highly doubt you wouldn't be able to see those arms from any shirt. They're wearing masks, so I can't completely make out their faces. But this male has tanned skin and devastatingly nice, full lips.

The other has curly, deep brown hair—cut short enough that it doesn't hang down his face, but long enough to see the defined curls. He's wearing a similar black suit, though has no tie, and the jacket is unbuttoned at the front. They have relatively the same build, and I really want to know exactly what that is since the fabric is hiding the details. His skin is more olive-toned and his lips more pouty—but still full, and definitely kissable.

They must have great senses and feel me staring, because they both pause to look around the large room until their gazes lock with mine. I snap back into myself and force my lungs to breathe again. Stunned, and a little embarrassed, I spin and walk quickly toward the door at the back that will take me to my rooms. The realm's two most beautiful males will not stop me from my mission of getting the hell out of here and sleeping off this wine.

Or maybe they will, because as I am reaching the door, I run directly into a hard mass of muscle. By the feeling in my chest, I know it's one of the two males. I also know the other one is standing behind me.

I look up at the male in front of me, seeing his eyes for the first time. Hazel, with small specks of gold. I could get lost in them…I find myself no longer wanting to move, but instead stare at him. I push that feeling down; Andras and I aren't together, but I get the impression that he would be upset with me for having thoughts about other males.

Before my hormones get the best of me, I raise eyebrows and speak, "What the fuck? Can I help you?"

His brows soften while his very soft-looking lips lift into a smirk. "I don't know, princess, can you?"

I take a step back at his audacity and run into another hard mass of muscle, not realizing the other male was so close. I turn to take another step away, so that they are both in my view—but now my back is against the wall, and I feel caged in. From my experience, a beautiful face doesn't mean a nice person.

"Okay, listen. I don't know who either of you think you are, but you can fuck right off because you're being very creepy."

The one with green eyes tilts his head and gives me a look that I assume is to showcase his amusement. His friend, who has eyes like the sweetest honey…one look at him has my defenses faltering. The room spins. He gives me a genuine smile, and says in a smooth voice, "I don't believe we have met before. Are you new to Ceross?"

"Why would it matter to you who I am and when I arrived here?"

The dark-haired one presses his lips together to keep in his laugh. Am I missing some kind of joke here? Why am I being interrogated and laughed at?

"I apologize. I think we have upset you. That was not our intention, we just wished to introduce ourselves. My name is Casmir, and this is Emrys. We are here visiting from Anloria." He gestures to Emrys.

Fuck. Casmir…as in Prince Casmir Vaintera? And Emrys, the prince's second in command? Of course—the one time tonight I cannot mask my annoyance just happens to be with Andras's guests of honor. I take a deep, deep breath. I'm going to need all the air I can get before Andras wrings my neck out once he hears of my actions. This ball is supposed to keep the peace between the cities, not have some idiotic female tear it all down.

Well, I am already in too deep; and if I'm honest, way too prideful to reel myself back in now. So instead I glance between them, doing my best to not lose myself in their gazes.

"Okay, great. Pleasure to meet you both," I spit, sarcasm swimming in my tone. "Is there anything else I can help you with, or are we done here?"

The prince barks out a laugh, and I would be lying if I said it wasn't more intoxicating than the wine I've been steadily drinking. Emrys gives me a look that tells me I've offended him, and I smirk at him just to piss him off more. Being under his intense gaze has heat rising in my abdomen; angry or not, I would pay to have him look at me like that every day of my life.

Shit, no. I can't feel this way about others. I don't even know them.

Casmir locks me in his stare as well, and it's as if I'm being stripped bare and having every inch of my body scrutinized, even though we are just having a simple conversation.

"Yes, actually." His voice sounds like the call of a siren. "I was wondering if you might accompany me in a dance? My hope is that—if I show you my less creepy side—you will honor me by telling me your name." He holds out a hand—a clear invitation.

I can't just say no to the prince, can I? Andras would be even more upset if he found out I rejected his guest of honor, than he would if he knew just how wet one look from these males has made me.

Gods, I need help.

"Okay. One dance, and then you both stop stalking me like animals." I smile sweetly while taking his hand. I feel his chuckle as he wraps my arm around his, pulling me closer and leading me into the mass of dancing bodies. I look back at Emrys, who is biting his lip, watching us walk away with his hands in his pockets. He looks like he's about to lose an internal war and come take me from the prince.

As we reach the center, a new song begins. He grabs my waist with one hand, my hand in the other, and we move around to the sweet sounds of the instruments; I focus on the violin, finding comfort in its notes, to keep myself from looking into the prince's eyes. I agreed to a dance, not to be trapped here, unable to look away from one of the two most gorgeous males I have ever seen.

"Are you new to Prince Andras's court?" I can feel his gaze burning its way through my face, and I'm wavering in my resolve to not look up at him.

"Yes, I am," I barely manage to choke out.

Is it suddenly a furnace in here, or am I going through menopause? Do fae even go through menopause? I am hyper aware of every place the prince is touching me, my skin an inferno under each point of contact.

"And what brings you here to his court?"

I do not have the mental capacity to come up with any lies at the moment. "I was living outside of the Veil, stumbled my way into the Veil, and Prince Andras found me. He has been helping me try to figure out my past, as it turns out I am fae and missing years of memories."

I can't help myself…I finally look into his eyes. He's studying me with a look of concern on his face, but wipes that away and smiles at me. *Gods*, I am done for.

"Well, I hope you find what you're looking for. I would be happy to help with anything you may require; Anloria has the largest library in the realm, and you would be welcome to search through it for any answers."

I can't breathe. The hollowness in my chest feels like it's bouncing around, pulling me every kind of way. Somehow, I can still answer Casmir. "Actually, I may take you up on that offer. We have been having little luck here, and I'm feeling discouraged that my memories will ever come back to me." I bite my lip to shut myself up and the prince's eyes catch the movement, watching intensely.

I am a hopeless romantic. One smile from the prince has me spilling all of my secrets and feelings. I have got to get it together, but that's not going to be possible. I'm ensnared by his eyes, and I suspect he may feel the same as he also hasn't looked away from me once. We are in our own world, nobody and nothing existing outside of our small bubble in this large room.

"We can certainly have arrangements made." He tilts his head, again looking down at my lips and back up to my eyes. "Well, have I proven myself at least a little less creepy? Possibly enough to know the name of the most beautiful female I have ever seen?" His smile is teasing. "Or should I just continue to call you princess?"

I think I stopped breathing. Again. Is he serious, or am I just stupid and falling for his shameless flirting? I guess it doesn't matter because I am completely under his spell.

"Nell," I whisper.

He ends our dance as the music does, capturing one of my hands in both of his.

"Nell." His eyes brighten—like when the sun first hits a forest in the morning. "I am very honored to have had this dance with you." He bends to hover his lips above my hand and looks up at me through his lashes. "I do hope I will see you again soon." He kisses my hand, and I see stars. He steps back, reluctantly breaking our contact, and bows to me. He walks toward the side of the ballroom where Emrys waits—who's staring at me with the intensity of a thousand suns. Casmir lowers his head to say something in his second's ear and looks back at me with a smirk on his face, winking. Emrys smiles and bows his head to me, following the prince back through the doors they entered from.

All at once, everything in the room comes back to me. The music of the next song is playing, but no one is dancing. Every fae in the ballroom is staring at me, some with their jaws hanging open. I feel very vulnerable. A prickling covers my neck and my eyes slide to the right where Andras's are throwing daggers my way; I thought me dancing with the prince would please him, though I guess Casmir's show of affection didn't go unnoticed. By anyone.

Unwilling to cower or apologize, I straighten my back, lift my chin, and walk out of the ballroom. I don't owe Andras anything, and he doesn't own me. It's not like I fucked the prince on the dance floor, though my interaction with him and Emrys left me feeling like that's exactly what I did.

I make it to my rooms and can finally breathe again. Ripping off this dress that has become way too hot, I drop to my bed in just my underwear and close my eyes. I disturbed Xamira's sleep in my haste, and she comes over to cuddle up next to me.

What happened back there? I still feel a tugging through the emptiness in my chest, but it's more muted now. It must just be a reaction to seeing those hot as fuck males after drinking so much wine. How is it even legal to look that good? I am way too tired to think about any of this. I pull the covers over myself and fall into a restless sleep.

Chapter 12

I wake up with a pounding in my head and a will to sleep for another three days. Unfortunately for me, the sounds my stomach is making tells me I need to at least eat before going back to sleep. Grumbling curses to myself, I walk into the closet and throw on a pair of grey shorts and a white t-shirt, not bothering with any formal clothing as Andras and I have been becoming more comfortable around one another. I'm feeling too much like shit to care if it bothers him, anyway. Sticking to my theme, I throw my hair into a quick messy bun and splash some cold water on my face. The movements have me feeling like I'm going to throw up all of my organs. I groan, scrunching my eyes closed, trying to keep the dizziness to a minimum. Did I really drink that much wine last night? Fen mentioned something about it being stronger than human wine. But fuck, she didn't say anything about it being *this* strong.

I walk to the dining area and hear voices, internally cowering. At least it's just Bren. He sometimes joins Andras and me in the mornings. I enter the room and stop dead in my tracks—what little blood I had in my face has drained and my eyes are so wide I could see Europa in the sky with little effort.

It's not Bren at the table with Andras…no, why would it be? It's the Anlorian prince and his second in command, sitting on one side next to Andras. I might actually throw up this time. All three of the males stop what they're doing to look my way, and I'm suddenly hyper aware of what I'm wearing. Not only are my shorts *short,* but I'm certain my shirt is a bit see through; and I know for a fact my nipples are hardened and putting on a show right now.

I must look like a complete mess. I don't want to embarrass Andras, but there is no way I'm about to turn around and run out of here like some scared little girl. If they want to stare at all the exposed parts of my body, who am I to stop them? It's just skin. Though I have a feeling Andras might disagree with that sentiment…because when I look over at him, he clenches his jaw, clearly upset with me.

That's his fault, though. How was I supposed to know these two male models would be here? I had convinced myself that my reaction to them last night was the wine taking over my body, but seeing them now confirms that was not the case. They are still just as gorgeous. The only thing different about them this morning being their attire.

Casmir is wearing a black shirt that is buttoned to the mid-point of his chest, the sleeves expertly rolled up. His nearly black hair looks like he just rolled out of bed and called it a day. But his eyes…his eyes remind me of the day I arrived in the Veil, with the beautiful color of the forest, the sun shining through some of the treetops. They're ethereal.

Emrys, sitting to the Anlorian prince's left, is wearing what appears to be leather. The vest fitting his chest like it was sculpted just for him, leaving nothing to the imagination. I have the urge to walk over and run my hand through his soft curls, and I almost do before I remember where I am. His eyes, though different from Casmir's, pull me in just the same. They look like the most seductive, swirling honey—I could watch them all day and not find myself bored.

I realize I've been standing here gawking at all of them and force my feet to move. I plant myself in the seat to Andras's right, across from Casmir and Emrys. This is going to be fun.

"Good morning, Nell," Casmir says with amusement lacing his tone. "It's delightful to see you again."

My eyes flit to Emrys, who's smirking at me. Then I glance at Andras and my suspicions are confirmed…he is also staring at me. It's more of a glare, and I can tell he wants to say something but refuses to do so in front of the other two. Having the full attention of each of them has my heart flying around my chest; I would be shocked if they couldn't hear the damage it's causing to all of my other organs. My lashes flutter from the being scrutinized, while my neck starts to heat and my palms dampen.

"You as well." I decide to keep my reply simple and cordial for Andras's sake.

To my utter relief, the males resume their conversation and I eat fruit in silence as I listen to them talk. Their discussion ranges from the ball last night to the state of their cities. The exchange is quite formal, and it almost feels forced. Like neither party wishes to talk to the other, but they do out of obligation. I wonder why that is. Andras said they have always been at peace with each other, and he's never had any issues with them.

Piers strides into the room, letting Andras know his presence is required in another part of the castle. He seems relieved by the excuse to leave the table and as he stands, it feels like he's about to make me come with him. But he thinks better of it and just dismisses himself instead. He hasn't said a word to me all morning. Could he be that upset? I haven't even done anything that would warrant such a reaction, though I suppose fae males can be territorial. And he saw how these two were looking at me last night.

And this morning, I guess, because when Andras is out of the room, my eyes drift up to find both Casmir and Emrys watching me. I suddenly remember the prince telling me I was the most beautiful female he's ever seen, and my cheeks heat at the thought.

Emrys bites his lip, and I hear his smooth voice clearly for the first time. "Nell..." His tongue curls around my name perfectly. "I must admit you were quite stunning at the ball last night. But this morning," his eyes drift to my chest and back up, winking at me, "you are absolutely exquisite."

My eyebrows shoot clear off my face, and I seriously wonder if they are just playing games with me and find my reactions amusing, or if they actually believe what they're saying? I look down at myself and decide it's the former. There is no way he is telling the truth when I'm dressed in wrinkled clothes, probably smelling like alcohol, with my hair in a knotted mess on top of my head. He's definitely joking.

Also, what is with the shameless flirting? I have never met such bold males…saying whatever comes to their head as if there is no etiquette in their court.

I lean back in my chair and cross my arms. "Thanks." I smile tightly. "But do I really look like every other female who falls for your bullshit?" Casmir runs a hand along his lips, stifling a laugh by clearing his throat. Emrys gives me a smug smile and rests his chin on his combined fists.

"No, you certainly do not," he confirms, his voice a little more rough. He licks his lips, and I home in on the movement, suddenly feeling another heartbeat. I seriously hope they cannot scent the wetness starting to coat my shorts…but with how focused they are on me, there's no way they can't.

What is it about these two? Since when does a pretty face, and a few sweet words, have me on my knees and drooling? I didn't even react like this when I met Andras for the first time—he also has a pretty face, but I could at least keep my head straight around him. Casmir and Emrys have me feeling like I've been dropped into a black hole, and I can't seem to find a way out. I need to get out of here so I can think properly.

I stand abruptly from my chair and open my mouth to say—what, exactly?

Thanks for the company? It was nice to see the both of you? Please leave me alone because my chest, and my pussy, are going to explode just from your presence alone?

Instead, I opt to say nothing. I close my mouth and look at them both one more time. With more effort than I'll ever admit, I peel my feet from the floor to swiftly walk from the room. As soon as I'm out of their sight, I break into a run—not caring if they can still hear me—and make it back to my rooms quickly.

I lean my head against the closed door and take several deep breaths. My chest is tight, and the pounding in my head has come back, but at least the light breakfast I had seems to have taken my nausea. I need more sleep before I can think about any of this.

I wake up as the sun is setting, feeling so much better than I was earlier. I have the urge to release some energy and stress, so I decide to change into my running clothes. I do not gather Bren because I really need to be alone with my own thoughts; instead I head down the dirt path in the forest that he showed me when we began our training.

Where do I even start? I'm frustrated about my memories, conflicted about Andras, and very confused about my reactions to the two Anlorians. Andras and I are not *mated,* or even have a verbal agreement to be exclusive to each other, so why do I feel so guilty for my feelings? I'm allowed to find others attractive, even if I was in an actual relationship with Andras.

I suppose I'm at odds with myself because, while I owe him nothing, I still feel like I do. He brought me to his castle and gave me a place to sleep, food to eat, and has been helping me try to figure out my memories. He has been so kind and understanding and has asked for nothing in return. Is his anger toward me because he feels an instinctual need to keep protecting me, or because he's hoping that we can develop a relationship, and seeing me flirt with others hurts him? He is a confusing male, always seeming so back and forth in his feelings. It's not my fault he's not very good at communicating his wants and needs; and I really shouldn't feel bad for just talking to other fae. Even if they are…*those two*.

And speaking of Emrys and Casmir, why am I fawning over them like a teenage girl meeting her ultimate celebrity crush? They are just males. Nothing different or special about them.

Even as I think that I know it's a lie. There is something different about them, but I'm not sure what. Maybe they're just really my type, or their smell is perfect for reeling my hormones in. Or perhaps I just have a thing for royalty; first I hit it off with the prince of Ceross, and then get star eyes at the first sight of the royals from Anloria. Whatever. I just need to accept that they make me feel crazy things, and those feelings will leave as soon as they do.

Unless I go with them, because Casmir did offer to let me use his library to see if I could find any information about my memories. All feelings aside, I want to figure this out more than anything. It has been weighing me down heavily, making me feel lost, though I try not to show it around Andras. I don't want to make him feel bad for not having been able to help me, but how could I refuse the opportunity to look in the other city for answers? He would have to understand; and it's not like I would be gone forever. I would come back to Ceross after I'm done searching, regardless of if I find anything or not.

I'm so focused on my thoughts that I miss the footsteps catching up to me.

"Hello, love," a familiar voice says. I shriek and lose my footing, nearly falling flat on my face before a set of strong arms wrap around my waist, spinning me and pulling my body into his chest. There's a pull under my skin at the leather and rosemary scent, and I immediately know it's Emrys who caught me.

His hands grip the bare of my back while mine lie flat on his hard, defined chest. Each place his skin touches mine feels like a shock to my senses. I meet his eyes, swaying with the effort to keep myself standing. I can feel Casmir watching the interaction and realize I'm gaping like a fool.

I push from Emrys, and he lets me go immediately. I look over at the prince and see they are both wearing shorts, though Casmir has on a black shirt while Emrys has gone without. Obviously, since I was feeling him up a second ago. I cross my arms, hoping to keep some semblance of my dignity.

"Why do you two keep showing up out of nowhere? Are you actually stalking me or something?"

Emrys gives me a feline smile and takes deliberate steps toward me, forcing me to back up unless I want a face full of his chest again. I mean, I definitely do…but I need to figure out their intentions first. My back hits a tree as they both cage me in and this is suddenly a replica of last night, just with fewer clothes. I don't feel unsafe, even though I'm being crowded in the middle of a darkening forest by two random males. I just feel insanely out of my depth.

Emrys closes the distance between us, leaning over to whisper in my ear but never actually touching me. "Love, if I was stalking you, I'd already have you choking on my cock—making sure there wasn't enough air in your lungs for you to spit that attitude you've been giving us since last night."

My jaw drops, and I huff out a breath as he leans back to his position in front of me. The look on his face tells me he is deadly serious. The *nerve* he has is admirable.

"And what makes you think you have the right to speak to me like that?" As hot as it was, I need to keep the upper hand. Emrys goes to step forward to show me exactly what gives him the right, and gods would I have let him if Casmir didn't put a hand out to stop his advances.

"All right, children," he directs at Emrys, "enough fighting." He winks at me and drops his hand before facing me fully again. "We did not come here to antagonize you, Nell."

"Then why *did* you come here?" My blood heats, their presence no longer clouding my head. "Because it looks to me like you cornered a random female in the forest, on the brink of full darkness, and are whispering dirty things in her ear about what I'm sure is," I look over to Emrys, and give him my sweetest smile, "a very nice, bite-sized dick. And then have the audacity to tell me that it wasn't your intention to upset me?"

Emrys looks like he's about to start swinging at my dick comment, but one glance from Casmir has him biting his tongue.

The prince looks back toward me, his brows furrowing. "You're right—I'm sorry. I suppose we did not think this through very well." He rubs the back of his neck; this is the first time I've seen him look at all uncomfortable. "I was hoping to talk with you about the issues you are having with your memory."

I had forgotten about that while I was being bombarded with new sexual fantasies. I lower my voice, no longer feeling the need to defend myself. "What about it?"

His lips quirk up into a small smile, and he leans against the tree next to me, folding his arms and looking every bit a god. His eyes narrow like he sensed my reaction to him, but he doesn't say anything about it. Instead, he answers my question, "You are still welcome to come to Anloria and utilize any resource you need to figure out what is going on. We will leave back to our city the morning after tomorrow and would be happy to escort you." His eyes meet mine after taking in every inch of my body, and he quirks an eyebrow. "That is, if you'd care to join us."

The way he said that makes it sound like a challenge; he's better than I thought, already knowing how to get under my skin. He thinks I wouldn't be able to handle him and Emrys during the journey to Anloria. I do love a good challenge. Emrys steps up to the princes side, hands in his pockets, smirking at me knowingly.

I want to say yes, but I'm still conflicted. Leaving Andras will be difficult; he's helped me with so much, and I don't want him to feel like I used him and then ditched him for another prince. I should talk to him before I give them my answer, to see how he truly feels about it instead of giving myself more anxiety.

Andras aside, can I trust these two? They seem to be genuine, and although they're very direct about what they want and what they're feeling, they have not tried to do anything without my consent. I have only known them for a day, but that's still better than just about every other male I've ever met. Instinctively, I want to say I can't trust them. Nothing good has ever come from a pretty package, as far as I'm concerned. But the pounding against the hollow pit in my chest is telling me otherwise; it's telling me that I could trust them with my life and going to Anloria with them is the right decision.

I don't need to say that out loud, though.

"I guess I'll think about it." I stand fully and rest my hands on my hips.

Emrys narrows his eyes and his voice deepens, sending shivers up my arms to the back of my neck. "Do you need to ask for permission first? Does Daddy Andras tell you what to do?" Where did that come from? Why is he so mad?

You know what, maybe this trip with them won't be difficult, after all. It might be fun to get on their nerves, especially crabby over there. I saunter over to him, planting myself as close as I can get without pressing our chests together. I have to tilt my head slightly to look into his eyes, but I make sure he can see the rage I have swimming in the grey of mine.

"No male will *ever* tell me what to do." I make a show of dragging my eyes slowly over his form, and then lean in so my lips are just a breath away from his. I whisper, "Not unless I want him to." I take a few steps back and raise my eyebrows at him in a challenge; but before he can respond, I turn around and make my way back to the castle.

Chapter 13

I'm sitting in front of the garden, where there's a white table and chairs set up for outdoor eating, waiting for Andras to join me. I asked Fen if we could have a little picnic set up, and she gave me a strange expression I couldn't discern. She almost looked scared before recovering and telling me what a great idea it was. I wanted to ask her if she was okay, but she quickly excused herself to arrange things. She did a nice job; the table is full of fruits, cheeses, and dried meats. She also had my favorite wine brought out, which I am sipping to help with the nerves. The taste of raspberries is heavy on my tongue.

I'm anxious to talk to Andras about leaving with Casmir and Emrys. I know he'll understand. I just don't want to hurt his feelings; he doesn't deserve that. My leaving for a short while doesn't mean our little fling needs to be over.

I see Andras walking from the castle toward me, wearing a white shirt along with his signature black trousers. His sandy hair shines in the sunlight, and I can't help but smile as he approaches. He smiles back and when he reaches me, bends down to kiss the top of my head before taking a seat.

When he sits, he realizes what we set up on the table and stiffens; his intense blue eyes shoot up, searching mine for something, though I don't know what. He looks back and forth from me to the picnic for a minute before I become concerned. Did I get this wrong? Does he hate picnics, or just eating outside?

"Are you okay? I mean, is this—" I try to look for the right words. "Did I do something wrong?" He watches me for a bit longer, and I become worried that I've gone and fucked this up.

Finally, he answers, his voice tight, "No, I apologize. I was just in shock. No one has ever done something this nice for me." *Lie.* I'm not going to press for him to explain, though. It's not fair of me to ask him to drag up his trauma when I have refused to tell him about mine.

"I just thought it would be nice to enjoy lunch by the garden today." I give him a reassuring smile.

He relaxes into his seat a bit, "You were right, this is pleasant. Thank you, my sweet."

We talk for a while about things happening around the castle and city. He opens up about his troubles with his council, which are noble families of the city who help Andras with decisions. They cannot seem to agree on housing expansions—it would be beneficial to provide additional housing to the fae that live here, but that would take a small piece of farming land. It's not currently in use, but it might be needed in the future, and they are having issues compromising on which is more important.

"That sounds…interesting," he laughs at my attempt to sound engrossed in the topic.

"I am glad I do not have such responsibilities. I'm not sure how you handle it. Just *hearing* everything you do has me stressed out." I take a sip of wine, preparing myself for what I need to say.

"Andras," he looks up at me from across the table. "I actually wanted to talk to you about something." He stiffens. I throw my hands up before he can say anything and blurt, "It's nothing bad, I promise."

He narrows his eyes, but nods. "Go on."

"Uh, well you know how we've been having a lot of trouble finding anything relating to my memories, past life, or even the god who could have done this." He dips his chin, watching me carefully. "Prince Casmir has offered to take me to Anloria so that I may look through their library to see if I can find anything. And I would like to go with him."

Andras becomes a statue; I swear I see darkness cloud his eyes briefly. This is not going how I had hoped. I can't tell if he's angry or sad. I sit and wait for him to tell me his feelings on the matter; and after several minutes, he finally takes in a breath.

"No."

"I'm sorry, I don't think I understand…no?"

"No. You will not be accompanying the Anlorian prince back to his city." His jaw is tight, fists clenched together. He's angry; but now so am I. Who does he think he is trying to boss me around? He may not like the idea, but he doesn't own me.

"Yes," I emphasize. "I will be going with them back to Anloria. I just thought it a courtesy to tell you I would be gone for a while, since you have been very kind to Xamira and me." I continue before he can speak, "It's not forever. I just need to know if there are any answers for me out there. *Someone* has to know who I am, and maybe that person is in Anloria since they are not here."

He stands, knocking some food off the table in his haste. "You. Will. *Not*. Be going anywhere with that prince. We will look elsewhere to figure out what happened to you." He leans forward and if looks could kill, I would be very dead right now. "My answer is final."

I tried to be nice, thinking he would be understanding. I've not seen such a side to him before, and although it has me feeling fear for the first time around him, I stand my ground because I will let *no one* speak to me like that.

I raise to his height so I can look him in the eye, and put as much venom in my words as I can muster. "Andras. You *do not* own me. You *do not* get to tell me what I can and cannot do. And you especially *do not* have any right to treat me this way when I have done nothing wrong." And because I cannot keep my mouth shut, I keep going to drive my point home. "Sure we fucked, and it was nice, but we agreed to not put a label on anything." I walk over so I'm less than an arms length away. "You have no claim to me and cannot force me to stay. I will be leaving in the morning. *My* answer is final."

His eyes become cold, unfeeling, and I don't have time to react before the back of his hand hits my cheek so hard I fly to the ground, rolling to a stop several feet away. I turn over to spit the blood pooling in my mouth onto the ground; I wouldn't be surprised to find a tooth missing. *What the actual fuck?* I've had him all wrong. This is who he is. Not some sweet talking, gentle fae male. But a cold-hearted prince who is clearly willing to do anything to get what he wants. I'm not sure why that's me, but I do not intend to stick around and find out.

I look up from where I am on all fours, blood still spilling from my mouth, to see Andras charging toward me. I fall back and try to crawl away from him, but it's no use. He is out for blood, and mine just happens to be the only option on the menu. His entire demeanor screams danger, and I find myself fearing for my and Xamira's life. What will he do to her if he locks me up or kills me?

He points directly at me and growls, "You are mine, an—"

"What is going on here?" A familiar voice interrupts Andras. One I am so thankful to hear right now. Andras stops in his tracks but says nothing.

Casmir walks into my line of sight, but I don't take my eyes fully from Andras. The Anlorian prince sees the blood on the ground, his gaze making its way up to my dress, which is also stained with blood…then to my mouth, where I can still feel it seeping from.

"Fucking gods, Nell, what happened?" He runs over and kneels down beside me, touching my face gently to look at the damage. I risk looking away from the demon in front of me to meet Casmir's gaze. He looks genuinely worried for me; but that's quickly replaced by confusion, and then rage, as he realizes exactly what happened. He looks over at Andras and exclaims loudly, "*You* did this to her?"

Andras still says nothing, looking conflicted between what he should do and what he wants to do. Casmir goes to stand, fury pouring from his skin. His intentions to attack Andras are clear, but I grab his arm; his raging eyes soften when they meet mine and I shake my head, silently imploring him to let it go. He sighs heavily, not wanting to listen, but nods and reaches for me again.

"Let's get you inside, princess, and I will help clean the blood from you." He helps me stand. Not that I couldn't on my own. I'm just in shock at the moment, not comprehending if any of this is actually happening.

Andras seems to snap out of his internal battle, and places a guilty look on his face. "Nell, I do—I don't know what happened. I just lost control of myself. I am so sorry." He reaches out to grab me, but Casmir places himself between us, not allowing him the opportunity.

His voice is lethal when he speaks to Andras, "You will *never* touch her again, unless she asks you to. If you so much as think about her again, you will find yourself without a head.

"And unless she wishes for me to deal with you now, we are leaving. My court, Nell, and I will be out of the castle tonight." He leads me away from Andras, who tries to call for me, but I ignore him and walk with Casmir to my rooms.

Emrys somehow finds us along the way. "Cas—what the fuck?" He stops in front of me, eyes wide, and I look away because I don't have the energy to deal with this right now. "What the hell happened?"

The prince gestures for us to continue walking before answering in a low voice, keeping his words between the three of us. "That fucking bastard hit her. I found her bleeding all over the ground while he stood above her, looking like he was excited to do it again."

Emrys replies and they talk quietly while we walk, but I hear nothing they're saying. I blink, and suddenly I'm standing in the bathroom, Emrys holding my hand and Casmir grabbing some cloths to help clean me up.

"I can do it," the words barely leave my mouth as a breath, but they both turn to me, having heard what I said. "I'd like to shower. It's not just on my face," I gesture to my dress where the blood soaked in, staining my abdomen.

They look at each other before Casmir nods. Emrys backs away from me as I move, looking out toward the room, not sure how to express what I need. Emrys gathers what I'm trying to say, though.

"We'll be right outside the door." He points to the sitting room. "We will not leave you alone, unless you would like us to?"

I glimpse myself in the mirror. I need to get everything off my body. The blood, his touch, my fear. It all needs to go.

"Thank you." They start to leave, but I stop them. "I would like to come with you, if that's still okay."

Casmir smiles and speaks softly. "I was hoping you would say that. Otherwise, I would have killed him to make sure he didn't get the chance to put his hands on you again."

I say nothing, because what is there to say? *He wouldn't do that again, it was just the one time.* I know deep down that it would certainly not be just once; Andras showed me his true self today, and I want nothing to do with it.

I get dressed after showering, making sure every single drop of blood was off my skin before I dried off. I pack a bag with the essentials; hygiene products, a hairbrush, and a few changes of clothes. I remind myself to grab some extra food for Xamira before we leave.

I walk into the sitting room and find the two males laying on the rug, playing with Xamira. She's chasing their fingers around, rolling over when she grasps one, only to get attacked with belly tickles. They laugh at her attacks, and eventually she relents. She rubs her face on Casmir's chin before curling up in the crook of Emrys's arm, where he's resting his head in his hand.

I realize then that Xamira was trying to tell me all along about the darkness hiding within Andras. She knew from the day we met him that there was something wrong; so maybe it's a good sign that she seems so enamored with these two. As if the pull inside that hollow place in my chest was right. Letting me know I could trust them, and now Xamira is, too.

I'm leaning against the wall with a big grin on my face when Casmir notices me watching, looking up from his spot on the floor. Emrys follows his line of sight, turning his back to see me standing here. Xamira gets upset, and reaches up to grab his face and pull him back down; my eyes widen at the action…is she *flirting* with him? Well, at least she has good taste.

"Xamira seems to like you," I direct the comment to no one in particular. But Casmir takes it upon himself to bask in the compliment, standing gracefully and walking over, stopping a few feet in front of me.

He gives me a wicked smile. "Of course she does. What's not to like?" I feel my eyes reach the back of my head, and turn around to take my bag to the door. "Hold on there, princess, did you pack everything you need?"

"I think so."

"Mind if I have a look? We will have to go through the Sunsor Mountains, which can get quite cold compared to the weather here." I shrug and hand him my bag. He looks through the meager contents and adds several more things to it. It seems excessive, but I guess I'm used to having nothing. I'm too tired to argue, anyway.

We gather everything we need from their rooms, and for Xamira, and head to the front of the castle where several horses and fae wait. I didn't realize they brought this many, though the other fae appear to be soldiers, so I guess that makes sense. It is their prince traveling across the Veil, after all. Of course they would need to be here to protect him if something were to go wrong.

"We're taking horses?"

Emrys gives me an unimpressed look. "Yes. Will that be a problem, love?"

Not wanting to admit my hesitation, I say, "Of all the technology in this realm," throwing my arms wide, "you guys couldn't at least bring over a better mode of transportation? Cars, trains, airplanes, or even bicycles, for gods sake?"

He barks out a laugh at my outburst, and I hear chuckles from some others. "We do have bicycles, *princess*," he mocks, "but horses are the best method of transport for this journey. It will take us several days to make it to Anloria, and I don't think you'd want to be peddling for that long."

He drops his face next to mine, speaking low enough for only my ears to catch, "But if you find yourself needing an extra leg workout, I have something else you can ride instead." I go to push him away, but he jumps back, laughing before I can touch him.

The mouth on that male will be the death of me. He watches me with a challenge swirling in his eyes, and I do my best not to smile but fail horribly. I turn around to Casmir before he catches it, because I will not give him the satisfaction.

Casmir notices the tension but doesn't comment. "Have you ever ridden a horse before?"

"I'm not sure."

He nods, understanding what I mean. "Well, it might be beneficial to have you ride with one of us until you are sure, or you get the hang of it." He looks between Emrys and me. I turn toward his second in command, a grin pulling at his lips because he knows my mind, *and pussy*, could not handle the dirty things he'd spend the entire ride whispering to me.

"I'll ride with you," I say quickly, and turn back to Casmir; the wicked curve of his lips tells me Emrys isn't the only one who plans to give me a hard time. He mounts his horse, a pretty black mare, and I walk over to her front, petting her soft nose to introduce myself.

Casmir helps me up, and I swing my leg over, planting myself in front of him. That was easy. I wonder if I have ridden a horse before, as this feels natural and familiar. The same feeling I had when I started training with Bren.

Bren.

The one fae here I consider a friend…and I'm not able to say goodbye to him, or at least thank him for helping me discover more of myself. I look back as we start riding away and see Andras standing in the castle doorway; wearing all black, surrounded by a sea of white. I sit up straighter, turning my gaze away from him, and focus on the path ahead. Casmir wraps his hand around my waist, letting me know that he's here. I look over to see Xamira riding with her new crush, laughing to myself at how ridiculous that sounds.

We make it out of the city and start heading through a forest toward the mountains. I have so many things to think about that I don't want to deal with right now. I'm *so tired* and start to drift off to sleep, but jerk myself awake each time, not wanting to fall off the horse.

Casmir tugs my waist, sliding me back until I'm flush with him. His other hand pulls my hair over my shoulder and his cheek presses against the side of my head. The touch sends shivers through my nerves.

"Sleep, Nell," he purrs. "I have you." I bite my lip, trying to hide the tremble I feel at the tone of his voice, mixed with all the places he's pressed against me.

He runs his fingers up and down my thigh, while his other arm continues to hold my waist. I do my best to control my breathing, trying not to let my hormones embarrass me. It doesn't take long before I feel myself relax into him, taking comfort in his touch and warmth. This new chapter for Xamira and I will be just fine.

Chapter 14

I startle awake, my eyes taking a moment to adjust to the dim light, and I almost freak out until I see two familiar faces laying next to me. We're still in the forest, though we must have made camp for the night. I don't remember getting off the horse, and I wonder what they had to do to get me down here. I was clearly more tired than I thought.

I rub my eyes and drag my hands down my face, wincing at the sharp pain that action caused in my cheek. I no doubt have a nice bruise taking shape; I hope it goes away before we arrive in Anloria. I do not need anyone else seeing it and asking questions; I just want to forget it happened and move on.

I still cannot wrap my head around how Andras went from a smiling, gentle giant to a raging, abusive asshole in a matter of seconds. Is that his personality all the time and he was hiding it from me, or does he only beat others when he doesn't get his way? I guess it doesn't matter. I still fell for his nice side because I was lonely and really hoping he wouldn't be like the rest.

I look up and see one soldier, a female with short blonde hair, leaning against a tree, carving a piece of wood with her dagger. She meets my stare and dips her chin toward me in greeting. I manage a sheepish smile, unsure if I should say anything, but she turns her attention back to the carving before I can think too hard about it.

She must be on watch as the rest of the camp is sleeping on bedrolls. I feel bad I didn't introduce myself or learn their names yesterday. I was just so out of my head. I'll make sure to talk with each of them today.

I lie back down on my bedroll and stare up at the brightening sky. I can make out a few stars through the tops of the trees, though we're covered pretty well.

I'm anxious about what happens when we get to Anloria. If I do find something to help me retrieve my memories, that would be amazing. Maybe I will figure out who I am and curse the god that did this to me. I'll regain access to whatever magic I have and use it to give Andras what he's got coming to him. That thought makes me pause. I never asked him what type of magic he possesses. Now that I think of it, I didn't see a single fae use their magic while I was in the castle. I wonder why that is? Do they just not use it often? I'll have to ask the others if they could show me that it actually exists, and it's not just another lie Andras told me.

But what happens if I find nothing? Do I stay in Anloria and try to make a life for Xamira and I? Go back to live outside of the Veil seeing as I would be magic-less, anyway? I scrunch my nose. No, I couldn't go back there. That world was colorless and sad, though maybe that's just because I don't belong there.

Here, it's like everything is so full of life. The colors are bright; the air is fresh, and the food even tastes better. There's no way I'd be able to live out there again, not after what I've experienced since falling through that impossible wall.

I hear a quiet mewling, and turn my head to see Xamira nestled in Casmir's arm, which is curled perfectly around her, almost like a hug. He's sleeping on his back with his head tilted to the side, so his cheek is snuggled against her head. I laugh silently to myself, thinking of how absurd it is that she is so attached to them already. Casmir's bedroll is nearly touching mine, enabling me to reach out and give the little traitor some belly scratches. She makes a quiet noise and settles further into the prince's warmth. The sight has the emptiness in my chest tugging at its restraints.

I take a moment to look at the male in his sleeping form. His skin looks so soft—I have the strange urge to rub myself against him. His dark hair is falling over to the side, looking messier than usual, and his face is at peace. I could easily stare at him all day. How the gods made these two annoyingly perfect individuals, leaving the rest of us scraps, is beyond me.

I feel a light touch down my arm, and turn my head to find Emrys laying on his side watching his fingers trail over the fabric of my shirt. He looks unguarded; like he walks through this life with a filter, and I'm catching one of the rare times he doesn't have it on. I don't think he realized I'm awake because his eyes snap up to me, showing me everything for a moment, before the walls are back up and his stare is guarded again. I say nothing about it. Maybe it's difficult for him to talk about and he'll bring those vulnerabilities up in his own time.

I roll to my side, facing him, and we share tired smiles.

"Hi," I whisper, hoping I'm quiet enough to not wake anyone else.

"Hello, love. Did you sleep well?" I nod, watching his curls shift as he settles closer to me. I want to run my hand through them so badly; I can't imagine there's another feeling like it. I wonder if he would let me if I asked nicely?

I don't have to wonder for long because one curl falls across his forehead and before I realize what I'm doing, my hand reaches to push it back in place. He doesn't move to stop me or say anything, so I take the opportunity to brush my fingers through. His hair is so soft that I have to wonder if he has special products made for it. The spots where my fingers lightly graze his skin send small zaps shooting through my arm. I feel my very essence, my soul, press against my flesh…almost as if his is calling to mine.

My hand makes it out through the side of his hair, and I watch my fingers trail down his jaw, in awe of how remarkable it feels to touch him. Something so simple. My fingers reach his chin and I focus on his lips, looking so plump and soft. I have to feel them. My thumb reaches up to touch them, but before I make contact, Emrys grabs my wrist and I snap out of whatever trance I was just in. Snatching my hand back, I feel heat rising in my face. What the hell was that?

"*Oh my gods*," I breathe, sitting up to rest on my elbow, feeling embarrassed. "I'm so sorry. That was incredibly rude of me. I don't—" I take in some air to calm myself, "I don't know what I was just doing, I'm sorry."

But he doesn't seem upset in the slightest. Actually, he's smiling at me, looking more content than anything. He grabs my hand, pulling me down to lie closer to him.

"Breathe, love." He takes in a deep breath and prompts me to do the same. I do. "It's okay. You never need to apologize for touching me. In fact, we could keep this exploration going because I have a certain body part that I would just *love* for you to discover."

I burst out laughing and immediately slap my hand to my mouth, trying to cover the sound. I hear a couple of the others mumble something, and adjust on their bedrolls before everything goes quiet again. When I'm sure I didn't wake the entire camp, I look over to Emrys to see him watching me, amusement coming off him in waves. I'm thankful for his ability to ease the tension, but I need to be careful. Andras said a few nice words, gave me a pretty smile, and I fell for it. I feel deep inside that Emrys and Casmir are not at all the same, but I still need to keep my guard up and stop fawning over them like they're my first crushes.

I roll my eyes at him and decide it's light enough for me to get up, eager to put distance between myself and temptation. I stand, turning to flip Emrys off, causing him to chuckle lightly. I make my way over to the horses to give them some attention and feed them before the long day of work they have ahead.

We've been riding for several hours and *fuck* do my thighs hurt. I'm unsure that I could stay on a horse—even if I was comfortable with the idea of riding alone—without Casmir holding me up. His arms around me are the only things keeping me from falling to the dirt.

After a light breakfast of fruit and bread, we made our way through the thickest part of the forest. There are still trees surrounding us, though they're more sparse, allowing the sun to warm our faces. Casmir mentioned we would be reaching Amsal just after sunset: a small village before we cross GodsPass: the path through the Sunsor Mountains. Apparently, it is the only way to cross the mountains, unless we want to make the climb up them, all but ensuring our deaths. No thanks.

I lean back into the prince, letting him take some of my weight since I feel my legs trembling from the effort of holding myself up. He slides my hair to the side, resting his chin on my shoulder.

"Something wrong?" I hear the smile in his voice, "Or are you just in need of more of my touch?" The hand resting on my thigh squeezes, sending my legs trembling for a different reason.

I move to sit up, too proud to admit defeat, ready to do anything I can to force my legs to work; but his other hand flattens against my abdomen, causing it to contract, and holds me tight against him. He tsks, a finger on my thigh tapping in time with each one.

"I don't think so, Nell," he teases. "I quite enjoy having you this close; the length of your entire body molding to mine." I'm not sure if I'll ever get used to the way these two talk. I try not to think about how many females their ridiculous, but effective flirting has gotten them.

I decide that I'll give them a taste of their own actions, but I can do it better. Before long, I'll have them on their knees panting up at me, and I don't even need their pretty little words to do it. Instead of resisting his hold, I relax further, adjusting my ass so it's pressed snugly against him. I feel him suck in a breath and smile to myself.

"Careful, princess," he whispers directly into my ear, and my breath catches.

I turn to the female that was keeping watch this morning before I lose myself in the prince. "I don't believe we were introduced. I'm Nell."

She returns my smile before telling me her name. "Ansa."

"It's nice to officially meet you Ansa." Not knowing what else to say, I awkwardly blurt out, "So what is it you do?" She raises an eyebrow in question.

"I mean, are you like a soldier or something? The leathers you're wearing make you look like one." And then I add, trying to redeem myself, "You also look pretty badass in them."

That earns me a laugh from everyone except the blonde-haired male toward the front of our group. I can feel Casmir shaking against me and look over to see Emrys trying hard to hold in his amusement. Did I say something funny? She does look badass; her leathers are thick and molded to every part of her body. She has two daggers, that I can see, fitted in small pockets attached to her pants. And large, brown boots that cover most of her calves. There's a sword strapped to her waist, silver with some kind of black material attached to the hilt; giving it an edge of beauty, but also practicality, as it looks like it was set in a way that allows for the perfect hand grip. It suits her look.

"We," Ansa gestures to the others, who are wearing similar attire as her, "are the Royal Guard."

"They manage the castle security," Casmir adds. "Each of them also helps to train, and coordinate, the Anlorian armies, with Emrys overseeing the entire division as captain."

I look over to Emrys and he winks at me, clearly feeling smug about his position. I'd like to wipe that look off his face, which gives me the idea that I will most definitely be challenging him to a match. Males *always* underestimate females, and I feel giddy thinking about the moment he realizes he will lose to a random human-made-fae who has no actual memories. We'll see how big his ego is after that.

The male with short, black hair interrupts my silent planning. "Since we're introducing ourselves, my name's Karis, that's Taryn," he points to the long-haired, brunette female, who gives me a warm smile.

"At the front is Sam." He whispers, "though he's always grumpy, and doesn't talk much, so don't expect any conversation from him."

"I heard that," Sam mutters, and Karis smiles like he meant for him to hear every word.

"And then last, and least, is Jorin." He nods his head to the fae behind us. I look back to say hello, seeing his black hair tied into a bun at the nape of his neck, a few stragglers hanging over his temple. But what catches my eye is his face. I almost give myself whiplash looking back at Karis, thinking I'm seeing things; but no, they have the same face.

Karis turns to me with a smile he can barely hold back, seeing the disbelieving look I'm sending his way.

"You're twins?" He nods, still finding my reaction entertaining.

I look at Jorin, who doesn't seem to find it as funny, though I see the glint of amusement in his eyes.

"Is that even possible with fae?" Stupid question. "I mean, obviously it is, but I was told it's really difficult to have children. So I can't even grasp the insane odds of conceiving twins." I must sound like a kid in a candy store, because they all share another laugh at my expense.

"Our parents were shocked when mom gave birth to me, and then a few minutes later felt his big ass head coming out," Karis jerks a thumb to his brother, and I have to cover my mouth to stop the laugh from escaping. I just met them and will be around them for a while, so I don't need one having a vendetta against me.

We fall into easy conversation, all of them taking turns talking about what they're most excited about when they get back to Anloria. It didn't occur to me before now that they have been away from their homes, traveling, for nearly two weeks already; and we still have a few days before reaching the city.

Their homesickness has me feeling the emptiness in my chest a little more today. I wonder what it's like to have a home? To have a place you love so much that it saddens you when you aren't there. I've never had that, at least not that I know of. All of my memories are of foster houses, where I wasn't wanted, and a cold, crappy apartment. The only good thing about any of those memories is Xamira. She kept me going when I didn't think I could do it anymore.

Then there was Andras's castle. It's upsetting that his castle, as cold and unwelcoming as it was, was the place I felt most at home. I think that was because of Andras. I felt safe and comfortable around him; he made me smile and helped me just *feel* something again.

Maybe that's what truly makes a home—not the place you are, or the things you have, but the individuals who surround you. Xamira has been my home for a long time; it didn't matter where we were...as long as she was with me, I felt at peace. It makes me wonder if there's anyone out there waiting for me. Was I someone else's home?

Part of me hopes so; it would mean the world to me to have someone I love on the other side of this, if I even can't get my memories back.

But part of me also hopes there isn't anyone. Not only would they have been waiting for gods knows how long, but I doubt I'm the same person I was before. Unless I have actually lived through all the traumatic shit in my old life, that I was convinced was my actual life, there's no chance I come back being the same person. I would just be a disappointment to whoever was waiting for me.

Chapter 15

We stopped in Amsal for the night, going straight to our rooms after a light dinner, all of us ready to pass out. I'm sitting at a table in a large open room, looking out at the village. It looks a lot like Ceross, just on a smaller scale. Though I quite like the warm energy the fae give off here; they all seem to be happy. The inn itself is cute; the upper floors hold all the rooms for visitors, and the bottom floor has a bathroom and the large room we're currently in.

The structure of the building is made from a dark wood, the tables matching, though they look more worn. There are random things being showcased on the walls; little trinkets, a blanket that was woven to look like a panther running through a forest. The panther is quite detailed. With its black fur, even darker spotting that catches in the sunlight, and intimidating, golden eyes. It almost reminds me of Xamira, though I think she would probably run for the hills if she saw that running at her.

I look over to see her sharing breakfast with Emrys, who is sitting across from Casmir and me. He is giving her some berries and cheese, and even grabbed an extra plate for her to use. If I didn't know any better, I would swear she was his cat, and they were best friends. As much as she likes him, he also seems enthralled with her. He's been very attentive these last couple of days; making sure she's comfortable, has enough food and water, and playing with her whenever she asks.

He looks up to see me watching them, narrowing his eyes playfully before turning to Casmir.

"The weather looks like it's going to hold. It should take us just over a day to get across GodsPass if it stays like this."

Casmir nods, pleased with the information. "Let's hope so. I do not want a repeat of last time, especially since little princess," he nods to Xamira, "probably doesn't enjoy getting wet."

"What happened last time?"

They both look over to me, Emrys speaking first, "There was a rainstorm when we crossed two weeks ago. It made the top of the pass cold, and slippery, and just unpleasant," he grimaces.

"Do you guys not have umbrellas here?"

"Of course we have umbrellas." Casmir casually puts his arm around my shoulders, pulling me into his side and bringing our faces dangerously close together. "*Someone* just forgot to pack them, even though he insisted he did."

I stare into his eyes, falling into a world of bright green and gold forests, barely hearing Emrys protest about how he *could have sworn* he packed the umbrellas. I'm so mesmerized that I don't realize I'm leaning forward to get a better look until a hand traces my non bruised cheek. I jump, coming back to reality, when I feel my lips breathe against his. I slide back from him, my heart racing, and I'm breathing like I just ran a marathon; something in my chest feels like it's tearing, forcing me to feel things I don't want to feel.

The prince is still staring at me with a confused look on his face. His cheeks are flushed and his breathing heavy, as well. I wonder if he was just under the same spell I was. What the hell is it? It doesn't feel like just a physical attraction; it feels like my soul is singing when they're near. Like I could burst into flames at their touch and feel more alive than I ever have. It reminds me of people who say 'love at first sight,' as if soulmates are something that exists. That is not possible with fae. Andras told me that mates choose each other. As in, they didn't feel like they were going to die if they didn't devour every single inch of the fae in front of them.

I look toward Emrys, who is watching the both of us with a calculating look on his brow. "Interesting," he mutters to himself before picking up Xamira and making his way out of the inn, patting Casmir on the shoulder as he passes.

This is strange. I feel strange. I can tell Casmir does, too; he normally doesn't look uncomfortable from much of anything, but he's rubbing the back of his neck and contemplating what to say.

I save him the trouble, "That was my bad. My head has been weird the last couple of days, and I seem to be forgetting myself."

His face smooths out and he flashes a serene smile, tilting his head slightly. "If you want to kiss me, princess, all you need to do is ask."

I huff out a breath, rolling my eyes. I'm not sure why I didn't expect that reaction. "*My gods*," I push him out of the seat, "you two are insufferable." I hear Casmir laugh quietly as we walk out of the inn, feeling his eyes on me the entire way.

I reach the rest of the group, waiting just down the road; I notice they're all standing with their bags and not any horses. Karis notices my confusion and explains, "Horses aren't able to go through GodsPass. It's too dangerous for them. That's why there's a village on each side to drop them off and pick more up."

"You're telling me we will be walking the whole way?" I groan, testing out my legs to see if they'll be able to handle the climb.

"I'm still open to helping you with those extra leg workouts, love," Emrys announces, winking at me.

"Or I could carry you, if you need." He holds his hands in front of him, like he's cupping something. "My hands could use something soft to hold for a while," his movements indicating I'd straddle his front while we walk.

I raise my eyebrows while the rest of their group tries, and fails, to not laugh. Even Sam seems to hold back something of a smile. I take a deep breath, needing all the calming energy I can get if I'm going to survive these next few days.

Not giving up on my little game, I step over to Emrys, nearly touching our bodies together, and look up at him through my lashes.

"You know what?" I say sweetly; Emrys blinks, not having expected my boldness. "*My* hands could really use something big and hard to hold on to." He swallows as I run my palm over his growing bulge, frowning. "It's too bad you can't help me with that."

I give him a devilish smile, and he looks about two seconds away from pinning me down and showing me just how wrong I am. Good. I turn to grab my pack and start walking, Xamira following at my side. I hear the group burst out laughing, Emrys telling them to shut up. There's annoyance in his voice, and I internally high-five myself for a job well done.

⁂

I crane my neck to look toward the top of the Sunsor Mountains, almost falling back with the effort. They look larger than I would have expected after seeing them from Ceross; the peaks have blinding, white snow. I can only look for a second before needing to turn away, since the sun is hitting them just right. I try to look ahead to see the path we will be taking through GodsPass, but cannot make out where it would be. The name of it is quite interesting.

"Why do you call it GodsPass?" I ask no one in particular.

Talyn makes a squeal, and I look over my shoulder to see an excited gleam in her eyes. She must find this subject interesting.

"Legend says that the top of the passage is where the gods enter and leave this realm. No one has actually seen it happen, but there are a couple fae who were alive during the War of Gods who claim that it is true," she scrunches her nose, realizing something. "Though I suppose they would be the only ones who could have started the legends."

I slow down to walk next to her, very interested in what she's saying. "Has anyone tried to go to their realm? Is that something that could be done?"

If it's possible to go to the gods myself, it would save me a lot of research and anxiety. She gives me a sad look before turning her eyes toward the mountains.

"I don't think it's possible for us to use the passage between realms. It is said that only the ones directly descended from the gods can use the passage from Earth to Europa.

"Though, it's also mentioned in some texts that the demi-gods, the ones who were originally created from the mating between a god and a mortal, can also go between realms. So I've concluded that it's not about having pure god blood, but about the parents." She looks over at me to make sure I'm following along. "If a parent lives on Europa, and has a child, I believe that child could use the passage. The issue is that I can't confirm the truth of that because none of the gods, or demi-gods, have been seen visiting Earth for centuries."

Well at least one would have had to come here to do this to me, and now I'm questioning why even more. If they don't visit and we cannot go to Europa, what the fuck did one of the gods have against me? What could I have done to offend one so badly that they cursed me to a life of suffering? Instead of getting upset over the things I cannot do anything about, I decide to change the subject.

"Is magic real?"

The twins chuckle, and Talyn tries to keep her face straight. I am just full of things to laugh at, I guess. Emrys steps up next to me, putting his arm around my shoulder. He holds out a hand and a flame springs to life in his palm. I think my jaw may have broke from how hard it dropped. I knew the types of magic that existed, but seeing it is something totally different.

"*No way.* That's insane. How do you do that?" I reach over to touch the flame, and he lets me run my fingers through it. I can feel the idea of heat, but it's not hot at all; and when I pull my hand back, there are no burns.

"I have fire magic, so I can manipulate flames to do just about anything I want." He gives me an example by shaping the flame into a rose and setting it in my hands. I look up at him, feeling a huge grin on my face because it makes my cheek sting a little, and he's watching me with awe in his eyes. I quickly look back down to not get caught in the tension.

"Are you taking away the heat from it so it doesn't burn me?" He nods, and the rose warms up just a little. Not enough to sting, but enough that it feels like I'm sitting in front of a fireplace holding my palms toward it.

"This is incredible," I breathe softly, more to myself than anything. "Do the rest of you have magic?"

I get various answers of affirmation, and they go around the group showing me a little of what they can do. Taryn makes an animal from water that looks just like Xamira. Jorin also shows his water magic, though Karis surprises me when he sprouts an actual rose from the ground and hands it to me. Emrys's hand tenses around my shoulder, but he says nothing. Sam and Ansa both have fire magic. It is so crazy to see each of them pull these elements into their control.

I look to Casmir, who is now standing on my other side, watching my reaction to everything. He takes my hand and stops me, letting Emrys's arm fall back to his side. I stand in front of him, his hands holding mine, waiting for whatever he's going to show me. He starts to lean in and for a moment, I think he's going to kiss me. But he moves his mouth to my ear instead, while I bit my lip to hide my disappointment.

"Close your eyes," he whispers, then moves so his forehead is hovering over mine. I gaze into his eyes, confused by the signals he's giving me, when he looks down at my lips, knowing exactly what I'm thinking.

"Trust me." And I do. I shouldn't—I can't—but I do. So I close my eyes, and he stays where he is. I wait for a minute, wondering what he's trying to accomplish since we're just standing here, in the middle of a field, breathing in each others air. It almost feels too intimate to have the others watching…and I know they're watching.

"Casmir, I don't understand. What are you doing?"

"Open your eyes, love."

I open them to see him still looking down at me. I lean back a little, confused about what I'm supposed to be seeing that's different. He looks the same as he did a minute ago, and I don't feel any different. I pull back a little more to look at the rest of the group, and at first I don't find them, but that's only because Casmir and I are hovering in the air; we are so high that I can see the tops of the trees.

My arms shoot around his neck, choking the life out of him, and I wrap my legs around his waist, straddling him in mid-air. I hide my face on his shoulder, trying to keep myself from looking down. I'm trembling a little; but I can't tell if it's because I'm floating in the air with the prince, or because I've attached myself to him. Out of desperation or not, this is quite the compromising position to be in.

"*Holy shit*, Cas, you could warn a girl!" I feel him laugh beneath me, and I suddenly want to look down to keep myself from thinking of this whole mess: all of my feelings and hormones. I sit back a little to peek at the group, standing not too far away from us now. Everyone but Emrys has some short of shock on their face, while he's standing with his arms crossed, looking like he's planning something evil.

"You're a damn show off, Casmir," Emrys mutters, and I laugh at that, causing me to slip a little and grip onto the male tighter.

"You're safe. I would never let you fall, even if you weren't wrapped around me." He gets a contemplative look in his eyes. "But this position has given me some interesting ideas." He lowers his head so his lips brush against mine. I'm too in shock to move. "Perhaps you would like to test these ideas with me?" He smiles against me, and I feel like I'm flying. I mean, technically I am, but my insides are also flying now.

The place our chests press feels entirely too strange. The emptiness that's lived there for years is slightly less…empty? Probably just my nerves going crazy at the moment. I'm so absorbed by everything that I forget what he just said. I hope he wasn't expecting a response.

His lips move with his breath, and I am still captured by his hazel eyes. Just like the night we met, everything around us falls away. All I see is him. These emotions are so confusing, and I don't know what to do with them. I just met him several days ago, and I don't know a lot about him. I guess that's not the full truth. I just don't know a lot about his past. But still, this is crazy. How can I feel like this so quickly?

"Cas," I didn't plan to give him a nickname, but the way he's looking at me tells me he loves it just as much as I do.

"Say that again," he pleads.

Every time one of us speaks, our lips graze, and it feels like lightning shooting through my entire being, threatening to split me into a thousand pieces.

"Cas, what are we doing?" Maybe he has a rational thought swirling around in his head, because I certainly don't. Do I want to kiss this male more than I've ever wanted anything? Yes. Do I care the entire group is watching us eye fuck, and might watch us do a little more than that? No. I couldn't care less about anything else right now.

He glances at my lips then back up, searching my eyes for a hint of refusal, but I just nod and close the distance between us, pressing our mouths together.

My vision goes white, and I know nothing else except the feel of his mouth on mine—it is the single most blissful feeling I have ever experienced. I'm falling through an unending void of fire and electricity. We pull back to look at each other, both of us feeling the same thing and not understanding what the fuck this is.

His hand grabs the back of my head, bringing me to him again; we meld together like one being, our souls intertwining just as much as our tongues and breath. Our hands move around the other's body, trying to find a way to press into each other more, even though it's not physically possible. My sight and vision are gone. The only things I feel are him and something in my chest frantically trying to rip itself out.

It could have been seconds, or hours, before someone clears their throat, causing Casmir and me to both startle and pull apart. We're breathing heavily, and he looks just as crazed as I do. At least I'm not alone in this strange feeling.

Another throat clears, and I look over to see that we're on the ground again, with Emrys standing a few feet away, smirking at us. The others are up the path, trying to pretend they didn't see a single thing. Everything comes back to me, and I realize I'm still wrapped around Casmir; I untangle myself, and he helps to set me down.

He's looking at me like I'm someone he's never seen before, his eyes searching for something I don't have the answer to.

"That—" he says in a rough voice.

"I know," nodding my head in agreement. He presses a hand to his sternum, and I briefly wonder if I hurt him before I remember the inexpiable feelings I just had. He must have experienced that, too.

We both start walking toward Emrys, who's looking concerned now. Needing to disperse the tension, I blurt out the first thing that comes to mind.

"So you have air magic…that's pretty cool."

A moment of silence follows my words before the three of us erupt with laughter, catching up with the group and making our way to GodsPass.

Chapter 16

We're almost to the peak of GodsPass when Emrys announces a little cave we found would be a good place to camp for the night. The climb itself has been easy; I'm guessing whoever made this path had earth magic, because it's mostly just smooth rock with flights of stairs once in a while. The guys made it sound like it was some treacherous climb that would have us all fighting for our lives; but now that I think of it, Karis was the one who told me more details about it. And from what I learned, he likes to dramatize things. I do see how a rain storm would make this part of the journey annoying. There are some places I imagine would be like walking on ice if they were covered in water.

Ansa uses her magic to start a fire at the mouth of the cave, picking that location to keep away any creatures living up here. I help distribute a small dinner to each person, Sam being the only one who doesn't say thank you. He just looks at me like I'm an annoying bug, so I slowly walk away, not wanting him to swat at me.

After dinner, we set out our bedrolls; Casmir and Emrys caging me in again, with Xamira laying at my feet. She walked most of the way today, so she's probably more tired than I am.

I'm staring up at the ceiling of the cave when I remember a thought I had earlier.

I turn toward Casmir, who's laying with his hands under his head. He looks like he already fell asleep, so I'm not sure if I should poke him or just try to remember my question tomorrow.

I'm contemplating what to do when he cracks open his eyes, a smile forming. "Yes, princess?"

"I was curious about your past."

"My past?"

"Well, yeah. I know little about you, and was wondering if you'd share some of it with me? I want to know how you grew up, when you became prince, how old you are. Whatever you're comfortable sharing."

He rolls to face me, with his head lifted and resting in his palm. He studies me for a few heartbeats before coming to some conclusion.

"I am ninety-eight years old, which is past the age most mortals will live, though it is quite young in fae years. I was crowned prince two decades ago when my mother became ill with some unknown disease, and my father wished to take care of her. I took over the title to relieve them of the stress. I spent my younger years fucking around, and fucking." He gets a remorseful look in his eyes. "I was always drunk or high, so it didn't matter to me who I fucked as long as it distracted me for a while."

Wow, that was a lot more than I was expecting.

"Is your mom…?"

"She's alive. Still sick, though she's not gotten any worse in years. She has her bad days, but she's doing quite well." I touch his arm, letting him know I'm here, and thankful that he shared this with me.

"She's going to love you," he says to himself, but I catch the words.

"Does she live in the castle? Will we be meeting her when we arrive?"

He searches my face again, pursing his lips before saying, "No, her and my father live in their own home outside of the main city."

He watches me carefully as I pick up on what he's saying…he wants me to meet his parents.

"Are you sure that's something you want? I don't think bringing some random fae to them, who doesn't even know who she is, would make them very happy." I find the sleeve of my shirt suddenly quite interesting.

"I'm sure."

My eyes snap up at his admission. His gaze is intense and heavy. I'm feeling things again. Before I can get caught up in those feelings, I turn my head to Emrys, who now has Xamira laying on his chest, purring at the soft petting he's giving her.

"What about you?" I say in a muted voice, not wanting to wake the others who are snoring in the back of the cave.

He looks at me and raises an eyebrow in question. I know he's aware of what I'm asking him. I can see it in his expression, but I press anyway.

"Your past. Anything you'd be willing to share?"

"No," he says in a tone that makes it clear he won't entertain any more conversation for the night. I feel a little hurt at the rejection, but I can't blame him. I'm not over here offering any of my stories, even if they aren't real.

I wonder if I will ever feel comfortable enough to tell anyone what happened to me. Real or not, I still have the memories. They still *feel* like they happened. That should be valid enough for me to accept how much they've fucked with my head, but it's not. I didn't actually go through it, so how do I have any right to be affected by it?

I wake, feeling the warm sun on my face. The scent of something sweet and familiar is heavy in the air. I don't remember falling asleep, but I'm glad I chose here to do so. It's so peaceful.

Wait.

I sit up to look at my surroundings. This is not where I fell asleep. I was in a cave, on the mountains, with Emrys and Casmir laying next to me. How did I get here, then?

I stand, and take in my environment; I'm in a field of tall, green grass. It's the middle of the day, the sun beating down on me, though I don't feel its warmth. In the distance, there is what appears to be…a city? It looks like different buildings, though I can't clearly make out their shapes. Behind me is an endless, grassy field.

I start walking toward the city, thinking maybe I could ask someone where we are and how I get to Anloria. I walk for what feels like hours, my limbs feeling tired. I look up to see how much longer I have before I reach the buildings and—what? How are they further away than they were before? I've been walking forever!

I look behind me again…still an endless sea of green flowing in the breeze. I don't feel a breeze. A wariness forms in the pit of my stomach, the hairs on my arms rising. Something isn't right. I turn and run toward the city, putting all the effort I can into it, but I get no closer. It's like I'm stuck in this one spot, unable to go in any direction, even though the ground under my feet is moving when I do.

This makes little sense.

I feel air on the back of my neck and spin around to find someone,—something—standing there. I scream and fall back into the grass, quickly righting myself just in case this thing tries something. I look them over, but I can't tell what I'm looking at. It has the shape of a person, the coloring of a person. I can see light hair and darker clothing. But everything is blurred. I can't make out any defining features other than a few smears of color.

The thing reaches for me, and I jump back, not wanting to go near it. But I have no idea how to get away when I can't run anywhere. It makes a noise, like it's trying to say something to me, but the words are muffled.

"What?" It tries speaking again, but the sound is no different.

"I can't make out what you're saying."

It walks closer to me, and suddenly my feet are in the ground. I'm breathing heavily, feeling terrified and wishing so badly I was with the prince and his captain. The thing reaches an arm out and grabs my throat, squeezing hard enough to cut off my air.

I wake up not knowing where I am, standing alone in the middle of a field, and now some random blob is choking the life out of me.

I struggle, trying to scratch at the thing, kick it, anything I can think of; but I go right through it each time I make contact. It's like air, and yet it's holding me up like I weigh nothing.

I'm going to die.

I feel my body start to give out, my vision going black at the sides and—

I shoot up off my bedroll, hunching to the side to cough, trying to get my lungs to work. I'm wheezing and coughing for minutes before I feel like I can take in enough air again. When I have enough oxygen in my body and become coherent again, I see Casmir and Emrys on their knees in front of me, looking horrified. The others are standing to the back, all with looks of worry on their faces.

"I'm sorry," I croak to them, my voice getting caught and almost causing another round of coughing. Emrys hands me water before I can, and I think I give him a smile in thanks; a few sips helps to lubricate the dryness in my throat.

Feeling a little better, and wanting less of an audience, I look to the fae in the back. "I'm sorry. I had a nightmare, I think. I didn't mean to wake everyone. I'm okay."

That seems to settle them a bit, though Karis and Talyn still look concerned. They all go back over to their bedrolls, giving me some space. I wipe my hand across my forehead, feeling so tired, and it comes back wet. My hands shoot up to feel my hair, which is damp. I reach around to my back, and it feels like I just went swimming with my clothes on. I could wring out my shirt and have a handful of sweat come back.

"What do you mean, *think*?" Casmir says in a hushed tone.

My head shakes since I'm not sure how to answer that. I realize I closed my eyes and am trembling, when a pair of legs surround my own and arms move to hold my torso. The smell of leather and musky earth hits my senses, and I relax a little knowing it's Emrys holding me.

"I'm all wet and disgusting. You really don't want to be touching me right now," I whisper, my voice cracking. He rests his chin on my shoulder, and places a light kiss under my jaw while he sways me side to side.

"You could be covered in the most revolting, foul substance in all the realms, and I still wouldn't hesitate to have you in my arms."

I don't know why that brings tears to my eyes, but I feel them run slowly down my cheeks. I think everything that has happened in the last two months is catching up to me, because as hard as I try, I can't stop the onslaught of emotions from taking over my body. Leaving Chago, falling into this whole new world, finding out I'm fae and missing who knows how many years of memories, dealing with trauma from memories I didn't actually experience. Then listening to my heart for once and falling for a male who just wanted to abuse me. Rushing out of the castle that was starting to feel like home…going on this journey with fae who I barely know, but seem to trust more than I've ever trusted anyone. And now this *thing* in my head that's trying to kill me.

It's too much to think about. But I'm unable to stop, and it all comes pouring out of me. I cover my face with my hands, trying to hide the river of sadness and frustration flowing out of me, but it doesn't stop the sounds; I feel Emrys tense under me when he realizes what I'm doing. Suddenly, I'm being lifted and placed into his lap. I decide to take the comfort he's offering me. Wrapping my legs around his waist, and my arms around his shoulders, I cry into his shirt for a while.

I probably sound obnoxious, smell gross, and look even worse, but I can't find it in myself to care. Emrys continues to hold me through all of it, and at some point I feel Casmir lightly massage my legs, letting me know that he's here, too. I should be embarrassed. I don't let *anyone* see me cry. I hate being looked at like I'm weak. But something tells me these two wouldn't ever think me weak or judge me for these feelings. So I let myself feel. I let myself get it all out, because that's the only way I'm going to get through it.

Eventually, my loud sobbing slows down to just ragged breathing and then that calms down, too, until I'm no longer shedding tears…just holding Emrys like he's my lifeline. Neither of them has said anything. They're just letting me process whatever is going on in my head, and I'm thankful for that. I couldn't explain how nice it is to just have someone here, with no expectations from me. That's not something I've ever had, besides Xamira. And though she is, and always will be enough, *this* is the kind of intimacy I've been needing.

A while later I loosen my grip on Emrys, hoping I didn't injure him at all, and sit back to look at him and Casmir. I realize we're sitting outside of the cave, down the path a little way. I feel a pang of warmth in my chest that they knew I wouldn't want to be near the others like this, and moved us to give me more privacy.

The prince is sitting just behind Emrys, his legs stretched out, nearly touching mine. He's leaning back on his hands with Xamira laying in his lap, both of them watching me. I turn my attention to the male still holding me, and wince when I see my tears have gone through half his shirt, those parts now clinging to his muscles.

"I'm so—" he covers my mouth with one of his hands, the other continuing to hold my back.

"*Never* apologize for your feelings," I almost protest, but the hard look in his eyes stops me. "It's just a shirt, Nell. It will dry, it can be washed, or I can always get a new one. It doesn't matter." I hear the implication in his voice: *I* matter.

Feeling a whole new wave of emotion inside my chest has me thinking of something to say so I don't have to deal with it; one breakdown was enough for tonight.

"I don't know what I mean," answering Casmir's question from earlier. I tell them of the dream, what I saw and felt. I do my best to explain the blurry figure that I'm pretty sure was a person; though I could be wrong, and maybe it was just a killer blob. They listen to all the details, and then sit in silence for a few moments, trying to figure out what it could signify.

"I wonder if it was a memory," I say into the quiet. They look at me confused and I frown, realizing Andras was the one that figured out the blurry people and places in my head were fake memories.

"When Andr—" I pause when their eyes darken. "When *he* discovered someone had fucked with my head, he asked me to think of memories from my past. I can make out details of things that happened, but I can't see any person's face.

"In my dream, it wasn't just their face that was blurred, it was their whole body. And all the buildings in the distance. It seemed so real and yet, not. I *felt* the thing grab my throat. I wonder if it was an actual memory of mine." I move my gaze between them to watch their reactions, hoping they don't think I'm completely insane. "It differed from my fake memories. That's the only thing I can think of other than my brain can't handle anything anymore, and is now giving me crazy real nightmares."

"I would have to agree." Casmir sits up further, giving me a sympathetic look. "Though I don't believe there is any way to tell if that's the truth without us getting your memories back."

I nod; he's right. I can speculate about it all I want, but I won't get any answers unless I can figure out this whole mess. It would just be a waste of my time and energy to think too much about it right now. I take a deep breath, feeling so much more clear-headed and calm. I look at each of them, Emrys's honey golden gaze shining sweetly in the setting moon. Casmir's eyes look darker; like the forest right before dawn, when everything is still and peaceful.

"Thank you," I tell them.

I lean forward and lay my cheek against Emrys's shoulder, feeling soothed by his heartbeat. I reach my hand out to Casmir, and he locks our fingers together, resting them on his thigh. I feel safe and content, something I've never been able to experience before. I drift off to sleep with the hollow part of my chest humming softly.

Chapter 17

After everything that happened last night, I am itching to get out of this place and back on the move. Now that I've had time to think, I feel unsettled about what everyone saw. The others insisted on cleaning up the camp. So I'm sitting on a rock, watching them, and picking at the skin on my fingers. Something I'm doing a lot of lately.

Karis is putting away the bed rolls and keeps shooting me concerned glances. Taryn has asked me a dozen times now if I needed anything. And even Ansa sat with me for a few minutes, making cute baby animals out of her fire magic. I'm doing my best to be pleasant and give them all smiles; I'm just not feeling right, so it's difficult. They must notice, though, because none of them have come over to me for a while.

I look to where Casmir and Emrys are having a conversation, far enough away that nobody else can hear. I know they're talking about me. One of them looks my way every so often; I'm not surprised I'm the gossip of the morning. After what they saw me go through a few hours ago, I wouldn't even be shocked if they decided to throw me in a hospital *for my own good*. Do they even have hospitals here? I don't recall seeing one in Ceross. How does anyone get help if there aren't any doctors? Now that I think of it, Fen mentioned fae heal faster than mortals due to the magic in their blood, and also rarely get sick because of it.

It's not impossible to become ill, though. Casmir's mother can attest to that. I look closer at him, noticing a slight darkening under his eyes. His hair looks like he's run his hands through it too many times to count, and there's clear tension in his body. Emrys doesn't look much different physically, though if he's at all stressed about anything, he's not showing it. He looks as calm and collected as ever; bored, even.

Something is happening between the three of us, and I don't know what it is. I don't think they know, either. I believe they're feeling the same things I am, from what I've seen, and none of us seem to want to talk about it. And as much as I've been trying to fight my reactions, not wanting to trust anyone again, I can no longer deny the way I feel when I'm around them. It's otherworldly. I have a hunch that whatever is happening between us has to do with whoever rearranged my brain, just like everything else that's going on.

I stand to walk down the path a ways, not planning to get so far ahead of the group that they won't catch up. I just need to move. I have to stop thinking before I drown in another stream of tears. I need to wait until I'm alone before I allow myself to feel it all.

So instead, I put down one foot after the other and take slow, deep breaths to help me regulate. After a few minutes, I see a random spot of color come into view. I wander over to it and realize it's a flower; it's not one I've seen before, but it's quite pretty. It has layers like a rose, with the bottom layers going from a deep purple to a light purple, and the inner layers a deep blue to light.

I bend down to take a closer look at the flower, because there's no way I'm seeing what I am. The colors almost look like they're glowing, circulating inside of the petals. I rub my eyes and look again. There's no glowing or movement any longer. It was just me. Going even crazier than I thought.

After staring for a moment longer, I look around and realize it is the only flower here. Just one singular stem growing out of the side of the path. That is strange; I wonder where it gets its nutrients, or how it survives the chilly nights? It seems like a flower that would prefer heat, but I don't really know anything about botany, so I'm not in the position to make such claims.

I hear noise down the path and see the group headed my way, Casmir focused on me. I stand, wiping the dust off of my knees, and offer a reassuring smile; though I can feel it doesn't reach my eyes, so I'm not sure it was convincing. Casmir's brows crease for a moment before he smooths them out, stopping in front of me and waiting for everyone to pass before he speaks.

He reaches up to touch my cheek lightly, a flicker of rage passing through his expression before it's gone. "Your bruise is looking much better. It should be cleared within a couple of days."

I nod, having nothing to say to that. I can see the concern in his green and gold irises. I must look worse than I thought.

Saving me from the dreaded *are you okay?* question, he says softly, "Ready to go?" I nod again, not trusting myself to speak. He holds out his hand in question, and I take it, wanting to feel the comfort his touch offers. My smile is genuine this time as we move to walk off these nightmare-inducing mountains.

We make it down GodsPass and to the village on the Anlorian side of the mountains. Veardale. I'm surprised it's not much different from Amsal, but I don't know what I was expecting. I guess I just assumed the places on both sides of the Sunsor Mountains would live differently.

I'm feeling lighter after a day of walking in the sun; there wasn't much talking amongst the group, which was fine with me because it gave me hours to clear my head and body of the horrid feelings that were taking root. Emrys and Casmir stayed near me the entire time, not asking me to talk or give them anything. Just offering their presence. They seem to understand me better than I do at this point.

We're walking along the main street that runs through Veardale, and I'm admiring all the shops they have. One, in particular, catches my eye; it appears to be a store that sells jewelry, and though I'm not usually one to like wearing any, I can't help but to appreciate a necklace that's on show in the window. It's a simple necklace, with a silver chain and a piece of what looks to be raw obsidian hanging from it. It doesn't seem like anything special, but I feel a pull toward it, regardless.

Someone in the shop—I'm assuming the owner—looks out of the window and right at me. She offers no smile or wave. In fact, she looks quite puzzled and just stares at me while we walk past. I guess there's strange people inside the Veil, as well.

We make it to an inn to eat and stay for the night. We all have dinner, and are sitting around a large, rectangular table drinking wine—well, I'm drinking wine. I have no idea what that yellow stuff is in some of the others' glasses, because it doesn't smell like beer. I'm seated at the end of the table, Emrys to my right and Casmir in front of me. The barkeep wasn't particularly happy to see Xamira with our group, but he clearly didn't want to refuse the prince. So she's happily laying in the middle of the table, swishing her tail, and occasionally reaching out to swipe at Sam's hair. With how much he seems to dislike everything, I would have expected him to kick her off the table—which would have earned some words and fists from me. But he cracks a ghost of a smile each time she plays with him, and I'm convinced he keeps leaning forward purposefully, making the strands of his hair sway.

Who knew a cat was all it took to make the male happy?

"How much longer do we have before we reach the city?" I ask.

"Nearly three days. We should be there by the end of the week, assuming no trouble arises." I nod at Ansa, who turns back to her argument with Karis. They seem to bicker about the most simple things. Anyone who takes a quick look at them might think they hate each other, but I know better. I see the longing glances they give each other when they think no one is looking. The touches that last a second longer than necessary. I wonder what their story is. Have they dated? Or maybe just fucked, and one of them wants more while the other doesn't.

I'm grinning toward the two of them making a minor scene when Emrys nudges my shoulder with his. I look up at him, and send a questioning look toward the fighting pair at the other end of the table. He catches on and gives me a small nod in confirmation with an amused smile on his face; I laugh at how he seems to love the drama as much as I do. Guess that answers that.

He leans back and puts an arm around my chair, running his hand through the back of my hair. "So, love, what are your thoughts on the sleeping arrangements this evening?"

I raise an eyebrow, knowing where he's going with this, but decide to play dumb. "What do you mean?" One side of his mouth quirks up, and he gives Casmir a look I can't decipher before turning his attention back to me.

"Well, I thought after you slept so peacefully in my arms last night that you might prefer the company of one, *or both,* of us so that you may continue to sleep soundly."

I huff out a laugh and take a big sip of wine. "Oh, *that's* what you were thinking? That you just wanted to comfort me while I sleep?" I pin him with an 'I'm not stupid' look.

He pretends to look offended, one hand going to his chest in distress. "Of course that's all I was thinking! What else could we possibly do alone, in a bed, with fewer clothes on?"

I roll my eyes and turn to Casmir, who is biting his lip to hold back a laugh. Emrys grabs my hair and tugs me toward him, his mouth landing next to my ear.

"Unless you'd prefer to be comforted in," he pauses for dramatic effect, before continuing in a husky voice, "*other ways?*"

I'm still looking at Casmir, whose eyes watch as I lick my lips at Emrys's comment. He's still gripping my hair and holding me in place when he places a kiss just under my ear, my eyes threatening to roll into the back of my head. I feel a painful throbbing start at my core, and clear my throat to try to break myself out of the spell.

But Emrys has other plans, continuing to torture me being his first. "It would be our absolute pleasure to service you however you need, love." His nose runs a path up the column of my neck, and I know for a fact this chair will need to be cleaned up once I move. I'm trying so hard to hold it together, but can you blame a girl? I have these two *actual gods* staring at me like I'm their prey, and fuck if I don't want to lie down and take anything they have to give me. My pussy clenches at the thought.

Casmir, who has been observing my reaction with growing heat in his eyes, smirks at my clear inability to hide my desire. The hand holding my hair lets go and I practically shoot out of my seat, not daring to look down and see the mess I've created. The whole table goes silent and everyone turns in my haste, making me feel very exposed. I need to leave before I do something crazy, like jump the males right here in front of the entire bar. I mean, I've never minded a little voyeurism, but I can barely handle the hazel and honey eyes on me; I would probably die if everyone in the room watched me be absolutely destroyed by them.

"I'm going to bed," I announce, my voice squeaking. "Good night." I make my way to the stairs, walking as fast as I dare, trying not to worry the others.

I get up to the room that is to be mine for the night, and lean my head against the door, taking a few deep breaths to try to calm both my heartbeats. I should just say yes and let my body have what it wants.

But I still do not know what this thing between the three of us is. Every time I touch them, I feel it in my soul, so what would happen if they were inside me? I'd be burned alive, and not make it through the night. Or that thing in my chest would finally rip its way through, and I'd die from the gaping hole it made.

I open my eyes and see movement to my right, yelping when I realize there's someone standing right behind me. I turn to face Emrys, his body just a foot from mine.

"I'm sorry, did you think me telling everyone I'm going to bed was an invitation for you to join me?"

He closes the distance between us, grabbing my lower back with one hand, and pulling me against him. *Hard.* I let out a surprised breath at the movement, and his other hand leans up against the door, allowing him the illusion of towering over me.

"Love, I don't need you to tell me you want me in your bed," he says with a sinful smile. "I can *smell* how much you want that." My eyes widen in horror…of course they're able to scent my arousal. What's one more thing in my life to embarrass me?

"And *fuck*," he practically growls, shoving my pelvis into him harder, "if it isn't the most divine thing I've ever smelled." He lowers his face, his nose touching mine. "I'll bet you taste even better. What I wouldn't give to run my tongue up your cunt and drink up every bit of your come for myself."

My knees just about give out from his utterly depraved admission. I have no idea how to respond to that; I don't even know what I would want my answer to be. Of course I want to let him do exactly what he just confessed, but I also want to say no. The last time I gave into my cravings, I ended up with a bruised cheek and more trauma to add to the ever-growing pile I stupidly refuse to work through.

"I—I don't know if I can," I say so quietly I'm not sure if he heard me. He searches my eyes for a moment and comes to some kind of conclusion. He nods, his expression softening in understanding.

He moves a piece of hair behind my ear and kisses my forehead, stepping back a little to look at me more fully. "I was being serious earlier when I asked if you'd like someone to sleep next to you. It seemed to help you last night."

I don't believe I've ever rejected someone, and they didn't immediately try to take what they thought I owed them. But instead of getting upset or angry with me, Emrys just…accepted it? And instead of trying to make me explain, just moves on and asks if it would help to have him sleep with me? I'm baffled at his response and yet, to be honest, I didn't expect anything else. It might be brainless of me, but I'm beginning to really trust him.

I nod, smiling at him, and grab the hand he has resting on my cheek to pull him into the room with me. The room itself isn't large; it has a decently sized bed, a bedside table, and a window. Very simple, but it has everything we need.

I change out of the clothes I'm wearing to pull on clean sleeping clothes, not caring if Emrys is watching me change. I turn around when I'm done to find that he is, though I wasn't expecting him to have a questioning look on his face.

"What?" I look down at myself, thinking I put everything on backward. But it all looks fine to me.

He opens and closes his mouth a couple of times before speaking. "Your markings. I have seen nothing like them before."

My eyebrows raise, remembering that Andras was the one who saw a good portion of them, and they've been hidden under my clothing since.

"That's what he said, too. I found nothing about them in any of the books I read, either. If I could figure out what they mean, I could find where I'm from and what happened to me."

He pulls his shirt over his head, leaving him in just a pair of sweatpants, and I feel no shame when I stand and ogle him. He is a well-defined, hard muscled, exquisite specimen. I can tell he works his body hard. I nonchalantly swipe my hand over my mouth to make sure I'm not drooling and Emrys catches the movement, smirking at my obvious gawking.

Instead of boosting his ego any further, I turn and make my way over to the bed, settling under the covers, and he follows. We lie facing each other, the only light coming from the window, just barely illuminating the features of his face.

"Thank you," I whisper into the silence.

He reaches out, sliding his arm under my neck and pulling me to his chest. I rest my hand over his heart, feeling comfort in the beat that matches the drumming under my skin. We hold each other for a while, not needing to say anything to just enjoy the other's companionship.

As I float away from consciousness, I hear him say, "Don't thank me. You deserve better than that."

I feel movement at my front and peer through sleepy eyes to find Casmir lowering himself into the bed. Emrys is now behind me, his hand draped across my waist. The bed is large enough for the three of us, but I pull at Casmir's side anyway, wanting him closer. He sits up slightly to place kisses on the corners of my mouth before pressing a light one on top of my lips.

"Sleep, Nell," he says into my hair and I feel myself smile, pulling him even closer before falling into a dreamless state once again.

*

I wake to fingertips trailing up and down my back. Not wanting to open my eyes just yet, I try to take in my surroundings. I'm half on top of one of the males; I smell a hint of jasmine and know that this must be Casmir. My face is smushed against his bare chest, one of my legs draped over his hips, and my arm is tucked around his waist, holding him tightly.

Emrys is on my other side, parts of his body touching mine; I feel him moving and guess he's the one rubbing me. I hear the prince's breath hitch and know the moment he realizes how we're tangled, because he tenses a bit before relaxing again, and uses his free hand to play with strands of my hair.

The two of them talk quietly about the plans for the day, and the remaining part of the trip. Both continuing to touch me and I keep my breathing even to not ruin this blissful moment before we need to leave. I may not be ready to fully admit all of my complicated feelings for them, but I will selfishly take the solace they're giving me.

"Do you think her nightmare has anything to do with her memories?" Emrys whispers, stroking the markings he can see from where my shirt rode up a bit.

"I think the timing of the dream was too perfect to be coincidence," he sighs deeply, "and that worries me. What if her life before was worse than the memories she has now? The fact that she has a memory of someone strangling her?" It seems like he's about to say more, but stops himself.

"What is it?"

I feel Casmir's head shift toward Emrys. "What if her memories were taken for a reason? Something that she chose?"

His second takes a minute to think before responding. "If that is what happened, then we will help her through whatever waits on the other side. I trust that she's trying to do the best for herself and Xamira. I will support her either way."

"So will I," the prince says, his tone harder.

They're silent for a while, both in their heads just as much as I am. I am about to get up when Emrys speaks so softly I have to strain to make out the words.

"You feel it too, don't you?" He sounds almost desperate. "In here?"

Casmir moves his hand from my hair to the place on his chest that sits just in front of my face and breathes deeply. "Yes."

"I've never felt anything like this before." Emrys sits up, making the bed droop before straightening out. "What is it? It has to mean something, but I can't think of a reason that would make sense."

"I've been wondering if it also has to do with who she is and the memories she lost. She clearly wasn't raised in Anloria or Ceross. Her markings are different from what we have. But where she comes from, I'm not able to place." He strokes my hair again. "I was not aware of any other fae territories, so it may be beneficial to try to find any that we can."

Could there really be other fae cities out there? I thought there were only the two in the Veil, but I don't even know how big the Veil is. There could be numerous places that have not been found yet. For the first time in a while, I feel a twinge of hope in my chest.

This means that if I cannot find any answers in the history books, I could search the lands for my home. Home. If that even exists within my memories. What if Casmir is right, and I asked for this to be done to me? Maybe I didn't want to remember my old life, and that scares me because if I thought that what I have now is better than what's hidden in my head, then how fucking bad would it have been for me to decide that?

They sink into their thoughts once more and I decide it's time for me to wake, ready to get through the rest of this journey.

Chapter 18

I'm sitting in front of Emrys while he holds me tightly against him. My legs no longer work after nearly three days of riding, but being constantly pressed between either him or Casmir is not something I will complain about. I feel safe with them. This time spent traveling to Anloria has fragmented my defenses, allowing me to become more comfortable with the both of them. I'm still wary of trusting them, and I feel like I'm giving off mixed signals, but my head is just confused over all of it.

I've known them for only a couple of weeks and yet feel so strongly. I don't want to give my trust out so easily, but I just know that they will not hurt me or betray my confidence. I can't explain how I'm so certain of their intentions, the knowledge is an intrinsic part of me.

Aside from the instinctual feelings in the hollow pit in my chest pulling me toward them, I am also starting to have a strong fondness for their touch, among other physical feelings. My body knows they're attractive, and is begging me each day to give into those basic desires; normally, I would have no reservations about fucking someone I'm interested in, but this is different. *They* are different, and I'm scared to find out what will happen if I get any closer to them.

Just being near them has every cell in my body screaming, and I know that's not a normal reaction because of how they are also questioning it. Kissing Casmir is still driving me mad several days later.

It felt so powerful and *right*. Kissing him felt like home. I don't know what that means, but seeing as we have no information on what would happen if we became more intimate, it makes me nervous to even think about giving into the impulses. The tugging in my chest is screaming that it's the right thing to do, to be with them, but what if that's just some kind of trick? What if the god who took my memories also did something else that causes me to feel pulled toward them, and our joining would actually harm all of us? That sounds ridiculous, like some villain causing chaos in a silly fairy tale. But after all the things I've experienced these last few months? I'm not going to rule anything out. It would break me if I accidentally hurt them. So, I'm stuck on the brink of needing them and also needing to be away from them.

I adjust myself on the horse, trying to get some blood flow to my legs, to no avail. I am way too excited to reach the city. To sleep in an actual bed, where the icy wind doesn't freeze my nose off; and to use a bathroom that has a toilet *and* a shower? I shiver at the thought of hot water.

When I thought about making the journey from Ceross to Anloria, I guess I didn't expect the lack of basic things that I'm so used to having. When you travel outside of the Veil, there are cars and planes to get you places, and in between stops you can get a hotel or go to a restaurant. You pretty much always have access to a roof over your head, a bathroom, and a hot meal…assuming you can pay for it.

Here, it is the complete opposite. I feel *so gross*. Having to relieve myself in the forest and not being able to wash my body when I'm covered in dirt and sweat? It's dreadful. And the best part of all is the fact that we carry just bread, with dried fruit and meat, as our meals. I mean, I can't say I ate a lot better when I was living in Chago. Most of the time, not eating at all. But after fueling my body properly for weeks, I am starting to feel just as weak and tired as I was when it was only Xamira and me in our apartment.

I look over at Xamira—her big, golden eyes shine brightly in the sun—and chuckle at the way she's wrapped around Casmir's neck. Her head is laying against his shoulder and her body is so long that her tail is resting on his chest, occasionally tapping him on the chin. She looks comfortable with her lounging arrangement, but I can tell the prince is tense; he's trying hard to not move too much, which would cause her to fall off him or get upset with him for disturbing her.

He sees me watching them, frowning at my amusement. He opens his mouth to say something and Xamira chooses that moment to whip her tail up, causing him to get a mouth full of fur. I explode with laughter when his eyes widen in horror, causing the rest of the group to look at the scene and finding his predicament to be funny, as well. Karis is full on cackling, the others in various states of laughter; I think I even saw Sam chuckle a bit before returning to his natural scowling state.

Casmir takes being the comedic relief in stride, giving Xamira a scratch on the head, and she responds by stretching even further around him, her front paws now extended and hovering in the air.

"We will reach Anloria by sunset," the prince announces.

"Thank the gods, *finally*," I groan, tilting my head back with a big sigh. Emrys squeezes me tighter, and I relax into his hold, resting my head on his shoulder.

The others begin to talk about what they plan to do when we reach the city, as Casmir has given them the next few days off from their duties. Taryn is excited to go visit her parents and little brother, whom she brings a gift for whenever she travels. This time, she found an interesting toy made from wood. It's in the shape of the letter y and has some kind of rubber band material attached to each branch, allowing the user to pull it back and shoot something from the toy at a target. It reminds me a lot of a bow and arrow, just for children.

The twins are also going to visit their parents, whom they don't see as often as they should. Ansa doesn't announce what she will be doing, though the looks she's sneaking Karis make it clear she does have plans.

Casmir is talking with the group, and the way he is so casual with all of them has shocked me since we first left Ceross. Andras was never like this with any of his staff. He only spoke to them when he had something to say related to his or their jobs. There were never any informal conversations, or laughs, shared with them; but they also didn't seem interested in being near him unless they had to. I don't know why I never noticed it before—I wonder if he treats them as poorly as he did me behind closed doors, and really hope that's not the case. Fen is such a sweet fae and wouldn't deserve any mistreatment. But you would think someone would have said *something* if that were the case.

I look over my shoulder at Emrys, who seems to be lost in a disturbing thought, so I try to distract him from whatever is giving him that vacant look. "What's Anloria like? I mean, compared to Ceross, I guess?"

His eyes shift over to me, coming back to life, and he gives me a smile in silent thanks before answering. "I would say it is better than that bastard's city." I huff out a breath. I want to get a genuine answer from him just once, instead of these surface level jokes he makes to hide his feelings.

"Why do you hate Andras so much?"

I feel him stiffen, his hand tightening on my thigh. "He hit you, Nell. That is disgraceful and cowardly. He should be thanking you for allowing him to live, because I would love nothing more than to rip his fucking head right off his body." I touch my cheek, no longer feeling the sting. According to the others, my bruise is almost fully gone, just a small yellowing left that you can't see unless you know it's there.

"While I appreciate the defense, I don't think that's quite true. I remember you and Cas clearly not liking him before *that* happened," I press.

He sighs, his eyes hardening and looking away from me. I turn forward, feeling like the conversation is done, and watch the dense forest go by. After several minutes of his silence, he opens his mouth to answer.

"We heard," he pauses, "rumors about him years ago. We haven't been able to prove anything, but I know they're true."

"What were the rumors?"

Another long few minutes of silence. "It was said that he was imprisoning fae. Torturing and raping them for his own sick pleasure. You don't need the details." His voice sounds rough and strained. I look over to him, taking his hand in mine as he appears to find this topic difficult.

"I spent months there and would never have thought that to be true." He opens his mouth to protest my ignorance, but I keep speaking before he can. "*But* I believe you. Especially after what he did to me. Just because I saw nothing doesn't mean it's not true, or maybe was true in the past but not now."

He sighs in relief at my reassurance, and I fold my fingers through his, attempting to give him a little of the comfort he's provided me recently.

He says nothing more; instead wrapping his arms fully around my torso, meshing our bodies together, and I have a feeling of rightness in my chest. That empty place starting to crack, telling me this is where I need to be.

The sun is getting further away in the sky while a curve in the mountains gets closer. I haven't seen a map of the Veil, so I wasn't prepared for Anloria to be right up against the towering rock. I understand the placement of the city, though. The only way to get there is through GodsPass, which is days away from the population. If someone wanted to go around the mountains, they would need to leave the Veil and enter on the other side of them, which would still leave them days from Anloria. It's the perfect place to have a city; not only is the location beautiful, but it allows the guards to see anyone coming toward the perimeter.

We crest a large hill, and I see my first glimpse of Anloria in the distance. There is a tall, stone wall surrounding what I think is the entire city, though it stretches too far for me to see for sure. The buildings look like they are built upon smaller hills, giving the impression that some are larger than others.

I am in absolute awe at the size of this place. I thought Ceross was quite substantial, with streets upon streets of houses and shops, but Anloria is at least triple that. It reminds me a lot of Chago. Not just in the magnitude of the city, but there is a river that seems to run through part of it, being filled by a waterfall on the side of the mountain.

I crane my neck, trying to get a glimpse of the castle to gauge how long it takes to walk through the city streets, but I cannot find it. We make it to the gates, the wall patrol immediately recognizing Casmir and his party, opening the doors for us to enter.

I wish I could take a photo of this view. The gates open to a large, paved street that extends for what looks like miles, but I doubt is that long. Stone buildings surround us, lining the path that seems to lead to the waterfall in the mountain. The sun is setting behind the one peak, leaving the sky a stunning orange-ish, pink color. The scene in front of me looks very much like a painting. I glance over at one of the buildings and find Casmir watching me instead of the path in front of him. The green in his eyes—being highlighted by the colors of the sky—is mesmerizing. This is his home, and it's clear he takes pride in his city and people.

We stay on our horses, heading down the long road ahead of us. There aren't many fae outside, but the few who see us recognize their prince, bowing and welcoming him back. He gives each of them a genuine smile, greeting them with a bow of his head. As we walk, Emrys whispers in my ear different places that we pass by. One that caught my attention being a crystal shop, which looked dark and gloomy. But that is completely my vibe, and I make a mental note to visit there soon.

We pass by what Emrys calls the *city square*, which is literally a square piece of open area in between buildings. There are benches to sit around the grassy patch, and a large courtyard that is used for different events Anloria has throughout the year. He mentioned a festival they have happening soon, and I feel excited at the thought of just doing something fun.

After an hour, I look toward the end of the road we are on and squint my eyes, not sure of what I'm seeing. It looks like there are spots of light coming out of the mountain? I peek at Casmir. It's just the three of us and Xamira now; the rest of the group waved their goodbyes and went to visit with their families.

"What are those lights up there?" I point to the anomaly in the distance.

He gives me a warm smile, looking to Emrys for a moment before answering, "That's our home, Nell."

My brows furrow and I look back over to the mountain, trying hard to concentrate on finding the castle. As we get closer, I think I can make out the general shape of it, though I'm not positive. I'll have to look when the sun is in the sky because it is impossible to see at the moment; I would have no idea it was there if not for the lights.

"I feel like you're playing a joke on me," I smirk at Casmir playfully. "I see nothing but those spots. There's no way you have a castle hiding right there."

"I guess we'll see in a few minutes," he grins and rides ahead.

Emrys takes our moment alone to grab my waist with both hands, using his thumbs to massage my back. I arch at the movement and groan, my head falling back.

"*Gods* that feels so nice," I murmur. He moves his hands down, massaging the crease of my hips, and leans forward to press his lips onto my neck.

"I could make it feel better," his breath warming my skin. "So much better, in fact, that it wouldn't be the gods names you moan." A shiver runs up my spine, and I turn my head to look at him, the heat in his gaze now matching my own.

"You have a filthy mouth," I say, my voice breathy. I glance down at his lips, having the urge to bite them.

He grins nefariously and places a light kiss to the corner of my lips, trailing them upward until he reaches my ear. "You're right, love. I could really use a drink to wash that filth down with." He flattens his palm on my abdomen and slides it down a direct path straight to my core, stopping close enough to get his point across.

I look into his eyes, feeling heat travel down my back, and want to give in and take everything he's promising me in his gaze. But I can't, no matter how badly my body is begging me to. Instead, I decide to return the favor and make him as worked up as I am. I close the distance between us, trailing kisses over his jaw and to his lips. I reach my hand back to grab his hair and hold him while I open his mouth with my tongue and devour him in a fervent kiss.

This idea backfired because I feel like I'm walking through the sky. My vision escapes me, and all I'm aware of is the feeling of him touching me. Lightning shoots through my whole body, pushing against the confines of my chest, trying to break free and claim Emrys as its own. The heat, and pressure, and utter euphoria take over my body. I nearly lose myself before I remember this is the same feeling I had when I kissed Casmir. This feeling has to do with whatever force is pulling the three of us together, and I need to pull away so I don't hurt him.

I break the kiss, both of us breathing hard. His hand is holding the back of my neck, which is now coated in a sheen of sweat. His pupils are wide, giving him a thin, shining gold ring around the center. My breaths match the pace of his, and we both take a moment to calm ourselves before I turn around without saying anything.

I look at our surroundings and see that he, thankfully, stopped us under a patch of trees, concealing our form in the shadows from any watching eyes. Our horse starts to walk again, coming through the trees to the front of an open gate, and the sight behind it has me questioning my reality.

"What the fuck? Did we go through some kind of Veil within the Veil, because where did *that* come from?"

Emrys belts out a laugh, his chest rocking against me in the process and reminding me of our proximity. "That, love, has been here the whole time. Cas wasn't lying to you."

I take in the incredible sight before me. The castle is huge, or maybe it isn't? It's hard to tell because I'm pretty sure it's just an extended piece of the mountain. The walls are made from the same rock as the large peaks behind it, rising in various areas to give it a mysterious, dark feel. Directly next to the castle is the waterfall. It isn't as loud as I would have thought, but it's quite pretty; lightly sparkling where certain areas are illuminated by the city lights in the distance. I can't imagine there's ever any open window on that side of the castle because it would surely flood the place from being so close.

I take in a deep breath, crisp petrichor invading my senses, as well as the hint of moss and herbs. I see Casmir standing at the top of the steps in front of the castle entrance. He's speaking with a female and a rush of adrenaline coats my veins. I startle, not knowing where that came from, and instead focus on dismounting the horse and not face planting into the ground because my legs no longer work.

Emrys reads my thoughts, catching me around the waist as I drop and holding me up into him. My hands land on his muscled chest, his leather scent intoxicating me.

"Thank you," I say too quietly, and push myself away from him before I make a scene in front of all the castle staff I haven't met. It takes a moment to get my legs working properly, awkwardly waddling until my muscles loosen enough to move normally. I slowly make my way up the steps to Casmir, and he pauses his conversation with the female to look over at me, laughing loudly at my struggle.

I get to the top and smack him on the arm, causing him to laugh harder. "You asshole! So sorry I don't have legs like yours that somehow work normally after days on a horse." I roll my eyes, crossing my arms to glare at him. The female next to us has her hand covering her mouth while she tries to hide her giggles.

"I'm sorry, princess," he says in a playfully mocking tone, stepping forward to grab my arms. "I know just how to make it up to you. You see, like Em, I am wonderful at helping with leg workouts."

I drop my jaw at his blunt insinuation that I know our company caught on to, but he continues before I can smack him again, "I am nothing if not generous, though." His lids drop as he grabs a piece of my hair, twirling it in his fingers. "Since you are so sore, I would be happy to have you lie on your back while I do all the work." I huff out an exasperated breath, looking to the female, who is finding this conversation highly amusing, and then back to the prince.

"Casmir Vaintera, I can—" He raises an eyebrow. "I will—gods, fuck you," I smack his arm again and walk toward the open castle doors, my cheeks heated from what those two are doing to me.

I step through the doors, not sure where I was intending to go, but stop short when I see inside. It feels like walking into the mountain itself; the walls being made of the same dark rock as the outside while the floors are a light wood color. There's frosted lighting hanging from different points of the tall ceiling, with lamps on the floor. There is one staircase leading up to the next floor and paintings hanging around the room that are stunning.

I walk up to one, struck by its beauty; it looks like a forest just after it rained. The surroundings are dark, but small bits of light shoot in from in between the leaves. The surfaces are dewy, and there's a light mist hovering above the ground, giving the impression that it's morning time. It looks so real, like an actual photo instead of a painting.

A presence steps up beside me, and I feel in my chest that it's Casmir. "My mother painted this," he says somberly. I look over at him. His hands are in his pockets and he's studying the painting as if it's also his first time seeing it.

"It's beautiful," he meets my gaze, looking over my face for something.

"She can't paint anymore; her illness makes her hands shake," he looks back to the painting. "It makes her sad when she's not able to get her subject just right." He sighs, and I reach over to link my arm through his and rest my head on his shoulder.

"But the worst part is that she's also sad when she doesn't paint. So it's a nasty cycle of her hurting when she paints and hurting when she doesn't." He lays his head on mine, and we stand in silence for a while, admiring his mother's art. There is nothing I can say to make his pain better, and apologizing won't help anyone but myself, so I say nothing. Instead, I just choose to be here for him.

After several minutes, he kisses the top of my head and whispers, "Thank you," before turning us to face Emrys and the mystery female, who are waiting just outside, giving us privacy.

"Leia," he calls, and she walks over with a polite smile on her face. "I would like you to meet Nell." *Please* don't let this be his girlfriend…I cannot deal with another sleazy male right now.

She bows her head, "It is an honor, My Lady. My name is Leia and I am the head manager of the castle. Please come to me for anything you should need." I hope the relief doesn't show in my face at her introduction.

I look to Casmir, feeling weird about the title. But I don't want to be rude, so I smile and reach out my hand. "It's nice to meet you, too." She gives me a very confused look, and I realize I'm an idiot and shoot my hand back to my chest. "I'm sorry," I wince, "outside of the Veil we shake hands when we meet someone new, and I completely forgot that's not a normal thing here."

Her eyebrows raise in surprise, but she gives me a friendly smile. "That's all right. My apologies for not recognizing the gesture. Prince Casmir mentioned you used to live with the mortals." *Used to.* That catches me off guard, and I lose my train of thought, thinking about everything that's happened since I was last there.

Casmir notices the shift in my demeanor and saves me from replying. "Please see that the horses are taken to the stables and food is prepared for Xamira. We will take dinner in my room in an hour."

Leia bows and walks off to take care of everything he mentioned. Still holding onto my arm, he leads me up the stairs and we make our way to the left, walking down a long hallway. Most of the doors are closed, and there are paintings along these walls, too. I want to ask if his mother did all of this, but that doesn't feel appropriate at the moment.

We pass a break in the rooms, coming to a large seating area with a window that overlooks the city, and a glossy, black piano sitting off to the side. I've wanted to learn how to play since I discovered the music from the instrument to be comforting, helping me through some very dark times in my life.

Several fae walk past us, each bowing their head to the prince with smiles on their faces, and he does the same to them. They seem to like him, though I just got here so I can't go around making such an assumption. I remember what happened the last time I did that.

Casmir stops me in front of a large, wooden door, gesturing to it. "This will be your room. Mine is across the hall, and that is Em's." He points to the door next to his. *Wonderful.* Just what I was hoping for, in fact; being in such proximity to them at all times. Though I am relieved, knowing that I will feel safer having them near me.

"Why don't you go take that shower you've been talking about for days," he smirks and then gets a pained look on his face. "I will bring you some of my clothes for now. We don't have any ready for you, since we weren't planning on meeting you and bringing you home when we left for Ceross. But I will make sure we get some tomorrow."

"It's really not a big deal, but thank you." I squeeze his arm once more and make my way into the room, closing the door behind me.

The room is beautiful; it has a large bed with dark bedding. The walls are the same rock that seems to make up the entire structure of the castle, but instead of light flooring in here, it's more of a dark wood. Walking into the bathroom, I find a lighter tile surrounding the vanity, and a large bathtub and shower. The shower looks quite interesting, with three of the walls being the mountain rock, and a glass door to close the space in. I look in a closet to find towels, setting one on the bench next to the shower.

I step into the hot water, and the feeling is orgasmic. I could stand in here for the rest of my days. I use the soaps on the shelves to wash my hair and body, taking more time than I need to scrub my skin extra, feeling gross from the days of travel. Once I feel like myself again, I reluctantly leave the shower and dry myself off. I see in the bedroom that Casmir hasn't brought any clothes yet, so I decide to look around while I wait.

I stride over to the sliding door on the opposite side of the bed and bathroom, wondering if this room is placed where I think it is, and step out onto the balcony to see the waterfall directly in front of me. I feel my eyes bulge at the incredible sight and try to take in the beauty of it. I was both wrong and right; the water isn't coming into the castle at all, but I do feel a very light mist every so often when the wind shifts a bit.

I'm leaning over the railing, trying to see as much as I can about the waterfall, when two powerful hands grab my arms and yank me back, my towel dropping from not being held up any longer. I squeal from fear, and spin around to see Casmir standing there with a horrified look on his face. I look down and see clothes thrown on the floor; he must have thought I was going to jump or fall.

I face him again and he's making a point of looking anywhere but me, which has me realizing I'm fully naked in front of him. I have no problems being nude in front of others, so I don't move to grab my towel.

Instead I put my hands on my hips and give him my best glare. "And what was that for? I was just admiring the waterfall."

He looks at me for a second before averting his eyes again, opening and closing his mouth like he's trying to say something but can't, and I burst out laughing.

"Are you serious right now? You and Emrys have been in my ear for *weeks* describing all the dirty things you'd like to do to me, and yet the sight of my body makes you uncomfortable? Was all of that just a joke?"

His eyes widen and he puts his hands up to explain, but looks down and realizes that they're hovering over my breasts; he quickly lowers them at his side again. I raise an eyebrow, finding his shyness amusing.

"Nell," his voice is strained. "I'm not uncomfortable because of your body. You are unbelievably beautiful. I'm uncomfortable because seeing you naked in front of me has my cock unbearably hard, and I am using every bit of restraint I have to not take you right here while you continue to *admire the waterfall.*"

I need to press my thighs together at his words. "Oh," is all I can manage.

"Yes, *oh.*" He looks down, taking in the sight of me. His pupils dilate, nostrils flaring, and he leans his head back, groaning. "So if you wouldn't mind getting dressed. Unless," he says suggestively, "you'd rather have me on my knees, admiring *you.* With my tongue."

I close the little distance between us, pressing my breasts and abdomen against him, slowly trailing my hands up his chest until I reach his neck, and grasp his jaw with my palms.

"On your knees is *exactly* where I want you," I taunt, pressing a kiss to his mouth, "but I'm hungry." I shrug and let him go, sauntering over to the clothes on the floor. I make a show of bending to pick them up, knowing he's watching me, and walk further into the bedroom to put them on without looking back.

Chapter 19

I'm sitting in Casmir's room with him, Emrys, and Xamira, all of us curled up by the fireplace after eating the first warm meal we've had in days. It feels so good to be clean and full; something I would have never known if I was still living in Chago.

I'm laying on a rug, basking in the fire's warmth, while Xamira runs around me pretending to get scared and attack me when I randomly tickle her. I go into a fit of giggles when she pounces on my abdomen and then stretches out fully, laying down on my chest. I smush her cheeks and give her a bunch of small kisses before petting her down her back.

"You are so funny." I scrunch my nose and tap it on hers. I remember we have an audience, and look over to find Casmir and Emrys both relaxing on the plush couch, a deep tan color, watching me with warm smiles on their faces. I quickly avert my gaze, not ready to face the heavy emotions soaring around all of us, and focus on petting Xamira.

After our situation on my balcony, the prince has been giving me many longing looks when he thinks I'm not paying attention. I can see the feelings written all over him, and I don't know what to do about it. He clearly is developing affections for me that aren't purely physical, and as much as I want to acknowledge that I may be, as well...I'm conflicted. I need to focus on figuring out what happened to me, which might lead me away from here. Away from them. Even if I allow myself to give in to things that feel so right, what happens when I leave? I just break all our hearts, and become a monster in their minds?

I believe Emrys is feeling the same, though it's much harder to tell with him. Where Casmir seems to wear his heart out in the open, Emrys keeps his in a steel safe, locked with a key he doesn't even have. I wonder what could have made him this way? Andras told me that he was basically adopted into Casmir's family, but I know nothing else outside of that. The way that he's reacted to my abuse, and the way he immediately understood and backed off when I rejected him back in the village…it all makes me think he has demons of his own.

These two very different males both look at me with such adoration. And I'm not so ignorant as to just convince myself I don't know how they're feeling. I just don't want to fully acknowledge it yet. Maybe that's selfish. Maybe that means I'm leading them on a little when I return some of those affections, not realizing most of the time that I'm returning them. Their presence puts me under some kind of spell. I wish I knew how to move forward with all of this, because being with them almost feels irrevocable, but is it the right thing to do?

Xamira looks deeply into my eyes and…nods her head? Playing along, I scratch her chin and ask, "Were you answering my question, silly girl?"

She nods again, and my eyes widen at the movement. There's no way she just answered what I was thinking. I've always thought she was smart for a cat, and can possibly even understand what I'm saying sometimes; but this is weird, even for her.

I look to the males on the couch who are both giving me confused stares—I'm going just a little crazy. Xamira uses her paw to pull at my chin, facing me toward her again and meows. I sit up and place her in front of me; she sits down and looks up at me expectantly. Waiting.

"Do you actually understand me?" I whisper, feeling eyes searing holes into the side of my head. She nods. Not just a dip of her chin that could be some kind of coincidence; she instead lifts her head up and down a few times, and then waits for me again.

"Have you always understood what I'm saying? Did you respond to my thoughts just now?" Okay, now I'm talking to my cat like she's going to start speaking and talk back. Definitely crazy, but I'm too stunned to care. Xamira nods, pauses, and then nods again. I think she just answered both of my questions in her own way.

"What the fuck," I mumble to myself. I think back to before we arrived in the Veil, remembering the day that she told me we should cross the bridge. I thought she was just being funny and wanting to go for a walk, but she definitely knew the Veil was here. I had asked her if we'd been here before and could have sworn she said yes; but with everything that happened, I completely forgot that I thought she was talking back to me.

Oh my gods. She was responding to me just like she is now.

"Xamira," my voice more desperate. "You said that you and I have been here, in the Veil, before. Is that true?"

She dips her chin.

"Does that mean you know what happened before we left the Veil?" Another nod.

"Do you know who I am?"

A slow, deliberate nod.

I sit back and cover my mouth with my hand. I stare into Xamira's eyes, trying to find something that tells me I'm making this up, but she's watching me like she is conscious of everything.

"Do you see this?" I ask Casmir and Emrys. "Please tell me you see this, and I'm not going crazy and creating things in my head." They both have a mixture of shock and confusion on their faces, Emrys sitting forward and studying Xamira.

"I'm definitely seeing the same thing as you," Casmir whispers.

I face those beautiful golden eyes again. "Are you able to talk to me in another way? Could you tell me what you know?" She nods her head again.

"Okay, uh, this is strange." I suddenly feel very self-conscious about everything I've done in front of her, thinking she didn't understand. "So why don't you do that? Whatever *that* is." I wave my hand in her direction, and she shakes her head this time.

"No?" I question. "Do you mean you can't?" A nod.

Holy shit. Casmir is now crouching next to me while Emrys is still watching Xamira carefully. "Why can't you, Xamira?" I say more to myself, but she shakes her head, regardless.

Unless…

"Is it because of me? Because of my head?" She nods.

"*Oh my gods.* So whoever fucked with my head did something to not only block my memories, but block you from communicating with me as well?" She nods fervently.

My head is spinning. I'm going to vomit. I stand up and run to Casmir's bathroom, making it just in time to throw my dinner up in his toilet. I feel someone grab my hair to hold it out of my face, while a hand gently rubs my back. After I feel like my organs are the only thing left to throw up, I rise to clean my mouth and bend over the vanity to close my eyes for a few minutes.

This is way too much to process. I have so many questions, and she can't answer them. Not really. I could try asking her a million things and hope I can figure out the answers with her head movements, but I have a feeling that what's happening is too complicated for that to work.

I don't understand how this is possible. But a couple months ago, I didn't understand how the Veil was here, or how my appearance changed and I have these strange markings. Nothing has made sense for a while, so this shouldn't be surprising. But that's not what's making me feel sick. It's the fact that she has been with me for *how long?* And was just stuck in her head, not being able to communicate with me, when she obviously was able to before? I thought I was lonely. I can't imagine how she's been feeling all these years.

And when she tried to communicate, I just laughed her off as a smart cat…never really taking her seriously. *Oh gods,* I'm such a terrible person. She must hate me for treating her like that.

I feel myself panic, my breaths coming quickly and my heart beating out of my chest. My palms are sticking to my head, and the edges of my thoughts feel fuzzy and chaotic. My chest is tight and if it gets any tighter, I won't be able to breathe. I begin sobbing into my palms, frustrated from this wave of emotions coming through me.

I feel arms pull me up and squeeze me to their chest. Emrys. The pressure of his hold oddly helps some of the mayhem inside of me, and I can breathe a little better.

"Deep breaths, love. We need to calm your heart and breathing down," he says softly, still squeezing me tight. "In slowly through your nose and out slowly through your mouth." He grabs my hand and lays it flat on his chest over his heart. "Do as I do, love."

He breathes in and I follow, taking in a large sum of air through my nose and then releasing it through my mouth when he does. We do this for several minutes before my heartbeat matches his, and I feel like I can exist again. I lie against him for a while longer, feeling comforted by the thumping under my hand; he continues to hold me just as tightly, putting relieving pressure around my torso.

I've had panic attacks before. I normally just curl myself into a ball and keep telling myself it's not real until it's over an hour or two later. I never thought that the tight squeeze Emrys is giving me would be helpful, considering it feels like my nerves are flying out of my body in all directions. But it is helping. A lot. That, and the steady rhythm of his heart, giving me something to focus on.

I eventually peel myself away from him, feeling exhausted throughout my whole body. "Thank you," I mumble, looking into his crystallized, honey eyes. He nods, not needing to say anything, and leads me out of the bathroom toward where Casmir is lying with Xamira in his bed. He sits up at the sight of me, seeming very worried but unsure of what to do. I walk over, not missing the sadness emanating from him, and wrap my arms around his neck, letting him know that he's done enough.

I've never had to worry about hurting others with my emotions before. I learned a long time ago that I needed to keep them deep within the confines of the mental cage I created and not allow anyone else to see them. Because they would use them against me. But I feel safe with Cas and Em. I feel understood. Loved. It's so new to me…being cared for and comforted by someone else.

I'm scared that I'm going to get too comfortable and allow myself to process all of my baggage. And in doing so, they realize I'm too fucked up to care for, and throw me to the trenches like everyone else in my life. The soft light of my soul tells me otherwise, but my insecurities won't let me escape that worry.

Emrys turns out the lights while the prince guides me into the middle of his bed. I'm too tired to protest. But I don't want to anyway, desiring their warmth and intoxicating scents around me right now. I lie on my back and Xamira prances over to curl up on top of me. I reach my hands out to either side of me, needing the connection between all of us, and hold on to the two males who are slowly working their way into my bones.

I open my eyes to a bright light filtering in through the glass door. Emrys and Casmir are not with me, and I feel a stab of disappointment before reminding myself that I shouldn't expect—or want—them to always be here for me. They've done too much for me already.

I grudgingly get out of the prince's bed, which is made of clouds, and head to the bathroom. After cleaning myself up and fixing my hair, I take a moment to look at myself in the mirror. I look tired. My eyes are still puffy from crying last night. My skin looks like it could use a bit more color, and even my hair seems a bit more dull than usual.

I turn away, not in the mindset to deal with this today, and decide to walk around the castle, needing something to occupy my thoughts. I consider changing, but remember I do not have any clean clothes with me. I shrug to myself and decide Casmir's dark sweats and shirt will have to do, even though they're both nearly falling off of me since I do not possess the sculpted, hard, and bewitching muscles he does.

I *burn* to lick my way up each one, wanting to memorize all the lines of his body and savor the sweet, masculine taste. Then I'll run my hands through each curl on Emrys's head, kissing my way down his toned body and letting him use my mouth for all the depraved things he purrs in my ear. *Gods,* I bet the sounds he makes are the finest ones I'll ever hear. I roll my eyes at my horny thoughts, stepping into the hallway outside of our rooms. But seriously, who gave them the right to be *that* good looking?

Walking down the hallway, I hear the soft notes of a piano. As I make my way closer, the music grows, sounding like a sad lullaby. My chest aches at the emotion fluttering through the space, and I have the urge to see who could be playing such a painful melody.

I peek around the corner, looking into the large sitting room, trying not to disturb the pianist. There's a sharp tug from the hollow pit inside of me when I see it's Casmir sitting at the bench. There's no one else in the area. Just him with his eyes closed, looking tormented by whatever is going through him right now.

I lean my shoulder and head against the wall, wrapping my arms around my torso and allow myself to experience what the prince is saying without words. The view of Anloria is quite the perfect backdrop for him. He looks vulnerable, but regal, and I get the sense that this is a part of himself he doesn't show others; always trying to be the strong, confident prince he thinks he needs to be.

I look from the city to find Casmir smiling at me, darkness prevalent in his hazel eyes. He tilts his head, inviting me to sit next to him. I feel my cheeks heat and walk over to join him on the bench. The smell of jasmine fills me up, drowning out all other thoughts and worries I had a few minutes ago.

His song slows—it feels like whoever wrote it found what they were looking for in the end. The light, happy notes filling the space before the prince ceases playing and the room goes quiet.

"That was beautiful," I murmur, turning to him and getting caught in his green and gold gaze. I want to hold him. I want to wrap myself around him and never let go, molding the colors of our souls together until they create a devastating piece of art. I want it so badly I'm struggling to breathe.

But I somehow find the will to pull my eyes away, breaking our cosmic connection. "I didn't know you could play," I say more quietly than intended, my voice straining.

"My mother taught me when I was young." He runs his fingers lightly over the keys. "I play for her sometimes, to see the light in her eyes again, even if it's only for a few moments."

I instinctively cover his hand with mine, curling my fingers around. "I'm sorry. I know it doesn't help, nor does it fix anything, but I am truly sorry for the things you all have gone through." I take a deep breath. "I wish there was something I could do to help you."

"Nell," he says roughly, and I turn to him. *You just being here is enough.* I hear his voice in my head, though the words don't leave his mouth. I'm just hearing what I want him to say. Instead he says, "Emrys and I picked up some clothes for you this morning. Regrettably, of course, because I do love seeing you wear mine." He smirks playfully, and I laugh with him, despite knowing there's something else he wanted to say.

My stomach chooses that moment to rumble, causing me to wince and cover the area with my hand. He chuckles, teasing me, "You're probably starving, seeing as you slept through the morning."

My brows shoot up at that. "Why didn't you wake me? I shouldn't be wasting a whole day passed out in your bed."

"I wouldn't call you in my bed a waste…but more of an opportunity," he winks, "and a necessity for my sanity, it seems." I don't want to get into what he all means by that comment. I'm still not feeling ready for that conversation.

I know how he feels about me, but knowing it and acknowledging it are two different things. If I let myself admit the truth of what is happening between us, I don't think there will be any going back. If I were to find out who I am and where I'm from, I would need to leave them. I can't allow myself to feel those things, and I need to stop falling into their spells. But the more time I spend with them, the more unavoidable it is.

I have to focus on the reason I'm here: my memory. After what Xamira showed us all last night, I'm even more determined to figure this out. The tug in my chest, pulling me toward the prince and his second, tells me that destroying the block in my head will give me answers with them, too.

Chapter 20

I decide to take a light lunch outside with me after Casmir mentioned there was a small courtyard behind the castle. I was confused at first because I thought they had built the whole back of the castle into the mountain; but actually, only the middle portion is attached to the rock, while the rest of the castle is built outwards on its own. It does look like the whole castle was attached to the mountain at one time, and some of it was taken away to open up this area. I'm curious to see what was built inside the mountain.

I look down at my new clothes, laughing to myself again. After sitting with the prince earlier, I went to change into something that he and Emrys brought back for me. I was shocked to see just how much they got; not only because it's just way more than one person needs, but also because I didn't know these two large, muscular males could shop for so much, so quickly. They definitely know my tastes, though: comfort clothing. There were different kinds of sweatpants and shirts, leggings, and even a few athletic outfits.

What I found funny, though, was the more intimate items they bought. A few sleeping sets that are made of satin, and too short to be intended for actual sleep. And then there were the bras and underwear…I think they had a little too much fun with those. They gave me maybe two practical pairs of cotton underwear, with the rest being lacy and revealing. There was even a crotch-less pair included, which I will definitely use just to get back at them. Maybe I'll wear those with one of the extra short *sleeping* slips they bought. I grin to myself at the idea of getting under their skin as much as they get under mine.

A light momentarily blinds my vision, making me look toward the waterfall. It is even more magnificent during the day. It's so tall I bet the gods could reach out from their realm and touch the top. The breeze sways in my direction, causing a small amount of mist to coat my face. I smile at the feeling. Water has fascinated me for as long as I can remember. I've always found comfort in its movement—the way that it will keep flowing even when something attempts to block its path. How it can be so calm that the world you see on its surface is a replica of what stands before it. How it can rage, causing even the largest ships to succumb to its will. Something that appears so weak, but is stronger than even the gods themselves. It's exceptional.

I rest my head on my hand and watch the waterfall, my eyes feeling heavy and—

"Nell!" Someone laughs and I jolt up, my mind having no clue where I am or what year it is. I take a moment to collect myself, recalling that I am sitting outside and the last thing I remember is watching the water. I must have fallen asleep.

I see Casmir sitting to my right, his hand attempting to cover his chuckles, amusement dancing heavily in his eyes, which look like a field of grass blowing in the wind on a sunny day.

"Did you have a nice nap, princess?" His voice is full of the laughter he's trying so hard to suppress.

"Why are you laughing at me?" I narrow my eyes at him, the scent of jasmine and leather hitting me, and I look over to see Emrys on my other side, also finding this funny. I peer down at my clothes, wondering if a breast is hanging out, but I look just as I did before.

Casmir is barely keeping it together, and I know there must be something on me that has him nearly suffocating like this. I look around me and still when I see that my lunch is still in front of me. I close my eyes and take a deep breath, because of course the gods would have me fall asleep on top of food that I guarantee is coating my face now.

I go to touch my cheek, but Emrys reaches out and grabs my wrist with his soft hands, preventing me from finding out what I must look like.

"Don't worry, love, I'll clean it up for you." He bends forward and runs the flat of his tongue from my jaw, across my lips, and up to the side of my nose. My eyes flutter, and my breath catches at the touch, but he just sits back with a devilish grin on his face and says, "Mmm, cinnamon is my favorite." He licks his lips to accentuate his point, and I have to look away before I slide right off my seat thinking of other places he could use that tongue.

Casmir calms his laughing down, and I see him wiping tears from his eyes, my jaw dropping at how funny he finds the embarrassing situation I've put myself in. So I grab the rest of the muffin on my plate and stand up to smush it in his face, making sure to rub it down his neck, catching the collar of his shirt.

"Not so funny now, is it, *prince*?" I cross my arms and smirk, and he feigns a horrified look on his face, but the intense heat in his eyes tells me I just made the wrong decision. Before I can comprehend what is happening, he grabs my hips and pulls me down onto his lap so I'm straddling him, while he pushes my back into the table, leaving me trapped here.

I huff a breath, "Excuse you—what was that for?"

He tilts his muffin covered face back to look up at me, biting his lip. "*That* was to give you proper access to your mess, since you're going to clean it up."

My face pales at his insinuation. "That's hardly fair! You were over here laughing at me. You had it coming!" I push at his chest, but he only flexes under my hand.

"Is that so, princess?" His voice is husky and I nod.

He pretends to think about what I said for a moment. "Hmm, that's not a good enough excuse for me to let you go," he smirks. "I expect you to clean this up. *All of it.*"

Playing dumb, I say, "I don't have a napkin. You'll have to let me get up so I can go grab one."

He chuckles darkly, taunting me. "Oh no. You'll be using the Emrys Method for this." I can feel him hardening beneath me, causing my core to heat and my brain to scream at me that this is not a good idea. But the pull in my chest says it's the best idea in history. I chew on my cheek, trying to decide what to do. I know that he'll let me go if I tell him to, but *fucking gods,* I've been waiting to slurp this man up since the day I met him. Maybe this is the best excuse I have to taste him just once. Purely to get it out of my system, so I don't think about it any longer. At least, that's what I tell myself.

I tilt my head and look at him through my lashes, bringing my face to his. "Fine," I whisper and swipe my tongue across his lips, making him shudder beneath me. If I'm going to do this, I might as well enjoy every second, which includes driving him crazy.

I sit back, making a show of looking over him slowly. Then I bend toward the part of his neck I got the muffin on and very, very slowly lick my way up, ending just behind his ear where I place a gentle kiss. His cock jerks under me, sending a bolt of pleasure through my center.

I take my time cleaning him up, ensuring I get every bit of his skin, whether it had muffin on it or not. By the time I'm done, we're both panting. My movements have been grinding me slightly against him, and I know he can feel me throbbing.

I sit back to admire my work, resting my elbows against the table, trying to appear nonchalant. His eyes are hooded with deep desire, and I clench my thighs at the savage look he's giving me.

I continue pretending I'm unaffected by the connection thrumming between us, and pat his chest right where I feel the buzzing in mine, causing him to jolt a little.

"There you go. All clean," I try to muster confidence in my words, but they instead come out thick and wanting. His lips curve up, and he licks his lips. Before I can devour them, I hoist myself up and pray that there isn't a wet spot on his pants. I'll never live it down otherwise.

I look over to Emrys who is sitting with his arms crossed, his face pained. "That was the hottest fucking thing I've ever seen," he mutters, and I have to turn around and remove myself from their sex-filled eyes before I do something insane. Like hop on both of them at the same time.

"Wait!" Em yells, making me pause but not turn around. He comes around and stops in front of me. One hand grabs my arm, while the other pushes my hair over my shoulder. "I'm sorry, love, you just did so good back there." His praise makes me stiffen, and I almost roll my eyes back before averting my gaze to hide my reaction, but his curious smile tells me he noticed. Thankfully, he doesn't comment on it. "Cas and I, before we found you in your…predicament, wanted to take you over to the library."

"Really?" He nods. "Well let's go," I wave my hands to usher him away.

We get into the castle, walking toward the center for several minutes before we reach a very dark hallway. My eyes widen as I realize this must be the part that's attached to the mountain.

"Wait," they both stop their advance to look at me, "the library is *inside* the mountain?"

Casmir nods, holding his hand out for me to grab, and I do. While we walk through the hallway, he explains, "It's good for the books to be away from the sunlight, and what better place is there than where the light can't reach? But that's only part of the reason this was the chosen location for the library, among other things," he says that last part quietly. "I once told you that Anloria has the largest library in all the realms, and that is true. But being the largest also means being the most valuable. We have texts in here that predate *everything*. Even before the gods created the balance. There's information in these texts that would be devastating in the wrong hands." He gives me a pointed look, and I know he's insinuating Andras has the wrong hands. "They could use the knowledge to gain access to a lot of power. More than any one fae should have.

"So we keep the library, along with other items, hidden in here. It's not impenetrable if Anloria were to be attacked and taken over, but it's the best we have for now."

The walls that we're in look like a cave, just with dim lighting illuminating the path. We eventually come up to a dead end and I look at Casmir, confused, but he just tilts his head toward the wall and whispers, "Watch."

He and Emrys walk forward and *into* the wall, disappearing from my sight. My forehead scrunches together, and I look around the passage to make sure they aren't playing a trick on me, but they're nowhere in sight. So I move forward, reaching my hand out to touch the wall and instead of a cold, rocky surface, I feel air as my hand goes through it. I snatch it back, but the tug in my chest is telling me to follow; I choose to trust it, and them, stepping forward to walk through the wall.

A second later I'm on the other side of it staring at an enormous library, my jaw dropping in pure amazement. In front of me is a floor lined with shelves upon shelves of books. I walk forward to a set of stairs and look down, nearly passing out from the sheer size of it. The stairs go down what must be at least a dozen floors, each looking like they hold their own enormous room full of shelves.

The lighting in here is dim, but I see a few tables that have lamps on them. It's also chilly, though I suppose that's important for the health of the books. The air is heavy with mustiness and worn pages.

"What do you think?" I startle at the sound of Casmir's voice, completely forgetting I followed him and Emrys in here.

"This is fucking incredible." They both smile at my wonderment, and I turn to take it all in again. "Where do we even start? There's *so* much here."

"I thought it might be best to begin with the older texts about the gods. That may give us an idea of who blocked your memories. And if the book talks about the magic they have that did that, it may also be helpful in figuring out how to undo it."

I nod my head in agreement and look around, waiting for direction.

"We'll find those texts on the fourth floor," he says.

My head drops over the railing. I glare down at the stairs, not wanting to even know just how many we have to descend, and then climb when we're done.

I laugh nervously, "Yeah, if I can even make it down there…my legs could barely handle a horse for a couple days."

"There's this thing called an elevator, you know," Emrys mutters.

I let out a disbelieving scoff. "Oh, *my bad.* I didn't think you guys would even *know* elevators existed, considering you don't have any other fucking helpful technology here."

He looks me over, humming to himself. "You are very attractive when you're annoyed."

"*Oh my gods,* you are insufferable." I march around his handsome, aggravating face toward the wall, hoping that the elevator will be where it *should* be; instead of floating in mid-air, or teleporting to random places, or something else crazy. Nothing here seems to work how I expect it to.

I sigh in relief when I see it just a small walk from where we entered. I tap the button and the doors open. Stepping inside, the males follow and Casmir presses the button we need. The doors close, and I become hyper aware of how small and dark this elevator is, leaving us all in close proximity. I smell their delicious scents, swaying on my feet and hoping this thing speeds up a bit so I can stop being tempted.

The elevator doors open and I push past them to run out and go over to the shelves. They follow and I go to ask Casmir where we should be looking, but spot a large book that conveniently says *History of the Gods* on the side; I figure that's a good sign and pick it up. Finding a table, I start looking through the text while the other two pick their own and join me.

After a couple of hours of sitting in silence, all of us absorbed in what we're reading, I come across a section of my book that has me sitting up straight. It's a list of each of the gods, along with their names, magic types, and what their job is.

I skim through the words, not paying attention to anything except for the one particular word I'm looking for, when I finally see it: *essence*.

"I found something!" I practically screech to them, wincing at my loud voice in the eerily quiet space. They jump out of their seats to look over my shoulder as I point to what I found.

Aeryn, the Goddess of War
Magic Types: Essence and Water
Primary Charge: The Goddess Aeryn maintains the balance of war be-tween Earth and Europa. War is an inevitable part of life, but too much war

will cause extinction among species. It is important for the Goddess Aeryn to step in when one of the two following situations arises:

Disagreements and fighting become too much for the species to handle
OR
The act of any war causes a disruption in the overall balance

I sit back in utter disbelief. Aeryn. The name of the goddess who did this to me, and she just so happens to be the Goddess of War. While this is a step in the right direction, it doesn't explain what I did to deserve her wrath and how I undo it. I close the book in frustration and lean my head over the back of the chair, looking up at Casmir and Emrys.

"That helps, but it also doesn't help," I murmur, disappointment coating my voice.

Cas puts a hand on my cheek, rubbing lightly, and I lean into the touch. "It's something, Nell. We know who blocked your memories. We now just need to find out if there's a way to get to her, or a way to remove the block ourselves." I put my hands up to my face and groan.

"Well, let's see if we can find anything else."

We spend another two hours looking through texts, and the only thing I find is an explanation of the different kinds of magic. The elemental ones are pretty self explanatory, but I don't know a lot about essence magic other than it can mess with your head.

According to the book, essence magic is exactly what it sounds like. The goddess can use that magic to manipulate the essence of *anything*. So, essentially, she has all elemental magic, but also can control living things like people and animals. It mentions that she can alter the essence of light, as well, which is pretty interesting, I guess.

Unfortunately, the book says nothing about undoing the magic. I shouldn't be so upset, because we've found more today than I have in months. I just want this to be over and to figure out the answers to all the questions that I have. I take a deep breath, trying to remind myself that this is progress, and I can come back and look again tomorrow.

I feel gazes on me and look up to see Emrys and Casmir watching with looks of concern on their faces. Em gives the prince a look, and they have a silent conversation. When they're done, they smile at me, and I just know that they have something wicked on their minds.

Chapter 21

"Come on, you guys, where are you taking me?" I whine, freaked out because I'm blindfolded and being dragged through the middle of a literal mountain by these gorgeous males. They've been ushering me along for what feels like an hour, but has probably only been ten minutes. For all I know, we're back in the castle at this point; though the air is heavy and wet, so I don't think that's the case.

"We're almost there," Emrys laughs.

"You're going to love it, I promise." I can hear the grin in Casmir's voice.

So I shut up and let them continue on. After a few more minutes, I hear a cascading sound that gets louder with every step, so I have the impression we're near the waterfall. Though I'm confused about how that could be since we were so far away from it. They must have tricked my senses and gotten me outside somehow.

The sound is loud now. We're definitely by the waterfall and the two males holding my arms stop abruptly, making me disoriented for a second. One of them pulls my blindfold off, and I drop my jaw for the second time today.

Oh my gods.

We're behind the waterfall, and in front of me is a pool of some sorts, made from the rock. The light from outside is just barely illuminating the space, giving it a secretive, but alluring, feeling.

"This is insane—how did you find this place?" I ask to no one in particular.

"We used to be little bastards as kids, and would explore these caves against Teryn's wishes," Emrys chuckles. Teryn, Casmir's mother; I smile at the thought of them as little boys getting yelled at for not listening.

"We've told no one of this place," Casmir murmurs, "and this part of the mountain is off limits to staff anyway, so you're welcome to come here anytime you need to get away."

"Yes, I'll be sure to take the paths I could see when we walked over here."

Casmir barks out a laugh, tilting his head back, and the sight of it makes me giddy. I turn away, admiring this incredible place, and walk forward to touch the water. It's a little chilly but not too cold to swim in.

I stand and face the males, assuming we're heading back to the castle now, and see them stripping their clothes off. "Woah," I spin, not needing to temp myself with the sight of their naked bodies. "What are you guys doing?"

"Swimming. Duh," Emrys's smart ass mouth says.

"All right," I swallow hard. "Well, you two have fun. I will find my way back to the castle."

I turn around and cover my eyes so I can only see below their knees. I move to walk out of the cave when Emrys steps in front of me and grabs my arms to lower them. "I don't think so, love. You're going to swim with us." Gods help me. I am just one female, and I only have so much self-control.

"No that's okay, the water is pretty cold," I try, but it doesn't work. Emrys throws a bit of fire at it and smirks.

"That should be warm enough."

I have nothing else to say in my defense, and he knows it. He steps back and drops his boxers, his only remaining piece of clothing, and I make sure my eyes are looking everywhere except where I want to look.

"Love, have you never seen a cock before? They don't bite," I hear the laugh in his voice.

"Yours might," Casmir announces, and Emrys does laugh at that, agreeing with him. Now I can't help but to look. Just a little peek to see what they're talking about. No, I shouldn't. I am too weak and won't be able to control my impulses. But my eyes betray me and glance down at him before I quickly look away; my brain frantically works to piece together what the fuck I just saw.

That male has a fucking third arm attached to his body. There is no way that is humanly possible. But he's not human, I suppose. Aside from his size, he has curled hair surrounding the area, though it appears to be trimmed a little. I'm about to fall to my knees and take a closer look at his impressive package, when I remember something: silver. I saw silver. I whip my head back around, not bothering to be discreet, and my hand slaps over my mouth when I see a metal ball peering around from under his shaft.

"I'm sorry—you have a piercing on your *dick*?" I say hysterically.

He looks down and wraps his hand around the tip, lifting it to show me the underside, a huge grin spreading across his face.

"Oh my fucking gods." I feel my face change from shock to horror to awe back to horror. He has five metal rods, with balls on each end, pierced down his entire cock. I feel myself drooling and quickly close my mouth, spinning and walking away to a rock that looks like it will work as a seat.

Emrys chuckles, slowly rubbing the bottom of his cock and I just about lose myself. "What's wrong, love? Afraid of a little fun?" He walks toward me. "I'm told these hit *just* the right spots. Shall we test it out?"

My head snaps up at that. "Me? I—there's no—I'm not—" Fuck me and my libido. "Uh, no thank you. I can't imagine how you don't tear yourself and every female you fuck."

He walks closer so that his hard length is directly in front of me, and I look up at his devilish face. "I can show you how."

I slide off the rock and squirm around his very hard, naked body, not deigning him a response. And come face to face with Casmir, who also is now fully naked, and before I can stop myself I look down at his cock. Please kill me now. I will not survive them.

"Are you absolutely kidding me right now?" I look between them. "Do you both just walk around with pythons in your pants all day? Or do you have some kind of spell you used to make them look larger?" They both laugh at my exasperation.

Before they can respond, I shoo them off. "Both of you in the water. I can't look at you anymore." They listen, both turning to step into the pool and I glimpse their asses; which are just as toned and nice as the rest of their body's.

"Come in, princess. We'll stop messing with you," Casmir promises, though I don't believe him for one second.

I sigh; it does sound really nice, and I feel like I deserve a relaxing swim after a day of research. That's the excuse I use as I go to strip off my clothes. Not feeling nearly as self conscious as them getting naked, especially since Casmir has already seen all of me. My sweater comes off first, followed by my leggings, leaving me in my undergarments. I'm suddenly thankful I chose a matching lace set today, knowing I look damn good in it.

I face away from them and unhook my bra, throwing it in the pile and then pull my panties down, bending just enough to let them get a look at what they can't touch. I step out of them and, without looking at either of the males, turn around and make my way into the pool. The water is warm like a bath and I groan, bending down to wet my face and hair. When I come up, Casmir and Emrys are both staring at me with wide eyes.

"What?" I already know what, but I ask anyway.

"I—you are…" Em doesn't finish his sentence, and just rubs the back of his neck with his hand, giving me a delightful view of his side.

I saunter over to him and say in a sultry voice, "I know." I slap him lightly on the cheek before gliding away from them toward the waterfall.

"Fuck," I hear him mutter to himself, but pretend I don't.

The edge of the pool is close to the back of the falls, and I lift myself up a little to lean further over. I look down but can't make out much because it's getting dark. It feels like we're pretty high up, though, so we must have climbed a bit to get here.

"We do have a reason for bringing you here." Casmir appears next to me, leaning against the rock. I raise an eyebrow in question. "This place is completely private, and we wanted to talk to you about something that cannot be mentioned around anyone else."

My curiosity grabs on, and I turn to face him fully, feeling Emrys's heat right next to me.

The prince looks to his second before continuing, "There may be someone who can help remove the block in your head, though I don't know for sure that she's able to."

"Are you serious? Who?"

"She is one of the last two remaining witches that practices blood magic." My brows furrow. I've not heard of this kind of magic before. "Blood magic is illegal and dangerous. This is because the user needs to sacrifice something to the Earth in order to take its energy for the spell. It is not a magic that comes from within a fae, but instead comes from the energy stored inside the realm.

"The main danger is in the sacrifice needed to perform the magic. The Earth always requires equal payment. Life for life. The more magic a spell requires, the larger the sacrifice needed." He watches me for my reaction.

"So how is that relevant to my problem?"

"Well, if Ivana decides she can remove the block in your mind, she could perform the spell required. But the sacrifice would be ours to pay."

I nod, understanding running through me. What if she could help me? I wouldn't need to find the goddess and beg her to reverse what she's done. But what would the sacrifice be? I would assume something quite large, since it is a gods magic that created the block in the first place; so Ivana would need a lot of energy to reverse it. I'll make the decision when I have all the information. There's no way I would say yes if it will get someone hurt; the sacrifice would have to come from me, and me alone.

"I suppose it couldn't hurt to just meet with her," I decide, looking between them.

Casmir nods. "I will have a meeting set up."

"Thank you," I murmur, taking his hand in mine. "The magic itself isn't just a risk. You said it was illegal, and no one else can know because of that. You guys would put yourselves in a bad situation if someone found out. Maybe I should meet with her alone."

"No," Emrys's stern voice rings around the cave. He steps forward and pinches my chin, forcing me to look at him. "You will do none of this alone, do you understand?" I nod slightly, having nothing to say to his demand.

His eyes look between mine for a moment before coming to a decision. In one quick movement, he has my back pinned against the side of the pool and his mouth crashing to mine. I let out a breathy moan at the impact, my hands automatically going up to grab his arms. All of my worries and thoughts leave my head. Fuck this distance I've been trying to keep. *I need them.*

I slide my hands up his very naked, very hard chest and grab the back of his neck, pulling him further into me and arching my back. His cock rubs against my core, forcing a groan from me, Emrys swallowing the sound. We break apart for a moment, breathing hard, and the desire on his face makes my breath catch.

"I need to taste you," his voice husky as he grabs my ass, picking me up to set me on the side of the pool. There's no warning before his mouth is on me, the sensation hitting me so hard I'm forced to fall back to my elbows so I don't hit my head. The flat of his tongue makes a long sweep up my center before he sucks my clit into his mouth, causing me to shiver.

"Oh my fucking gods, *yes,*" I breathe and lean my head back, letting him do his thing.

One of his hands reaches around to press down on my pubic bone, using his thumb to circle my nerves while his tongue slides inside of me. The pleasure is overwhelming, and I can't think any longer.

"Em, please. I can't." My words are just as jumbled as my brain.

He continues to fuck me with his tongue, curling it at the top in a way that makes my eyes roll back. The heat building low inside of me explodes, and I come with his name on my mouth, riding out the waves that seem endless.

I lift my head just as he takes one last taste, standing to his full height and looking down at my exposed body like it's the most valuable piece of art in the realm. Casmir is standing to the side, still leaning on the rock, watching us with a smirk on his mouth and heat in his gaze.

I feel Emrys swipe a finger through my folds, causing me to jerk from being oversensitive. He holds his finger out to Casmir, never taking his eyes off mine. The prince steps forward, grabbing Em's wrist and sucks me off of him. Both of them are staring at me, watching for my reaction. My mouth drops at the action, and I can't tell if I'm disturbed or more turned on. But the clenching of my inner walls answers that for me.

Casmir releases Emrys's finger with a pop and turns to me, licking his curved lips. "You are delectable, princess," he says in a deepened voice. I blink, too stunned to do anything else.

Casmir grabs my hips and lifts me off the rock, settling me around him, and I feel his cock at my entrance. I hold his face between my hands, and kiss him with the ferocity I feel strangling my chest. He returns the kiss with an intense passion, and I feel like I could stay here forever and be perfectly happy.

I feel alive.

I feel full.

I feel like I need more of them.

Casmir sits down on the steps, leaving the bottoms of our legs in the water, and I take the opportunity to sit fully and slide myself across his impressively large dick, causing him to moan into my mouth. The sound of his pleasure has me turning into a feral animal.

I lift and go to impale myself on his length, but he grabs my hips to stop me, breaking our kiss. "Not yet. Let me savor you," he whispers onto my lips and proceeds to pull me up his body until I'm seated over his face. I move to protest, but he holds me tightly and wastes no more time before sucking my whole center into his mouth, causing me to moan loudly.

Emrys steps out of the water, and I immediately grab his cock, pulling him over to me, and looking up at him with a feline smile on my face. I hold his eyes as I lift his shaft and run my tongue along his piercings, the cold of the metal feeling nice against my flesh.

"*Fuck*," he groans, running his hands through my hair and grabbing the back of it. "You are incredible."

I suck his tip into my mouth, and he jerks in my hold. I slide him in deeper, watching his reaction just as Casmir enters me with two fingers. The feeling of his soft skin being inside me makes me fall forward more, and Emrys hits the back of my throat.

I try to pull back, but he grips my hair and keeps me there, nearly choking me. I look up at him and his lips part.

"Good girl, Nell, just like that," he praises, and his words, along with Casmir's savoring, have me coming for a second time. I moan over Emrys's cock and he hums. He fucks my mouth. *Hard.* His piercings glide across my tongue as he slams himself into my throat; I'm drooling all over myself, and the sounds of slurping are loud, even with the waterfall right there.

I'm going to have bruises on my throat tomorrow, but I can't seem to care—I've never felt better in my life. Seeing both of these males come undone by me is euphoric. So I take everything Emrys has to give me, using one hand to massage his balls while the other is holding the back of his cock where my mouth can't reach, both working in tandem.

He holds himself deep, forcing me to gag, and I relax my tongue, swallowing. His head falls back at the action, and he growls, "I knew you could take it. You're doing so fucking well."

Casmir rides out the wave of my orgasm and immediately jumps back in for more. I can feel him moan against me, finding his pleasure in mine. The hand he doesn't have thrusting in me is gripping his cock, his one hand moving at the same time as his other. He swirls his tongue around my clit while his fingers swipe against the part of my walls that makes me see stars.

I'm so close to coming again, and I can tell Emrys is, too. I suck a little harder, and I feel him stiffen for a moment before he releases into my throat with a moan that I will dream about. I swallow each drop and clean him off when he's done.

I'm sitting up from Emrys when Casmir hits every spot exactly right and I come for a third time, this one stronger than the others. I have to pay attention to holding myself up so I don't suffocate him, but he pulls me down hard, and I squirm because the pleasure is too much. He forces me to take it, making my orgasm last for ages, while Emrys stands back and watches me grind against his best friend's face with a smirk on his.

I finally come down from the high and slide myself down Casmir's body. I take his cock into my mouth, needing to swallow him as well.

"Fucking gods, Nell," he breathes, keeping his hands to himself and letting me take control. And I make it so good for him; I use my hands in time with my mouth, sucking and gagging, and he watches me through his lashes, clearly enjoying the sight. It doesn't take long before he stiffens; with a heavy groan, he starts shooting into me, and I devour every single bit.

When his orgasm comes down, I give him one last lick, kissing the tip and then make my way up his body with more kisses. I take my time, having wanted to taste them for so long. I make it to his neck, and give him slow, deep kisses until I reach the corner of his mouth.

I pull back to look at him, and the emotion in his eyes makes me grip the rock harder. He's looking at me like no one has before. Like I'm his beginning and end. Like I'm the answer to every question he's ever had. Like he couldn't live another day on this earth without me. It hits me hard, and the tug in my chest literally pulls me down to his so that they're touching. My breath hitches at the weird feeling, and I have the urge to connect myself to the prince in every way possible, and never let go.

I don't know how I'll ever go back to ignoring the pull to him and Emrys. This feels so right. *They* feel right. I don't know what that means yet, and I'm afraid to find out.

Chapter 22

I'm reading through new books, just as I've been doing for the last two days since Casmir and Emrys showed me how to access the library. While this place is moody and peaceful, it's also a little creepy. Cas mentioned that there was indeed a librarian, Ender, who basically lives in here; but I have yet to see, or even hear, him. So while I'm alone, weaving through these dramatic shelves and dusty books that are almost too heavy to carry, I don't always feel alone. Sometimes there's an awareness pricking the back of my neck that makes me think I'm being watched, but when I observe my surroundings, there's no one there. I haven't voiced my tense thoughts just yet, as I'm waiting to see if Ender will introduce himself. Maybe he just enjoys solitude, and who am I to judge?

I think back to the zealous event that occurred between Emrys, Casmir, and I, and I have to bite the inside of my cheek to keep myself composed. I daydream about their beautiful bodies; being so absorbed in my need for them to touch me that I'm struggling to focus on what I have in front of me.

Something shifted between the three of us in that cave. Sure, the physical experience was transcendental, but it's so much more than that. Ever since we left the pool, the void in my chest has been absolutely pulverizing my insides. It feels frantic, like static on a television; it's disorienting and, at times, I struggle to breathe, knowing deep in my soul that the only solution is giving myself to them completely. I'm not certain how I know this; it's just an instinct. Something primal. Essential to my sanity and continued existence.

I'm terrified of what this means. I know they're enduring the same thing. I can feel their turmoil when they watch me. None of us have dared to discuss what's happening, though. I think we're all scared of not knowing.

I understand that this is my fault. I'm the reason we're all grappling with…whatever this is. I feel guilty for causing this to happen, and I'm wrenching every bit of information I can from these texts to try to find a solution, even though I know I won't. The only answer to this is in my memories. But I will work my way through these books, regardless, hoping that I can help them, in some way.

Casmir has been wildly affectionate, needing to always be around me, making sure I'm protected and happy. I've seen him trying hard to distance himself, probably for my sake, not wanting to smother me.

Emrys is a little trickier. He definitely is experiencing the same thing, though he is much more resistant to it. When he unconsciously comes closer to me or touches me, I can see the moment he realizes what he's doing and forces himself back. I wish I knew what he went through to cause the devastation and distress in his eyes during these moments, but it's not my place to ask him to relive that for me.

I sigh and drop my head to the table, closing my eyes and breathing sharply through my mouth. This much stress cannot be good for anyone.

A tingling sensation crawls down my neck, making the hairs on my arms rise. I sit up and turn to look in every direction, but all I see is the faint illumination of the stairs and the dark aisles of the shelves. This awareness feels different from when I expect Ender to be near. This feels stronger. I lift out of my chair, hoping to make it to the elevator before I go down from a heart attack.

A light snapping sound has me whirling to my right. I'm definitely not alone any longer, but who here would want to scare or hurt me? Maybe someone recognizes me and has come to finish the job. I feel my blood heat, sending adrenaline throughout my body and preparing me for whatever is going to crawl out of the shadows. My palms are sweaty, and I rub them on my leggings while simultaneously backing away from the sound, careful not to move too quickly or turn my back to it.

My foot touches the floor behind me, my rapid breathing the only noise in here now. A hand suddenly grabs my mouth, pulling me into a hard body, their other arm grasping my torso and locking my arms. I start to scream and flail my legs, fear overtaking all my senses. Then I remember my training with Bren, something that he said blinking like neon lights in my mind:

Find your calm.

If I let myself succumb to the panic, I won't be able to focus, and this fae will have free rein to do what they want with me. I will not let that happen ever again.

I take a deep breath and reach my leg in between theirs, pulling it out from under them and forcing us to fall back. They loosen their grip enough for me to grab the wrist that's holding my mouth, pulling it over my head and twisting it while I twist myself around to straddle them. I continue wrenching their wrist to the side until I hear a loud crack, the fae screaming in pain. The voice sounds familiar, but I don't give them a chance to see me hesitate. I sit over them and drag my hand back, intending to smash their nose in like a pug, but stop when I see Emrys's dark, crystallized honey eyes looking at me with pain and awe radiating from them.

"Oh my gods, Em. Holy fuck. I'm so sorry, I didn't know it was you." I feel tears gathering at the pain I've caused him, but he laughs. A full belly laugh, shaking me and fusing my pelvis to his. My shoulders drop, and I blink the tears through my lashes to see him better, needing to know if I'm making this up or not. No, he's laughing. I've broken him; physically and mentally, it seems.

Full of disbelief, I say softly, "Em? Why are you laughing? I just broke your wrist and almost crushed your face."

His laughing slows to a soft chuckle, and he peers up at me, his amusement evident. "Love, this," he holds up his wrist, "is nothing. It will heal quickly. I'm laughing because imagine my shock when this beautiful, soft female manages to take down the captain of the Anlorian armies." He laughs a little more, and the tension peels away from my bones.

"I did not know you could fight like that." He grasps a piece of my hair before sliding his hand to my neck and pulling me down so that my lips hover over his. "You are astonishing," he whispers, and reduces the distance between us. "Devastating."

The kiss starts soft, but quickly transforms into something suppressed and hungry. He grips me with both of his arms—his wrist must be healing already—and I hold on to his jaw, drawing him further into me because I can't get enough. His leather scent mixing with the mint on his breath captivates my senses, and I moan into his touch, the soft sound floating heavily through the library.

I instinctively begin to grind against his growing erection, both of us becoming more frantic in our need for each other. The hollow of my chest blooming through every fiber of my being, wailing at me to join with him.

Wait.

I don't know if I can do that yet. I'm still unsure of what it means, regardless of how *right* it feels. I have to forcefully remove myself, pushing on his chest and sitting up. We stare at each other for a minute, the question we both have agitating the space between us.

I compose myself enough to stand and offer my hand to help him up. "Is your wrist okay? I'm sorry." I pinch my nose, frustrated with myself. He squeezes my chin, forcing my gaze to his. I expect to see anger directed at me, but there's only understanding, and something else I'm not ready for.

"It's okay, my love. It's already healed, see?" He shows me the not at all injured wrist, and my eyes widen in surprise. How does that work? My cheek took several days to heal, and that was just a bruise.

Emrys answers my thoughts. "You don't have access to your magic at the moment, which is a large part of the quick healing. You will still heal faster than a mortal, but it will be slower without your magic." I nod in understanding.

I stroll back over to the table and remember why I had hurt him in the first place. Spinning around, I throw a punch to his arm. "That's for being a dickhead and scaring me," I mutter with no wrath in my voice.

He raises his hands up placatingly, smiling at me. "I didn't know it would scare you so much that you'd turn into a certified badass, okay?" Shaking my head, I take my seat so he doesn't see how his words threaten my nonchalant composure.

"What brings you to this lively place, anyway?"

"I wanted to see you." I roll my eyes at his flirty tone. "But seriously, Nell, I am sorry for scaring you. I know you have," he pauses, attempting to find the right word, "*things* in your past that make those situations difficult for you. I didn't expect that to be one of them, but you have my word that I won't ever do that again." His eyes bore into me with a sharp severity.

I watch several emotions pass over his face. Consent is something he takes seriously, that much I can tell. But why? What happened in his life that caused this level of distress?

"Why is that important to you?" I blurt out, hoping I'm not pushing it too far. He tenses, understanding what I'm asking between the words. I get the impression that he and I aren't so different in our trauma.

"Let's just say I also have *things* in my past," he utters quietly. We stare at each other, both of us aching to share our stories and bond over things we can't change, but neither of us speaks. I'm afraid he'll see me differently if he knew. That he'll look at me with disgust instead of tenderness, and I don't believe I could handle that. Not knowing everything I feel for him.

He interrupts the silence, "When I was eleven, Cas found me living alone on the streets." I listen, longing to know anything I can about him. "I didn't know he was the prince's son, so I told him to fuck off. But he saw what I looked like: skinny, pale, dirty—and ordered me to come to the castle with him." His lips curve at the memory.

"No one orders me around, so of course I knocked him in the face. His guards found us brawling in a random alley, trying to take each other down. They brought us both back to the castle, where Niair and Teryn were speechless because the law would've had me executed for trying to kill the royal son, but I was just as young as him.

"Cas defended me, telling them he started the fight because he wanted me to come to the castle, and I wouldn't listen. They gave me a bed, a bath, and a hot meal that night; I remember crying so hard because the idea of sleeping in a bed was beyond anything I could have dreamed for." He sucks in a breath and blinks several times, coming out of the memory. "After that, they took me in. I felt like the most undeserving boy in the world, but I was so happy. Ever since the day he found me, Cas and I have been inextricable. He helped me through more than I want to remember. I can't explain it, but I've always felt like we were meant to be in each other's lives."

I watch Emrys lose himself in thought, stretching my hand out to grab his in a silent show of solidarity. He opens my fingers, examining each one before tracing the lines on my palm. His simple touch sends sparks weaving through my body. I rest my head on my other arm, closing my eyes and savoring the feel of his skin on mine.

"I did want to see you, but I also came here to tell you the festival is being held in the city square tonight," he squeezes my hand, "if you'd like to go."

"Are you kidding me? Music, dancing, and food? We have to go!" I grin and his eyes catch the movement.

"Well you better get ready so we don't miss anything."

I'm standing in front of my bathroom mirror, cackling to myself at my outfit. I haven't had much of a chance to tease Casmir and Emrys for the lingerie they bought me, and tonight is perfect for it. I'm wearing a pair of flowy, black pants and a black, mesh top that showcases every bit of the lace bra I chose. I also put on the matching panties, but they unfortunately can't be seen through the fabric of my pants. My hair is hanging down my back, with light waves running among the strands.

I feel pretty. I'm starting to appreciate my markings as a part of me. They tell a story of a life that I have yet to learn but want to know. I get caught in my grey eyes, captivated by the strong, full of life female I see there. I wonder if my past self would be proud of me. If she would think I'm doing the right thing, making the right decisions. I hope so.

I shouldn't be allowing these negative thoughts in tonight.

No.

Tonight is going to be fun. I'm going to let myself smile, and dance, and not worry about any of the million things plaguing my mind. I kiss Xamira on the head and her snoring stutters, pulling a laugh from me. Then I take a deep breath and leave the room before I bring myself down too far.

I told my escorts that I would meet them at the entrance so they weren't standing outside my door waiting for me. After a few more words of encouragement, I make my way to them.

I glance up as I stroll down the stairs, a deep satisfaction rolling through me when Em and Cas notice what I'm wearing. The prince's jaw unlocks, parting his lips slightly, while his second bites his lip and makes no effort to hide his scrutinizing gaze.

Finally reaching them, I feign confusion and say sweetly, "What? Is something wrong?"

"That doesn't look like what I told you to wear," Emrys's tone quiet with severity.

"You said to wear something nice and comfortable. I thought I looked nice, and I'm quite comfortable." An idea comes to mind, and I decide to press them harder. "Though I could do without the shirt, it's a little itchy."

I give them a feline grin, basking in the possessiveness emitting from them. "I didn't think so." I pat them both on the chest and walk to the door, smiling to myself.

We wander into the square, and I am shocked. I imagined there was going to be a little food stand, and a few fae dancing to the live music, but this exceeds all expectations.

There are vendors set up around the barrier of the square, a large, packed dance floor in the middle, and various types of seating areas in between. There are lights hanging across the space, giving the event a small amount of illumination. I hear what sounds like upbeat, instrumental music, but I can't tell where it's coming from. The festival is lively and packed with fae from all across Anloria; the sight saddens me a little, knowing there was never this kind of community outside the Veil. I was always alone and doing everything on my own, even when I was around others.

The festival almost reminds me of a fair, just without the murderous rides. I excitedly grab Em and Cas's hands to drag them with me while I look at everything. The prince insists I can purchase anything I'd like, and my heart catches in my throat. Not at the idea of buying things, but the fact that no one in my life has ever taken care of me like this. Nobody has even cared for me at all, unless they wanted to use me for something. But the looks of pure adoration that these two are sending my way right now are leaving me powerless against every worry I had about them.

I turn away, reminding myself that I will not think about any of that tonight. Tonight will be fun and freeing.

Emrys and I are sitting on a bench watching Casmir greet a group of fae who approached him. I remember when Andras took me into Ceross, and looked uncomfortable each time he had to meet someone. Cas is the complete opposite. He has a genuine smile on his face, and is focused on each fae he talks to. He's listening to, not just hearing, everything they're saying, and laughing with them at whatever jokes are being made. He looks like a prince who loves his people and sincerely enjoys spending time with them.

I drag my gaze to Emrys, who is watching the interaction with a warm smile.

We're both working through a large, airy, sugar-coated donut, and it's near orgasmic. I shove the last piece into my mouth and moan in appreciation. Emrys chuckles at my display of affection for a pastry.

"Oh, shut up," I laugh with him. "I am allowed to cherish my food, thank you very much."

He reaches out to caress his thumb over my lips, pulling it into his mouth and sucking off the sugar that was on me. His eyes, which look like a deep, rich amber in this lighting, stay glued to mine. My lips part at the simple but sensual action, and the heat in my body is no longer from the swaying fae behind us. He is exceptionally handsome; his black pants, half-buttoned, tan shirt that exposes his smooth skin down to the top of his abs. Deep brown curls falling slightly over his forehead, temping me to run my hands through them. His bronze skin gleaming in this atmosphere. The rare, unmasked grin softening his face and revealing his white teeth.

All of him has me captivated, though I'm definitely not the only one. I've caught several females giving him *fuck me* eyes, and I may or may not have discreetly threatened them with my own. It's not that I feel jealous others appreciate his body. No, it's more than that. A need to claim and protect him, even from harmless gazes. I know the fae can be territorial, but my reaction seems a bit much. We're not together, or mates, or exclusive in any way, so I have no actual claim to him; but that doesn't make the powerful feelings disappear.

A couple hours later, and a few glasses of wine in, I find myself on the makeshift dance floor, surrounded by fae I've never met, but am having the best time with. A young female comes up to me—she looks around eight—and grabs my hands to start spinning around. I help her spin in time to the music, laughing at her infectious giggles, and the warmth in my chest takes over my body. I'm happy in this moment.

A sheen of sweat covers my neck, even with the cool night air. Lila, I learned when we yelled through the blaring music what our names were, and I dance with each other for several songs before she finds someone else to spin with. She has just left me when there's a tug in my chest so hard it forces me to lurch forward. I immediately know what it means, and spin to find Emrys and Casmir both watching me with warm smiles. A blush creeps up my skin, warming my face and neck.

I decide to act with my soul tonight, going with the theme of not letting my worries consume me. I saunter over to my males, not hiding my appreciative scan of them, the wine making me bolder than I normally am. I would be this bold in private, though there's likely many fae watching since Cas is indeed their prince. He and Em don't seem to mind, however; so once I reach them, I grab a hand from both of them and bring them up to my mouth to give them each a gentle kiss. Releasing their hands, I give the prince a wink before turning to Emrys.

"Dance with me," my voice ethereal. I reach out my hand, showing that I won't force him if it's not something he's comfortable with. His brows lower as a wave of emotion passes over his face before his lips break into a lopsided smile.

I could never refuse you.

His voice plays through my head like a euphoric song, and I wonder if it's the wine and music making me hear things.

He holds onto me as I lead us through the crowd of dancing fae. He's tense, though I can tell he's trying not to show it. I rotate so I'm facing him, grab his face in my hands, and pull him into a kiss. I fill it with all the passion and emotion I feel for him, longing for him to understand the things I can't admit yet. I also hope it helps to calm his nerves.

I pull back and smile when his muscles loosen. He wraps his hands around my waist and presses me into his chest, his heartbeat crashing against the frantic energy strumming through mine. I grip the back of his neck, massaging his soft hair, and we watch each other in silence. Both of us are afraid to put a voice to the sensations humming between us, but understanding we each feel it.

"Although I'm finding it very difficult to stop myself from going after each fae that's admiring your body through this bold fashion statement," he pinches my back lightly, "I think you look radiant tonight." My cheeks heat, and I suppress a smile.

"Thank you," I choke, closing the distance between us and hold him in a soft hug while we continue to dance. The world melts away. It's just me and him for this moment. This is where I belong: in his and Cas's arms. The empty space in my chest fills with light each time I'm near them. It tells me I am safe, that they are my *home*. I understand that now. I may not know where this connection comes from, but it's clear that it's important; I've been denying the truth, trying to find excuses that would give me reason to refuse it because I'm scared. I could never trust anyone besides Xamira. I know what it feels like to want to be loved so badly that you naively give your heart to the first person that shows you attention, only to have them betray you. I've known since I met them that Casmir and Emrys would never do that to me.

My soul calls to them. Recognizes them.

I know I still need to figure out who I am, and where I come from, but maybe all of this happened for a reason. Maybe I wouldn't have met them if I didn't go through all of this, and I would've continued to feel empty inside for the rest of my life. If my memories return and I find out I live far away from here, I will stay. They are mine and I am theirs. That much has been clear since the moment I locked eyes with them in Ceross.

The song ends and Emrys whispers in my ear, "Thank you." I hug him tighter, making the moment last just a bit longer. "I think you have another admirer."

I turn and follow his gaze to Casmir, who is standing behind me with his hands in his pockets. He looks enchanting under the dimmed lights, with his dark, messy hair, casual attire, and tender eyes that are swirling with deep green and affection.

He lifts my hand, bowing to me just as he did the first time we danced, and smirks as if he knows where my thoughts are. "Nell, would you honor me with your next dance?" I nod, unable to keep the grin off my face at how wonderful he is. He pulls me into him as the next song starts, and I curl my arms around his head, needing to feel the strands of his hair as well.

How could I not let myself fall for him when he's looking at me like I'm his reason for living?

I flutter my lashes, trying to dispel the tears threatening to come out. I should be an expert in processing my emotions after all the years I spent with a therapist, but I still suck at it. So instead of feeling all of them, I decide to tease Casmir as a distraction.

"And what is His Highness dancing with me for? I'm sure there are *so* many females here who would leap for a chance to dance with their prince."

There is only you, his voice loud in my head with the words I want to hear. But then he says out loud, "There is only you, princess." Am I hearing things?

I sputter a few jumbled syllables, my brain freezing up from the declaration. His sincerity is disarming. All I end up doing is nodding, words leaving me for good, and holding him tight like I did Emrys during our dance.

I see several females glowering at me, but I ignore them. They can certainly come find me later, and meet my fist, if they think they're getting anywhere near my males.

Gods, I am crazy.

My males. That's the second time I've thought of them as mine tonight.

I relax into Casmir, and we stay locked together for two more songs, the thrumming inside me glowing brightly.

Chapter 23

Emrys, Casmir, and I are wandering back into the castle after spending a few more hours dancing, and enjoying the freedom from being who we are. Cas is grumbling about a council meeting he must attend tomorrow—or today?—while his second teases him about how he has no meetings and can sleep in all day. I'm laughing quietly at their bickering when we reach the junction between our three rooms. I stand awkwardly, not knowing what I should say after a night of pure intimacy between us.

Thanks, good night?

Sleep well?

Just fuck me already?

None of those seem like the wrong—or right—thing to say. Casmir saves me from my straying thoughts, stepping in front of me and grabbing a strand of my hair. The dark walls and low lighting give him an ominous aura. His tender, jasmine scent, mixed with a hint of wine, is difficult to ignore.

"Nell…" He pauses, struggling for the right words. "I think we all realize there's something manifesting between the three of us." This feels like forbidden territory, since we haven't discussed it with each other before.

He goes on. "Something special that even I, or Em, do not understand. But we all feel it," I nod, almost needing to hold my chest because of the strain I have inside.

"I want you, Nell. In any way you'll let me have you." His hand slides through my hair to grab the nape of my neck, peering so deeply into my eyes that I'm convinced he could tell me the color of my soul.

I sense Emrys feels the same way, but I don't expect a declaration from him; at least not yet. He is more reserved than Casmir in voicing his feelings, but that's perfectly okay. It's what makes him *him*.

I nod again, answering the prince the only way I can right now. I feel overwhelmed, though I can't tell if it's from anticipation, nervousness, or the thing in my chest desperately trying to break out.

I didn't realize Emrys stepped behind me and startle when he pulls my hair over my shoulder. His breath tickles the side of my neck, and my lips part in suspense. He doesn't move to kiss me, but his knuckle traces lightly up my spine, causing my breath to hitch and my back to curve inward. That simple touch has me trembling already and craving so much more.

Casmir guides my lips to his in a fierce, demanding kiss, igniting every part of my body. A breathy moan leaves me as Emrys marks my neck and runs his hands up my sides until they grasp my waist. Both males are pressed against me, and my blood expands as it boils, causing my skin to flush. Cas pulls away from our kiss, and spins me around, where Em immediately begins to greedily devour my lips, sucking my tongue into his mouth and clashing his teeth against my own.

Perfect.

So beautiful.

Fuck, your skin is unbearably soft.

I can't focus on what they're saying with the disorienting sensations crashing through me. Though I'm not sure how they're getting a word out when both their mouths are occupied.

I release Emrys to suck in a breath and he lifts me, wrapping my legs around him and kissing his way down my throat. Casmir leads us into his room, and I'm deposited on the bed, where both males stop to look at me lying before them.

Emrys strips my pants off, leaving me in my lace panties. He runs his nose through the wet fabric, and his head falls back in satisfaction. "*Fuck.*" He stands, putting an arm on each side of my head so he can capture my eyes.

"We're going to make you feel so fucking good that the gods will hear you screaming for them," his voice is rough and threatening.

My mouth nearly drops open at his heavy promise. But before it can, a force whips my arms over my head and confines my wrists together. I'm then dragged to the middle of the bed and let out a squeal of surprise because Emrys is still leaning on the bedding, staring at me intensely, and Casmir is leaning against a bedpost with his arms crossed and a wicked smirk on his face.

I attempt to sit up and find that my torso is also being held down. "Cas," I say, my voice breathy, knowing it must be his air magic rendering me immobile.

He doesn't answer, but continues to find amusement in my struggle as his second crawls up the bed to hover over me once more. He sits back on his knees and grins devilishly as he bends my legs and runs a finger down the inside of my thigh. My core feels hot, much more so than I would think is normal. I peek down—

"Holy shit." My panties are in flames and burning off me at his command. I can feel a small amount of the heat, though it is not harming me or the bed. Impressive.

And sexy as fuck.

I swallow loudly as the flame changes, and an orange-yellow snake inches its way up my abdomen. I'm shaking in my restraints with fear and excitement, knowing he wouldn't ever hurt me. But there's still a literal fire snake crawling over my body, which would wring the adrenaline out of anyone.

"Emrys. No fucking way." I can barely get the words out through my heavy breathing, my eyes locked on the slithering creature. The snake loops around my breasts, burning the fabric of my shirt and bra off, before lifting its head and lurching forward to bite one in the center. A ragged noise leaves me, but not from pain. It feels like a small pinch, shooting bolts of energy straight to my core.

It slides up to the base of my throat and levels its sight with mine, so close I can taste the flames swirling around its body.

"Em," my voice is hoarse. I focus on the snake, hoping my unease isn't showing through. After what feels like a lifetime of it watching me, it hisses, sounding like sputtering flames. The creature leaps into the air and dives straight for the hollow point in my chest. I yelp, trying to move, but still being held down by invisible hands. The snake makes contact with my skin and dissipates, almost feeling like it's disappearing inside of me, though it's not.

"What the fuck was that?" Emrys chuckles at my incredulity.

"Just a little fun, love," amusement is heavy in his voice.

"Ready for some more?" Casmir teases. Before I can answer, I'm spun around to my stomach and my arms pull back to my breasts, though they're still restrained. My legs are lifted, forcing me to my knees, so that my face is buried in the bedding while my lower half is on display for the two dangerous males.

"Oh my gods," I sigh into the soft fabric.

"They can't hear you yet, love."

A mouth descends on my center, lapping at my growing arousal, and forcing a shuddering groan from me that the bedding catches between its stitches. I'm being eagerly devoured, Emrys switching between licking and sucking. Just when I start feeling close to the edge, he pulls back, driving a whine from me. He adjusts on the bed and presses his legs against my thighs. I'm not sure when he took his clothes off, but there's no complaint from me. A hand lands on the center of my back, forcing me to arch further. His erect cock runs a path through my folds, the cold metal a pleasant contrast to the overbearing heat. I push into him, needing more friction than he's offering, and he pulls back, tsking my action.

"No misbehaving, love," he teases in a seductively dark voice. "We'll give you what you need."

He runs fingers through my lubricant before sliding them inside of me so slowly I nearly lose my mind. "We have to make sure you're ready for us." He pushes a third finger in, the stretch causing a slight burn before it melts away into pure bliss. He's pumping his fingers unhurriedly, and it's all I can do to restrain myself from moving and causing him to stop again. I sense another presence in front of me right before a hand grabs my hair and lifts me into a kneeling position.

I'm facing a pair of hazel eyes that are dripping with desire, the look making me clench around Emrys. The prince jerks my chin up with his hand, his lust filled gaze catching on my mouth.

"Open," he orders, and I do without hesitation. He drives two fingers into my mouth, pressing at the back of my tongue, and I gag from the movement. "Suck," his voice is deadly and powerful. My lashes flutter in anticipation as I do what I'm told.

"That's my princess," he praises, and if I wasn't being held up at the moment, I would have melted into the sheets.

He pulls out just as Emrys does, reaching down to take his place while his second begins to swirl around my other hole. I bite my lip, preparing for his entrance. I've done anal before, though never with anyone their size…but I'm not one to back down from a challenge.

"Have you had anyone here before?" I nod in response, and he growls at my back. "As much as it infuriates me that some other male touched what wasn't his, that will make this easier for you." His possessiveness is intrinsic and euphoric.

He pushes a finger in, and a guttural moan leaves my throat at having both of them inside of me. "That's it, love, you can take it," he groans into my hair. Another finger from each of them enters, and Casmir captures the sounds leaving me with his mouth. I am at the brink of insanity, the tugging in my chest snapping every bit of stability.

"More," I breathe against his lips. I can't wait any longer. "I need you. Now," I command, my voice regal and otherworldly. The restraints around me disappear, as well as the hands inside of me. I force Casmir to his back and straddle his lap, having an unhinged need to claim these males. I lift my hips, and lower myself onto his cock, his size stretching me so good. We both groan at the invasion, and I ride him fervently, needing more. But it's not enough, not this time.

Every cell in my body is reaching for them with a demand to bond our souls together. I know it won't be sated unless I have them both.

"Emrys. More," I barely whisper, and he is behind me instantly, his length already covered in lube as if he expected what I would want. He wastes no time inching his way into my ass, his large dick pushing me to my absolute limit, but I don't care. I feel as though my body will shatter into a million pieces if I don't have them. A primal need has taken over me, and I must obey.

Once Emrys is fully seated in me, we all take a second to breathe before my body moves on its own, taking everything it craves from them. Casmir lifts himself to suck on one of my breasts, palming the other and rolling my nipple in between his fingers. His ragged breaths are coating my sternum, and a gratifying pang flows through me at being the one to pleasure him in this way.

Em has a hand gripping my hip so hard I know it will be bruised in the morning, though I don't feel any pain. I feel nothing except completeness. He grabs my hair to turn my head and force my mouth to his, kissing me with a passion I didn't know existed.

We stay locked in a swarm of tongues, teeth, hands, and bodies moving methodically. The sounds of our moans, and skin slapping together, fill the room. All of us lost to each other. Pressure builds low inside of me and they must feel it, too, because their movements become more frantic. Cas circles my clit while Em bites down on the sensitive spot below my ear.

I feel them everywhere. Every burning cell. Every damaged part of my body. Every thought I've ever had. All consumed by them.

Nothing exists outside of this moment.

They are everything my heart has been crying for.

One more thrust and I lose it. "*Oh my fucking gods*," I scream, my vision going white as I fall into an orgasm. I feel both of the males tense before warmth coats my insides. The pleasure is too much—I swear I'm floating in a different realm. The emptiness in my chest is filled with blinding light and emotion, overwhelming every nerve in my body.

I have the sense that I would cease to exist without them. It's no longer a want to be with them, but a fundamental part of my being. I don't know what this is, or what we'll do with it moving forward, but I don't care right now. It feels *so* right. I feel complete.

My head finally comes back into focus after an eternity. I'm laying on Casmir's chest while Emrys is laying on my back. We're still tangled together, neither of them having pulled out, and breathing hard. I shift, a little uncomfortable, and Casmir grabs my face with urgency.

"Are you okay?" He says, eyes full of worry. I kiss him lightly and nod.

"Just tired, and I think a little sore, but it's hard to tell right now." That makes him chuckle, putting pressure on my inner walls and, yes, I'm sore.

We pull apart, and I wince at the motions. I've never been with one guy as big as either of them, but then to have two...*at the same time*? I was really out of my head. I fall to my back, not possessing the energy to do anything else, and Emrys follows my lead, plopping down on the side opposite of Casmir. We lay in silence for several minutes.

What the hell was that? I have never known sex to be anything other than a simple fuck, but that was something completely different. My hand goes to my chest. The thrumming has died down, so I can think again. The pocket sitting under my palm, trauma that's normally vacant, is now resting partially full. I always thought the feeling was something to do with the depression Sarah claimed I had. That there was something wrong with me, and I would never feel whole or fulfilled. That was something that I accepted about myself, knowing that everything I've been through had to have caused some everlasting damage.

As of right now, I no longer believe that. I still feel the trauma and anxiety waiting in the sidelines of my thoughts, ready to take over at the first sign of weakness; but now I know that those are not attached to the hollow area near my heart. All along it meant something else, and I can't help but to wonder if it's Casmir and Emrys's presence directly causing this change in me, or if they're just helping me change myself. Would I have discovered this connection had I not met them?

"That was—" Casmir whispers into the stillness.

"There are no words for what that was," Emrys finishes for him, sounding just as shaken as I am.

I was worried about acknowledge my feelings for them. Worried that it would somehow hurt them, and me, if I did.

I was wrong; nothing that feels *this* good, and *this* right, could hurt anyone.

I'm stirred awake by tender kisses being trailed over my shoulder. A sleepy moan escapes my throat, and I grip onto hard muscle and pull it closer to me, needing to fuse myself to the warmth. The body behind me takes the hint and presses closer, wrapping arms around my torso and holding onto the other body in front of me. The smell of leather and jasmine and sex float through the air.

Emrys and Casmir. My brain wakes a bit more, and I remember what happened between us last night. A wave of contentment washes through me and I sigh happily, settling into my males; not wanting to unwrap our little cocoon.

I crack open an eye to peer at Emrys, who I'm draped over. The morning light filtering in through the window is painting the hard lines of his chest. He is tragically perfect in this moment. I trace my fingers around him, sketching an invisible line up to his face that is peaceful in sleep. His curls falling to the side of his head, where he's facing me. I grab one of the strands to twirl my fingers through its softness.

Beautiful.

I look down at his voice to see he's watching me with a tired smile.

"Good morning, my love."

"Good morning." I smile at his words.

It doesn't take long for us to touch each other, needing to feel our skin colliding again. He drives into me slowly, savoring each moment. Where last night felt desperate and demanding, this feels lazy and precious. My muscles hurt even more than they did several hours ago, but the pain quickly dissipates as he fucks me with unmasked longing. Our foreheads and mouths are pressed together as we slowly consume each other. Once we both find our release, not as Earth shattering as last night but still transcendental, I see Casmir is still sleeping. I crawl over to wake him with my mouth and tongue, which quickly has him breathing my name; I suck him deeply and slowly, smiling up at him when I finish cleaning his cock off, and he pulls me close for a devastating kiss.

We shower together, and I have more than one straying thought of what it would be like to have them rail me against the stone of the mountain that make up all the walls. Would I bleed from the rough edges? Would it be too painful, or just enough to add to the pleasure?

I need to get my head together. I thought that giving into my desires would help ease them for a while, but it seems to only have made things stronger. Casmir informed us that the witch he knows, Ivana, agreed to meet with us today. That should have my full focus; I could get my memories back. After years of struggling through a life that didn't feel like mine, and then these last few months of knowing things are missing, but not being able to do anything about it…I'm so ready to find out who I am. I'm trying to not get my hopes up, because we're not sure if she can even help, but it's impossible not to. This could really be my chance to figure everything out, including this connection between Cas, Em, and I. I'll also be able to understand what Xamira has been trying to tell me.

My head feels much clearer after reminding myself what's at stake here.

The prince leaves to go to his council meeting while Emrys follows to grab us some breakfast, insisting that I shouldn't have to get out of bed, even though we already were.

When they leave, a small tug returns.

Chapter 24

I hold Casmir's hand as we make our way through the tunnels of the mountain to the hidden library. He explained that nobody in the castle can know we are meeting with the witch, so Emrys snuck her in while the prince and I occupied ourselves elsewhere.

We enter the library, and I remember to ask how it's kept hidden since it is an illusion; as far as I know, no fae have magic like that. Apparently, when this castle was built centuries ago, there were more witches alive than the two left today. His father paid a powerful one to create an illusion spell along the entire border of the library so that anyone who didn't know it was there wouldn't be likely to find it. Unless they tripped and fell into the fake wall, I suppose. That is the only entrance and exit to the large room, making it even more difficult to find.

We depart the elevator on the bottom floor, where there are no lights or books, but rooms that are used for storing valuable artifacts and holding meetings like this. Casmir leads me through the extremely dim light with a hand pressed to my back. I tap my fingers against my thigh, suddenly feeling more nervous than I was before. If she can't help, I will truly feel lost and defeated. There's no way for me to reach the god who did this unless she comes to Earth, which could take hundreds of years, if not millennia. My palms begin to feel sticky and my cheeks flush. Now is not the time for me to panic over something I don't even know the answer to yet.

Casmir senses my whirring thoughts and stops me. "You can do this, Nell," he encourages, caressing my cheek with his palm. I lean into the comfort. "All we're doing is talking to her. Whether she can help or not, there's absolutely *nothing* you need to agree to. You can walk away at any point, and I will support your decision."

I nod my head, silently thanking him as my breath feels less constricted. Entering the room, Emrys is sitting on one of the two black couches facing each other, the witch on the second. A fire is illuminating the space, but no other lights are on. There is a table made of the mountain rock seated in the middle of everything. That is all that's in here. The space is compact and intimate; also private, which is what we needed for this meeting.

I take a hesitant seat next to Emrys while the prince lowers himself on my other side. Raising my eyes to Ivana, I take in her appearance. Her skin shows wear, and I would guess she's in her forties, though I have no clue how long witches live. If their lifespan is anything like the fae or more like humans. She's wearing her black hair in a bun, several strands falling out and surrounding her narrow face. A deep red gown covers her body, along with a black cloak that I'm assuming she used for her way in here. She has a gold chain clasped around her thin neck, with a large pendant sitting just above her cleavage. The pendant is a gold band holding what appears to be a small vial filled with a red liquid.

Blood.

I lift my gaze to hers, expecting her to have a cunning and grim aura around her, but her deep red eyes are crinkled at the edges from the wide grin she's giving me. Maybe witches are only mean in fairy tales?

"Hello, Nell. I'm Ivana," she nods her head in greeting. "I assume you've been told who I am and what I'm here to do?" I look over to Casmir, who nods, telling me I can trust her with this information.

"Yes. I seem to have missing memories, and have been trying to find a way to free them so I can figure out who I am. I've had no luck, and was hoping maybe you would be able to help."

She smiles warmly. "I will see what I can do, though I will need to look inside your head first to determine if I can help."

My brows furrow. "What do you mean 'look inside my head?'" I question.

"I will just feel around for the magic that was used on you. I will also be able to see what exactly was done to your memories."

I clasp my hands together, nervous to have someone else in my head when I'm trying to get rid of the last one that was there. But I knew this is what I was agreeing to; I can't expect her to help me without poking around my brain at least a little.

With my decision made, I look back up to her, nodding. "Okay," I whisper.

"I will have you sit next to me, as I need a physical connection to do this." I stand and move over to her while she continues, "This may feel uncomfortable, but it will not hurt. I'm just looking for now and will do nothing more." She adjusts herself to face me.

"Are you ready?"

I glance to Emrys and Casmir, both of them looking concerned but trusting me to make this decision for myself. I offer them a reassuring smile before turning back to Ivana.

"I'm ready."

She stretches both arms to touch my temples. "Close your eyes." I do.

After a moment of silence, I feel a pressure in my head and recoil at the sensation. Like she said, it doesn't hurt, but it's strange. It feels like thick smoke traveling through every crevice of my brain, searching for something specific. After a few minutes, the heavy feeling evacuates, and I take a deep breath at feeling fully myself again.

Ivana jerks her hands back, folding them in her lap, looking spooked by something.

I'm hesitant to ask, but I need to know. "What did you see?"

She raises her chin, jaw clenching. She's clearly conflicted about something that she learned. "I can see your memories have been blocked, as you suspected. Numerous times, in fact." I rear back, wondering what the hell that means, but let her continue before I bombard her with questions. "The magic used to create these blocks was not that of the Goddess Aeryn." Okay, now I'm even more confused. How is that possible?

"It was blood magic."

My face pales as the knowledge sinks into my skin, leaving me itchy and uncomfortable. Casmir said there were only two witches left, and if it wasn't Ivana who did this to me, that leaves only one option. But even worse, that means someone in this realm did this to me. I would assume they live in the Veil. There's no way I haven't been recognized if that were the case. Someone lied to me.

"That means the other witch…" I can't finish the sentence, but Ivana nods anyway, knowing what I mean.

"My sister." My eyes snap to hers. Her *sister* did this? What could her sister possibly have against me?

"I have not spoken to her in over two centuries," well that answers one question, "and was not aware she was abusing magic in this way." She seems ashamed of her sister's actions. I don't blame her, but I understand her sentiment.

"Do you know why she would do this?" Emrys asks sharply. I give him a look to tone his attitude down, because she's just trying to help. He relaxes his shoulders a little.

"I apologize. I do not know," she ducks her head.

"It's okay," I say hastily, grabbing her attention. "It's not your fault, and I wouldn't blame this on you." I move on from the who and why. "Is this something you'd be able to fix?"

A haunted look passes over her features before she recovers and nods. "I can, but the cost will be high."

"I'll pay any amount you require to help her," Casmir sits forward, eyes pleading with Ivana.

She gives him a solemn smile. "No, Your Highness, that is not the cost I speak of." She takes a deep breath, preparing herself for whatever she needs to tell me.

"In order to obtain the amount of energy needed to undo what has been done, the Earth will require something just as powerful."

The crinkles next to her eyes are now from distress. Her posture is tight, nearly as tense as the males sitting across from me. Each of us watching her, waiting to hear what sacrifice will be required. Anxiety is flowing through me, and I swear I feel Casmir and Emrys's, too. I'm about to shake the answer out of her when she speaks.

"A piece of your soul."

The room is spinning. "I'm sorry. I don't think I heard you right. You said a *piece of my soul?*" I sputter incredulously. She offers the barest of nods.

I lurch out of my seat to pace the small room, tapping my fingers to my chest in a weak attempt to ground myself. I do not want to have a panic attack in front of anyone, but the gods have never been on my side. It's becoming hard to breathe, and I need to get out of here. I turn to the door, only to find Emrys stepping toward me.

He envelopes me in a tight embrace, just like last time, and I start to calm. The pressure grounding me better than I can do for myself. He sways me side to side, and I focus on his heartbeat, seeking to match my rhythm to his.

"You're okay, love," he whispers. "You don't have to decide today. You can take time to think about it, and we'll be here for you no matter what you decide."

"If you would like to move forward with this, I will meet with you in a week's time, at midnight. There will be a full moon, which is the time the Earth's energy is most abundant and powerful. It would give us the best chance of removing each spell."

A week? I'm not sure how anyone would live with a piece of their soul missing. I need to decide what's more important: my soul or my past life.

I'm leaning over the edge of the pool behind the waterfall. I told Casmir and Emrys that I wanted to be alone for a while, though I feel guilty for not including them. I just needed some time to my own thoughts, especially after everything that was revealed by Ivana yesterday.

She said there were different blocks inside my head, not just one. I've been gripping onto every reason I can find for why that would be, though not one makes sense. I suppose none of this makes any sense. But, the fact that I have multiple blocks tells me I created new memories after the original ones Ivana's sister wanted to suppress. How many times has she done this spell on me? And why does no one recognize me? None of these questions will really matter unless I go through with removing them from my head.

A piece of your soul.

Ivana's words ring through my head again and again. I asked the witch what it would mean to lose part of my soul, but she had no answer for me. This is not a sacrifice she has seen made before and knows no one with a fractured soul. Would it change me to lose it? Would I feel like a different person?

Maybe the hollow area in my chest will grow. When I'm with the prince and his second, it's like the essence of me lifts from the darkest depths to join my heart near the front of my body. The void that I normally feel there begins to fill up with ancient promise and ethereal light. Is that what a soul feels like? Because if so, then I've already lost a part of mine, and maybe I could handle losing another part.

I'm curious if the sacrifice for Ivana's sister was taking small parts of my soul each time she performed the spell. Forcing me to pay for her choices, and live through her layered consequences.

If I don't do this, then she wins. She gets what she wanted, for whatever reason she wanted it. But more than that, I won't be able to help Xamira. She has been by my side for much longer than I think I realize; she's been suffering along with me and she's warranted the help this would give her.

I also may never understand this connection between Emrys, Casmir, and I. It seems too important to ignore. They deserve to have answers, regardless of how I feel about it. All of that has to be enough for me to say yes.

I can do this. Live with this. *For them.*

Even if the sacrifice was my entire soul, I still might be inclined to agree for their benefit.

I hear a light splash behind me and whirl to see Emrys joining me; rolling my eyes, I chuckle at his inability to stay away.

"Technically, I did give you a while," he appeases playfully, and I give in, opening my arms to invite him over. He lifts me so that I'm straddling him, and presses my back to the rock behind me. I hiss at how cold it is, but he quickly fixes the crispy temperature.

"I may not be able to help with your decision," he discerns, his honeyed voice matching the complexion of his eyes. "But I *could* help in other ways." I bark out a laugh at his insinuation; he always knows how to turn every situation into something sexual.

"You and Cas are insatiable, dirty-minded, and insufferable," he chuckles, gripping me tighter and igniting sparks of electricity under my skin. "Thank you for the offer, but I'm sore as fuck from earlier." I sit up straight, my entire body tensing. Earlier. When we fucked, he and Cas coming inside me *again*.

"What?" He questions at my obvious anxiety.

"Em," I breathe, "I don't want to get pregnant right now. We haven't used condoms or…anything." I am so foolish. Before coming into the Veil, I thought that one of my particular *incidents* with a man when I was sixteen left me unable to have children.

My head is pounding. I feel weak and tired. I keep my eyes closed, not ready to face the light of day and make this headache worse. Just as I'm about to slip into unconsciousness again, everything comes back to me.

A large man. A dark alley. Pain and screaming and blood.

Another man who thought it was okay to use my body for his own pleasure, even when I said no. Except this time, I fought back. This time, I was so sick of being hurt that I used my jagged fingernails to claw his eyes out.

It didn't work.

He grabbed my throat and slammed my head against the wet concrete; my vision went fuzzy, and I no longer had control of my body. I tried to continue fighting back, but I was so dizzy and nauseous. He didn't stop there because why would he?

After he finished fucking me, he proceeded to pulverize my body. He drove his boot into my stomach several times before using that same boot to knock my face, covered with tears and shame, into the brick wall next to me. The entire time telling me I'm worthless. I'm a bitch for scratching his face. I'm going to die for that.

Die for defending myself. That makes sense.

That's the last thing I remember before now. I crack open my eyes, groaning at the pain of such a simple movement. The room comes into focus; I'm in a hospital bed, a white room surrounding me, the overhead lights dimmed, but not enough to keep me from wincing. There's a blue chair next to my bed, as if someone has been sitting here with me. I don't know who would. I don't have anyone.

There's a whiteboard on the wall next to me that says Jane Doe at the top. I guess that's expected since I don't have an ID, or anything, and no one would have come to claim me. A beeping sound collides with my ears and hacks away at the last of my sanity. I move to turn the machine off, or bash it into the fucking wall, but the door opens just then.

A woman with long, caramel hair, pulled back into a ponytail, walks in. She's wearing a pair of baby pink scrubs. The top has farm animals printed all over it. She's looking through some papers on her clipboard when she glances up, doing a double take.

"Oh my darling girl, you're awake!" She rushes over to my side, and I cringe back. "I'm sorry, I don't mean to frighten you, sweetie. Do you know where you are?"

I nod. "A hospital," I attempt to say, but my voice is weak and brittle.

She turns to grab a cup of water, holding the straw up to my mouth. "Take a few sips, but not too much, or you'll hurt your stomach." I do. Once I settle back, exhausted from that small task, she sits in the blue chair.

"Do you remember what happened to you?" I nod and she purses her blurry lips mournfully. "You have been unconscious for six days." She lets that sink in, but I sense that there's something even worse she needs to say, so I don't respond.

"You were in…poor shape when you arrived. Doctor Walsch needed to perform surgery to stop your internal bleeding," tears form in her eyes, and I steel myself for what's coming next. "I'm so sorry, hon. The damage was too much, and you needed to have a few organs removed. Because of this, you can never have a baby."

My head spins. I'm not even an adult yet, so I've never thought about having a child of my own. But to have that choice taken from me? By a random man, that took other things from me?

I feel sad, but I was expecting to die in that alley, so I'm not shocked at what needed to be done in order for me to live. I keep my expression neutral, listening to everything else she's telling me. Six broken ribs, a cracked nose, damage to my bladder, and a ruptured appendix. That doesn't include the bruises covering my body, or the split in my head; which, lucky me, doesn't look like anything but a minor concussion.

She then mentions a rape kit that was done, and my eyes snap to hers. "We were able to gather…evidence from what the man left. I hope the police will catch the guy."

Spoiler: they never did.

She talks about the different things I should expect for recovery, and how long I will need to stay in the hospital. After a while of me half paying attention, she stands and steps over to the whiteboard.

Erasing the Jane Doe at the top, she turns to me with a warm smile.

"All right, my dear, what is your name?"

But now I know that memory never happened, it was just planted in my head. I've always used condoms with humans, when the sex was my choice, because it just grossed me out not to. With Andras, he never came inside me, thank all the gods.

But I haven't used any form of protection with Cas and Em, never having needed to truly think about it before. I haven't had a period yet..actually, now that I think of it, I haven't had a period in years. Does this mean I can't get pregnant? I would rather assume I can, and take precautions, because I *do not* want a child right now.

"Hey, get out of your head, love. There's nothing to worry about."

"What do you mean there's nothing to worry about? I'm sorry, Em, as much as I lo—" I take a deep breath before my emotions have me admitting things I haven't come to terms with yet. "As much as I care for you and Cas, there is no fucking way I'm about to get pregnant. Does Plan B even exist here?"

He plants a tender kiss on each of my cheeks before speaking calmly. "It's not a worry because a lot of males choose to have a procedure done when they're of age that prevents us from impregnating females. When we're ready to try for children, we can have the procedure undone. Cas and I have both had the procedure," he winces, but continues. "You can't imagine the amount of females who would love nothing more than to have the child of a royal."

That's smart because, no, I never thought of how many females would try to do that. Also, the males are the ones preventing birth? No hormones or extremely painful surgeries involved? I laugh at how crazy that idea would be outside of the Veil.

"Thank you. I was freaking out a little." I give him a sheepish smile. He presses his lips to my forehead, and I melt at the vulnerable gesture.

"I wish I could stay here with you all day, but the guard are back today, and I need to have a meeting with them."

I dress and walk back to the castle with him, determined to say yes to Ivana. A piece of my soul for everything else seems like a fair trade.

Chapter 25

My eyes widen as I walk into the training arena. It's on the top floor of the castle and takes up the entire west wing, it seems. There are floor to ceiling windows being utilized as three of the walls, with the waterfall being just outside. The back wall, where we entered, is made of the same rock as the mountain. I ache to come up here during a sunset; I bet the view is incredible. I put the thought on my mental to-do list.

There's a deep red sparring mat in the middle of the room. Behind me is a wall of weapons, not unlike what I saw with Bren back in Ceross. There's also an indoor track circling around the room, though I'm not sure why you couldn't just run in a circle without the lines? There's different equipment stationed throughout other open areas; instruments that look like they belong in a gym.

What's most interesting is one wall of windows has four different elemental stations to practice magic. There is a small, raised pool in one section, a fire pit in another, and a compact garden in a third. The last section has a few random objects in it, so I assume that's just meant for air. I notice that there is no space for essence magic, but I suppose that makes sense since only the Goddess Aeryn possesses it. She would have no use for a training arena on Earth.

Casmir insisted on bringing me here after Emrys informed him of our incident in the library the other day. My muscles tense in anticipation, because I know I'm going to shock the both of them. They saw me running at the Ceross castle, but they know nothing of my ability to fight. I haven't trained since my time with Bren; a twinge of sadness swipes through me at the thought of him.

I shake it off, my body straining to release the tension and stress that have built since meeting with Ivana. I'm nervous about what will happen—

No.

I will not let myself think about any of that right now.

"And why have you guys been hiding this place?" I place my hands on my hips and give them my best 'are you kidding?' look.

Em stretches his beautiful muscles and I watch, not hiding my keen appreciation. He meets my gaze. The color of his eyes looks like smoldering caramel in the afternoon light that's gleaming in through the windows.

"You never asked about it." I roll my eyes at the tease and entertain the thought of getting him back. I turn and saunter toward the mat to hide my smile, knowing exactly what will throw him off balance.

I stand in the middle of the deep red and hold one of my arms with the other, pasting an uncomfortable look on my face. It must work because Cas stops in front of me and grabs the nape of my neck, placing a light kiss on my nose.

"You'll do great. We just want to see where you're at in skill and help you improve," I quirk, one side of my mouth nodding.

"Thank you, I appreciate that." The smile that raises on my face is genuine.

Emrys steps onto the mat with a stern look on his face. "When you took me down in the library, I was stunned, so I didn't quite grasp what you did. But it was impressive, nonetheless. So let's see what you got," he motions for me to get into stance.

I move my legs apart incorrectly and hold my arms up at an angle, feeling foolish, but the look on his face will be priceless when he realizes what I'm doing. He sees my stance and attempts to hide his laugh with a cough, trying not to embarrass me.

"Uh, more like this, love," he moves my body into the correct position. "Okay, so I'm going to attempt to pin you, and you just do your best to not let me. This will help me determine where we should start training." I nod, peeking over at Casmir, who's giving me a curious look. He definitely has a suspicion, but thankfully is keeping his mouth shut about it.

Emrys lunges at me, and I discern that he's going to grab for my right arm, most likely to fold it behind me and knock me onto my torso. I let him.

This time.

I make a grunting noise when he pins me and he immediately lets go, focusing on helping me up and glancing over my body to see if he hurt me. He sighs in relief when he realizes he didn't, and amusement takes over his face.

"That was an okay start. Let's do that same thing again, but this time I want you to hold yourself in your position and try to block me." I almost feel bad; he's trying quite hard to be nice about this. But this is what happens when you tease me, so he has it coming. I nod back coyly, my blood shuffling in every direction when he falls for it.

I turn toward Cas and give him a wink, because his eye roll tells me he's very aware of what I'm about to do. I face my sparring partner and lower myself into the stance once more. He charges me, and before he can grab my arm, I step to the side and kick my leg out, tripping him and he falls on his face. Casmir barks out a loud laugh, and I have to bite my cheek to not follow his lead.

"Oh my gods, Em, are you okay?" I reach for him, feigning concern.

He stands, looking confused about how I knocked him down. "I'm good. You did good. Let's go again."

He runs toward me a third time, but I decide I've had enough fun playing with him. I leap and swing my leg over to catch him at the neck, using the power in my motion to bring his body with me, twisting him around until we're on our backs. I crunch my body upwards, grabbing his arms and folding them over his chest; I use them to swing myself over his body and land straddling his hips.

Keeping him pinned beneath me, I grin at the look of pure disbelief coming from him. "How was that?" My voice is musical. He attempts to push me off so he can stand, and I use my unusual strength to hold him there a moment longer before letting him go, making sure he knows he won't be winning another fight against me.

"I can't believe you fell for that, Em. She was clearly playing you," Cas chuckles, teasing his companion.

Emrys ignores him, instead looking at me with blatant confusion on his face. "How did you do that, Nell? Where did that come from?" I shrug because I don't have an answer to those questions. I just know what I'm doing and I assume it, like everything else in my life, has to do with my blocked memories.

"I'm really not sure, I just do it," I explain lamely.

"Well okay...lets go again." And we do. At least a dozen more times, though I lost count after the sixth, because he came at me pretty aggressively. I could tell he was getting increasingly frustrated that I kept taking him down, but one thing I've never been called is a good sport. I'm exceptionally competitive and wouldn't even let Xamira win against me. Some may call it a flaw, but I call it vitality.

After pinning him down again, I back up and opt to press his patience. "So...what do you think I need to improve on, Captain?"

Casmir covers his mouth and hops away, removing himself from Emrys's alluring wrath. I bite my lip and raise my eyebrows, taunting him.

A wicked gleam grows in his eyes and he marches toward me with purpose. "You know what? Sassy girls get punished," his voice gravelly as he picks me up by my hips and throws me over his shoulder. I squeal at the motion, and giggle hysterically from the adrenaline and anticipation. He carries me over to one of the walls; I'm not familiar enough with this room to know which way we're headed, especially when all I can see is his round ass. I grab it tightly, making him jerk forward and smacking mine sharply.

Before I can say a word about how hard that was compared to what I did to him, I'm flying back over his shoulder and being dropped into a pool of water. The icy feeling spreads across my skin, causing me to cringe inwardly.

Oh my gods, I am going to get that insufferable male.

I lurch upwards, standing and facing my very good-looking assailant. "Emrys, I swear to the gods you're going to pay for that," I laugh with a determined strain to my voice. I step out of the pool, lifting my hand and stepping forward to spin around and throw a mass of water at his face.

It hits him.

I just threw a sphere of water at Emrys without touching it…and it hit him exactly where I wanted it to, causing him to fly backward and roll onto the sparring mat. My vision blurs, and I faintly notice Casmir running over to his second to help him up. I'm staring down at my hands, trembling, because *I just used magic.* I've been trying for months to feel—or do—anything and haven't been able to. I think that the ability to know what magic I have, and how to use it, is locked inside my head with the rest of my life. But this? This was pure bodily instinct, just like my ability to fight.

I have water magic.

I don't know how long I'm standing there, hearing my two males try to talk to me, and feeling them touch me. Their voices sound muffled, as if they were speaking low through the other side of the hallway door. Their touches are distanced, almost like an actual memory would feel, I imagine. Eventually, the room comes back into focus, and I can think again. I peer up to Casmir and Emrys from my spot on the ground—I must have sat at some point during my episode—and they're seated in front of me with worried looks on their faces.

Casmir has a sheen of liquid in his eyes, and I feel guilty for not saying something sooner, knowing how deeply he feels. Emrys feels just as strongly, though he's much better at hiding it. He watches me with his brows furrowed, but no tears ready to escape, just his rich curls dripping water down his cheeks.

"I don't know how I did that," I whisper lightly into the disorienting silence. "I just had a feeling in my gut telling me what to do and I *did*." I tell them how I've been trying to find out what magic I have since I arrived in the Veil. I explain my theory on how the mind and body have different memories; how the witch who put the blocks in my head couldn't also put them in my muscles, and that's why I think I can fight and use magic now, apparently. I don't mention how Andras helped me come to that conclusion, not wanting to say his name ever again.

They both listen intently, Casmir twirling his fingers through mine the entire time.

"So you have water magic. That's amazing, Nell," Em says sincerely. "With everything you've been through, I wouldn't expect you to take all of these new discoveries in stride." He scoots forward to grasp my face in his palms. "I'm proud of you."

I swallow hard, tensing my abdomen and holding my breath, trying not to let those four words affect me. I nod, not trusting myself to speak, and my eyelids flutter with pent up emotion. Why does that mean so much to me? I've *never* had anyone tell me they were proud of me; but still, I shouldn't be so worked up over it. I take in a shaky breath, willing all thoughts to go away so I can focus on what's in front of me.

Casmir brings my hand to his lips, kissing the back. "You are everything, princess," his throaty voice catching me off guard.

I lean forward to grab both of their necks, planting a demanding kiss on each of them before we decide to be done with training for the day. I'm curious to see if I could replicate what I did in the arena. Maybe if I get my body in a certain emotional state, it will allow me to. But I let the thought drop, not wanting to get my hopes up and have something else go wrong.

Chapter 26

I 'm lounging in the seating area near my room, attempting to read through another book to keep my mind occupied. It's not working so well. As much as I want to know more about the *Characteristics of Magic*, my thoughts stray toward everything else going on.

It's been three days since I decided to go through with the sacrifice, in exchange for my memories. Random anxieties plague my conviction, and I just have to keep reminding myself why I'm doing this. I'm doing this for me; to find out who I am, where I'm from, how old I am, even. I'm doing this for Xamira, who was there when everything happened and stayed with me even after. I'm doing this for Casmir and Emrys, who I have a strange connection with, and they deserve to know why.

I'm thankful they have been sleeping with me each night, or I would look like a zombie right now. Their touch seems to keep the panic and nightmares at bay, and allow me to wake up rested.

I look up to see Leia approaching with a determined look on her face. Closing the book I'm reading, I give her my full attention with a smile.

"My Lady," she says with a small smirk, and I roll my eyes but don't comment. I've asked her so many times to call me Nell, but she insists on the formalities; though I'm convinced she continues the behavior just to tease me.

"Prince Casmir has requested your presence at a party that is being held later this evening in the castle."

"Party? He hasn't mentioned anything about this before?"

She nods and, in a more quiet tone, explains, "This is a party held once a year for the Anlorian council members. It is a more intimate, private event, and would not have been announced to anyone except the attendees."

Interesting. I wonder why Casmir didn't mention it. It must have just slipped his mind, since this doesn't seem to be a big event. Picking up the books I have gathered and standing, I turn to Leia, ready to do anything else except be consumed by my own head.

"Should I wear anything specific? Or is it just more casual?" I say, gesturing down to my leggings and fitted long sleeve shirt.

She grins, an amused glint appears in her eyes, "The Prince has had an outfit delivered to your room for you to wear." My brows furrow. If he wanted me to attend, he could have at least prepared me.

"Thank you, Leia." She offers a small bow, letting me know she will find me in an hour, and heads back the way she came.

I stroll over to my room, curious to see what Casmir could have possibly picked out for me, anticipation running through my veins. Closing my door, I see a dress laying on the bed and scrunch my nose, confused because there's no way he'd want me wearing *this* to a party? Especially a party full of the council? I think the only time I've ever worn a dress around him was when I met him and Emrys at the Solstice Ball in Ceross. But this is definitely not a gown.

I slide the dress on and look in the mirror, my eyes widening in surprise. This seems rather scandalous for the occasion. The top of the dress is a mesh, black fabric; the sleeves are long and puffed out slightly. The bodice is a corset, with fabric the same black mesh as the sleeves, and there is a dark boning around it. At the top of the two middle boning pieces is a circular piece of opaque black fabric, which is *just* enough to cover my nipples. The flattering ridge of the bodice dips into a heart shape, forming around my breasts and doesn't cover but a couple inches above the center, leaving me feeling like they will fall out at any second.

The dress changes at the waist, sticking out a bit from the layers of black mesh all sewn together, but not enough to make me feel overpowered. The fabric from the waist stops just below my ass cheek, meaning that if I bend in any direction, everyone will get an eyeful of everything down there. The prince was generous enough to include a thong with the dress, so I at least have the semblance of coverage. He also left me a pair of matte black heels, which make my legs look quite nice.

I pick up a small box I find under the clothing and gape when I open it. The necklace. The silver chain with obsidian that I saw in Veardale…how did they know I was looking at it? I admired it for only a moment.

I'm grinning to myself, feeling giddy, as I clasp the chain around my neck. It looks nice with the outfit he and Em picked, but more than that is I have the same pull to it that I did back in the village. Not as intense as what I feel with my males, but it's there. I remind myself to thank them later.

I decide to leave my hair mostly down, pinning half of it up in a messy bun and leaving some strands out to frame my face. I survey the dress further and decide to add a little liner to my eyes along with a tinted gloss that makes my lips look puffy and shimmering with pink.

After one last look in the mirror, I conclude this party is being held at a nightclub.

I'm almost tempted to put on one of the other dresses in my too large closet, but Leia said this was delivered for the party, so I'm going to trust Casmir and risk wearing what is basically lingerie. I take a deep breath, scratching the top of Xamira's head while she purrs, and wait for Leia to collect me.

Never mind.

I suddenly do not feel like this dress is scandalous at all. In fact, compared to what the other females are wearing, I feel like I'm dressed quite modestly. I look to my left and see one has on a red, silk dress that is so short you *actually* can see her bare ass. The top of the dress dips down and rests below her heavy breasts, so they are fully out. But she is wearing red heart stickers over her nipples.

Another is dressed in a bodysuit that is made of one piece of deep green fabric. It wraps around her neck, and is pulled down in between her legs so that her breasts and vulva are covered. She turns to whisper something in her companions ear, and I see that the fabric ends up in a thong, running up her spine and connecting to the loop around her neck. Interesting, though I can't imagine that's at all comfortable.

I look around the large room; the front seems to be an area used for mingling, while there is a table at the back large enough to seat everyone here.

I can't make out many details. The space is very dark, the only lights are sporadically placed lamps on the walls, and even those are barely illuminated. I would be more creeped out if I didn't get sidetracked by the dancers. There are four platforms, one in every corner on this side of the room, surrounded by black caging, each containing one or two fae.

The cage closest to me has a male and female dancing intimately to the instrumental music playing throughout the space. The female is wearing only a little slip of cloth in between her legs, while the male is wearing nothing, and his cock looks painfully hard. I wonder if they're going to fuck?

I get my answer when I spot another cage that has two female fae, both naked and covered in paint. Deep blue, burgundy, and black streaks envelop different places on their bodies, highlighting their curves and muscles. At the moment, one female is leaning against one side of the cage, her legs open in a split and resting on small platforms attached to the bars on either side, allowing her to bare herself to the room in mid-air. The other female is on her knees, absolutely devouring the first female's pussy. The music must be louder than I thought, because I can just barely hear the moans coming from their direction.

There are more fae here than I expected, though I suppose the council members would probably bring guests to an event like this.

This is not the party I was expecting, and I feel out of my depth, especially since Casmir didn't think to warn me ahead of time. Actually, knowing him, he most definitely kept me in the dark purposefully. That impossible male; he may be sweet and calm on the outside, but he is just as depraved as Emrys on the inside. Em just likes to flaunt his wicked thoughts.

While I'm a bit uncomfortable, I find nothing wrong with enjoying pleasure, even in front of others. It's just not something I've ever partaken in. I wonder why this is the type of party Casmir has for his council…and why the council seems to like it? They're basically at a sex party with their coworkers. I've been in the Veil for months and still find things about the fae culture to be surprised about.

I feel a tugging sensation and turn my gaze to a shadowy part of the room, spotting Emrys standing with a drink in his hand, watching the others enjoy themselves. He appears quite bored, leaning against the wall in his black pants and fitted shirt that shows off every one of his spectacular muscles. I saunter my way toward him and when his eyes find me, my knees almost buckle.

His lips part while he takes in every inch of my body. The heat in his inspection has me feeling like I'm walking through a raging fire. He licks his lips, shaking his head, while his free hand comes up to run across his mouth and chin. He looks like he's fighting for control within himself while also struggling for air, and I smirk.

I come to a stop, my breasts brushing his chest, raising an eyebrow in amusement at his reaction to me. I mean, I thought I looked good, but not good enough to make this male nearly die at the sight of me.

"You look," his voice gravelly, "*deific*. I want to bend you over this fucking table and claim you as mine in front of all of them." He steps closer, pinching a barely hidden nipple between his fingers until it stings, rubbing the pain out with the pad of his thumb. I gasp at the motion, feeling my pulse race at the thought of others seeing us.

"But what I want more is to rip the heads off every one of these bastards for being in your presence. *They do not even deserve the concept of you*," he growls, grabbing my throat and smashing his lips roughly on mine in a demanding kiss.

A moan stumbles out of me at his dominating words. My arms find their way around his neck, and I grab his hair to pull him closer to me, wishing I could swallow him whole. I know the stretching of my body probably has my entire backside hanging out, but I can't seem to find it in me to care right now; my sole focus is on the perfect male in front of me.

Emrys breaks our kiss too soon, gripping my throat tight enough to restrict my air, but not tight enough that I can't breathe. He hovers his lips over mine, breathing me in, and says in a deadly voice, "You are mine, Nell." All I can do is nod, taken by the possessiveness radiating off of him in waves. I'm not sure where this intense side of him came from, but I'm starving for more.

He lets me go, spinning me to face the room where it's clear a few of the other fae were indeed watching us, but turn their attention somewhere else when we look their way. Emrys rests his arm over my shoulders, ensuring there are no questions about who I belong to, and I feel a torrent of butterflies swarming my insides.

I'm not one to let *any* male control me, but I will play his game with a smile on my face tonight. My thong is already feeling too wet at the thought.

"Where is Casmir?" I say with a feathery tone, trying to rein myself back in enough to make it through this party.

"He is usually the last to appear at these things."

"And what, exactly, is *this*?" I gesture to our surroundings, now full of more pleasured sounds and heated looks, "I don't understand why this is the kind of party that's had for the council?"

Emrys drags his fingers from the base of my throat to the bottom of the corset, the touch sending heat to every part of my body. "Teryn began these parties decades ago to show his *appreciation* for the council, but it's always been to just feed their egos. They like to feel powerful and important.

"Cas continued the tradition, but made the parties a little more," he leans down, his mouth hovering next to my ear, "fun." A tingling sensation shoots up my spine, and I swallow hard.

Before I can ask anything else, he continues, "Normally I find these things to be rather annoying, but I have a feeling my opinion will change tonight." He presses a kiss just under my ear, making me shiver, and my head tilts to offer him better access.

If this is how they'll be acting all night, there's no way I'm going to make it through alive. I'm already throbbing so hard it hurts, and he's barely touched me.

I go to ask what he means, but the conversations of the room die off as the prince walks in, and *gods* does he look good. He's wearing black trousers with a white button up partially tucked in, sleeves rolled up to expose his forearms, and only buttoned to the bottom of his sternum, showing a good portion of his hard chest. I bite my cheek to keep my sound of appreciation from exiting my mouth. I'm so turned on I almost walk over to lick his exposed skin and thank him afterwards. Emrys keeps me planted with his arm tightly holding me, probably knowing exactly what I'm thinking.

He must feel how much I'm struggling, because he reaches his hand further down to tug on my nipple again, giving me a little of the friction I crave, but it's not even close to enough. I lean back into him and Casmir finds us, an evil grin spreading across his face when he sees how we're standing.

He turns to the rest of the room and announces that everyone is to migrate to the table for a meal.

Chapter 27

I walk with Emrys over to where the others are now getting seated; the large armchairs are so tall they're grazing the underside of the table when they move. I realize that out of the two seats left open at the table, there are only Casmir, Emrys, and me left standing.

"You'll be sitting with us tonight, Nell." I startle at the prince, who is now on my other side. He shares a look with Emrys, though it's too dark in here to make it out properly. Casmir grabs my waist and leads me over to his seat at the head of the table, Emrys to his right. The rest of the council, and their guests, are filling up the other seats. He lowers into his chair, and I now understand what he meant, because he pulls me into his lap. His hand holds my abdomen while he pushes the armchair further under the table.

I know exactly why they didn't tell me about the party...this is a game they're playing, and I am their pawn. Emrys confirmed that in not so many words a few minutes ago. I tremble at the thought of what they plan to do.

Staff bring out various dishes and line them up across the middle of the table, separating our view from some others. It's too dark to see them anyway, but the layout is interesting, and I wonder if it was purposeful.

Casmir fills up a plate full of roasted vegetables, herbed chicken, and diced potatoes covered in a garlic and dill sauce. He takes his time feeding the both of us, not allowing me to reach for anything but my wine. It feels strange to be fed, and the others must think so, too, because they keep sending intrigued glances our way. I let him continue, though, ready to be their toy for the night.

After he's satisfied with how much I've eaten, he sets his utensils down, grabs my hips and presses a kiss where my neck meets my shoulder. I arch back into him at the contact, letting his jasmine scent seep into me. Before I can move any further, he whispers into my ear, "Em and I chose your outfit tonight for one specific reason." Goosebumps slide over my skin at his dark tone.

"What's that?" I say, feeling like I'm about to find out just what they're planning.

He smiles into my neck. "Easy access." Before I can comprehend what he said, one of his hands grabs my thong and rips it clean off my body. I jerk in his grip, not having been prepared for *this* kind of game. I thought maybe they'd taunt me with vulgar words and watch me try to hold myself together. But I should have expected more—they are always more.

I've never been shy about enjoying different sexual adventures, but this has me feeling a twinge of fear. How far are they going to take this? I'm suspicious, but excited to find out the answer.

Casmir pockets my panties, and I look over my shoulder at him, only to find a playful look on his face. I just know whatever he has planned is utterly sinful.

He sits back in his seat, using his knees to press my legs open and hold them to the sides of the chair. I freeze, not sure what to expect from here, but I'm wound so tight from anticipation that I tremble every time I feel a light breeze. Interestingly enough, there shouldn't be any *breezes* in this room.

We sit for a while, just listening to the conversation some of the others are having. I can't concentrate on a thing they're saying when I'm waiting in complete suspense. Casmir hasn't touched me further, except to rest a hand on my thigh, leaning his head against the other. I squirm, need thrumming through my body at the speed of light, but he has my legs pressed so tightly against his that I can't move very much. I feel him chuckle beneath me, and the motion has me clenching. This impossible male is going to find himself cock-less if he doesn't do *something* right fucking now.

"Cas," I say, my voice breathy and strained.

"Yes, princess?" I hear the smile in his voice   he knows exactly what he's doing to me, and he's enjoying every second of it. "Can I help you with something?"

"You know precisely what you can help me with," I practically snarl. If their game was to work me up and then tease me to death, they're succeeding.

"Hm," he feigns ignorance, "I don't think I do. Would you care to be more specific?" The hand on my thigh tightens, causing me to tremble even more. How am I this feral and he hasn't even touched me?

I groan, knowing that my begging will get me nowhere right now. He wants me to suffer. I lean forward to grab my wine, taking a large drink, and Casmir decides that's the perfect time to shove two fingers inside of me. I cough my wine back into my glass, trying not to choke. I continue to sputter into a cloth napkin, having gotten some wine in my windpipe. The contractions from my cough only make me clench around him, and I bury my face in the napkin, trying to hide my reaction from the rest of the table.

My coughing slows, the pleasure increasing as he slowly massages my inner walls, and Casmir leans forward, saying innocently, "Are you all right?" To the rest of the table, he looks like a concerned prince, but I see the laughter in his gaze.

I narrow my eyes at him and nod, mumbling an apology to those who turned my way in concern. Once everything has settled, and conversations return to full volume, Casmir pulls me back into his chest and I go willingly, at the edge already.

"That was fast, Nell," he murmurs into my hair, taking in a deep breath of my scent. "All it took to make you come undone was one thrust of my fingers," he curls them with his words, making my walls clench. He presses his palm to my center, and I stifle a guttural moan as the orgasm rips through me. I bite my cheek in an attempt to hide the pleasure from my face.

"Seeing you come while the others watch, knowing I'm the one who's inside you, making you feel this way? *Fuck,* you are perfect." He removes his fingers from me, and I watch as he reaches up to suck them off, his eyes rolling back at the taste before returning to mine. One corner of his mouth lifts as his knees somehow widen my legs even further, and his hand returns to my pussy.

"Now be a good girl, and give me another," he demands as he circles my clit. Feeling too vulnerable to look at everyone else, I rest my head on my fist, covering my mouth. My eyes find Emrys, and he's staring at me like I'm the answer to everything.

I stay locked in his gaze, not daring to look away, while Casmir pumps his fingers in and out of me, using his thumb to put pressure on my very sensitive nerves. My eyes threaten to find the back of my head, but I keep them forward, looking at Emrys. I know that if anyone else glances our way, they could definitely tell what's going on.

Casmir picks up the pace, and I'm doing my absolute best to suppress the sounds trying to come out of my mouth...I can't tell if it's working.

I can't focus on anything except for these two males, who are driving me to the brink of insanity.

He curls his fingers just right, sending me over the edge, and I scrunch my eyes closed to keep quiet while I practically convulse in the prince's lap.

Emrys lifts my chin, narrows his eyes and demands, "You will look at me while he makes you come." I open my eyes more to hold his, the honey golden color glowing with desire. "That's it, love," he praises, sending me into oblivion. I grab onto Casmir's thigh and feel him laugh, probably enjoying the form of torture they've decided to bestow on me tonight.

I come down from the high, sweat lining my brow and my breathing erratic. Casmir removes his fingers, causing me to whimper at the over stimulation. Just then, Leia walks over to our part of the table and bows.

"My Prince, you are needed in your study."

"I am busy at the moment, Leia, can it not wait?"

She nods, lowering her voice so the others cannot hear, "You asked to be retrieved upon the arrival of a certain letter, Your Highness. It was just delivered and placed in your study."

He tenses at that, thanking her, and she makes her way back out of the room.

"I need to take care of this, princess. I will only be gone for a moment," he puts his hands on my waist, letting my legs go so that I can stand with him. "In the meantime, you will sit with Emrys." He kisses my temple, and moves me toward his second, who has a wild grin on his face.

I turn to face Casmir, concerned about whatever requires his imme-diate attention. Emrys takes that moment to grab my hips, pulling me hard onto his lap, and slamming his cock fully inside me. My eyes bulge out of my head while I scream at the intrusion. I force myself to cough to cover up the embarrassingly loud noise that comes out of me.

After a moment, I look up to see the entire table staring at me, and smile sheepishly, my body trembling at the cool metal running along my walls. "So sorry, I'm not feeling my best today," I try to wave it off, and most return to their enthralling conversations, while a few stare at me curiously for a minute longer.

Once the attention is off me, I look to Casmir, who's standing in front of his seat trying to hold in a laugh. He winks at me before walking off to take care of whatever is in his study.

Emrys pulls my hips back further, causing his thick length to move inside me just right. I whine at the insane amount of pleasure I'm experiencing, deciding that this is the worst form of torture.

He leans forward a little to talk in my ear, and I spasm at the movement. "You're doing so good, love," he purrs. "Seeing you take me like this is mesmerizing." He follows his words with a hand, dragging it to my lower abdomen, pressing in and causing my whole body to vibrate.

This is insane. Perfect, but insane.

I might die if he doesn't start moving.

I lean forward, resting my elbows on the table and arching my back; I use that hold to lift my hips the slightest amount. Emrys takes advantage of the little space I created and begins to gyrate, sending me spiraling into a black hole. I know nothing outside of this feeling.

I press my face into my hands, playing up the lie that I'm not feeling well, the freedom allowing me to not mask my facial expressions. Emrys continues to fuck me slowly with small thrusts, his piercings pressing in so good.

"Fuck," he murmurs, pressing harder into my abdomen. I can feel the pressure building at my core, and I know just a few more thrusts will have me seeing stars. Emrys must feel it, too, because he grabs my hair to roughly pull me back against his chest, forcing me to drop my hands. I peek at the others, who are still animatedly talking with one another, and Emrys turns my face to the side, where a pair of forest green and gold eyes are watching me. I have no idea when he came back to the party, but I don't think I'd know if the room was on fire at this point.

I turn my head more, my lips brushing against Emrys's. "Em," I whimper, lowering my forehead to his and breathing in his sweet scent.

He groans and says in a strained voice, "*Gods*, the sounds you make right before you come are hypnotizing." He lifts me off of him a ways before slowly sliding me back down his thick length, moving my hips back and forth when I'm fully seated. I release a stuttering moan into his mouth, thankful I'm facing away from the rest of the table, so they can't see the undiluted pleasure on my face.

He pinches my chin, forcing me to look at Casmir. "Watch him while I make you come. Let him see just how good I'm making you feel," and I do. Emrys reaches down with the hand not pressing on my abdomen, circling my clit lightly, and I lose it. I bite my lip so hard I taste blood, trying to suppress the moan I need to let out.

Casmir smirks at me, looking down at my hands, which are gripping the table so hard I'm surprised pieces aren't broken and falling off.

"Good fucking girl, Nell," Emrys whispers sharply in my ear. The tone of his voice tells me his restraints are snapping. He and Casmir share a look while I come down from the orgasm, coming to some kind of agreement between each other.

"Out," the prince says loud enough for the room to hear. All the noise stops, the other fae turning to look at him, confused.

"Out. Now." he commands, his powerful tone making me clench my thighs together. "The party is over. You can talk amongst yourselves elsewhere." He rests his head in his hand, looking annoyed, and staring each of the other confused fae down until the room clears.

"Thank gods," Emrys says, lifting me up off of him, and I don't suppress my moan this time. He stands, pushing my hips forward into the table, and swiping everything in front of us to the side, causing plates and utensils to clank against each other, some crashing to the floor from the aggression. He then grabs the back of my neck and forces me to bend, pressing my cheek into the cool wood. In the next second I feel him lift my dress up before thrusting his cock back into me, fucking me hard and fast, like he's not able to hold back any longer.

I'm taking everything he has to give me and enjoying each second; I'm definitely going to be sore tomorrow, but I don't give a fuck.

He reaches around to massage my nerves, adjusting himself to press his piercings right into that magical spot. I feel him stiffen, his cock growing slightly before spilling into me, causing me to go with him. Both of us are a panting mess by the time we come back to Earth.

He pulls out of me, and I sag into the table; he allows me no rest, lifting me to stand, and turning me to where Casmir is lounging in his chair, stroking his beautiful cock.

"We aren't done with you yet, love," Emrys says. I take the hint and saunter over to my prince, who looks downright godly. I stand in front of him and lift one leg at a time, straddling him, before slowly sinking down onto his incredibly impressive length.

We both groan at his entrance, and I pause when I'm fully seated, grabbing his face to kiss him. I give him all the passion and frustration I've experienced in these last hours. He returns my fierceness, wrapping his arms around my back to squeeze me into his torso. I break the kiss, resting my forehead against his, and ride him slowly, savoring the control I have in this moment.

I whimper at the sheer intimacy and intense pleasure. Casmir nods lightly to my unspoken words and whispers, "I know, princess."

So perfect, I hear him add, but his lips don't move. I would think more about it, but he tightens his hold on me while he stands and sets my ass at the edge of the table.

He pushes me to my back, taking my hips in his powerful grasp, and starts ferociously driving into me. He spits on my sex and rubs his fingers around my clit, sending my eyes rolling.

My hand reaches out, searching for my other male, and I pull him down to me to claim his mouth with my own. His tongue presses at the seam of my lips and I immediately open, inviting him in eagerly. He massages my breasts, our tongues dancing together and teeth clashing. Casmir continues to thrust, and I almost don't think I have it in me to orgasm again, but he lifts my hips with his free hand, angling himself perfectly, and I explode. Emrys inhales my scream of pleasure while I feel Casmir stiffen and find his own release inside of me.

After a few minutes, our breathing calms down; the prince is leaning over me with a hand on either side of my waist, and Emrys sitting on the table, brushing my hair with his fingers.

I don't think I can move; I am so tired but so content. Casmir pulls out and I wince, already feeling the effects of being fucked hard by two immortals.

I sit up, and our combined juices begin to seep out of me. Emrys walks over, reaching his hand under my dress and scooping his fingers through my folds, gathering some of the mess.

He lifts his other hand to my mouth, grabbing my cheeks and squeezing, forcing me to open.

"Suck." He orders, shoving his fingers to the back of my throat. "Taste how good we are together." I nearly gag from the thickness of his fingers but eagerly swirl my tongue around, taking in every bit that

I can. The sweet and salty taste makes me moan, causing Emrys to lick his lips. He pulls his fingers out, bringing them to his mouth to clean up anything I missed.

Casmir steps forward, grabbing my chin and pulling my face to his. He pins me with a hard look. "You're ours, Nell."

"Yours," I nod, and he plants a sharp kiss on my lips before lifting me in his arms. I snuggle into his warmth, feeling happy, and fall into a deep sleep before we're even out of the room.

Chapter 28

My head jerks to the side with the force of Ansa's punch; I feel blood pool in my mouth and run my fingers over my lips to see them come back covered in red. I laugh, probably looking like a maniac, but whatever. This is exactly what I needed.

Our meeting with Ivana is tomorrow night, and I've been gushing pure anxiety for days. After Emrys and Casmir's fervent *distraction*, as they called it, my worries have been growing larger by the minute. They both needed to leave the city to visit where their north army is stationed. It's not far from Anloria's outer wall, so they shouldn't be gone all day. But I was going to crawl out of my own skin pretty soon if I didn't do *something* and, thankfully, Ansa had a great idea.

"That was a good hit," I chuckle, licking excess blood from my lip. I've been training every day for the last week, and am much more comfortable with my movements now. My focus has sharpened, my muscles have woken up from a long sleep and are growing more in tune with my mind. After feeling so weak for years, it's incredible to be able to defend myself.

It's also a fun bonus to best every fae I've fought with; the prince, his second, and a few guard members, now including Ansa.

"After watching you spar with the others, I know damn well you could have blocked that," she says accusingly. She's right. I could have. But I let her make the shot, hoping that a little pain would help dampen my buzzing nerves. I was also right, though I am feeling tired. I've noticed I get worn out much easier than the rest of these fae, which tells me that I haven't conditioned my body in a long time. The thought sends a twinge of hatred through my veins, and I suddenly have a renewed sense of energy, ready to pretend Ansa is Ivana's sister.

I will continue to push my body and train myself to be better. I'm determined to be strong enough, mentally and physically, to confront whoever the fuck asked the witch to mess with my head. I'm about to find out exactly who that is, assuming Ivana's spells work.

I shrug at Ansa, smirking, and get back into position for another round. I spot movement to my right and turn to see a small flame floating in the air. Before I can say anything about it, I'm being tackled, a huff of breath leaving my lungs as my back slams into the mat. She used her fire to distract me. Impressive.

I hook my arm around her neck, pulling her into me and using the momentum to roll us. I jump off her, but she's already on me; grabbing my legs and throwing me over her shoulder, I tuck my head and roll into a standing position. My back is to her, so I spin and see a ball of fire headed straight for my face. I duck and right myself to glare at my opponent.

"That is certainly not fair, Ansa."

She smiles devilishly. "The enemy will never fight fair. You must use all available resources to your advantage." She has a point, as much as it annoys me. I haven't been able to harness the ability to manipulate water again, so I will have to be smarter than her magic.

We quarrel for a while, neither of us letting the other get the upper hand. I'm getting frustrated at her use of fire, since it's not something I can punch or kick my way through. She straddles my waist and throws two strikes to my cheek and jaw; I think I hear a crack, but I don't feel it or pay any attention, focused on taking her down. Before her hand reaches my face again, I jab her throat, causing her to choke and fall back with the effort of trying to breathe.

I lift into a crouch, but don't have time to feel guilty for taking it too far before she growls and heaves a large mass of fire at me. My body reacts to the threat, and I feel static rise, lingering just under my skin. I raise my arms and curl my hands. The fire stops just in front of me, and I shove it back toward her, spinning one hand in a circle, forcing it to restrain her in ropes of fire. I make sure it doesn't burn her, not wanting to hurt her yet, but instead taunt her. I pull water from the pool behind her, and hold it just above her head, letting her know I could drown her without a second thought if she tries anything else.

"NELL!" she screams. I don't listen. I move a rope of fire up to cover her mouth, shutting her dramatic voice up. She attacked me. What else does she expect?

Something appears in front of me; no, *someone*. Emrys. He's grabbing my shoulders and shaking me. I blink, awareness seeping through my pores, and unadulterated horror takes over my body. The static sinks back into the depths that I can't reach, releasing Ansa from the hold I had on her. I push Em out of the way, stumbling my way over to her and see Casmir already there.

"Ansa…I do—I—" I have no idea what just happened. "I'm so sorry." I whisper, shame flowing through me. How many times have I apologized for hidden skills that have hurt others? I'm such a disappointment. I just keep letting my body take over, and harm everyone in my life that I care for. I feel tears well in my eyes, mortified and guilt-ridden.

"Nell, it's okay," Ansa moves in front of me. "Seriously, it's fine. Crazier shit happens during magic training; and you didn't even hurt me. Though I would've easily healed if you had." She's trying to make me feel better after what I just did to her?

"You don't understand," my voice shaking. "I was going to drown you," I admit, looking up into her bright eyes. There's a flash of shock before she recovers.

"But you didn't. You weren't in control, Nell," she pleads. "This was my fault. I shouldn't have thrown the fire at you. I was angry and not thinking rationally, and your body responded just as it should have to my assault." I nod, not having anything else to add since my protests clearly won't be heard.

"Wonderful, we're all friends again. But are we not going to discuss how the *fuck* Nell just used water *and* fire magic?" Em declares to the large room.

"What's the big deal?" I say, frustrated. "You saw me use water magic the first time we were here. So I can apparently use fire, too. Just another secret hidden behind the blocks in my head."

"Princess," Casmir moves some stray pieces of hair behind my shoulder and caresses my arm tenderly. "What he means is we don't know of any fae who possesses two types of magic. As far as we're aware, nobody has *ever* had more than one type."

Oh great, more anomalies to add to the list. First my markings, then my fighting skills, and now my magic. All of it different from the fae that live here, which just further solidifies my decision to go through with meeting Ivana tomorrow.

I'm walking with Casmir and Emrys up a small path that leads to a flat area next to a cave in the Sunsor Mountains. We left the city and walked for an hour before climbing several large rocks to find this path. I was wary of climbing in nearly pitch black, the only light from the full moon that's taunting me, but my males have been here before and helped lead the way up.

A chill runs over me, raising the hairs on my neck, the smell of frost and gloom heavy in the air. A part of me is cold, even wearing a fleece-lined jacket and leggings, but the potent chill I feel is mostly from what I'm about to do. I am willingly going to let this witch inside of my head to undo what her sister did. I know Em and Cas trust her enough, but I barely know her; and to be honest, the idea of letting *anyone* in my head for this makes me nauseous.

We enter the clearing, none of us having spoken the entire way here. I can sense they are just as stressed as I am. Sure, this could work and I could have my memories back and answers to all these buried questions. But it could also go the opposite way; what if it, instead, just adds another block to my memories? Leaving me clueless about anything, including who the prince and his second are? I'm scared. But I need to do this.

Ivana comes into view; she's wearing that same large, black cloak I saw her in a week ago, and she's looking up to the sky, basking in the moonlight. Her crimson eyes find mine as the three of us approach, and she offers no smile or greeting this time. Her face is stern and ready to perform powerful magic.

"You came. I assume that is because you've decided to pay the cost required for this to be done?" Her voice is resonant and full of power.

"Yes."

She nods. "Before we begin, there are things you must know." I take a deep breath, and steel myself for the coming events. "First, this will hurt. A lot. I am removing things that have been melted through your head and are now a part of your body." I stare at her, having already expected that.

"Second, once we begin, we *cannot* stop. That is essential. If we were to stop during the spells, you could lose your memories forever. You may end up with mangled ones, never being able to piece together your truth. Or your memory store could clear out completely and you would be, in essence, a blank canvas. How babes are when they're born.

"You must agree to follow through, because I cannot help you if it is stopped." I also expected this, but I'm still hesitant. She seems confident that, as long as I keep going, we will remove the blocks. But I don't think it's that simple. Either way, *I need to do this*. Thinking about it further will just worsen my anxiety.

"I understand," I say sternly, and turn to my males while she prepares herself to begin. I take a hand of theirs in each of mine, and look them both in the eyes. Casmir's look like the forest on a dark, rainy day; he's scared for me, but he trusts me and won't stop me from doing this. Emrys, who is stoic in most situations, is watching me with his brows creased and lips trembling slightly. His beautiful, honey eyes are a deepened caramel in the moon's light.

They both understand what's happening here. I am going to get my memories back; figure out who I am, and who did this to me. I've been so certain for a while that none of that matters in the long run, because they're my home. I will be with them no matter what moving forward. They are mine and I am theirs. I haven't had the strength to admit this to them yet, and now doesn't seem like the right time, so they will just need to trust me.

"Cas," I glance at him again. "Em. You must promise me that no matter what happens, no matter what you see or hear, you will *not* interfere. Please."

The prince nods, warring with his need to protect me, and his need to trust that this decision is mine. Emrys doesn't move. He watches me, searching my eyes.

"Nell," he breathes, his voice wavering. "Whatever happens, you must know that I lo—" I cover his mouth with my hand, stopping him from saying something I can't hear right before I'm about to step into a possible death sentence. But they don't need to know my worries. They have enough of their own.

"Shh," I smile warmly, moving my hand to cup his cheek. "I am not going anywhere. We will get through this and be back home by morning with answers that we need." He opens his mouth to speak, but I shake my head, "Please, Em. Say it to me when this is done."

He relents, nodding hesitantly. He grabs the back of my neck and pulls me in, colliding his lips with mine. I hold on to him tightly, wanting to savor this moment in case it's the last I remember of them. We break apart, and he kisses my forehead. A tear slides down my cheek as I turn to Casmir and jump into his arms, kissing him with fervor. His fingers dig into my skin, as if he's unwilling to let me go, and for a moment I almost agree to it. But I pull back, holding his face and resting my forehead against his.

Lowering from him, I give them both my most reassuring smile before turning to face Ivana, my face dropping from panic. I move to stand in front of her, longing to take one more look at my males, but not trusting myself to continue if I do.

"Are you ready?"

No.

"Yes."

She turns her palms upwards and closes her eyes, speaking in a language I don't know. It sounds Italian, but I don't think that's correct. A sheen of sweat begins to cover my body, and my breathing becomes labored. Is this my own panic or the spell working?

I have my answer a moment later when a force as strong and sharp as a bullet slams into my head. I drop to my knees, my hands covering my ears, pressing at the pain and the noise. Is someone screaming? My throat burns from the force of being used.

I'm the one screaming.

The sharp, singular pain morphs into what feels like barbed wire being slowly pulled through every crevice of my brain. I'm screaming into the rock below me, barely able to hear myself through the blinding agony coursing through my head.

"KILL ME," I screech to anyone who will listen. "KILL ME." I can hear the males through the storm.

You have to keep going, Love.

You're doing so great.

Keep going and once it's done, it's over.

They're right. I agreed to this. I need to do this.

I understand I can't stop, but that doesn't help the sheer torture I feel; the burning, throbbing, stabbing, aching pain that is making me feel like my eyes are going to pop out from the pressure of whatever the witch is doing in my head.

No, I can't do this. I have to stop; I have to tell her—

Something bursts in my head, and a small amount of pressure dissipates. Are those memories? I see images of Xamira and I in our Chago apartment, but it looks different. Images of me at a job I don't remember working. They're flashing too fast for me to focus on one, but that doesn't matter because another bullet flies through my head, and I scream again.

My vision goes dark. I'm thrashing on the ground, begging the gods to just kill me already when I feel another burst. More memories. More pain. This happens twice more, more blocks being removed before the breath is stolen from my lungs.

This is the last block, but it's also the largest and most complex. I can feel its restraint to the spell. I can feel it warring with Ivana for control.

Oh, fuck. This is going to hurt.

White hot, searing pain tears through my body, my soul. This must be part of the sacrifice, as well. I can't feel anything any longer; I don't know where I am or how long I've been here…I know nothing. The pain lessens and then comes back full force, in waves. I sense my body is seizing at this point, and I can't imagine what Casmir and Emrys are seeing, and thinking, right about now.

The pain becomes so bad that I go numb; I think I passed out, though I can't tell for sure. Just when I think this is the end…that I walked right into my own death, and I prepare to say goodbye to the world, regretting not letting Emrys share his feelings, there's one final burst in my head. It takes all the air out of my lungs with it; it steals every part of my energy, but then the pain is gone.

When my senses start coming back, I realize I'm on my hands and knees, heaving. My lungs burn from the lack of air, my throat feels like thick claws have mauled it, and I taste blood in my mouth. But I'm alive.

I'm alive, and I know who I am. My memories are back.

All of them.

They're shuffling through my life at an impressive speed, and my heart lurches with all the things that were taken from me. Flashes of daggers, pain, and war go through my head as I try to grasp the reality slamming into me.

I can't believe I let this happen. This is my fault for being so naïve. I need to go back. I need to warn them. They won't have a clue what's happened here and what he plans to do.

I take a deep breath, needing a moment from the decades of memories slamming into my consciousness. I cross my legs and cup my head with my hands, attempting to slow my heart rate and breathing. I look up to see Casmir and Emrys and—

Oh my fucking gods.

"No," I wheeze into the silence, truly seeing them for the first time. This is so much worse than I thought it was.

No.

Fuck.

They're my soul bonds.

Chapter 29

I walk through the trees surrounding the back of the castle, heading towar the lake on the other side of the small forest. I'm going to meet Andras; he said he had a surprise for me, and tingles start deep in my stomach thinking about what he could have planned.

I'm starting to have feelings for him, though I cannot decide if that is a good or bad thing. I'm not new to the attention, or touch, of males but I have never felt the love and deep connection I always desired. I want someone to look at me like I am the one holding their world together; like if I left, or were taken away, they would stop at nothing, overcoming every trial and enemy to get me back.

I want to feel the passion I have read about in mortal books…to be kissed by someone like I'm their favorite taste, not being able to keep their hands off of me, and staring at me when they think I'm not looking. I want that. I know that's not realistic for me. I have heard stories in Europa that completed soul bondings are like that; having all the passion, pleasure, and love that I crave. Those are only assumptions, though, since none of the other gods have ever bonded.

Accepting my soul bonds is not realistic for me; I'm the only child of gods to ever be born. I have expectations I need to meet, and responsibilities I need to uphold in Semiria. And if I accepted my soul bonds, my status would be taken from me, and I would no longer be allowed on Europa. Gods cannot have both: love and power. In order to keep proper balance of the realms, Gods need to be objective and focused. My mother told me that those who are bonded do not have this ability, because their life purpose shifts from upholding the balance of the realms to protecting and loving their soul bonds.

Because of this, Gods must choose one or the other, responsibility or bonding; if they choose their bonds, they are stripped of their god status, so they can no longer enter Europa or be a part of the balance of the realms. They are to live on Earth with their bonded for the remainder of their lives.

That is why I wouldn't even bother looking for my bonds, since I would just torture myself knowing they are the only thing that I want but can never have. Touching them for the first time triggers the bond, causing irresistible longing for each other until the bonding ceremony is completed. Once the bond is triggered, it is nearly impossible to refuse. I cannot allow that to happen to me.

So, I will enjoy my time here with Andras, making sure he knows it could never be anything serious. I will need to return to Semiria, to my home, once my training here is complete, and he could not come with. It could never work between us long term, but there is no harm in enjoying the time we have together.

Sunlight filters through the trees, telling me I will be to the clearing in front of the lake soon. Why am I so nervous? I have never felt so giddy in my life; I can feel my stomach tingles heading up to my throat. The crisp scent of the morning making me smile even wider. I suppose I am just excited for whatever surprise Andras has planned for today, though I am holding a little hope that it is something romantic. A little romance before I go back home can't hurt, right?

I spot the clearing up ahead and quicken my pace, ready to rid myself of feeling the need to vomit my nerves. Jogging my way through the last section of trees, I stop in my tracks when I see the familiar hue of sandy, golden hair shining in the sunlight. Andras sits on a blanket in front of the water, leaning back on his elbows, face toward the sky, seemingly enjoying the peace. He's wearing black trousers and a loose short-sleeve shirt that's the color of the sky at midnight. He looks majestic at this moment, and I can't help but smile to myself at seeing him appear so carefree and content. He sits up to look at me as I approach, a beautiful smile fixed on his handsome face.

"Hi," I say breathlessly.

"Hello, Anellah, you look beautiful," he says.

I purse my lips trying to hide my smile, though I am definitely not hiding the blush tracking up my cheeks. He chuckles, probably since I am never this shy. What is going on with me today? He is just a male; I have had plenty of male companions, so what makes him so different? He's not one of my soul bonds, I would feel it in my chest like a spark of electricity, and I do not feel that when I look at him. But I do feel happy; ever since I have come to the mortal realm, Andras has been so patient in showing me around and caring for me. He has taken an interest in all the things I talk about, and answers my endless questions without annoyance clouding his beautiful features.

Am I so weak to be brought to my knees by the first male to show me romantic attention? My past male companions and I just fucked and went on with our days, just needing a release in our stress, but courting is not something we do in Europa. We do not have dates, stolen kisses, or longing looks. This is new. Different. And I must want it more than I am willing to admit to myself if such simple things like this can make me so giddy.

Looking at the scene before me, I notice a basket and realize what this is. "You set up a picnic for us? That's the surprise?" Excitement overtaking my voice.

"Sort of—it's part of the surprise. I thought it would be nice to have a quiet moment to ourselves, away from everyone and the stress of running a city, or being a god." He gives me a knowing look. I roll my eyes at his attempt of humor.

"This is really nice, thank you."

I sit on the blanket Andras brought, and we talk while we eat the berries, grapes, and cheese that he brought. It is refreshing to just talk to someone with no expectations; in Semiria and Anclona, the two cities on Europa, nearly every conversation is business. You are always expected to bring something of importance, otherwise what is the point of you talking?

Calix and I share laughs once in a while, but even conversations with him are pretty much short and to the point, and I consider him my closest friend. Talking with Andras is like a breath of the freshest air, and I am thankful that it was him that I met when I transferred to Earth. I could be anywhere, with anyone, learning more about the mortal realm, and its history, but Andras found me and has been so kind in helping me learn what I need to, while also showing me the fun side to life.

I never realized what I was missing at home and, even though I won't admit it out loud, staying in the mortal realm after my obligatory years of training here would be nice. I would have to forfeit my god status and would be a complete disappointment to my parents, so I couldn't ever go through with it, of course…but a girl can dream.

"Nell?"

I jump in my spot on the blanket, realizing I was staring at Andras without saying a word. Gods, can I do anything right? I am always messing things up, and now Andras probably thinks I'm too strange to even be friends with.

"Are you okay, Nell?"

Shit, I'm still staring and still not saying anything. "Yes, I'm sorry. I was in my own world for a minute," I mumble hastily.

He gives me one of his dazzling smiles. "It's all right, you are quite beautiful when you're thinking. I mean, you are beautiful all the time, but I just meant you get this look about you when you're in your own head," his brows furrow. "Not in a bad way at all, you are beautiful no matter what you're doing, I was just—I uh—I am messing this up, aren't I?" He lowers his head and swipes his palm over his face, appearing stressed.

Is he nervous, too? Are we both feeling things for the other? Or does he just not know what to say after my outburst?

"Andras, you are not messing anything up. This has been the most lovely morning, and I have enjoyed my time with you. Not just today, but the last few months, as well."

He looks at me, hope blooming in his eyes, "Listen Nell, I haven't done this in a long time, but I feel like we are both tip-toeing around what we want to say, so I am just going to say it," he faces me fully and smiles. "I like you. A lot. You are beautiful, funny, and so smart. I would love to spend more time with you, and get to know you more intimately, if you would like the same?"

I am at a loss for words. Is that what the culture is like here? To be so open about one's feelings, instead of ensuring they are never talked about?

"Yes, I would like that," taking his lead and speaking what's in my heart.

His smile grows wider, showing his white smile, and he glances down to my lips, then back up. "Can I kiss you, Nell?"

My stomach drops to the grass. "Yes."

He leans in and stops just a breath away from my lips. I can taste his scent, a mix of clean linen and roses, and before I have a chance to ask why he stopped, he grabs the back of my head and presses his lips to mine. It's a pleasant kiss; his soft lips fit comfortably between mine, and he tastes of the berries he brought.

He runs his tongue along my lips, and I open for him immediately. Heat builds low in my abdomen, but before I can think about taking this any further, I start feeling a pulling sensation in my chest. It's just a little at first, but quickly starts to build until it feels like the very essence of my soul is being ripped from me. I pull away from Andras and grab at my chest, opening my mouth to tell him something is wrong, but stop when I see the smirk on his face.

"Something the matter, my sweet?" His words dripping with sarcastic amusement. He cups my face and leans in to kiss me again, but I tug away, giving him a confused look.

"What's going on? Why do I feel like this?" I'm panicking. I try to summon my magic, but it doesn't come. My limbs begin to falter, and I grow weaker.

His face goes cold at my rejection, his eyes burn with a rage I have never seen before. He grabs my throat and shoves me to the ground; my arm that was holding me up is locked at a painful angle under my weight. He's squeezing tightly, cutting off most of my air, and adrenaline courses through my blood.

He hovers over me and bends down to lick between my breasts up to the bottom of my lips. "You taste divine, my sweet Nell. I have missed the feeling of raw power. When they find out what I have taken, they will give me what I've been after for centuries."

My chest feels heavier, tighter, and my head spins. I can't breathe. I attempt to ask what he's talking about, but I can't get any words out. I'm going to die.

He bends down to capture my lips again, and the feeling in my chest intensifies to a point where I am positive my body is withering away. I have never felt such pain or pressure, but I can't scream or call for help. Actually, I can't seem to do anything anymore…my arms will not move, my legs are not listening to the commands I am internally screaming at them. I'm frozen.

Andras pulls away and takes a deep breath, power radiating from his every pore.

My power.

I can't even speak to ask him how he did this to me. All I can do is blink and move my eyes, everything else has been taken from me.

He looks down at me, laughter heavy in his blinding eyes. "Okay, I get it. You're probably freaking out since you can't move, right? Well, long story short, sweet Nell, I took your magic from you. Unfortunately for you, you seem to have a great deal of essence magic, which means you are mine to do with as I please," he chuckles and runs his thumb over my lips, "and I think you are definitely going to please me, my sweet."

A siphon. Oh, gods. Siphons don't exist. Siphons are created, not born, when a god is stripped of their magic. Gods cannot live without their magic, so their body goes into survival mode and begins siphoning the magic of others to stay alive.

Wait…that means…

My eyes widen in realization. Andras has been watching me and seems to be pleased with my reaction. "I was wondering how long it would take you. Yes, I am the god you read about in your history books, the one who started the war," he rolls his eyes. "Though I'm sure they do not mention me by name. I have been waiting for this for a long time, Anellah. It's finally time I take what I am owed, and I will. But in the meantime, you and I are going to have a lot of fun." He runs his hand up my thigh and grabs my hip to emphasize "fun."

Andras. The executed god. The books said he was dead, killed by the other original gods. They thought they killed him. Yet here I am, not in control of my own body, while he picks me up and begins walking toward the castle.

Chapter 30

I hear muffled voices, though I can't make out what they're saying. Jasmine and leather scents filter in through my nose. My body feels stiff and heavy, as if I haven't moved in ages. My throat feels sore and scratchy; I could use a whole tub of water right now. There's a prickly feeling running over me from my dream—

My dream. Andras. The witches. The pain. My memories.

My eyes fly open, and I recognize Casmir's bedroom. I'm in his bed, alone in the room, the muffled voices from earlier are gone. There's no light filtering from outside so it must still be dark, though I'm not sure how they brought me back to the castle so quickly, considering they would have needed to carry me down the mountain.

I attempt to take stock of everything that I know. I live on Europa, and I was sent to Earth to complete one of my last trainings before transitioning to my role as the Goddess of Nature. Which was Andras's original role before he started, and lost, a war and my mother took over his responsibilities.

I met Andras when I arrived here, having left GodsPass after deciding to walk toward Ceross. I didn't know he was *the* god when I met him. We all thought they killed him; my parents told me themselves they helped execute him. I don't know how he survived that, and then somehow survived by siphoning fae magic to live?

Gods are far more powerful than fae, so he would have to regularly take magic from several fae at a time in order to live…

That's right. I asked him that after he took my magic and used it to control me; he showed me the castle dungeons, where he crams fae into cells so that he always has enough of a supply of magic to sustain him. At least when he had me, he didn't need to take from them, since my magic was enough.

But I fought back. I tried everything I could think of to hurt him and escape him. It just made him angry, and he had the witch, Imogen, take my memories and watch over me outside of the Veil. At least he was generous enough to let Xamira come with me, since he kept her locked in a cage, too.

I remember every five years Imogen, or Sarah Gardner I should say, put another block in my head so I wouldn't question why I wasn't aging. They wanted me to continue living there, unaware, until Andras was ready for me. But that didn't work how he planned, because Xamira led me back here after twenty-one years of suffering.

And of course, my idiotic self fell for his charm again. I think back to when he hit me, and it reminded me of the day he kissed me by the lake. If Casmir and Emrys weren't there, he would have siphoned my power again. But he couldn't as they were watching, and he's not strong enough to take them on alone.

Then there's the two males I never wanted to meet. I allowed the bond to be triggered. It's going to break me, and break them, to tell them I need to leave. I can't be with them for so many reasons.

I have to go back to Europa and warn the rest of the gods about Andras. Then I need to take my place as the Goddess of Nature, and help with the balance of the realms. I can't do that if I stay with them…I'll be stripped of my status, never to be a sanctioned god. My parents would be so disappointed in me; they already think I'm weak and naïve, and I guess they were right. I am not ready for the lecture I will receive when they find out what Andras did to me. It's my fault.

I need to go back.

I hear a light meow before Xamira jumps on the bed, and I reach for her with tears welling in my eyes. "I am so sorry, my sweet girl. I'm so sorry for everything I put you through. I can't believe you stayed with me, thank you," I cry into her fur, not able to hold my emotions in right now.

I will always protect you, Anellah.

"I know, and you tried to tell me. It must have been so hard not being able to talk." I sit up and look into her molten gold eyes. "We need to go back, Xamira. We need to tell them what happened, and what he has planned."

We do. I'm with you, always.

I hug her again, her voice leaving my head, and silently thank the gods for her. Xamira is a Sorid; they are our third bond, and usually the only one we meet. They live on Europa, and when a god is in need of a Sorid, one bonds to them and is sworn to protect them for their entire lives.

Xamira came to me the day I was born. My mother told me she found her sleeping next to me when I woke from a nap. She has been by my side for nearly seventy-five years, and is the one soul in my life I can forever count on.

I hear the door creak open, followed by a sharp intake of breath. Before I can even turn to see Casmir, he's sliding onto the bed beside me. His everlasting hazel eyes are red rimmed, and he has dark circles under them. The time with Ivana must have been really hard on him, too. He moves to grab my hand but I force myself to pull away, knowing that I can't allow any more connection between the three of us.

"Hi," I croak. My voice is weak and hoarse.

"*Oh gods*, Nell, you're awake," Emrys runs into the room and slams himself onto the bed, next to Casmir. Em tries reaching for my leg, the bond begging us to be touching constantly, but I shake my head at him.

"I'm sorry," I try, but it's strangled with emotion and bruised vocal chords. He sits forward to grab something off of the table next to the bed, and hands me a glass of water.

"Drink, love, you're very dehydrated." My forehead scrunches with confusion and I look outside, seeing that it's indeed still night, so I shouldn't be that dehydrated. He catches my silent question. "You've been unconscious for five days, Nell. We got you to swallow some water a couple of times, but you haven't been awake since we were on the mountain."

My eyes widen in horror. Five days. That's nearly an extra week that Andras has had to plan something. I need to go back immediately, before he does something horrible, like hurting the ones I'm close to.

"Do you remember anything?"

I nod, my lip trembling, and I bite it to keep from crying. This is going to be hard, but I need to tell them. They deserve to know the truth, especially considering the turmoil I'm going to put them through when I leave.

"Ivana left this for you," Casmir holds out a sealed letter. "She insisted you be the only one to read it." I take it, breaking the seal and folding the paper open to reveal the written words.

Anellah,

I saw your memories and figured out who you were, but you must know your secret is safe with me, even from your soul bonds. I did not get the chance to explain that the Earth did not require a piece of your soul as a sacrifice for removing the blocks in your head. You are a god, which means your magic and life force are very, very powerful. You have more power than can be sustained on the Earth.

When a god visits this realm, the Earth takes some of their magic, which allows them to stay in the realm for as long as they need.

My dear, you have been here for decades. *You have been feeding the Earth with your magic, and already paid the cost of the spells I used.*

I know who did this to you, along with my sister. Please be careful. They are strong, and Imogen is cunning; they will do whatever is necessary to keep you because you are the ticket to destroying the other gods.

Be smart. You know where to find me if you need help.

Ivana

I read over the letter a couple times, stealing a few minutes of silence before I need to face the two beautiful, kind, perfect males staring holes into my heart. I close my eyes and, for the first time in years, summon my magic, burning the page to nothing. After a few deep breaths, I steel myself and look to Em and Cas, who are watching me with wonder.

"I will tell you everything, I promise," my voice sounds stronger. "But first I'd like to use the bathroom and change." I don't give them time to respond and skip to the bathroom, closing the door and leaning against it. The tugging in my chest is painful and tense, like it knows what I'm about to do and is begging me not to.

I clean myself off, brush my teeth, and look at my markings in the mirror. I was so confused about what these meant before, but I stare at them now with recognition and determination. I trek out of the bathroom and into Casmir's closet, not bothering to cover my body. Nudity is not something that is shamed on Europa, like it is for the mortals. I throw on a pair of his sweats and a t-shirt, wanting to get this conversation done with so I can grab my things, and Xamira, and go back home. Every cell in my body is telling me that's the wrong decision, but I was raised to think with my head, not anything else.

I join them back on the bed, too cowardly to look at them right away. But I decide to just rip the band-aid off and twist my hand in the air, creating a wall that is soundproof to anyone who would try to listen to my next words.

"What did you just do?" Casmir reaches over to feel the wall. He knocks his fist against it, before he and Emrys give each other questioning looks.

"I put up a sound barrier. What I'm about to tell you is not to *ever* leave this room." They nod and I begin my story.

"My true name is Anellah, but I go by Nell sometimes. I am the daughter of Hale and Aeryn, God of Balance and Goddess of War." Casmir's jaw drops to the floor in pure shock, while Emrys's eyes bulge out of his head.

I try to keep my explanation short, telling them of why I am on Earth, what happened with Andras, and everything since before I met them. They listen, clearly wanting to ask questions but not interrupt me.

"So you're saying Andras had you under his control for *three years* before sending you to live in a different kind of hell?" Em asks and I nod, focusing on my hands. "And what did he use you for during that time, exactly?" His voice is dripping with barely controlled rage. I shake my head, not wanting to hurt them anymore.

"What the *fuck* did he do to you, Nell?" He yells and I wince, fearing his hatred and disgust when I tell him about the rest of it.

"You know what he did."

"Say it," he spits.

I look him in the eyes, cold hatred pouring from them, but not directed at me. "He stole my magic. He sucked nearly. Every. Drop. From me, leaving only enough to keep me alive. He raped me. He would press my face against the windows while he took me over and over, showing me what freedom looked like while using my body for his pleasure. He did it so I would know that he owns me, and I would never have that freedom. He would fuck me in front of mirrors, and make me watch as he forced my body to come, so he could tell me that I secretly liked what he was doing.

"He tortured me for information." I sit forward, making sure he hears every word I'm saying. "He would skin different parts of my body. He would listen to me scream, and laugh, as he cut limbs off while I was awake, and then sewed them back on with a dull needle. He would pull out my teeth, slowly, and watch in delight as I choked on the blood. He became so deranged by the end that he cut off my fingers and fucked me with them while they grew necrotic.

"But, in his *generosity*," I growl sarcastically, "he made sure to put all the parts back, and give me just enough of my magic so that they would heal themselves, and we could start all over again. Is *that* what you wanted to hear, Emrys?" I'm trembling from reliving those horrors, and being so fucking angry at Andras for doing this to me. Angry at myself for being so naïve to let it happen.

"Thank you for being concerned on my behalf," I try to calm and speak to them with a level head, "but I am enraged enough for the both of us. Andras *will* get what he deserves, and it *will* be by my hand."

He no longer has fury radiating from him, but sadness. Defeat. I look to Casmir, who has silent tears trailing from his eyes, and I have to look away before I let my own fall. All those years of torture and still the worst thing I will ever go through is leaving them. They deserve to know.

"There's one last thing I need to tell you," I murmur and continue before I talk myself out of it. "There's a reason the three of us feel so connected. Every god has two, what we call soul bonds, that live on the mortal realm. You're mine. That means that you each have a piece of my soul inside of you, as well as a piece of each other's. That's why you came together at such a young age; you were always meant to be a pair."

Deep breath. "However, it should have never come to this. I was the catalyst in triggering the bond, causing these feelings and urges between us. I never intended to meet either of you, and I am so incredibly sorry for that."

"Why would you be sorry? That sounds like it would be a good thing…" Cas questions hesitantly.

I explain the rules with either being a god or having your soul bonds. I describe why I can't complete the bonding ceremony. Both of them get more tense as my words continue, as if they know what I'm going to say next.

"Because of that, and everything happening with Andras, I need to return to Europa. I must warn the other gods so that we can execute him for good, and then I must take on my title as the Goddess of Nature."

They sit in silence with this information. The prince looks like he's trying to figure out if there was anything false in what I said, or a loophole he could take advantage of.

Emrys grows angry again, heat radiating from his skin. "Are you fucking kidding me? After everything that you've been through, everything that *we've* been through, you're just going to leave us?" I open my mouth to respond, but he pins me with a glare that shuts me up. "You just said yourself that the three of us are meant for each other, meant to be together. We have a part of your fucking soul, Nell!" His voice cracks, and I swear my heart shrivels into dust at the sound.

"You can't leave us, Nell. You're ours. We're yours. You said you have a choice…choose us." Emrys's voice shakes deeply, and his cheeks begin to gather the moisture seeping from his eyes. *Gods*, his feelings run so much deeper than I thought they did. I want so badly to hug them both and tell them everything will be okay, but it's not that easy.

They don't understand the magnitude of the decisions I make, and how important it is for me to go back home.

Home.

The building in Semiria has never felt like anything but a place to sleep. Not like Casmir and Emrys. No, *they* are my home. I've always wanted a home. I want them. They want me. Maybe I should think about this more.

I stand from the bed and lower the sound barrier, needing a moment to myself, and to pack my things before I leave. Whether or not I choose them, I still need to warn the other gods of Andras.

"So that's it? You're going to dump all of this on us, and then walk out the fucking door without even a goodbye?" Emrys shouts, and I turn around slowly to face him as he and Cas get off the bed. "Do you even care about us? Or is this just some game to you? To play with the little fae on the *mortal realm,* while you sit high and mighty on your throne of power?"

I rear back at the accusation and the harsh tone of his voice, his anger directed at me this time. "Are you kidding me, Em? Do I care about you?" I laugh manically, and run my hands over my face; I don't have the strength to stay calm any longer. "Of course I care about you, but that's not the fucking point!"

"Then what is the point, Anellah?" His voice is deadly and low, and I wince at his use of my full name.

"The point is that I never wanted to meet either of you!" I gag from the admission, not even wanting to think about my life without them in it. "I never wanted it to come to this, because I know how hard this is going to be. Once a bond is triggered, it's nearly impossible to reject. I was warned, before coming to Earth, to leave wherever I was immediately if I felt the zapping in my chest that I did when you two crashed right into my life at the ball.

"The second I looked into your eyes, I knew it was over for me. Even if I had my memories, I'm not sure I would have been strong enough to walk away then. But I'm trying to be strong enough now. This is so fucking hard that I might die of a broken heart. You stupid," I push their chests with each word. "Fucking. Insufferable. Males made me fall in love with you! And now I have to rip myself away from you, and it feels like I'm being torn open from the inside!"

I press my hands to my chest, heaving from the tears I can't stop. "I have felt so *empty*, right here, for decades. But being with you two has filled that void and has made me realize that my life is worth living. I love you both so fucking much that it's *killing* me, Em, so don't you dare accuse me of not caring for you, when I'm leaving because I—"

I can't finish my emotional rant because Casmir has me locked in a greedy, fervent kiss. If I was a better female, I would push him off and distance myself from them.

But I'm not.

Instead, I shove him onto the bed and straddle his hips, continuing to kiss him with every last bit of sanity I have left in my body. He yanks my shirt off, desperate to touch me, and palms my breasts before kissing his way down my neck.

I look to my side, where Emrys is still standing. "Em, get the *fuck* over here," I demand, leaving no room for protest. He looks at me with longing streaming from his eyes before his resolve splits, and he's lifting me up from Cas, who rips my pants off. He nods to the prince, who backs against the wall, and pushes me into him roughly, sandwiching me in with his front.

He captures my lips with his, filtering all the anger and frustration through our connection. I can make out some of his strongest thoughts, now realizing that I've actually been hearing them in my head all along. Soul bonds can speak to each other through the bond once it's triggered, and if the ceremony is completed, it grows to include emotions and physical senses, as well.

Cas buries his face in the crook of my neck, and my hand reaches back to grab his soft, messy hair. I turn, needing his lips on mine again, and as we kiss, Emrys shoves his cock into me, and I scream from the burning intrusion. He reaches over to hand Casmir the lube, who makes quick work of getting himself ready before he follows his second, and thrusts into my other side with no mercy. They fuck me hard and fast, holding me by the legs and hips. The rough pace is slightly painful, but this is what we all need.

Em reaches down to massage my clit, and I cry out at the release; the contractions of my inner walls send them both over the edge as well. I lean my head back to Cas's chest, and he plants soft kisses over my shoulder and neck. Sweat is coating my skin, as I'm trapped between the inferno that is my two males. *Mine.*

"Nell," Cas whispers, holding me against him, "you belong with us. It's not possible for you to leave." I don't say anything; tears fall again because deep down, I know he's right. Rejecting them is going to destroy all of us.

They lift me off of them, causing me to flinch, and I realize I was the only one with any clothes off. I face them, not bothering to care about my nudity, as I'm going to my room to shower again.

"I need some time to think," I whisper, looking between the both of them. "Please." They stare at me for a moment; Cas looks like he's about to get on his knees and beg for me to stay. I bite my lip to try and hide the trembling, wondering if I'm already feeling their emotions, or if this utter turmoil is all my own. Em has a war of emotions swirling through his eyes; I can see that he is so angry with me, but desperately longs for me at the same time.

Cas steps forward, rubbing his hands along my arms. "Okay, princess," he murmurs, and kisses my forehead before releasing me to walk to the bathroom. Em searches my eyes for a moment longer before nodding and following his prince, leaving me alone to let my tears fall freely.

Chapter 31

After a long cry, and maybe a little panic, I took a few hours to think about everything while Cas and Em slept. I'm not going to make a decision about our bonding just yet. Now that I've had time to reflect, I realize that it was incredibly selfish of me to tell them I was leaving without even considering their needs. I am their bond, too, and they are going through the same unrest that I am over this. The only difference is that they don't have the balance of the realms in their hands. I guess I don't either, yet, but I hope they can at least take that into consideration. I will compromise with them. They didn't ask to be my bonds, and they didn't have a clue what they were doing when they met me. This isn't their fault, and they deserve a say in the outcome.

Ultimately, it will be my decision, but it's important that I listen to them as well. It wouldn't even be a question what I would choose if I didn't have so many expectations on my shoulders. But I do, and that makes this so incredibly hard. I nod to myself, solidified in my choice to wait and think it over for a while before deciding anything.

That leaves the other big issue warring in my head at the moment: Andras. He's planning on using me to bring the other gods to Earth so he can kill them. He wants revenge for them stripping his magic, and forcing him to live life as a fae, while having to take other faes' magic to survive. He spent all those years torturing me to get me to give him information about them that would allow him an advantage.

Unfortunately for me, he needs to wait until my thirty years of training on Earth are completed before the other gods will wonder where I am and come looking for me. He couldn't send me back because only gods can cross the border between realms, and he wouldn't have leverage any longer. So he's kept me locked up; first by him directly, and then by my own head. He's a monster.

And I intend to wring every ounce of life from him with my own hands.

But first, I need to travel back to Europa. That will require Xamira and I riding to GodsPass, so it will take a few days. Maybe two if we push it. I know that the prince and his second are going to insist on coming with me, but I can't let them. It will only make it more difficult to say goodbye, spending more time with them, and then I would have anxiety about them making it back to Anloria safely.

I walk down to the dining area on the bottom floor of the castle, preparing myself for what I hope is an easier conversation than our last. Cas and Em are sitting at the small table, both looking somber, but their gazes shoot to me when I enter the room. I can't stop the warm smile that spreads across my face. These two males have taken over my life, and as much as I hate how difficult that makes things for me, I can't bring myself to regret it.

"Good morning," my voice is quiet, interrupting the consuming silence, as I sit down across from them; this moment reminds me of the day after I met them. I breathe in the smell of fruit, bacon, eggs, and toast. My stomach turns painfully, and I remember that I haven't eaten in a week.

"Good morning, my love," Casmir returns my smile with a genuine one of his own. The green in his eyes is full of shadows and deep, golden light. Emrys doesn't speak, looking like he's straining to not ask me what I've decided on.

I nod, not wanting to keep this from them any longer. "Okay," I breathe. "Before I tell you where my thoughts concluded, please just promise you'll hear me out first. I don't want us to be angry with each other."

I raise my hand to encase the room in a sound barrier. Emrys tenses, expecting the worst. Cas nods, and gives me an encouraging smile, being kind even when I'm not.

"Neither of you asked for this, and obviously I never intended for it to get this far. But it has, and there's no undoing it. I can't remove my feelings for you just as much as you can't for me. It was wrong of me to make such a big decision for all of us, and I apologize for that." I look them both in the eyes, attempting to convey my sincerity. "I think it would be best if we all made this decision together, but not right now."

Casmir's brows furrow in confusion while Emrys moves to speak, but I hold my hand up, silently imploring him to let me continue.

"I'm not saying no, and I'm not saying never. Just not right now. This is a *big* decision, you guys. Please try to understand my side of things." I feel tears coming back, but I harden my emotions before I lose to them again. "I have so many expectations of me. I was created to take over what they stripped from Andras. That has been my duty, and only goal, for the last seventy-four years.

"I want to stay with you both more than *anything*. My soul aches at the thought of being without you. But giving up everything I was raised for? Having the realms depend on me? My parents? That makes this incredibly difficult. I need time to think. And when a decision is made, we will make it together. No matter what, I will come back to you."

Casmir, who's leaning on his fist, rubs his hand over his lips, thinking deeply. A wave of sorrow crosses his eyes before he hardens them, coming to a conclusion. "I understand." He leans forward, piercing me with a tender look. "Nell, I will wait for you until my dying breath, if that's what it takes." I can't help it. I reach out to hold his hand, certain that he can feel me trembling.

Emrys shifts, crossing his arms and sitting back in his chair. "So that means you're still leaving?"

"Yes," I say. "The other gods need to be warned about Andras. He is torturing other fae and taking their magic so that he can live. He's planning revenge against the gods for what they did to him. He must be stopped, and that means I have to go for a while."

His eyes, the color of crystallized honey, search mine. I reach out my hand in offering, but he doesn't move to take it and continues to look for something inside of me. I keep my hand outstretched and hold his gaze; after what feels like an eternity, his defenses lower and he leans forward to hold my hand, his quivering more than mine.

"We will be coming with you to GodsPass, then. I need to make sure you're safe," Casmir's voice faint and suppressed. This is where I lose them. They're going to hate me for lying, but I'm stronger and more powerful than they are. Than anyone else on this realm. So, I can ensure my own safety.

"Okay," I utter, the lie tasting cheap and repulsive on my tongue.

⁘

I'm leaning over my balcony, listening to the waterfall, and waiting for the right time to leave. Casmir and Emrys both went to bed two hours ago, and I asked them to give me some space for tonight, to which they reluctantly agreed. Now, my packed bag is sitting next to me, and Xamira is waiting on the bed. She's not happy about the plan, seeing as she's also bonded to me and feels very protective of them. But she understands the importance of not involving them in this, for their own safety.

Once I think we've waited long enough, I turn to her. "Are you ready?" I ask. "This is going to be a hard journey. We need to get back as quickly as possible."

I am ready.

I nod, and we sneak out of the castle easily, as Xamira is able to tell me where any staff or guards are, and my essence magic allows me to manipulate the light and render us invisible. We are out by the stables within several minutes, and taking off through the gate not long after. The guards there were easy enough to fool, as they know how important I am to the prince and don't want to deny me anything. I'm not sure if they'll run to warn him, though, so I fly out of the city as quickly as I can with Xamira sitting in front of me.

Once we're out of the city gates and up the hill that will take us toward GodsPass, I stop the horse to take one more look at Anloria, my true home, before leading us into the dark forest.

It's been a day and a half since Xamira and I left Anloria. We had to stop once to allow the horse to rest, but were back on the trail quickly. I feel horrible for pushing the mare this hard, but I'm thankful we've made it to Veardale so she can rest. I tell the stable hand to give her extra food and care, grab food for Xamira and myself, and then we begin our walk.

It's morning, so we should be to the top of GodsPass by nightfall, if the weather holds. I am a little disoriented, having only slept a couple hours, but I keep reminding myself that I can't stop. The more time I waste, the more time Andras has to plan, and the more time my males have to catch up to me. Assuming they're even following.

I haven't tried to reach out to them through our bond, not knowing what I would say.

Hey, so sorry for lying, see you soon!

Please don't follow me, I'm fine.

I don't think they yet realize they can reach out to me if they wanted. I haven't blocked my connection to them, selfishly hoping that they will figure it out before I'm off this realm.

I'm not sure they would even want to talk to me right now, considering what I just did to them. I hope they don't think I was lying about coming back for them, but I wouldn't blame them if they did. I didn't have a choice, though. They are *everything* to me…my entire world. I can't let them risk themselves for me like that, not after all they've already done.

I sigh, not wanting to think about dreary emotions right now, and continue the climb with Xamira.

It's just after nightfall when we are coming up to the top of GodsPass, where the Filicity flower rests. I remember having some sense of familiarity when I saw the flower on my way through with Casmir, Emrys, and their guard. The Filicity flower only grows naturally on Europa, but was placed here by my father to mark where the stone is that's used to travel between realms. The flower was spelled to never die, so it needs no food or water. If someone were to cut it down, it would just grow again. It will always be here, marking the way back.

I spot the flower up ahead and heave a sigh of relief at almost being there. I stop in front of the flower and grab my dagger, moving to cut my palm and place my blood on the stone behind it, but I hesitate. Should I reach out to them before I go? Just to say goodbye? Yes. I would be hurt and panicked if I didn't know they were okay.

I close my eyes to pull on the connection between us when something sharp pierces my leg, and I cry out from the pain. There's a dagger in my calf. I look up and see several fae, all wearing brown fighting leathers, marching toward me.

Xamira, hide.

I hear her groan of protest in my head, but she does as I command. I need to figure out who these fae are, and what they want, before I let her out of her shell. I pull the dagger out, wincing at the renewed pain, but push the sensation aside and prepare to defend myself.

"Who are you?" I demand in an ethereal voice.

One of them snickers before they all attack at once, coming at me from every angle. I home in on my magic, using it and my body to fight off my attackers. I manage to drown one from the inside, and injure a few others with foul smelling burns, but I don't last long. More keep coming, and by the time I fall to the rock, I have a broken left arm, bruised ribs, blood in my mouth, and several more daggers sticking out of various places in my body.

How do they know how to fight so well? They're all standing over me, watching while I sputter blood, and I will my body to heal faster so I can run. There's no way I'm winning against this many well-trained fae. Two soldiers part by my feet, and my soul drops out of my body.

Xamira, go. Find Casmir and Emrys.

Let me help, Anellah!

NO! He will just lock you up again, and then we'll both be trapped. Please, go find them! Tell them what's happened.

I will come back for you.

She takes off through the shadows, and a weight lifts from my chest, knowing she's going to be okay and keep the other two away from here.

"Hello, Anellah," Andras drawls in a mocking tone. "I was hoping I would find you here. I've missed you."

I spit my warm blood at him. "Fuck you."

He chuckles. "You know," he crouches in front of me, "I was going to let you live with me, and not touch your magic until your thirty years was up, but you just had to question things and then leave with them, didn't you?" I don't answer, and he smiles at my look of disgust. I can feel my body pushing the blades out; if I can keep him talking, maybe I can run before he does anything.

"How did you do it?"

"Do what?" My voice is pure venom.

"Get your memories back. How?"

"I don't see why that's important. It's already done, Andras." He chuckles.

"No matter," he waves his hands, making his soldiers back up a little. "Imogen already has a good idea of how you did it." The blades are just about to fall out of my body, so I shoot up and punch him in the face as hard as I can, hoping it hurts worse than when he hit me.

I get up to run back the way I came when a sharp pain hits my spine, and I'm shoved back down, my face cracking against the stone. Tears pour out of me; I'm more terrified than I was the first time, knowing exactly what he plans to do with my body.

Find your calm.

I take a deep breath, grimacing at the blade being held in my back. I send myself into the depths of that familiar nothing that I forced myself to feel in order to make it through Andras's torture last time. He sits on my lower back, putting terrifying pressure on my hips. I feel him lean forward, brushing my hair out of the way. I try my best to move him, and not let him touch me, but I've done this before...I know it won't work. He has me.

The pulling sensation I had become so accustomed to begins, and I shriek, pure terror working its way through my body. Before my connection to Casmir and Emrys is gone, I reach out to them, feeling their shock when they recognize me.

I love you. Xamira will find you. Don't come for me. I couldn't live with it if he hurt you, too. I love you.

My connection breaks off as Andras sucks the life from my veins, his mouth pressing to my neck in what I'm sure he thinks is a sensual kiss. I feel him hum in satisfaction against me and recoil, but my body can no longer move.

"My sweet, Nell. I've been waiting a long time to play with you again. We're going to have so much fun," he breathes in my ear.

I feel the light leave my eyes, my magic going with it, and pray to every god that Emrys and Casmir don't come for me.

Epilogue
Casmir

I exhale a sigh of relief at seeing Veardale come into sight. Em and I have been racing nonstop to GodsPass since he found Nell missing from her room and her traveling bag gone. I'll be having a word with the guards who let her through and did not inform me.

It's been two days since we left Anloria, pushing ourselves, and our horses, harder than ever. But I refuse to stop now; I will run all night if I have to, and beg the gods that we make it to her before she travels back to Europa.

Anellah.

My goddess—*our* goddess. I glance at Emrys, who has had the same scowl on his face since we left the castle. I know he's angry. I am, too. She lied to us and then left us without even saying goodbye. But I can't think about that right now. I need to find her.

Em explained he had awoken in the night with a deep, heavy sense of dread slamming into his body. When he retrieved me, I woke with the same feeling slithering through my veins. We knew something terrible was going to happen, though we didn't know what. There was no question that we needed to leave immediately and do everything in our power to make it to Nell.

We leave our horses at the village stable and begin running through the streets into the forest. We just make it to the trees when a sharp, hurried sensation takes over my head, and I stop in my tracks. Emrys must feel it, too, since he has the same confused look on his face. I don't have a moment to say anything to him before I hear *her*.

I love you.

My wide eyes meet Em's. Her sad, panicked voice is resonating through both of us.

Xamira will find you. Don't come for me. I couldn't live with it if he hurt you, too.

Fuck. We didn't make it…this is the dread we were feeling. We failed to save her from whatever is happening.

I love you.

The connection cuts off, snapping me back to reality, and I nearly vomit from the horror coursing through me. We need to hurry. Maybe there's still time to get to her. We take off running, both of us using every bit of energy we have to quicken our steps; running for what seems like days, though it has been only an hour or two. I refuse to let myself think about what's happening to her, knowing that will slow me down. I need to keep going.

A howling noise sounds up ahead, but I ignore it, focusing on trying to make my body go faster. Another noise, this time closer and above us. I look up, dawn beginning to illuminate the sky, and see a pair of wings headed straight for us. What is that? I can't make out many details with how dark it still is.

Emrys halts his advancement, and I follow, preparing for an attack. The winged creature lands several feet in front of us, but makes no move to approach. With the close distance, I can see it's a black feline. A large one, with black, feathered wings attached to its back. It steps forward and beams of the dawn light melt along its face.

It's a panther, with shiny, smooth fur. Intense, golden eyes stare back at us and—

Golden eyes. A pang of recognition hits my chest.

"Xamira?" She dips her head in response. "How?" I breathe, needles running rampant over my skin. Nell hadn't mentioned who Xamira was to her before leaving, though I suspected there was something different about her after the night she had a conversation with Nell.

Xamira will find you.

Emrys's thoughts are the same as my own. "Where is she?" The panther bows her head, sorrow surging off of her in waves.

"Xamira," he snaps, and I can sense he's barely keeping it together. "Where. Is. Anellah? Where the *fuck* is our soul bond?" His shouts surround every bead of silence the night had remaining. He falls to his knees as tears stream down his face. He's come to the same conclusion I have.

"He has her, doesn't he?" I whisper, not at all ready to face what I already know to be the truth. "Andras." She dips her chin once more in confirmation, then throws her head back to let out an agonizing roar, filled with pain and regret.

He has her.

And it's my fault.

Acknowledgements

Writing a book is more rewarding than I expected it to be. I have wanted to write a novel for years, but could never push myself to get started because I always thought the process would make me hate it, in the end. I was completely wrong. I fell in love with my story, and characters. They are such a big part of my life that they feel like family, and I'm so excited to share them with all of you.

I'm grateful to my friend, Payton, who has been my biggest supporter throughout this project. She read every single draft I gave her, helped me with ideas, and was always enthusiastic about anything I did for the book. She even helped find songs for the playlist, and aided me in ideas for getting the book out into the world. I'm thankful she was there to encourage me, and I'm excited to go through this process again on the next ones. Thank you for being there, Payton.

Next, I want to thank my husband and sister, who took time out of their very busy schedules to read through my drafts and offer me different points of views on things. I found it so helpful to have people who do, and don't, read fantasy go through everything and give me their opinions. You both were so important in this process, and I can't express my gratitude enough.

I know that I would have never done this if it weren't for my younger self. So, I want to say thank you to the child in me, who was obsessed with reading and writing. We lost our spark for a while, but we got it back. Thank you for reminding me of what I was missing.

Lastly, I want to thank *you*, the reader. I hope you love this story as much as I do. I came up with the idea for this series intending to write *my* perfect books, but I still wanted to share them with others. I hope you find something to cherish within their pages. Thank you for reading, I'll see you in the next one.

Pronunciations

Characters
Aeryn — Air-in
Andras — On-drass
Anellah — Uh-nell-uh
Ansa — On-za
Casmir — Caz-meer
Emrys — Ehm-riss
Hale — Hey-uhl
Jorin — Jore-in
Karis — Care-iss
Leia — Lee-uh
Niair — Neye-air
Sambril — Sahm-breel
Talyn — Tay-lin
Teryn — T-air-in
Xamira — Za-meer-uh

Places
Amsal — Am-zall
Anclona — An-clone-uh
Anloria — An-lor-ee-uh
Ceross — Sair-oh-ss

Chago — Sh-ah-go
Europa — Ear-oh-puh
Semiria — Seh-meer-ee-uh
Sunsor — Suh-n-zer
Veardale — Veer-day-ll

Also By Dakota Monroe

The Curse of Gods series
Of Gods and Pain
Of War and Realms

Shadows of the Crown series
Shadows of the Crown
Essence of the Throne
Mark of the Aetarys, 2026
ROTC, TBD

Standalones
Her Lovely Curse
Laced in Longing, 2026

About the Author

Dakota Monroe lives in a dark world and dreams of even darker fantasies. She has been a fantasy-obsessed reader since she was a child and now brings hers to life through her writing. As a neurodivergent woman, Dakota has always felt out of place with her thoughts and ideas; but books have been her savior, and a nonjudgmental place for her to escape the colorless world we call reality. She hopes her characters, and stories, provide an outlet for others, even if just for a little while.